MORE CRITICAL PRAISE FOR LAUREN SANDERS

FOR *WITH OR WITHOUT YOU*

"[Sanders's] vibrant, vigorous second novel is a sendup of America's obsession with pop culture, B-list celebrities, and prison life . . . In lyrical, potent prose, Sanders navigates the terrain of loneliness, obsession, and desperation with the same skillful precision as her vulnerable, calculating protagonist." —*Publishers Weekly* (starred review)

"[A] wickedly crafted whydunit . . . Sanders shows a surprising ability to simultaneously make you feel infuriated with and sorry for her borderline-schizo heroine. A-" —*Entertainment Weekly*

"This psychological 'whydunit' provides a compelling and sympathetic look into the mind of an obsessed fan who can't quite explain what went wrong. Part coming-of-age story and part prison novel, the story explores the fragile relationship between celebrities and our fascination with their lives. Recommended for larger public libraries." —*Library Journal*

"Startling, shocking, and heartbreaking . . . dark adolescent noir that gets to the heart of why an obsessed fan kills the object of her desire." —*Philadelphia City Paper*

"I hate the term poetic, but Lauren Sanders's writing has such a slick mean surface and her subject is such a truly bad girl, a murderer. I mean, so that *poetic* suits *With or Without You* just fine. It's a hot poetic book I wouldn't kick out of bed." —Eileen Myles, author of *Chelsea Girls*

"Lauren Sanders's new novel packs a wallop. With skillful precision, Sanders paints the vivid worlds of hardened young women in prison, aimless teens on Long Island, and the narcissistic world of B-list celebrities. Wicked, fun, disturbing, and heartbreaking, *With or Without You* is a fearless book that pushes every boundary. It captures perfectly the torment of modern-day adolescence, as well as the utter loneliness of obsession." —Nina Revoyr, author of *Lost Canyon*

FOR *KAMIKAZE LUST*

- Winner of a 2000 Lambda Literary Award

"Like an official conducting an all-out strip search, first-time novelist Lauren Sanders plucks and probes her characters' minds and bodies to reveal their hidden lusts, and when all is said and done, nary a body cavity is spared."   —*Time Out New York*

"This sexy little novel isn't afraid to be steamy—but it isn't too jaded for romance either."   —*The Advocate*

"Lauren Sanders is a writer of extraordinary skill."
                                                        —*Bay Area Reporter*

"Without wit or heart, this much sex would be unsexy, particularly if the author were using the titillation factor as mere bait for jacket blurbs. Instead, it serves a broader purpose, illustrating that the boundaries we use to demarcate civilized society are largely an illusion, and that labels like 'porn star,' 'cancer patient,' and 'lesbian' are meant to signify— falsely—'people nothing like us.' Here sex bleeds so naturally into life, and life into sex, that books that shy from this human realm begin to seem prissy and suspect."   —*City Pages* (Minneapolis/St. Paul)

"Sanders zips and zooms through Rachel's overturned life with prose as sharp, quick, and deadly as any suicide mission."   —*Out*

"The fact Sanders can so overtly take on sex and death, write almost exclusively of their relationship to each other and their effects on a developing personality, and not sound clichéd, is a monumental achievement in itself."   —*Toronto Star*

"*Kamikaze Lust* is a whirl of New York neurotic fast-quipping with a line or two courtesy of Miss Sandra Bernhardt, but who better to borrow from than the Princess of Pith?"   —*Time Out London*

"Great courage must account for such complete disregard of political correctness, and great sensitivity for such sadness."
—Amanda Filipacchi, author of *The Unfortunate Importance of Beauty*

THE
BOOK
OF
LOVE
AND
HATE

LAUREN SANDERS

BROOKLYN, NEW YORK, USA
BALLYDEHOB, CO. CORK, IRELAND

©2017 Lauren Sanders
ISBN: 978-1-61775-582-8
Library of Congress Control Number: 2017936089

Akashic Books
Brooklyn, New York, USA
Ballydehob, Co. Cork, Ireland
Twitter: @AkashicBooks
Facebook: AkashicBooks
E-mail: info@akashicbooks.com
Website: www.akashicbooks.com

People do not die for us immediately, but remain bathed in a sort of aura of life which bears no relation to true immortality but through which they continue to occupy our thoughts in the same way as when they were alive. It is as though they were traveling abroad.
—Marcel Proust

SUDDENLY, LAST SUMMER

Ben Gurion Airport, August 9, 2008

Fury is an airport in summer. Even in the desert there's a sickly freeze piped in, people throwing bare legs up on vinyl chairs, chewing too hard on day-old sandwiches. Cranked-up book covers. The numbness of waiting.

I have made it to the security line where I stand with the rest of the locals, faking it.

Outside Tel Aviv is wilted to its roots. If I step off the line and drive fast I could be at the beach in ten minutes, dipping my feet into the deep blue sea. And isn't that what we're all here for ultimately? Not some drummed-up notion of a spy novel. But we love stories, even airport security in the toughest departure zone in the world can't get enough of them, anything to break the monotony of interrogation.

Dress matronly, I'd been told, and was unsure how to execute having never been a mother and harboring only shadows of my own. It's not a genre I've ever gone in for. But this is a matriarchal culture. Nobody will bother you if the details hold. Here's the deal, though: I am tall enough to stand out—always have been—and dressed in a long floral skirt, loose T-shirt, and sensible shoes that feel particularly suspicious. A lavender beret highlights the nondescript light-brown wig made from real hair—don't ask. All the ladies do it. The back of my skirt is soaked.

An armed security officer approaches a man a few people ahead of me in line who presents his passport, Israeli, and the back and forth begins. I make out a few words . . . *nothing* . . . *I go to travel* . . . *Paris.* Closer to the checkpoint, I fear the religious posturing might be all wrong; everyone hates the Orthodox. I take several deep inhales, counting backward . . . *Ten,* exhale, *nine,* exhale, *eight,* exhale . . . a technique from my days in competition, those last few minutes before pushing off onto the ice, when you're led into position based on a coin toss. Random. Waiting for a signal, the gunshot, and it's do or die. Counting was the only way to clear my head. Still is . . . *four,* exhale . . . *three,* exhale . . .

I continue breathing and counting while keeping an eye on the officers, there are no women today. Another moves into a line full of tourists, fingers playing his M16. The army has a code peppered with words like *humanity* and *dignity.* Soldiers respect their rifles. No solace as they advance, and I know I'm doing something I shouldn't be doing, and probably for all the wrong reasons: guilt, loyalty, worst of all worsts, love. My father says all people are motivated by sex or money. Even those in the business of doing good are channeling some deep-seated vice or crack of shame for simply being born. As a teenager, declaring myself the opposition, I'd float examples to ruin his theory, and ask about, say, nuns. "Sex," he replied. "God is sex." The president (we had been watching Bill Clinton give his state of the union): "That's too easy, Jen. Look at the corners of his mouth, his fist, those eyes . . . and all of those congressional fairies and chosen ones standing like puppets, the eyes of the world upon him up there at the podium, you know he's doing it all for the friggin' lead pipe in his pants." What if it was a woman up there? I asked, and he laughed. *Dream on, little girl.*

I am a dreamer. Otherwise I would not be standing here doing his business, the last cry of a rabid, old tycoon. On the other side of the windows the tarmac steams, monstrous 757s nose up with military planes, crews flagging luggage trolleys, security officers fatigued and loaded with ammo.

Anyone here will tell you it's easier getting out than in. But decades of terrorism have refined suspicion of air travel into policy. After traveling around the States a lot, the first thing you notice here is no one removes their shoes. It's almost silly, when you've got staff trained in espionage asking random questions to make even the most seasoned traveler squirm—not to mention all of those guns. Years ago I flew to Tel Aviv from the southernmost tip of the world and was detained for a gold-plated switchblade before I could even get on the plane. At the bottom of Argentina, more men in camo-green, boys really, laughing at the knife and me, shaking their heads. *Look at this girl trying to take a weapon into Israel!* As if they would have let me take it anywhere else in the world.

I was bringing the knife for my brother, so we could cut blocks of cheese and tomatoes. We were set to travel together.

When the soldiers finally get to me, I'm as hot as the city outside and long past counting. I try to forget I'm crammed with secret positions and records, where two nights earlier my father's lover had trailed her heated tongue, all the spoils of his dirty little war.

Perhaps it is his dream to die in the holy land—how sallow and resigned he looked in that hospital bed despite the doctor's assertions that he would make it through this time. It wasn't a real hospital, not even sure the doctor was real either. My father told me he was not long for this world, otherwise he'd never ask me to do what I am now doing. He'd always been scrupulous about keeping his shadier dealings away from us, even after I went to work for him I knew almost nothing about what was really going on.

"Who is taking care of your children?" a security officer interrogates in English. I'd just explained my status, recently arrived from America, extended family in Paris. Common migratory patterns.

"My sister-in-law." I am suitably religious, maternal, uxorial.

He nods, mama's boy through and through. Part of me thinks it's too easy, and another part feels like skating or how sex stops time, the world heightened into a short incandescent stretch, and maybe that's the big secret of crime: it's exhilarating. The officer flips again through my passport, then slaps it back and forth against his palm. "Why are you carrying only one bag?" he asks.

"It's all I need."

"No gifts for anyone?"

"I'm cheap."

He smirks, and I am sent through the X-ray machines: mule, liar, my father's emissary. I'm feeling closer to him than I can remember, but he's warned me—there are undercover security people on every flight. In the passenger's lounge, I open my computer and log onto the Internet, hoping for a sign, though everything has been wiped from my hard drive as a safety measure. No saved messages from him . . . or his lover. I have a sudden, intense urge to return to her once this job is done, which catches me. I am usually drifty with lovers, a strand of take-it-or-leave-it the essential part of my MO, one of the few pieces that's remained consistent throughout a decade of sobriety.

I stare out the window until my flight is called over the loudspeaker and I walk with a line of women and children all speaking Hebrew. Maybe they should have hired me a kid, it's easier to fit in if you have the right props. But I'm doing okay, settling into my seat next to the window, packed in tightly by two teenage girls in skirts to the floor, ballet slippers, and button-downs, carrying stale paperback Bibles. *What's that like?*

The captain says we are about to shut the doors, all cell phones must be turned off. I look out beyond the bouncing heat of the afternoon, a smoky haze rising from the tarmac into a bright yellow sky down low, blue-gray tint against the windows I'd just been sitting next to on the other side, and there she is, tight curls framing those lips I'd kissed two hours straight before she asked me to do what I'm doing, do it for him, because he is dying, and we need to move things "under the covers." Like I'm not being watched, I said, and she told me no, nobody knows. You have been erased. Then she pushed my fingers into her so deep my wrist snapped.

Something clamps beneath my seat, I'm on the wing. Then the plane pulls back from the gate and she is gone. We will not see each other again, if all goes well on the other side in Paris. I can live there for some time, they've set everything up with one of the hedge fund managers. Or maybe I can just go home.

PART I

AT HOME ON THE EVE
OF DESTRUCTION

Tel Aviv, Late December 2008

War begins with a whimper, streetlights twitching into purple sunset in a town of a thousand histories. There's a fire in my right calf, appeased for the moment by elevation and two sobbing bags of ice, as evening flickers on below like a soundstage, the BBC droning in English from an old stereo receiver. Earlier this morning, the army dropped leaflets from airplanes alerting families in their sardine-packed huts across the checkpoints that troops were coming and they should get out while they had the chance.

"*It's extraordinary,*" says the commentator with breathy traces of the Queen's tongue. "*No other country does this! After the Americans bombed Hiroshima, they dropped leaflets encouraging surrender, telling people to turn themselves in, the worst had come. Propaganda. But this is truly astonishing, the army telling people we are coming, this is no joke, set yourselves free. How humane this is . . .*"

I hitch up my leg slightly, sending an electric pang down through my ankle, about a six on my scale, though the chill from the bulging ice packs on top of the brittle evening makes it stronger. I shiver, crying out like a muted bird. Nobody hears.

Outside, on the terrace of a seaside apartment at the dawn of winter, the dawn of another war in a country built on violent conquest, and for one second I think maybe it's a sign, I should not have come back. But I am not one for easy answers and in many ways I do what I am told. In 1989 I was called to this country by my brother and I came, though I had a feeling even then that it would be the undoing it turned out to be. I am psychic sometimes, can see things others might bypass, and it's gotten stronger since I've been sober. Now my father is calling, indirectly, and though I have the same feeling that nothing makes sense and everything is destabilized, I need answers. There is no form to it yet, nothing to grab onto. Only the pain keeps me grounded, always has. I am, in some ways, a junkie for it, seeking to bear the weight of what's inside in a way that will ultimately peak and soothe. Physical therapists talk about pain as relative, no two people experience it the same. If you're serious about sports you don't care about anyone else's scale, you need to learn your own. I have devoted much of my life to this pursuit.

Foot traffic increases steadily below, life pushing into the backdrop of headlights as if it's your average evening. Everything normal. Copacetic. These revelers had fought long and hard for their right to be like everyone else and no cries of unfair escalation or two-state solutions can take that away. Couples sip red wine at outdoor tables in the café across the street, mostly gay, or at least same-gendered, from what I can tell. This is a hip if slightly disheveled part of town. The café is called Movie Star, and I can make out a few of the old Hollywood posters through the front window, the Garland version of *A Star Is Born* most prominent, they're crazy for Garland. Others promenade in stiff hair and pressed denim, heading to the boardwalk with puffed-up dogs. A man shouts his dinner reservation into a cell phone, repeating the same series of numbers, or that's all I can make out, the knife pinch squeezing deeper into my lower leg, and I hear the great lady singing: *The road gets r-r-rougher, it's lonelier and tougher . . .*

Or maybe she's speaking it. Or it's the commentator talking about the long road to war coming out of this most recent incursion. Besides, I am here for love, not war, and it bites harder when all your love is gone. Two more things you should know straightaway: I lie sometimes, like before when I said I do what I'm told. I was told to stay away from this country, to burrow back into my life as if everything this past summer could be erased along with my tracks. Maybe I don't do what I'm told all the time, who does? The second is more thorny, along the lines of this: I am a stubborn cow. Once I get an idea in my head I carry through. Time for a parable, perhaps?

In the thirties, Natalie Barney booked passage to Russia to pursue the desultory contessa—imagine it's 1920 and you've already cycled through all the women in Paris, in walks a gorgeous countess, you'd follow her anywhere, even across the frozen tundra. I've done the same, though my countess is a war hero gone underground. We made love only once and I cannot stop hitting repeat. This is the stuff of obsession, might make a good story if it were happening to someone else.

And then of course there's her other lover, my father, who might also be lurking around too if he's still alive. In the two weeks I've been here I've locked onto hundreds of sets of eyes pinballing back and forth on the blazing streets, searching for the man who gave me life. I have talked to almost no one, save for the waiter at the Movie Star who now knows I'm serious when I ask for a third cappuccino in the morning and the guy who lives in the flat across the terrace and wears colorful sarongs. He says things about the weather in English when our ships pass. "You are here for some time," he said the other day, and it took me a few seconds to realize it was a question. Yes, I said. He asked why and I said personal reasons.

Tonight I am longing to let someone in, as less than an hour away people steady themselves for the onslaught of war and everything feels futile. I am lonelier than Garland and the closest I've come to slipping in years.

My sweet girl, says a voice, maybe the radio again, though it feels more deep in the bones and directed at me. *Sadness is the way of the world.*

The wind sweeps in like a small whirlpool, hurling a plastic beer mug over the railing. I lean in slightly, so I can watch it fall, slowly as if guided by a parachute.

The voice on the radio says it's on.

After two days of stretching and ice, I venture beyond my own street, walking the three short blocks to the beach. I sit and stare out at the waves. On day three I walk up and down the boardwalk all afternoon and make it through the evening without ibuprofen, which is a no-no, even low-grade pharma posing certain challenges for someone of my disposition. But I am not a friggin' saint.

The next day I walk to the queer center for a yoga class. I am ready for stretches. And I can do them in Hebrew, mirroring the tight-knit line in front of me no matter how many of the words I get. Meetings are harder, I need to know what's bubbling up. There is an English-speaking group here at the center, which is really a few connected rooms in a nondescript concrete building stuck between a couple of tatty beachside hotels. A new center, years in the making, is set to open very soon in a famous building with state-of-the-art everything and more meetings. People are skeptical, but the where hardly matters. I need to bury myself in the dull cadences that scared the shit out of me as a first-timer. The voices keep me centered, stop me from trading in on the new identity and saying yes, how sweet of you to offer, when the wine comes. Before I pulled the muscle I'd been visiting bars, maybe not so smartly, retracing the steps I took last summer, hoping they would take me to Gila.

She is a former army pilot, one of the first women to fly planes into Lebanon, or so she said. She is also a corporate spy.

Lost in her now I can barely follow the simplest of poses and need to pay attention. *Center thyself! Breathe! Bend, for shit's sake!* Three lines of young women in spandex with logos from European sporting companies, a few men in tight shorts and bare backs in between, all queer or queerish, guide me forward. The teacher prompts in Hebrew, sometimes repeating in mellifluous Sanskrit, and I sink in deeply, overtaken for a few beautiful moments by the synchronized bends and stretches.

Afterward I can barely walk. I fish a large plastic water bottle from my bag and sit down on a wooden bench outside the yoga room. There's a corkboard behind me with taped-up messages in at least five languages, mostly apartment rentals and odd jobs. A sign in English speaks of an antiwar protest later tonight, next to it a litter of messy chocolate lab pups for sale. They were rescued from an empty field near the airport. I imagine Gila and me adopting a puppy.

"*Slicha.* Excuse me. Do you speak English?" A figure emerges in front of me in the sticky fluorescent waves, so close I need to lean my head back to take it in. She's Anglo, American most likely, pale skin and almond-brown hair, dressed in khakis and a flannel-lined jean jacket with an *Obama '08* button on one pocket, a *Free Gaza* button on the other. Two younger women follow behind her, maybe in their late twenties, one with a pierced eyebrow, the other in a pink biker jacket and mohawk, Mediterranean features, Arab most likely. Each has a stack of flyers.

"Didn't I see you at the *Dignity* protest the other night?" the Anglo says, American indeed. "You're with one of the watchdog groups. Or the journalists."

Dignity is the name of a ship, not just an aspiration for how we should treat one another in this big, cruel world. The capital-D *Dignity* set sail from Cyprus with a group of activists, doctors with tons of medical supplies, a former US representative and CNN reporter in tow. Some say the activists are of dubious origins, connected to terrorists and arms smugglers, or maybe to these women here. In any event—depending on whose report you believe—they were either slammed by or simply collided with Israeli patrol boats.

I have been shaking my head no or saying something, though I'm not sure the words have come out.

"Are you a lawyer?"

"What?"

"I don't understand why you're here."

"I'm traveling."

"In the middle of a war!" At this the Arab women snicker. "Even the State Department said don't come."

"Who listens to the government?"

She smiles. I know how to flirt, even when I'm not flirting. This has been a problem for me in the past. But the American seems curious, exactly what I've been trying to avoid. I inch forward in an attempt to stand, but the pain in my lower leg has its own agenda. I clear my throat and ask for a flyer.

"You should join us. It's going to be unprecedented tonight," says the American as the pink girl removes a piece of paper from the bottom of her pile and leans down with it. "The opposition is growing stronger every day. It's apartheid and everyone here knows it. Now's our chance to show the rest of the world."

The pierced girl nods along, then digs a *Free Gaza* button

out of her bag. She hands it to me saying I should join them. "We meet by the fountain and then take the streets. We are calling this government down for its dirty war."

"Perhaps I'll come," I say, wishing them away because my feet have filled with lead. The Israelis have named their war Operation Cast Lead. They began during Hanukkah and thought the nod toward casting a dreidel was funny. Who knew dreidels were made of lead? The song says clay. Apparently you'd forge the lead like a bullet, though bullets haven't been made of lead for decades and this war is nothing but a nuisance for me.

Looking out beyond the activists, I see the center has filled up, flashes of hair color moving in pastiche . . . *Don't they have others to enlist?*

"Please do come with us," says the pierced one. "I'd really like that." She turns over one of her flyers and pulls a pen from her ear, writing down a few numbers. The American glances at her, half-cocked, then turns down to me.

"You're from New York, aren't you?"

"No," I lie. "I live in Paris."

"But originally New York. I know we've met before, you look so familiar."

"People tell me that all the time," I say, trying to stand her down while seated, hold her gaze.

"No, it'll come to me. I remember everyone I've ever known."

"That sounds annoying."

"It's just who I am." She nods, taking a step back as the pink girl taps her on the shoulder saying they should go. The pierced girl hands me the paper and smiles with a perked eyebrow as I survey the digits, hers no doubt. I watch her slide into the traffic, tracing the outline of her back as long as I can.

* * *

People recognize me. Less so these days, but on occasion there is someone who's skated or another who grew up with the Olympics being her favorite televised event in the eighties, before the Internet made everyone famous. For these people my face sticks out.

I was a rising star. Barely twelve years old and taller than my mother, taller than most girls' mothers, I had what people called a presence. It was the money, perhaps, that conveyed a sense of belonging to the world in a fundamental way. I could have done anything. But all I wanted was to skate. Then skating brought other rewards. Not that I was inexperienced—I wasn't. You don't get a body like this and say I think I'll save it for my wedding night, especially when you're starting to sense that things aren't necessarily meant to go that way. We'd had an au pair from Spain, and is it even right to call her an au pair if she didn't speak French? Her name was Sofia. She was with us one summer before stealing $5,000 from one of my father's secret drawers stacked with crispy bills. "Never be stuck without cash," he told me often. "Never. Never. Never. You don't know when you'll need an escape route. Fast cash. Run money. Whatever you want to call it. Without it you're a sitting duck."

It's funny remembering that now since he's run so far, so fast, tapping the curiosity of the FBI, Homeland Security, not to mention the Jewish mafia—if nothing else, my father has given me the makings of an interesting life.

He wouldn't have known Sofia had taken the money, he had so many hiding spots for his cash, and had she asked I would have drained every last bank account to have gone with her, that is the kind of undying love one experiences in adolescence, but she had to do things her way and her way was old-world polite. Three days after she'd left, a thank you note arrived postmarked from Florida. She was on a boat, she said. Heading to an island where she could make a new life. She wanted to tell him how much she'd enjoyed her time with our family and appreciated his generosity. He snorted, "Generosity! That's fucking rich."

"You could go find her," I said. He had no idea what she'd meant to me. Or to my brother, apparently, but that came later, when I was well into competitive skating and out on the road. She returned to New York and got a job as a back rubber in a fancy strip club. Marc was still underage but old enough when she got back in touch.

"Oh, please," said my father. "These gals are a dime a dozen. We'll find another . . . maybe a real French one this time."

"But I want this one."

He turned toward me with a gaping look, like he was waiting for me to fill it with something that made sense. But how do you say this to your father? One month earlier she'd taken me into the second study near the laundry room, bumping her hand into my front pocket. There had been other boys and girls with fidgety wet kisses, mercilessly rubbing each other into oblivion. This one with her hand in my front pocket knew her business. "I want to show you *someting*," she said, the accent alone debilitating. I nodded my head, *yesssss*. And like that we were kissing. How do you say I want those kisses back, can you get them back for me?

"Forget it." I shrugged it off.

We got a new girl. Then another. All of whom made Sofia stronger in her absence. What stays most are those few weeks of kissing in the study, the kitchen, up on the roof, and, despite the collaborative dance of hormones, a strong feeling that it was something I needed to get through. To understand.

After Sofia, I knew where I stood in the world.

I left school a couple of years later for a series of tutors and coaches, their well-choreographed plot hinged on the power solidifying in my thighs and my father's money. I could skate faster than anyone I knew. Weekdays I commandeered our New York apartment, mornings in the gym to augment the vessel with weights, knee bends, up and down twenty flights of stairs, running madly on plastic sheets to make the floor feel like a rink. Afternoons I met with tutors in my favorite study. Austere in its dark wood and thick Oriental rug, Tiffany desk lamps, like a hidden cul-de-sac in the public library. My father had the books imported from a used bookstore in London, first editions of the twentieth-century book bullies—Faulkner, Hemingway, Eliot, Pound—none he'd never read. Only I got that sentence. I hated these books, preferring journals of numbers and studies of the natural world, the science of my own elliptical strength far more salient than any feeling. Later, when I got sober, I would come to see the duality of science and emotion, how I'd overloaded on the physical.

Weekends we traveled to the oval in Connecticut and eventually to Lake Placid so I could let loose on the big rink. Training so vigilantly it's hard not to believe what they're telling you through cold breath clouds on a crystal-clear night, the oval lit up like a space station . . . *You are strong. You are lightning. You are a winner.*

My coach, the one who got me to the Olympics in Calgary, had a name so lovely I could barely pronounce it. I called her Tree. She had serious legs like mine and a celebrated cocaine problem. She was in love with me. Or me, her. And either way, what of it? I'm left walking along the Mediterranean with a pair of binoculars longing for the coldest winter in Canada. Seasons connect us as much as countries, places, or perhaps the weather grounds us in the Calgary of the mind.

Tree fed me a series of pills—speed, steroids, painkillers, muscle relaxers—in concert with macrobiotic shakes.

Like me she lived the inconsistencies. She taught me to study my enemies, know what's motivating them, their weak spots, how much they need to win. But I never really paid attention and became more interested in the desultory nights. People saw me as rebellious.

"You're too fast," Tree said, trying to get me to focus on technique and build what she called epic endurance. It's everything in long track. Inhabit the air, she'd shout from the sidelines, push into it, own it. In training you learn you've always got more in you, inside and out. She would repeat this later too, as I sat on the smelly rug of a hotel room floor trying to keep the tears in check as she patched my bleeding toes, sometimes ripping the skin of my big toe even farther so it could heal faster. She'd pump an amyl under my nose to get me on the ice the next day, taking care of me in a way nobody ever had. And I loved her for it.

As an adult it's easy to look back on the people who manipulated you and hate them for it. It's harder to acknowledge how you worked them back. I've gotten reamed for saying this in nearly every therapeutic context. *You were just a kid. You wanted to be cared for. To be loved. You are not to blame here.*

What happened in Calgary broke Tree's heart. I had the whole world in front of me, watching me, and she had invested so much time in crafting a winner. Time. Philosophy. Drugs. Her music collection. The rhythms helped charge endorphins, and she always played it, the kind of stuff I'd loathed before her: Led Zeppelin, Lynyrd Skynyrd, Cream— masters of the seventies hard rock Olympics and potheads. To this day I can't listen to bad stadium rock, even those that came later, without feeling my throat close up a little, and it's Tree's hands wrapping around me so tightly my breath closes in. I still can't talk about Calgary in terms of my own loss. It hurts less to focus on her.

Years later we were both clean and working through it.

I wanted to make amends but she wouldn't let me. "Come on, Tree," I said, in a telephone call, trying to persuade her to meet me. "We're in the same place now. Let's make it right."

"There is no right for us."

"Just let me see you."

"You're off the hook. I forgive you."

"What? I'm the one who's supposed to forgive . . ."

There was a click on the line and she was gone.

Somehow the holidays have passed by the stormy sea and it is a whole new year: *Hello, 2009.* From my apartment I could hear the fireworks along the beach. My calf has healed nicely but I am tired, growing weary of why I've come back here . . . *in the middle of a war!* like the American activist had scorned. Why I hate political people, let me count the ways. I've been steering clear of anything that reeks of protests and never called the pretty girl with the pierced eyebrow, who might have been a happy distraction. Stopping a war is just not my thing. Instead I wallow over to the new immigrant center, where I pick up a schedule of groups and services and drip into the computer room. There are four empty PCs, screens dusted green-gray, crumbs caught between the blackened keys. The room is empty. I take the station in the corner, booting up from the external operating system I carry with me on a jump drive, the only way I'll put my password into a machine and I'm still careful to check for cookies and re-boot before leaving. I learned this system from Melissa, who runs my professional life and now so much more.

She forwards pages of e-mail messages, all precisely photographed and vying for my attention. I tell her how to answer, authorizing transfers of public funds to build a plaza, save an after-school coding program for brown-skinned girls, sponsor a summit for petty tyrants, mostly just yessing her decisions—she's better at me than me.

There is some news of my father. Apparently the government is closing in on him, rumors of his death greatly exaggerated, says Yearling, the agent who's been trailing me. Everyone on the Internet's a fucking comedian. I catch myself laughing out loud, then lift my head. Turning left and right I confirm I'm still by myself inside the crackling beige walls and filthy keys. I take a deep breath and let it out with a flutter, then shut down the machine.

The government agent has a sense of humor . . . somehow this frightens me more than anything else I've heard all week.

I know a little café in the old port of Jaffa where Gila and I dipped our pinkies in each other's water glasses last summer. It was just before my father died the first time, his breath trickling down in a sequestered hospital room reserved for long-ago war heroes, politicians, Jews with money. Men from the Orthodox kibbutz he'd founded provided cover, praying throughout the day in small groups at his bedside. The ID tag outside the door claimed he was a rabbi. I'd left a gaggle of them praying over him though they knew he couldn't recite one sentence from the holy book— for years he'd been running money through the kibbutz, the country's largest purveyor of hard goat cheese, and that was loyalty enough for his men, most of whom were not really religious anyway. They wore covers on top of covers.

Gila met me outside the café, quickly grasping both of my hands in hers. It was a hot night and she was visibly sweating at the brow. "I know this is difficult," she said, "but you must trust me."

I followed her inside and we were taken to a private table in a cave-like dome along the sea, not unlike the hospital room I'd just left. Together, we devoured the heavy summer sun dipping into the blue-green expanse, a sailboat in the distance that looked like a Viking ship, as she told me about my father. How they'd met a few years earlier and fallen in love, or in her words, *embraced our deep and mysterious connection*. No matter that he was more than twice her age and still married to wife number three, whom he'd described as having grand features and a grinding take on marriage that had begun to wear him down. She was trying to go back on the written agreement they'd made not to have children. So he stopped sleeping with her, which he told Gila was inevitable anyway once he met her, Gila, and took her on as lover and accomplice.

This happens, Gila said to me. Even the most beautiful woman can become ordinary when the sheen cracks and you see what's underneath. It opens a room for someone else.

What's wrong with ordinary? I teased. Gila said it's just not me, and the back of my throat tickled.

We made love only once, the night before my father supposedly passed from this world into the next as I successfully carried a jump drive stuffed with secrets through Israeli security and out of the country in a burst of filial loyalty, manipulation, self-preservation, love . . . my motives changing on a dime.

One kiss is enough to fuel a thousand fantasies, a face a thousand ships, none of them called *Dignity*. I can still hear her coming when I close my eyes.

Now she's disappeared from Google searches and Melissa says our people can't find anything. The hidden café is all I've got on this cold night in January, rain cozying up along the coast as darkness blankets the unlit side streets. I should have hired a car. Most people in the city have them and there is never enough parking. No luck with a shared taxi, I flag down the bus, though there is risk in mixing with students out for the night, Arabs, workers, all of us crammed together behind the steamed-up windows. Life insulates, I tell myself, as if it were a prayer.

A boy of about seventeen with thick, dark hair sits directly across from me. Every few seconds he shoves his friend who's broader and sandier and they play punch each other into streams of laughter, as oblivious to the rest of us as to the ominous splash of rubber wheels beneath our feet. Soon they will be carrying rifles, policing borders in tanks, or training to become software engineers in the elite unit. But for now they chide each other in a way I find vaguely intimidating, not their countenance but the bond. I can't take my eyes off them, almost missing my stop just outside the market.

The streets are wet, rain zipping down in pellets. I pop up my umbrella and walk outside the market, lights dimmed but for a few restaurants with thick awnings and foggy plastic shades pulled down to protect the outdoor seating. I let the rain push me forward, though I can't help looking behind the metal gates at the stalls, all of the tools, the rugs, plastic shoes, and jewelry, and what is it with Russian nesting dolls at flea markets? Everywhere you open and unearth a smaller version of the same painted face, each a little more vacuous than the last, it's disturbing. I continue on toward the busy two-lane boulevard that divides the market from the coastal streets. Tonight the cars move slowly . . . deliberate? I check faces in windows while crossing diagonally into a smaller square that leads to the beach; behind me footsteps, heavier than mine. I move left toward a row of concrete apartments, splashes coming closer, my heartbeat riveting, I shouldn't be out alone at night. I'm an idiot. I walk faster, catching an alley on my left, and jump inside as if it had been my destination. A crash hits the street like a cymbal and I cave, heart amped like a drum machine. A fluffy white kitten mews and nuzzles into the shelter of my umbrella. I let it coo against my thigh, as I breathe . . . *Ten*, exhale, *nine*, exhale . . . regrouping for a few seconds before leaving the alley. The kitten will find a doorway or crawl under a car. Strays live forever sometimes.

I breathe quickly as I move through the last blocks before the café, thinking nobody knows I am here, nobody knows . . . not even the people I'm looking for. There is no one after me. Even so, I run faster, triggering the pain in my lower leg that had just recently evacuated, tomorrow I'll ice again. When I arrive at the café my toes are soaked and my heart won't quit.

Inside I shut myself in the bathroom for fifteen minutes just breathing, before taking a seat at the bar and ordering a club soda with a twist of lime. The bartender smiles. "I remember," he says. "You were here some days ago looking for a specific woman. I remember your accent. The American from Paris."

"I'm impressed."

"You changed your head." He touches the top of his own to indicate my new crew cut. A disguise, I'd thought.

"Why would you take out all of your hair? It looked better last time."

"Thanks for your opinion."

"This is what everyone wants from the bartender. Show me one bartender who doesn't say bold things and I will say he is a very poor man."

"I thought it was about making drinks."

"That is part," he says. "The other is human relations. I am born with this. The drinks I've learned."

The bartender lilts on about himself and I am grateful for the listening. He tells me he never made a drink before walking into this bar a few years ago. Says he's absorbed everything he knows about bartending from the Internet and experience. He studies music at the university. Someday he would like to be a sound mixer and work in movies, make his parents proud. They are second-generation immigrants from Morocco. Next year they will celebrate as he weds an Israeli-born girl who colors animated filmstrips at a cable television station. He will miss being a bartender, he says. It has taught him about appropriate measures, how things blend together. Not unlike sound frequencies. "Some who tend bar, they are like a chef," he says. "Always experimenting with the drinks, which vodka tastes better in a gimlet, the same one for a martini, but for me it is more precise, like a baker. I am looking for the right reaction. What happens when you add an organic egg white, a few drops of evaporated cane sugar. That is where the magic comes. Would you like to taste the perfect winter cocktail?"

"No thanks," I say. "I don't drink."

"Oh, I can make without alcohol. Or maybe just a little so you won't notice. It's just for tasting. You will see."

He turns his back, setting up for the perfect winter cocktail, and I am sad he's gone. I dig the sound of his voice, like a low-key motivational therapist. The bar is empty but for an older man with salted hair and a tight brown leather jacket sitting at the other end eating creamy pasta with a fork and knife, napkin tucked into the top of his shirt like they do in mafia films, lonely and satisfied, too deep into the food to be any trouble for me. Peeking behind I see a few couples dabbling over dimly flickering candles, each in their own little world. They say the city of Tel Aviv is itself a bubble, insulated from the consequences of history by trendy cafés and good jobs and a spoonful of sugar.

"You take eggs," says the bartender, directly in front of me once again.

"Please. I don't—"

"Trust me. You are not vegan."

I shake my head slightly.

"I didn't think so."

He turns and I hear the split of an egg, bottles clinking against one another, the spinning of liquid over ice cubes. I think about what I'll say, why I can't while I've let him make such a show of it. Another part says, maybe it's okay, things have changed, and a drink might calm you down.

It's a slow night so he takes his time, stirring dramatically to fizzle the egg white.

"Here we have it." The drink sits in front of me, the color of almost-not-there amber bleeding into heavenly foam, a few sandy lines on top in the shape of a dove. He calls it A Mix of Sun and Clouds.

Sometimes change comes in a second, the time it takes to lift a glass to your lips. I have a few times pretended to drink in social settings, sipping lightly and exhaling into a cloth napkin. Once when I was dating the Republican lobbyist, I sniffed from a bottle of brandy she said was 250 years old. It tasted like fire.

I lift the glass and smell. "It's lovely."

"You haven't tasted."

His eyes on me, nothing but a cocktail napkin to cough up into, I'm screwed. But the truth is I want escape, I want to swallow not spit, to recover some lost piece of myself I didn't even know I was looking for. And this country of tattered souls reminds me of a time I was thrown into it with my brother, the king of pain himself. We drank so much that summer it ruined my career, what was left of it anyway. But what a beautiful way to go.

I look at the bartender. He's waiting for something, as if he's been following my thoughts. I take a long sip.

"Well?" He hovers.

"You say you're as good with sound?"

"Even better." He smiles, then excuses himself to help

an attractive couple who've landed next to the man eating pasta. I take another sip of sun and clouds and think maybe it is a virgin, I can't taste any alcohol, though the next sip beckons and I know I'm lying to myself. But it's okay. Because it feels steady, more than familiar, and for the first time in days I want to laugh. What was I thinking all those years?

The music comes out of hiding, Israeli disco, bass lines exploding through the half-empty bar. After my final go at rehab, when I was serious about quitting, I avoided bars entirely. They said change your patterns, your people, your places, anything that reminds you of who you were. It almost worked.

The bartender returns with a new drink and I eye it skeptically. He says look around. The crowd has hit its momentum. There is that point when the bar realizes its promise, he says. Like when a girl becomes a woman. I give him a pronounced *huh?* "I am serious," he continues. "You can't tell when it is or what's made it this way—I'm sure, of course, we know what's made it this way in the philosophical sense—but from the outside you can't say that moment, it is just one day there. And it is the same way each night for the bar. And so tonight, my sad, sweet lady, we have finally arrived."

"Does your girlfriend—"

"Fiancée."

"Your fiancée, sorry. She knows how much you cavort with other women?"

"The thing she understands is I love her more than life itself. She knows we will have a beautiful family together and I'll protect her and take care of things and also push the kiddies down the street in a stroller, I am not a machismo man. This is important for us. And you?"

"What's important?"

"Of course."

"Depends on the day. Mostly I'm trying to find a reason to stay hopeful."

"In that way I can help." He smiles and I'm bulldozed by a craving for sloppy wet kisses, the graze of someone else's skin against my own. Before I can go any further, he speaks again, timing impeccable: "Your woman was here last night."

"Excuse me?"

"Okay, well, maybe it was not her, but it was the description you left me. Short with the tight curly hair and very good body."

I raise my head slightly, pick up the glass, and gulp down the rest of the drink. It tastes even better than before. "That's not what I said."

He shrugs. "Maybe not."

"So what was she doing? Why was she here?"

"I do not know that."

"Then what exactly do you know?"

"Just that I saw her come in with a couple of men. They were very tall."

"Let me guess . . . you don't know anything about them either."

"I am just a bartender." He taps his forefinger in front of my glass. I raise my head slightly. Yes.

As he turns I catch myself: *You are drinking.* He pivots back, says something, or it's the music that seems more tinny and acrimonious by the second, and I feel a resurrection of sorts is coming. I put my hand in my front pocket and finger the wad of cash inside, hoping it's at least twenties. I try to hand the bartender something when he returns with my drink. "No, no," he says. "All expenses are paid."

I wake up in a ball at the top of my bed, covers down by

where my feet should be, unsure how I arrived. It had something to do with the weather and a bartender. Yes, the man who drove me home and then politely left.

My head is all church bells and tractors. Slowly I rise to find the bottle of ibuprofen I've been dipping into judiciously for the leg injury that seems in check, though maybe it's just lost prominence this morning. My entire body is throbbing. I drink three glasses of water then bury myself back underneath the covers.

When I get up again it is early afternoon. I shower and cross the street for a cup of coffee, slowly coming to life as I read the news, put off by the date, the eighth day of the new year, and what have I done, where am I? When the waiter brings me my coffee, he shakes his head, somberly says, "Terrible day yesterday." It takes a second for me to realize he's talking about the war and not me.

Yesterday saw some of the most brutal bombings since the fighting began. More leaflets were dropped near the border with Egypt urging residents to leave. The bombs and soldiers were coming soon. In the *Jerusalem Post*, a woman in a floral headscarf raises her open palms to the air: *Where are we supposed to go?*

They stayed and got pummeled. Forty air strikes in all hit the small territory overnight and it was not lost on anyone that forty is a sacred number, the number of days of the great flood, the number of years the banished Jews spent wandering the desert, the number of nights Moses spent up on the mountain to prove his people worthy of the Ten Commandments, the number of years the Jews had peace before unraveling and invoking the spirit of Christ; and now, these holy bombs launched methodically in their Hanukkah war after a day of ground incursions, rockets, and explosions that left seventy Palestinians and five Israelis dead—the fighting so treacherous at one point that Israel halted all attacks for three hours, calling it a humanitarian break. Today they're back at each other's throats.

Forty is also the number of years I've been alive. Take note: it must mean something.

Though I feel like I am one hundred years old this afternoon.

In the Movie Star Café, it's business as usual: there's eighties music, the incessant click-clack of laptops, steaming cappuccino machines, shift workers nursing war-TV hangovers, their bloodstained eyes and tense cheekbones the only clue anything's slightly off, as we sit together in the shadows of Garland, Hepburn, Deneuve, praying into ceramic cups. The poster girls are not having it today, either.

I will run later and find a meeting, I promise the great dames.

Above it all, comes a familiar tune: "*It's the end of the world as we know it, and I feel fine . . .*"

At home I find my neighbor slamming his palm against his front door. He is wearing a terry-cloth robe, white scarf wrapped around his head like an ancient queen. "Ah," he turns to me, jittery, "I am so glad you've come home . . . See, what's happened is I've locked myself out. If you have a screwdriver inside, I can pop it out, the lock."

"I don't have a screwdriver."

"What do you mean you don't have? What kind of house does not have a screwdriver? A small hammer . . . duct tape. You never know what is going to be here and the landlord, he is a pig. He will not come for things like this, he doesn't care." He is distraught, clenching his fists, then pounding, his face violent yet despondent.

"It's all right," I say. "There's got to be something we can do—what about a locksmith?"

"No! There will be no locksmith!"

"Okay, no locksmith."

"You don't understand," he says, "nobody can come here, nobody . . ." He slowly lowers himself to the floor, careful to keep his short stubs of thigh together and not inadvertently expose more than necessary. Sweet, though I wouldn't have cared. He buries his head in his hands and whines, "I am a terrible person."

"This isn't about a lock, is it?" I kneel down next to him. "What's going on in there?"

"I have broken a rule, a very big rule for someone who's doing what I'm doing. You know who I am, no? I run the van with the condoms and medicines, I work with many shelters, and now . . . I promise this has never happened before. You don't know me, you won't believe."

"No, I will."

"I can't . . ." He is crying.

"Yudi, it's okay, trust me."

"I have fallen in love with a client and he has fallen in love with me, he thinks at least, he doesn't really know. What can he know, he is barely a person yet and what he's come from . . ."

Through his heaving, I get this: The boy behind the door is sixteen and from Gaza. He escaped through one of the tunnels used to float weapons, supplies, food, everything in from Egypt, crawling a mile underground, then traveling by night into the Sinai. There was money he'd been saving for years, money earned the only way he knew, though it brought shame upon his family. It's miraculous he's survived, Yudi says. One of the boy's brothers cut off his left pinkie, the finger that sent messages. Another dipped his penis in ice water and kept a sharp blade at his throat as he added block after block of ice. His mother stopped looking at him, spoke to him only through a veil, and when passing him on the street cast her eyes to the ground. That was

most painful for the boy, Yudi says. To have to choose between your mother and your God-given nature. Thoughts of
his mother had become synonymous with suicide. The boy
had appeared around Yudi's van for weeks before he took a
piece of bread, a condom, mouthing, *Thank you*, in Hebrew
without a sound. It broke Yudi's heart.

"For twelve years I have been doing this work," he tells
me. "Twelve years and there have been crushes, sure, but I
don't pay attention really, you see them for what they are.
But this boy . . . it's like he came to me directly from God."

I tell him again that I understand, but I don't.

Yudi says this boy has been hustling for years and is
addicted to crystal meth. He won't quit the life, it's all he
knows, and they fight monstrously, he and Yudi, so bad it
often turns violent. Now the boy has locked Yudi out of
his own apartment. I take him inside with me, give him a
T-shirt and pair of boxer shorts. He says he's never worn
boxers. They are for lesbians and American basketball play-
ers. We sit down on my bed, drinking tea and talking more
about the boy. Yudi could lose his job, though he helped
create the program and is more dedicated than anyone. "*Ha-
matzav chara* . . . I am a terrible person," he repeats.

"Maybe," I say, "but that's not really helpful thinking."

"Have you heard anything I've said? I've broken the covenant with my organization, broken the laws of the state of
Israel, my board will not like this at all, and if he turns me
in . . ."

"He won't and you know it."

"You are, I think, a little bit prejudiced against the
Palestinians."

"This has nothing to do with the Palestinians."

"Do you see we are at war?"

"Yes, I see, it's all anyone talks about around here."

"You don't understand."

"Oh, please. You're fucking a client who happens to be a minor. That's your problem and it's bad enough. Don't complicate it with thousands of years of history."

"You want they should send him back to the fanatics who raised him? They should cut off another finger! I would sooner have flaming arrows shot through my heart, hurl myself into a pool of maggots. Not for my life . . ."

Again he covers his face with open palms, shoulders shaking, though not making a sound. We sit next to each other on my bed, which somehow I got it together to make before heading to the café. I put a hand on his shoulder, though I'm not really a comfort person. *Ten*, exhale, *nine*, exhale . . . At a meeting once I heard someone say you could learn new emotions, fake it till you make it. Yudi stirs and leans back slightly, throwing both of his arms behind him, and says thank you. "I don't even know you really."

"You helped me shave my head." I had been clipping it out on the terrace when he'd come outside the other night. I trusted him with the plastic razor right away.

"Yes, but you are so calm. So having it all together."

"I fell off the wagon last night." My words surprise us both.

"*Ma zeh?* Off wagon?"

"I got drunk. So drunk I can't remember things."

"But you said you are not drinking? Oh . . ."

"There was this bartender. He gave me drinks. I don't know, I woke up in his car and had no idea how I'd gotten there. He was driving me home."

"Was he thinking for sex? I mean you know, I am of course aware, but that head, you are so positively not for men."

I laugh. Then a thought hits and I can't believe it took so long. The bartender talked about Gila. He fed me drinks, then took me home, as if there were some logic to the whole evening. Now he knows where I live, information that could be dangerously passed along to someone looking for something; everything's been compromised. My face must be ghastly white with fear, though Yudi misinterprets the origins.

"I understand," he says, reaching out and gently rubbing my upper arm.

I shiver slightly, but settle in as he keeps his hand there, not too tight, as if he knows my limits. It's the first time I've been touched in weeks and it's okay, nice even. You forget what it's like, another person's fingers on your skin, why from the youngest age I've worshipped the body and why it also terrifies me. Yudi turns toward me, hand still affirming, saying we both have much to make amends with. We agree that we can help each other.

I went to rehab, the final time, after crawling out of a taxi one morning in my late twenties straight into hell. I am not being melodramatic. My girlfriend at the time, hopelessly addicted to love and heroin, hauled around enough theatrics for us both. Addled to the point that rendered sex passé, hardly worth the effort, we carted each other back and forth to bars along the West Side Highway, near my apartment. That sultry morning, still end-of-night blue and wretched, I had the sense of being watched beyond the idea of everyday exhibitionism I carried with me back then.

We'd left the Boiler Room after my girlfriend had roughed up her thigh trying to find a super vein in her groin and was threatening to hang herself. I was taking her home to sleep it off in my bed with the steel-gray sheets, when climbing out of the cab she nicked her leg on a stray piece of metal, the doorframe, perhaps, and there was the vein she'd been looking for. It made a bloody mess of her leg. Upon noticing the ooze, she screamed and spilled onto the sidewalk.

I reached out of the taxi to grab her, but someone else had a hand on her shoulder. A thick, freckled hand, well manicured.

"What's the matter with her?" said my father.

"What are you doing here?" I shot back, stiletto-fierce, eye makeup smudged across my shirt like a grease stain.

"It's Marc," he said. "And it's serious. So help me get her up and back into the cab."

"She's not going anywhere. I love her!"

"No. You don't. Don't bullshit me and definitely don't bullshit yourself. There's no time for this. Your brother is hanging by a thread."

He bent down and felt her pulse. I was suddenly guilty. It should have been my job. Why didn't I think of that? If I focused on my girlfriend the rest would go away. My father lifted her up and swung her over his shoulder, her dirty-blond hair streaming down his back. She started pounding his lower back with both fists, screaming, "Put me down!"

"Keys." He held out his free palm.

"We don't want your help! Put her down!"

"Let go!" She tried to dig her knees into his stomach, but he gripped her tighter.

"Damnit, Jen, give me the fucking keys or I'll strangle her."

I detached the chain from my belt loop and opened the front door. He brushed past me with my girlfriend still shouting and pumping her fists into his back.

Upstairs he ordered me to open my door and followed me inside. My girlfriend had nodded out somewhere along the two flights up, her entire body deflating like an air mattress no longer needed. He dropped her facedown on the bed, which I hadn't made in days, and quickly looked around. "This is where you live?"

He had never been to my apartment, a stark loft with

next to nothing on the retouched brick walls. I liked the openness—the towering ceilings and exposed pipes. It felt new and industrial and alive, the opposite of where I'd grown up, where he still lived. I liked that it appalled him.

I dropped down to my knees, stroking my girlfriend's hair with fervor.

"Listen to me," my father said. "Marc's probably not going to live."

A cold spear shot through my breastplate.

"He slammed his car into a goddamn mountain. He was speeding. Going way too fast."

I felt my eyes shut and wished I could keep them sealed for a very long time. Opening even a crack would unleash something fertile, something furious. *Keep it in*, I thought. *Just keep it in.* My girlfriend stirred, muttering something I couldn't make out. I had it in mind that I could serve her, save her. That was all I needed.

"Get your keys, wallet, whatever. We have to go," my father said.

"I'll be there later," I responded, and before I realized I had no idea where *there* was, my father was lifting me by the shoulders and shaking me.

"Goddamnit, he needs you now, so snap out of it!" He slapped my face.

It stung. And sunk a deep weight into my chest where the spear had been.

My brother was in a coma, my father said, as we walked back downstairs and into his car with the tinted windows, and for the first time his words stuck in me. Nobody even knew Marc was back in the States. Last we'd heard he'd been living with a woman south of Sydney. I had letters in blue airmail envelopes, some never opened, because I was still mad at him.

My father said Marc had been trying to see my mother.

He'd broken up with his girlfriend and was distraught. She'd sent him the plane ticket.

"You talked to her?"

"She's at the hospital."

In minutes so were we. But it didn't matter. He never woke up again.

At the Movie Star Café this morning I realize half of January is gone and here's what I've got to show for it:

—One meeting at the queer center, where everyone looked like they were just out of diapers and I did not say a word

—Seven dinners on the terrace of my apartment, when it was not raining, four of them with Yudi, one with the boy too

—At least ten walks along the beach, and a couple of long runs on the boardwalk, slowly   c o m i n g back into the thing that saves me from the other thing

—Two yoga classes

—Read countless online articles and abstractions about the war

—Almost thirty cups of cappuccino

—Absolutely no protests or pierced girls

—Nothing of Gila Zyskun

—One night at the bar in the old port in Jaffa, where I didn't stay long enough for a glass of water

I'd gone back to the bar, despite the shaking fear in my toes, to find the bartender who'd juiced me, but he was gone. Someone who might have been the manager said in Hebrew that he would never be back. My spine curled up. I now look even more closely over my shoulder, burying my skin beneath hoods and sunglasses when I go out on the street.

Yesterday the Israeli army hit relief offices in Gaza. It's always "yesterday" in the café where we gather over the papers. Reports say a bomb had been fired from the building first, which the relief workers say is ridiculous and typical, first the Israelis turn back a ship carrying food and medicine, now they've bombed a building with supplies for hundreds of thousands of people living in the war zone. Relief workers are calling for more resources, help for the people.

"It is somehow not right," the waiter says, "that we sit here and drink coffee."

"Have you been to the protests?"

He shakes his hand dismissively. "What good is that? I am going to join the relief people. They are coming from everywhere. You should too."

"Maybe . . ." I look away. I can't even make it to a meeting.

This morning I ran five miles on the boardwalk in a light-gray rain and still the pull of a glass of wine is even stronger than yesterday. Hours to go before I'm safe. I order another coffee so the waiter will leave me alone and open the *Christian Science Monitor*, shifting my sunglasses on top of my head. I need a meeting . . . and I need a drink. I used to get rattled when people came drunk to meetings. Nothing stated outright but you just knew. And then there were rumors, the stages of denial, if you're showing up the actual behavior is less significant, you're onboard with the grand design. Getting clean is active: like sports.

"What makes you think you'll be different this time?" my father asked, when I begged him to send me away again after Marc.

"I don't know."

"I need to hear more conviction than that." He loathed weakness in any form and addiction was about as weak as you could get. For me it wasn't half as decrepit as asking him for help with something so personal. That's how bad I was.

"You know, there are people who say it's chemical," I told him.

"Oh bullshit, Jen. That's just bullshit. You need to toughen up and you need a purpose. So work on thickening that taffeta you call skin and I'll figure out what we're going to do with you."

The coffee grinder churns me out of it and I am torn apart wondering whether that glass of wine might not be the best alternative today. The waiter appears at my table, asks if I'd like another coffee. I request a menu. Reading the English side, I zero in on the name of an old Jewish army, reminiscent of my trip here with Marc and how we drank like rebels ourselves. I'd once read that the average beer is 95 percent water, a good liquid.

The waiter stands above me, hovering. Not like there's much for him to do, the café is empty today.

It happens so fast I almost don't recognize my voice. "No, not coffee, I'll have a beer."

It is just past noon, still a bit gray out, normal for this time of year, but the sun is struggling. I can feel it gasping to break through the soft cover of clouds. My Maccabee arrives and I briefly think, you don't *have* to drink it. But I do.

At twenty-five, this sort of struggle made sense. At forty, it is most undignified.

As is chasing my father and his lover halfway around the globe. From what I'm told she was his watchdog, his eyes on the inside, whatever that means. My own eyes burn slightly, throat drier than a camel's ass. My thoughts are interrupted when the café's door opens and someone walks in, staring straight at me. He is young and beautiful and queer-like, if not queer. I can't help thinking I've seen him somewhere. Or this beer is making me paranoid.

"May I join you?" asks the man-boy, hanging onto the light so I can't see his features . . . but that voice.

"Oh my god, it's you."

The bartender takes a seat across from me. "You were looking for me."

I sigh.

"I left my position very quickly after we last saw one another."

"I heard."

"It is not what you think."

"What do I think?"

"That I was fired for making too much in the drink. For having your head on the bar when the owner came in and he was very angry. He said get this woman out."

"Is that what really happened?"

He affirms, just as the waiter appears, and orders a beer. Now we are two sitting in a stuffy café on a shifting winter's day. The bartender comments on this, tells me he is working at a new bar, gives me the address, which I will forget in two seconds. His beer arrives and he holds it out toward me before sipping.

"Then why were you fired?"

He pivots his head back and forth. "No, no, I was not fired. I was promoted to the next bar. It is even more fancy. The cocktails are very serious."

I am confused and wish I wasn't drinking, but the warmth, the comfort is just marvelous.

"You want to know what I really think?" I say.

"Of course."

"You wanted to know where I lived. Someone wants that information. And you gave it to her."

He smiles. "That is not it."

"Then what?"

"I thought you might have more interest in me. Maybe we can be friends."

"Friends? Seriously?" I laugh, and he looks down slightly, wiggles his fingers against his glass.

"Okay, okay . . ." He stands abruptly. "I cannot stay longer, but you are correct in one thing. I have come to tell you something. Give me one moment."

He calls over the waiter, talking to him in Hebrew, almost whispering, I can't make out a word. Though I see some money pass into the waiter's hand. The bartender pats him lightly between the shoulder blades. Then he leans both palms on the table and looks down at me. "Go home," he says.

"I have things to do today."

"That is not what I mean."

"Who sent you?"

"Go home, Jennifer Baron."

He stares a second more, then pushes back slightly on his arms. Being dramatic, no doubt, but he knows things. I never told him my name.

"Wait." I grab his elbow. "Please, is it Gila?"

He sighs, removes my hand. "Just take my words. You are not in your league, you are not even on the field, and you will not save anyone despite these ideas you've built up in your head. You will only cause more trouble. Now, I must be going."

He turns and walks out of the café. Before I can stand, the waiter brings over another beer and says courtesy of the gentleman.

I say thanks.

And drink the second beer, staring up at the goddesses I've come to believe in more than the highest power in the world. This is the only field I need. There is no home anymore. And that's what's keeping me here, Judy Garland and all.

* * *

I have been circling the same three blocks downtown in the newborn heat, looking for the meeting, but I keep rounding back on a street that isn't there. In between the sidewalks there is sparkling-gold sand. But for the banana-yellow of an old Caterpillar tractor and a young man standing beside it in a hard hat eating french fries, the scene could have passed for an urban experiment. The street that was a sandbox.

How can a street be a sandbox?

As a child, I was often asked to explain things. How does water boil? But why does the flame come up when you click the knob to the right? What happens if you put your hand over that pretty blue-gold mass of fire? It turns your fingers into marshmallows, I once told Marc and he giggled. I gripped his belly as if he shouldn't be laughing, as if not believing his fingers would become squeezably soft and sticky was like crying over spilled milk—stupid. It was a game the two of us played, testing each other to do the one thing that went too far.

"Well, if you don't believe me . . ." I tempted.

"It's stupid."

I shrugged, pushing my upper lip above my teeth, eyes wide. Others thought I was tough. In fifth grade I beat up the strongest boy on the block, twisting his wrist behind the back of his head and making him scream, "I'm a faggot!" louder and louder. I was a bully. And sure enough a faggot myself. My cheeks tingle when I remember this. When I remember Marc at nine, my mother gone, and for some reason I'm back from training and bored.

Marc shouts at the top of his lungs: "I won't do it! You can't make me!"

"And they all say you're so smart."

"Stop it!"

"What?"

"Stop looking at me funny, I'm not doing it."

"Oh well. I thought you were different. Thought you were so *special* . . ." I draw out that word, the one adults used all the time around him. Then I turn my back on him, like my father.

"You're not my sister! You're a sadist!"

"How do you know that word?"

"Fuck you!"

"Why are you getting so mad?"

"Because you suck."

"Remind me again why they say you're so smart."

"Because I know your fingers don't turn into marshmallows on the stove. It's not possible."

"Then why are you so mad?"

This is the one question that irks him more than anything. He has a temper he cannot contain. Throughout his short life, all the drinking, the drugs, the shrinks, nothing will help. He is a terror to himself and early on I learn how to rouse the beast, the one that jumps from rooftops, rides his bicycle deep into the ocean. One time he tries to dig out his ankle bone with a Swiss Army Knife because it's not supposed to be so big. I had told him it meant he was retarded.

I walk past him and click on the flame. It burns into a bluish-gold triangle. We stare over it, me giving him the look, his cheeks growing pinker by the second. Like a cartoon, you can see the steam rising behind his head. Then his shoulders release and he bends toward the flame. He sticks his fingertips right into it. My chest clenches. "Okay, enough! You win. Stop it!"

But once he crosses over it's never enough. He moves his palm just above the flame as the skin begins to bubble and you can smell it. Worse than hair, flesh has a tar-like scent.

I reach for his hand, shouting again, "Stop it! Stop it!"

His eyes roll up high in their sockets. I pull his wrist, scraping the back of my own hand against the flame just for a second, and it burns like fuck. "Ha!" he shouts, and now I'm mad.

I dig my nails into his skin where's it's bubbling and wet.

He screams so loud I know I've gone too far. He falls back slightly, staring up at me, and I remember the squirrel we'd bonfired alive a couple of years earlier, the white of its eyes slowing fading out.

I let go of his hand and the back of his head hits the floor. "Marc!!!" I shake him.

His arms are dead weight, eyes shut.

"Aiii! *Dios!*" Sofia screams behind me, comes running, then drops down to her knees. She touches Marc's cheek lightly and his eyes flutter open. He turns his head and smiles at me. She stands, blows out the flame.

"Jennifer," she says, "call the ambulance."

"You call," I reply, because right now I am down on the floor with Marc, hugging him like I can, because I'm the only one who understands.

The hand hits my back, then the Hebrew words come. The man who had been eating french fries one by one stands in front of me pulling me up by the elbow. From what I can make of his words, the crank in his eyes, and the scratchiness between my fingers, I must have sat down in the middle of the street that wasn't a street and started digging.

"This is not a beach," he says, finally, in English.

I shrug. "Whatever."

Still holding my elbow, he leans into me and leers, as if I'm fucking up something important, not just lunch.

"You are drunk," he says.

"No I'm not! You can't even say that!"

"*Yalla*, let's go, move out . . . crazy fucking tourist," he says, letting go of my arm and scuttling back to his tractor.

I stand very slowly, trying to stay stable so he'll see his mistake. But he doesn't seem to be watching. I shake the sand from my pants and walk right past the tractor. Two men are inside now, concentrating as the nose dips into a vat of wet concrete and drools it over the sand. I head toward the beach, craving a landscape that makes sense, sand where it's supposed to be. When I hit the beach I take off my sneakers and walk far along the shore, passing the wind surfers, the people bathing with dogs, the nudists, though they are sparse today, it's still officially winter. So I walk and walk, arriving at a rocky corner late in the afternoon, I think. I do not have a phone and realize I've forgotten my watch at home. No wonder I missed the meeting. It is getting colder, temperatures dropping fast into evening.

Marc had a third-degree burn, the skin cut to the bone. He never told them it was me who dug in worse, that would have been a violation of us and we were all that counted. He had a quick operation to reconstruct the skin from a patch on his ass, scars he carried like a medal. I thought all siblings loved each other this violently.

I lean back on the sand and feel him close, perhaps because we'd spent time here together, just the two of us. A shorebird dips into the ocean, working with the dusky rays to spot out its prey. The lazy orange sun sinks beneath the waves, and I cannot take my eyes from it, because it's this— the fix of beauty and being, of place and pattern—that's been said to release endorphins, not unlike eating a piece of dark chocolate or gossiping with a coworker. And I am a hog for endorphins; most athletes are.

It's like I'm breathing for the first time today, all week maybe.

I take another deep breath and hold it. Letting it out
through my mouth with a big sigh. My eyes adjust again
on the horizon, then shoot in closer. A figure rises slowly
from the ocean, like a diver who's been under for a bit. It
walks toward me, no mask but a silver cape tied around
its neck. My eyes are playing tricks or I drank more than
I'd thought. I remember three Maccabees, or was there a
fourth? I blink tightly. Open. And it's still there, the cape so
silver but roughhoused a bit, less heroic, more survivalist,
as if Astroman had been living under the creaking boardwalk where the kids on crystal play all night, and it occurs
to me then: I know him.

There's a bit of sand in his hair, but other than that he's
completely dry. Does that point in favor of a ghost? Or is it
the whatever-percent alcohol in beer . . . Okay, let's get this
straight: the shifting dusk always reads slightly ghost-y, but
I swear there are lavender beams bouncing from his electric
cape. He is stronger too. The most familiar beach smell is
oil or fish and he seems a creature of both. He hasn't shaved
and the little hairs on his face have gone scaly, something he
would never put up with in life.

When he's about three feet away I say, "Dad?"

He nods.

"You alive?"

"Not really," he says, a light cloud of breath trailing his
words. I think the black tights and shirt might be a wet
suit. "I'm here right now, in this moment. And in some ways
these moments are all we have. What amounts to this thing
we call life."

"Is this for real?"

"You know, Jen, there was a time I was afraid of dying.
Now I'm fearing for the living. For all of you. How's that for
the mindfuck of a lifetime?"

Dead or alive, he is exactly the same, all full of himself

and oozing bad philosophy. I have an urge to smash his head in the sand.

"Oh, and you'll love this—I've reunited with my parents! We've been having tea together in the afternoons. Your grandparents. Remember them?"

"Yes. They wore big hats, especially your mother. There were parties in Brighton Beach. Caviar. Herring. Champagne. Why are we talking about this?"

"Because I bring regards."

"From the afterlife?"

"Don't be so cynical," he says, and despite all signs pointing toward absurdity, the air between us sweetens— the idea that my grandparents in heaven or wherever are thinking of me. I stare at my father and he does look serene.

"What's going on here?"

"I could ask you the same thing. You were not supposed to come back."

"I had to."

"Why?"

I turn away, knowing my face will reveal it's about a girl. We are alike in this, though it's the first time we've staked the same turf. Behind him the sky bruises, wind charting small ripples in the sand, waves coming stronger, louder. He sighs, starts walking backward toward the sea. "She is no good!" he shouts.

"Gila?"

"Yes, Gila. She's a cheater and a killer. Stay away . . . trust me!"

"I don't."

"Then let me go."

"Let you go? Where?"

He's still walking backward. I stay put, so we are screaming now. "I'm speaking metaphorically," he says. "We are all metaphors! That's it!"

At the shoreline he turns around and faces the water. "Dad!"

He looks over his shoulder, shouts: "Don't worry, I'll see you soon!" Then he hops a few steps on one leg before diving into the sea. I run down calling to him, but he's disappeared into waves. He does not come up again. I sit down on the wet sand and dig my fingers in, grateful it still feels like earth.

PART 2

BRIEFLY, BEFORE THE WAR, THERE WAS HOPE

New York City, Early November 2008

Sun rises late in the middle of fall, leaves still dangling from the maples and honey locusts around Trinity Church, a few beginning to flirt with color. Tickling rays lend hope to the battered notes on Wall Street. The markets had not expected the Democrat to win—neither did we, and I must confess: I voted for him, my first time dipping in the ritual of electing a president. My father would have been livid.

I have walked this street from beginning to end hundreds, thousands of times across the decades, the light bounding in shifts and shards that dwarf the mightiest titan. Today I am headed into the family foundation, which I try to do on Fridays, though I can't remember the last time I've shown up. The contractors have spent the past several months turning our three floors inside out, keeping me away from the office more than normal, though, in truth, I'm more often required to be at a restaurant or banquet hall than behind a desk. I've grown weary of the drop-ins probing about my father's disappearance, can no longer keep the government names straight—Parker, Hernandez, Washington. And my guy, Yearling.

But I do need to monitor the goings-on every so often, talk to a few people, make my presence known. Seems the least any foundation president would do in the best of times; now there's additional reassurance necessary with my father gone and the economy in the gutter. I like this part. More than the meals with other money people, heads of old stalwarts and hip new companies, venture vultures, anyone with an idea smacking of goodwill and in need of large sums of cash, the office keeps one foot in front of the other. Still the young ones hate you. They don't understand why they have to be here at all. If the work is so important, right, they'd do it for nothing. But they don't want to work, they want meeeeeeeeaning, an existence dripping with personal satisfaction, as if that's a prerequisite, not a perk. I like working-class kids better. They see right through your bullshit. Not that there's much to see. The foundation's work is on the level, its reputation impeccable. Our thing is infrastructure and we've steered a fortune into hospitals, middle-income housing, museums. "We must avoid controversy," my father told me early on. "Politics, causes, opinions, anything that reeks of too much sentiment . . . it's not for us. We do the stuff nobody can argue with."

As it turns out, it's also the stuff that can survive the lowest of downturns. And we have not stopped prospecting. Most people I know, beginning with my father, are classic libertarians, firm in their conviction that left to their own devices people will do the right thing and take care of one another.

I linger down the street in the sugary sunlight, the East River twinkling blue as the Mediterranean, and feel a surge of anything is possible. In the lobby, I swipe my badge through security and smile at the guard. You'd have no idea we owned the building and half the others in this new boom; we rent out most floors to banks and hedge fund people, 20 percent to do-gooders at a reduced rate. Stepping off the elevator on the fiftieth floor, I am greeted by a girl in a tight green sweater dress and pink high-top sneakers. It crosses my mind that pink sneakers are perhaps not appropriate for your first interaction with a somewhat conservative foundation, though her hair is tidy, a sheen of black with crisp bangs against her forehead. Still, would you trust a woman wearing pink sneakers?

"May I help you?" she asks. Condescending enough. I like them to have an attitude. One shouldn't feel too welcome in a place like this. You should feel elite, chosen. Like your past has added up to something and now you are ready to share it with the world.

"You want to help me?" I say. "Maybe start by losing the sneakers."

"I'm sorry, did you have an appointment with someone?"

I walk by without consequence. Later she'll ask who the woman was in black jeans and cowboy boots, and she'll feel contrite, stupid. I would be lying if I said I didn't like the idea, but it doesn't last long. As I turn a few corners, wrap myself down the wide spiral staircase to our first floor, I am blindsided by a new level of stupidity: I have no idea where my office is.

Within minutes I'm back at the girl with the pink sneakers. "Okay," I say, "give up the game: where is my office?"

"Who are you?"

"The name on your paycheck."

"Arnold C. Correola?"

My accountant. The actual name on her paycheck.

"That's right. How do you do?" I put out my hand to shake hers. She barely touches my fingers. I give the attitude back, all eyes. She reaches for the phone and dials Arnie, who's not picking up.

"Is Melissa here?"

"Okay, I get it. This is a joke, right? I saw something like this on the news . . . A couple of fanatics went to Planned

Parenthood and pretended to be a drug company? They said they wanted to make this huge donation, but there were cameras and bugs and they ended up calling the police . . . It was right before the election?"

Ignoring her, I take out my phone and text Melissa.

"We can't just let anyone in? You know?"

Melissa texts back immediately: *Stay put.* I roll through the messages on my phone, continuing to ignore the girl who's buried her head in a large computer screen.

"Jen!" Melissa storms through the glass doors, her arms flung open dramatically.

I hug her, whispering, "Where the fuck is my office?"

She pulls away smiling. "Come."

I follow her through the reception into a corridor with brown walls and nicely spaced prints, one clearly a Rauschenberg, the others less obvious. In the beginning my mother selected the art. When she first met my father she was a painter who worked with oils on tiny canvases, the biggest the size of a street sign or shoe box. They were meant to be shown in groups, the pieces together far surpassing their individual parts, like the human body or anthills, she used to say. Why she married my father was anyone's guess. Her family had money, and she was a star among the up-and-comers at the Art Students League. She wore platform shoes and flowers in her hair.

When I was seven or so, before their marriage collapsed in a flurry of dreams gone bad, I'd overheard my mother at a dinner party. I was on display in a blue silk dress—this was before I'd called the moratorium on formal wear. I was once a traditional girl, though even I find that hard to believe.

A man approached my mother, one of my father's partners with butt-plug fingers and a jagged smile, old enough to find his hairline receding no matter how much coke kept him perpetually startled. He swept the strands back as best he could with wax or something equally shiny. All of this in my now-mind, at the time I remember thinking he looked like a stuffed ox. He toddled up to my mother by the window. The view behind her—Cole Porter romantic—a million red and white lights on the streets below.

"Hello, sweetheart!" He smiled, the corner of his mouth rising and falling as if wired. Some babble into it—she could charm anyone, my mother—he asked if she was still painting.

I saw her lips broaden into a slight arch. "Are you still masturbating?" she replied. A couple nearby turned simultaneously, then looked away. I wouldn't say the inquisitor himself was shocked, he brokered millions of dollars an hour, remember, but he was hardly quick enough for a comeback, so to speak. The thing is, even at seven, I'd heard her say this before. The first time I looked up the word in the dictionary, I was led to a book on the shelf called The Female Orgasm. Masturbation was normal, just touching, but the man skulked off in defeat and I knew the word was more loaded, more daring than it seemed.

When my mother left several years later, I was elated. She absorbed too much of the spaces around me. What bothered me most was she left all of her clothes behind, as if she'd died and we were stuck to disperse them to charity. My father made a phone call and within a few weeks everything was gone, save the one pair of platform shoes I stole from her closet, black Mary Janes, chunky as bricks, shoes I would outgrow by the following year when my feet wouldn't quit. Like my father I have giant feet and long thin toes. I kept the shoes for years. They reminded me of illicit talk, the sweet smell of bourbon, tight white couches, the Velvet Underground, masturbation, and art.

There are no paintings in my new office, though the windows reveal an expansive view of the river all the way out to New Jersey, pinkish light backing the rise of an ambitious skyline, ferries streaming in all directions, the Statue of Liberty winking above it all. It's a corner office, of course.

I run my hand along the mahogany desk, then sit down behind it. My laptop is turned on and running. The phone in my pocket buzzes, but I ignore it.

Melissa sits in front of me. "What do you think?"

"I like the view."

"I know, right? How are you?"

I look at her, trying to gauge what she's asking. As far as anyone knows, my father is still missing. The man I'd watched fade away almost three months earlier was pretending to be a dying rabbi whose minions made hard goat cheese and bred right-wing political candidates—neither of which my father had much of a taste for. His body was laid to rest in the Mount of Olives. But Yearling thinks he's turned up something new. He'd sent an e-mail this morning with a red exclamation point saying, *WE HAVE TO TALK!!!*

I brush off Melissa. "Fine, I'm fine. What's new? How's Robert?" I've learned to stroke people by taking an interest in them, asking about boyfriends, girlfriends, babies, stray dogs found behind the amphitheater in Central Park; this does not come easy for me. Robert is a relatively new find.

"We went skiing in Patagonia last month," Melissa says, and walks behind my desk to show me pictures on her phone. There they are in front of a blue-white glacier, faces ruddy under colorful hats, Melissa's is bright orange with a tassel. She looks happy; I cannot remember the last time I traveled for fun. Melissa senses my growing anxiety and shuts off her phone. She leans against my desk, looking out toward the harbor, so close that if I swiveled my chair I could grab her by the hips and get my face up her skirt. She's sexy, in an uptight way, like you want to roll her around in the mud or stick a finger up her ass right away and watch her crinkle. I always hire women who attract me in some way, and it's a test to keep the boundaries. Being sober helps. As does being lost in another person, even if she's disappeared behind a curtain tighter than death.

I push my chair backward in the other direction and walk to the window.

"We're doing well," Melissa says, moving next to me so we're both looking out at the water. Behind us, the phone on my desk rings in muted tones. If you put this scene in a movie it would be ridiculous. "I know this sounds crazy, all things considered, but people aren't asking for enough money. They had too much wrapped up in the banks and don't trust the economy. They're in cutting mode, not building."

"Then forget them. Don't look at anyone who's asking for less than a million. Put it right up front in the RFP."

"That never works. It just brings in the wrong people."

"Then you keep the money. Buy a Jaguar. Take your boy-friend on another ski trip."

You know who I sound like. It happens the second I step into this office, like his spirit coils down the walls and up through my feet, taking residence in my head, the way he'd command a room, kicking off his shoes, throwing his feet up on the furniture, and barking for a drink, the *New York Times*, someone to sit next to him and tickle the inside of his elbow as he opined on the day's top stories. It's where my obsession with the news started. Seeing him so powerfully now, I wonder if this is what *missing* is: absence smattering a canvas prettier than it ever was.

"We'll figure it out," I bring myself back to Melissa. "It's only money."

"You know, you've got to have money to say something like that."

"And you've just told me we do. Which is astounding because nobody else seems to."

"I'm worried about how we're positioning ourselves. There are too many people asking questions."

"People?" I back up slightly. She pretends she doesn't want to speak, but she will. We've known each other almost a decade, having met under circumstances not discussed outside of church basements with folding chairs and cardboard coffee cups, which means we really know each other. I touch her arm lightly. "It's okay, just tell me."

"That FBI guy's been around. He was asking about you and your father, he said he had a warrant to look at our books."

"Let him look."

"That's exactly what I said. So he did and nothing turned up, but you need to give me more to go on."

"I told you, I don't know anything else."

"Where have you been?"

"Home. Around. Come on, I e-mail you twenty times a day."

"I know but . . . something's different. Since you got back from that conference. What happened over there?"

"Nothing *happened*. It was a bunch of NGOs and development people who don't know the first thing about money, talking about money. Oh, and I got offered a job in Namibia. Think I should go?"

She smiles. "You're being secretive, which for people like us is never a good thing. You can trust me, you know that, right?"

My right pocket pulses again with a call. I guide Melissa lightly by the arm in the direction of the door. "Listen, can you get away for an early dinner? We'll go to Nobu."

She nods. "Seriously, Jen, I want to help. I really can help."

"Later, okay."

She leaves, and I shut the door behind her, taking a deep

breath and holding it in until my lungs hurt. When I first hired Melissa my father warned me against it. Never bring in anyone you know socially first, he said. The other way around's okay, but friends have expectations, they think they're special. My phone buzzes once more and I grab it out of my pocket. It's a text from Yearling: *Financial Times. READ IT NOW!!!!!*

I sit down behind my big desk, light streaming in so hard it pulses against my forehead and evaporates everything on my computer screen. I swivel around, looking out at the sun and water in front of me as the article loads. Then, in big letters across the top, comes the marquee: *Billionaire Fugitive Found Dead in Jerusalem.*

Before my mother left, she sat Marc and me down together in the big living room. The space was a contradiction, the walls cut up with Picassos and Miros but the furniture, lamps, rugs were Oriental, with lots of patterns and strings, seemingly from another era. In the beginning, I liked how dark it felt, how thick with secrets.

"This has nothing to do with you," my mother said after we'd sat down next to her on the couch. I had to turn awkwardly to see her face. "I simply cannot live like this anymore."

"Like what?" I asked. I was going on twelve and obsessed with details.

"Like a camp counselor. I never realized how much silence I need, the way people can bury me alive. Maybe you'll understand this someday. Maybe you'll hate me forever. But that's what I'm taking on. You are both strong. I've been watching and I know this to be true. You two are my core, you always will be, but I can't take one more minute of this life."

"Fuck you," I said, more because I wanted to show her

up than anything else. I'd learned to curse beautifully by then and had already had my heart broken by Sofia. I was on my way to becoming the fastest female skater in the world. My mother was nothing.

"You have a right to be sad, not angry. I opened my legs to that madman for you. I harbored you in my womb for ten months, Jennifer . . . Yes, you were that late. But I hung in there and when they ripped you out of me like a bloody tumor, you were perfect, and you are perfect, both of you. Trust me, my puppets, you don't want to watch your mother dry up like a lizard in August."

"What do you mean?" I stood up from the couch, mostly to show her how tall I was, to revel in the prominence of my electrified thigh muscles. I was an athlete and that was all that mattered.

"I'm dying here, Jen."

Marc leaned into my absence, sidling up next to her. "I'd like to go with you, if I may," he said, as though they were talking about a trip to the corner for a hot dog. Molded as delicately as a crystal goblet, my brother seemed otherworldly, ancestral like the furniture. He hated our father with a physical passion. Once when the old bastard—our name for him behind his back—had gone to pick him up at school in first grade, Marc claimed not to know him. There had been a string of kidnappings on the Upper East Side, so the school took his words seriously despite my father's protests, which, as Marc would later tell the story, went something like this: "I'll have you all strung up by your shoulders, after I skin that obstreperous little punk alive!" You can't blame the school officials, though the police settled the matter quickly when they arrived, and Marc was sequestered in his room for days. My mother visited him every few hours and from behind his door came deep snarls of laughter.

"You darling boy," she said. "How can I make you understand? This whole thing is against my nature. I'm an Aries. I cannot suffer one passion to fulfill another."

"But what about *my* nature?" Marc said. "He'll kill me too, don't you see? I should go with you. That would be best for all of us."

"No, trust me, love . . . this is better for you. It's what you need. I truly believe that." She cradled his head close to her breasts, saying how terribly sorry she was, how torn apart she was, but this marriage was the biggest mistake of her life. "Not you, my pet," she stroked his hair, coddling him, "you are the best thing I've ever done. That will never change. I just can't make this work for us." He bawled, and she held him tight, the way Sofia used to hold me, her grip stronger than any tears. I remember watching them, thinking about the Oscar party at our house in Greenwich a few months earlier. A movie about a woman who leaves her husband and kid behind to go find herself got most of the statues. Watching the ceremony on giant screens set up throughout the living room, the adults seemed stonier than usual, talking mostly of Meryl Streep's beauty and how adorable the kid was. My mother sat silently, and I swear she was smiling.

"It's not him." I speak loudly into my phone, our connection finicky in the gusts along the lower tip of Manhattan. I took the long away around to clear my head, but Yearling wouldn't let me have any space. I picked up on his fourth try.

"Uh, they're pretty sure it is," he says.

"Do they have DNA?"

"They're working on it."

"Good luck with that."

"Funny you're not happy. You're finally free."

Wind excruciating, I scrape my left hand through my hair to steady it, but it catches in a clump of gel, too slick for anything but show, not unlike the smarmy fellas who used to hang around my father. I sigh. Yearling says listen closely, he's got a few new details for me.

He begins to relay dates, names, who discovered what, when, and his theories. I am doing my best to follow but the wind keeps hitting me straight on, making me tear up, and I can't get the gel off my fingers without wiping them on my stiff-as-new jeans that you're not supposed to wash more than once a year. A word stops me: *rabbi*. Did he say rabbi?

"I'm sorry, what?"

"I'm telling you this is where it gets weird. You have to pay attention."

"What?"

"Remember last summer there was that rabbi who died? Big procession to Jerusalem, nobody drove for a week, that sort of thing . . . Well, you know this, of course, but your papa was bankrolling him, funding side businesses."

"Lots of Americans do that," I snipe at him, clearly defensive.

"You were there right before the rabbi died."

"No I wasn't." Gila said I was erased, no record of having been in the country, it would take very good intelligence to pin me to the woman who left, much better than the FBI could string together.

"Strange . . . your assistant told me you were at a conference."

"Yes. In Auckland."

"Something's not adding up. I'm trying to map certain logistics around. I have a spreadsheet."

"That sounds helpful."

"Are you sure you didn't got through Tel Aviv?"

"You want the conference schedule? Witnesses?" What's

amazing is how strongly you can start to believe your own lies. I am feeling righteous.

"You didn't see your father?"

"No," I say, and in that second I understand why Gila told me I couldn't call or write, not even under a fake name. Any ties could break the shroud.

"Okay, so here's the thing," Yearling says, "last week there were a whole bunch of gravestones turned over. Marble smashed all over the place. Vandalism, you know? Arab kids. Usually happens around the holidays. But, uh, when the police got there one of the totaled graves was for this rabbi who had just checked in, really, when you think about it. And the thing is, once they moved all the broken slabs of marble, there was nothing inside."

"Nothing?"

"Absolutely nothing."

I take a deep breath.

"Yeah," Yearling says, "this is what I'm thinking too."

"I don't understand."

"You don't?"

"No."

I saw my father lying in a hospital bed, the life draining out of his face, a determining factor in what I would do for him twenty-four hours later. Gila closed the deal. Then I was safe in Paris for a few days when his buddy Armond told me he'd passed. He and his wife Helene took me to an ancient synagogue on the Left Bank for Friday-night services. We all cried because we couldn't attend the funeral, which would be huge, my father mourned as a powerful rabbi as they lowered his body into sacred ground. The actual rabbi would disappear. Even in death my father could make people disappear.

I questioned why he couldn't just die and Armond told me it was a financial decision, easier to move out of reach of the government as a missing person. Once the estate went public everything would stop and we could all be held accountable. "Accountable for what?" I asked, not being naïve. I really didn't know the extent of what my father had been up to. I didn't want to know. Armond tapped my hand and said, "Don't worry, we'll take care of you."

But Yearling has a new thought. He says the empty grave is the kicker. Maybe there was a body moved or maybe it was never there, and it could have been anyone, really, there's nothing traceable, the stony remains doused in oxygen bleach, a sign of professionals. "Then a week later a guy fitting your father's profile gets blown out of a hotel in the Old City."

"What?"

"Oh, uh, yeah, I was getting to that . . . There was a bomb."

I stumble at the word *bomb* and grab onto the railing with my left hand, still sticky with hair gel, balancing the phone in my right. The boardwalk is lousy with sightseers enjoying the remaining rays of autumn, bird watchers with lenses so big they can scope past Brooklyn, cyclists in electric tights, all crowding for a quick glimpse of the green lady or stray sailboat as steam shoots from buildings across the river. I was right here when the second airplane hit the south tower on a different, stunningly perfect fall day. I watched the great fireball explode a rack of steel, the north tower still spitting a thin line of gray-black smoke into the air, upper floors hanging like ash from an untapped cigarette, pieces lightly falling. Later we learned those were bodies. My father managed to get me on my cell once I'd escaped farther east. Long past composure, he cried, "Chuckie was up there! He was eating breakfast!" His lawyer and best friend had been finishing up a cozy meal at Windows on the World with a woman who was not his wife. It took months before my father could say his name without shaking.

A bomb in a Jerusalem hotel? Sounds fishy.

Yearling is still talking, something about how they'll need me to identify his body. They would fly him home first, of course, and then notify us.

"I think you'll find the closure helpful," he says. "I've seen people in missing persons cases seriously lose it the longer they wait."

"Okay," I say.

"But Jennifer?"

"Yes?"

"Once we've got him and can start digging into things, you may have to account for your own whereabouts last summer and any connection to one missing rabbi."

"You mean the dead one?"

I hear him snuffle on the other end of the phone. "Just don't do anything stupid."

The night the towers went down, I couldn't return to my place so I camped out with my father in the apartment I grew up in. We ordered a pizza from the joint on the corner that was staying open all night for people in the neighborhood. When he delivered the pie the young guy with pale brown skin said, "God bless," and I nodded. I gave him a ten-dollar tip. We ate in silence, my father, Suki, and me, then sat together in the den. He'd closed all the windows though you couldn't smell it yet, we were far enough up-town. I remember the smoke and burning leather catching my throat as I walked north in silence with hundreds of other zoned-out people. When I shut my eyes I saw the building crumble, before it started mixing with TV images. We'd watched the clip over and over again on the news until they stopped showing it, because people said they were being traumatized by the footage. Now it was a lot of talking heads. My father kept his left hand tight around his cell phone waiting to hear from Chuckie, sure that he'd somehow got out, because Chuckie was like that, an escape artist. Suki told my father he was being ridiculous and he snarled at her, "Shut up, you fucking bitch! Get away from me!" She cowered off into the kitchen and I followed. It was only a matter of time before he turned on me too.

Suki poured herself another drink, filling a tall glass more than halfway with Scotch, topping it with a dash of seltzer. She looked like she'd been crying all day, which she had been. I put on the kettle for tea.

"He didn't mean it," I tried to comfort her.

"You think this is about some big tragedy?"

I stared at her.

"He's a pig every day. Why should this one be different?"

"He's in pain."

"I have a river I want to sell you—yes you," she said. "It's called De-Ni-Al. Get it, De-Nial . . . De-Nial . . ." She laughed. I mean, she really laughed, and I thought this is what trauma does, and this is how we perpetuate it, something I might have said in a meeting though I wasn't entirely sure what I even meant. I returned to my old bedroom and turned on CNN, which was all static, apparently the big antennas had fallen with the towers, and called Melissa. Her message said she was okay and with her family on Long Island, and I wondered if I should do the same. Instead I left the apartment despite protests from Suki and walked to a church on Third where I knew there were meetings. I sat with a bunch of tony white people I didn't know and together we tried to make meaning of what had just happened to our city.

Two days later Yearling calls again. "You're not going to believe this," he says, "but the body's gone."

"Gone?"

"Uh, yeah. Gone. Mossad is trying to keep it tight, but it's a little embarrassing losing such a big fish. A big dead fish."

Israel is a very small pond. Nothing like the city my father and I call home, where you can slip into a crowd and emerge as someone entirely different. These thoughts take hold as I listen to Yearling, this time sitting at my kitchen counter, fingering my passport. He warns again what might happen if the body does not turn up and we are back to square one, only this time we've got two missing bodies.

"Two?"

"The rabbi, remember?"

"I don't understand what one has to do with the other." I'd practiced this, my words and approach: ignorance above all.

"You are not convincing me. In fact, you're making me more suspicious. The rabbi is his man."

"His man? How do you figure?"

"I'm this close to pulling you in and polygraphing you."

I sigh, as if I'm fed up with the whole thing. "Go on then."

"I will. Soon."

"Why don't you just find my father? This other stuff is wearing on me."

He doesn't respond, sighs himself. Then repeats his theory of my involvement somehow, saying he'll figure it out eventually, and it will be worse for me.

One more time: "You sure you have nothing to tell me?"

"No," I say. "I don't."

If my father has bred anything into me, it's never trust the government. I'd pegged this more to money than criminality, though I am losing faith. Armond has not answered any of my calls or e-mails. I hang up with Yearling and try Armond again. Nothing.

Then I call Melissa. "Okay," I say, "I need you."

My brother Marcus Victor Baron was named after the painter Mark Rothko, who himself was born under the achingly Semitic though far more vibrant moniker Marcus Yakovlevich Rothkowitz, and, if you believe the biographers, was turned onto painting at the Art Students League, just like my mother. She loved Rothko and gave my father no other options for the stamp of his only son. She would not compromise as she'd done with me. Juniper is what she would have called me if my father hadn't put a stop to it—as he's reminded me many times throughout the years, how he saved me from the hippie linguistics of the day and how I should be more grateful given the way things turned out. "You see any feminists out there called Juniper?"

"I'm not a feminist. You mean lesbian."

"Semantics, Jen. Semantics."

I like this memory because it's the part of my father that softens, exactly what I need this morning as I head north on the Taconic in a car Melissa rented at the bottom of Hudson Street, inside a campus of parking lots, just as the sun was beginning to creep west. She used her own personal credit card.

We are practicing together how to move without tracks. Not so easy in this heavily coded world.

At first she questioned my motives for the early-morning drive through the misty caverns, something I would normally do in summer, as close to the day as possible, but this year I'd been in Tel Aviv (don't tell Yearling, I joke to myself). I am headed back in a couple of days, armed with a new passport, forged credit cards, bucketloads of money wired ahead and waiting in escrow. Melissa has helped me organize it all. I am some sort of venture capitalist, apparently. The state of Israel loves venture capital.

My phone blinks and buzzes at once, startling me. I see Melissa's name flash across the screen. She is checking in. Before I took off, she'd given me a plug and showed me how to attach it to a USB port in the car, warning me to keep my BlackBerry on. I can talk into it without using my hands, tell it to play music . . . but that's a bit much. The phone lights again and I shyly say, "Answer." Nothing happens. It calms and I look out the window in silence, a shifting set of blues behind tentative branches.

"Are you sure you want to do this?" I'd asked Melissa yesterday. We were sitting in the Starbucks in Grand Central Station, laptops open, filtering the details of our plan through an encrypted e-mail program and browser.

She nodded, so calm you'd think she was some kind of spy. You really can't tell what people are capable of sometimes.

"Remember when we first met?" she said. "The worst thing, right? The worst. It wasn't giving up all the shit, you know? I mean, if you drink enough coffee you can almost get that same kind of buzz and still stay up all night and fuck . . . I'm right, and you know it, Jennifer Baron. Coffee's the world's best drug."

"I thought that was Coke. Not your kind . . ."

When we'd first started hanging out, her nose wouldn't stop bleeding and she always had a headache. She needed two different septum surgeries, she'd literally torn hers in half. Both times I let her recover at my apartment.

Looking at her all put together these days, you'd never know—unless you do.

She smiled. "That's not what I'm saying, I don't know what I'm saying, just something dies when you stop. It's a freaking funeral like any other, you know?"

"Of course, that's what they tell us."

"No they don't, they tell us it's all giving up control and letting go and all that higher-power shit. But the thing is, you can make amends with as many people as you want, you're never gonna be right until you grieve for the part of you that's gone, and that is the worst part. I still miss myself every day."

"Okay . . . ?"

"Don't be such a dork. You know I'm right. You know that's why I'm sitting here."

"I do," I said, "and I guess it's the same here."

"Of course it is. We have a higher risk tolerance than most mortals."

I laughed. "That's one way of looking at it."

"Be careful, Jen."

"You be careful," I said.

About an hour and half outside city limits is the spot. At least I think it's the spot, it was difficult to determine the first time I'd come, two days after Marc's accident, which was eerily similar to my own, if you substitute a car for skates, boulder for wall. The police report said the town was Pleasant Valley, which I'd circled on a map I still have from the Adirondack Mountain Club, though it's so frayed the edges feel soapy on my fingers. And I know the spot, if it really is the spot, just past the state park, where the concrete curls slightly, revealing a little shoulder followed by a giant piece of shale jutting out. The thing is, it's easy to miss, easy to see how one might spin out of control and slam into the rock, but it was summer and not raining and, though this byway is beyond dark, Marc knew how to get around cars, he'd been steering since he could barely see over the wheel. Our drivers had schooled us both; they thought it was cute. Marc loved the green MG Midget with its leather seats and stick shift. I can still see his skinny hand powering the vehicle up and down the unmarked roads across the border in Connecticut, our exit a bit lower down, off this very road.

Sun fully up now, it dodges between a net of clouds, soft like the palest smoke. I pass the park, spotted with evergreens, pine, slowing down to forty-five. There is barely anyone else on the road, the Taconic falling out of favor among commuters, its rigor too intimidating before coffee. Every winter you hear about a doctor or nurse crashing into a sidewall or the railings just outside the city, cautionary tales. But it is a breathtaking road, in every season, with barely any rest stops and long stretches of hills and trees, still the longest parkway in New York State.

I spot the boulder and slow down even more, pulling off to the side. Shut off the engine and inhale deeply.

Opening the door, a gust of wind hits my face. I stand up into it, then slam the door behind me. It shuts cinematically. I open the back and pull out my bomber jacket, quickly wrapping my arms inside and turning the fuzzy collar up against my cheeks. Then I grab the giant bouquet of flowers, hot on asters and lilies and anemones, goldenrod spiking far beyond the edges of the plastic cone. Another loud *schwoop* inward as the door shuts.

The ground is leafy and damp, smell of winter testing. I can see my breath in the air. When we were really young, Marc and I used to play dragon, seeing whose breath could reach farther into the deep country night.

I have visited this spot every year since 1996 and not once have I felt a sense of peace. In cities personal vigils persist through the seasons, a pair of high-tops tossed over telephone wires, ghosted white bicycles chained to signposts, they have a longevity difficult to find in nature—apart from actual graves. Marc is buried somewhere in Queens, but that marker feels irrelevant to who he was in the world, which is what I won't let go of, the last conversation we never had.

Every year I put flowers on the side of this pretty highway, unwrapping them carefully and taking the plastic back to the city, so everything here returns to earth like it's supposed to. Easier to understand flowers, how they bloom and shed and brown into eternity. It's the same with bodies but we don't like to think of it that way.

My father had no time to decompose, if he was ever really dead the first time. Or the second.

Twelve years ago he never had the chance to say goodbye to his son. None of us did, not even my mother. It was her fault he was on that road, she'd bought him the plane ticket, and they'd all accepted the idea of suicide so easily—they didn't know him like I did.

A car swishing by kicks me back to my purpose. I position the flowers around the bottom of the stone, so you can see the bright purples and yellows from the road and know they mean something, likely obvious *what*, it's the *who* that's buried in a time capsule. I want to speak eternal words but settle for the obvious . . . *Wish you were here.*

PART THREE

IF GHOSTS HAD FEELINGS, AND THE TRUE NATURE OF EXISTENCE

Tel Aviv, Late January 2009

The boy finds me sitting outdoors at the beginning of another cold, sunny day. He says he wants to get lost but can't find the key. "Can you climb?" I ask, tilting my head up toward the half-open window into Yudi's flat.

He smiles. "You will help me?"

I nod. He sits down at the table across from me, stares at my coffee cup. Next to it is my watch, a steely platinum residue of my old life and far too expensive for this climate. I almost want to pick it up but fear looking distrustful, racist. Instead I lift the coffee cup.

"You want?"

He nods.

I stand up and walk inside. Fill the kettle from the tap and light up the stove. I drink Nescafé at home like half of this nation and it sucks. As the water boils, I grab a folding chair out of the closet, here, I suppose, for guests. Or abetting a break-in, as it turns out.

Something I don't get in translation: how a gay Muslim from Gaza learns English through comic books and the Internet. There was one computer in his apartment building outside Gaza City, where he sat for hours until the four-story building was slammed by an Israeli shell and the electricity was blown out. This was months before the war, before his mother began to shun him and his brothers sliced off his finger. I did not hear this from the boy, but remember it from a conversation with Yudi. He told me the boy's brothers are still looking for him. They ask around and seem to know where to go, almost as if he's left a trail.

The water boils and I make a cup of awful coffee for the boy. I bring it out to him at the table, then go back in for the chair. I carry it out and over to the window, quickly coming back to the table.

The boy takes a sip of coffee. "I am not for using today. I promise to Yudi. I wash my face and have new clothes."

"That's fine," I say.

"But today I work. You will not tell Yudi, okay?"

"No."

"Okay," he says, and sets down his coffee cup. He walks to the window and climbs up the back of the chair, balancing with his palms against the wall until he reaches the window and pushes it up as high as he can before slithering through the small hole.

His work is giving blow jobs on the outskirts of the market, something that promises a little pocket money, which of course he spends on crystal, despite his vows to stay clean. He can say anything he wants. He is an addict.

Though it is a perfect day to get lost—clear skies, sun kicking into high gear, a red bird battling its shadow against the window. I have a memory of Central Park, the view from my childhood apartment. Once a tiny yellow bird landed on our terrace and got its wing caught on a bicycle spoke. My father, in a rare weekend morning at home, bent over and detangled the shocked creature, smaller than his fingers, lifting it painstakingly with his thumb and forefinger and placing it on the stone wall. The bird clucked its beak into the concrete, leaned down slightly, as if to say thanks, then flew off. I looked up and saw my father watching it fly away, eyes wet. My legs felt weighted, like someone had loaded them with sandbags and twisted my throat so I couldn't sing. I wanted to say something big. I was five or six and hung up on what was important. I'd never seen my father near tears. He walked to the outer edge of the terrace and put his palms on the concrete. "Nice day," he said. Then turned and pulled the ties of his silk bathrobe tight before returning inside.

The boy opens the front door of Yudi's flat and walks out. His clothes are new, face shiny, hair neatly combed. He is carrying a faded brown leather shoulder bag, which must be Yudi's.

"You won't tell him where I go, okay?"

"I won't," I say. I cannot stop staring at him. At sixteen, he's improbable, ineffable. He doesn't smile, tilts his head up into the air slightly.

"Then I get lost now."

"Wait." I put my hand up in front of him. "Just a sec. I have something for you."

I walk inside to get my wallet—it's how I've learned to push the world forward, and if he can buy another coffee, lunch, not enough to score, that has to help. I dig ten shekels out of my wallet.

When I return to the terrace, the boy is gone. So is my watch. The boy and I understand each other. I sit down and stare at the empty space on the tabletop.

Obvious as it sounds, technology has blown out travel. In some ways it's harder to disappear, some easier. It used to take time to hash out an itinerary, make hotel reservations across continents, find ways to connect with home, wire for money. What I remember most from *Tropic of Cancer* is not the sex but Henry Miller's daily walks to the American Express

office in the center of Paris to communicate with those left
on the other side of the Atlantic. There is weight to what we
leave behind, a compressing of time and space and everything we know as home.

I do not call across the Atlantic. Instead I create a new
e-mail address each week and tap Melissa through encrypted
code. She says we're good, says everything is proceeding
normally as the days pass. She is living in my apartment,
texting with Yearling and others on my BlackBerry as if
she's me, answering my e-mail messages, careful to deploy
sarcasm at precisely the right moments, walking to and
from the office occasionally in a short brown wig and my
favorite leather jacket, beaten up like the bag the boy held
tight, taking a piece of Yudi out with him, and somehow
this made the lie okay. *Everything is working,* Melissa writes.
You have nothing to fear. Our lying is okay too.

I am in the front seat of Yudi's van, driving to Dizengoff so
we can park in view of the fountain spinning its faded color
wheel, the height of all things grotesquely modern. It's a key
spot on the Bauhaus tour, an eye toward the Germans and
what they made of this little town by the sea. It is also the
first stop for us tonight. Yudi had grabbed me as I was coming back from the café, where I won another battle against
the Maccabees and simply ordered a plate of hummus and
cherry-flavored soda water for dinner. I have not picked up
in over a week. He asked if I wanted to come along with him
tonight in the van.

"That's okay?"

"I have freedoms," he said.

"Apparently . . ."

He looked directly at me. "There is no reason to judge
me."

"It was a joke."

"You joke like Americans and it is not funny. Take a jacket if you are coming. The offer is over in two minutes."

We sit silently at the fountain, which seems designed by a child, bland primary colors on the slats, water spewing. At night it glows like a ride at a run-down amusement park. Beneath the square there is street life—drugs and sex mostly, though not nearly as much as you'll find deeper into the beach. Yudi first saw the Arab boy here at the fountain. Sitting below the English scrawlings, *Fuck You* and the like, his head tilted back against the concrete, eyes wide open as if in a coma. He had stowed away in the cargo area on the bus from Eilat a few days earlier, the end of an impossible journey, his body ravaged by pneumonia and shingles, the sores in his shins so deep you could see his bone. Amazing, Yudi told me, that he was alive.

The evening is quiet, so we move on, hitting all of Yudi's spots. The air hangs like a nervous sibling, omnipresent and slightly needling. The deeper we go, the more I want to return to the dirty fountain and jump inside, pocketing the pennies from the floor and dipping my head into the sputtering color wheel. I want to scream, *FUCK YOU!* as loud as I can into the night.

"Can we go to the beach already?" I whine.

Yudi barely glances at me, as if turning his head is too much effort. "Be patient," he says. "We always go to the beach in the end."

I am getting antsy and really want a drink. In my world there are only two reasons to be awake after midnight.

"You must relax," says Yudi, reading me in a way I find uncomfortable.

"Will he be there? The boy?" This is what we call him together, when he is not around.

"No. I hope."

"You don't know?"

"I cannot keep him locked away. Then I am no better than my government."

It is a struggle not to be sarcastic about the global weight of everything in this country. We felt it briefly those few weeks in New York, when you couldn't start so much as a film review without saying something along the lines of, *In light of recent events . . .* Then one day, everything was normal again. I turn my cheek to the window and stray into the hazy stream of headlights.

We cut into the side streets to avoid Ben Yehuda. There is only one beach for us this evening, Yudi says, heading south toward our flat but pushing farther out into what seems like a film set. Bright lights set off an enormous square of sand, sending rainbow beams in every direction, the sky and shore spinning like a color wheel, everything the ugly fountain wishes it could be. Techno pulse-throb syncopates the beams, controlled like planetarium streaks in their condensed infinity. You can literally see the music move through the thick, damp air. All of this before we come to the crowd smothered in Day-Glo T-shirts, 3-D glasses, kids in costume. The music gets vaguely chant-y, vaguely hip-hop, boom-boom pounding beyond language. There are Ortho punks, Arabs, schoolboys and girls, foreign travelers dancing barefoot in the sand.

"It's a circuit party," Yudi says. "The Yeshiva kids started them to get closer to God. The scene has exploded."

"Huh."

"Yes, my dear, there is a way to God for everyone."

"Are you trying to convert me?"

He smiles, looks out into the crowd.

I am overwhelmed by an enormous shudder, another craving. If this is religion, sign me up. If this is prayer, I'm in—the way the kids flare up their arms toward the sky in collective bounce, tranced out. Yudi says it's the crystal revving everything up beneath the hot lights, the end of a long, long winter at sea. I remember the drug-induced sweat of dance floors in the Meatpacking District, early nineties, Madonna at the Clit Club, between rehabs, before my brother died but after he'd left New York, and all I wanted was to fuck and dance. If I could slip back now, I would, maybe fall in love with the right person early on and have a whole other history, one that doesn't put me in van on a beach with a social worker who's babying me as much as the kids he picks up. But this game goes nowhere.

"What do we do now?" I pull myself back into it.

"We wait."

"For what?"

"For whatever comes."

People know the van. They know Yudi and why he is here and the kids embrace him for it. He makes no pretense of being anything but a miracle worker, never calls the cops or forces anyone to do or not do anything. Every night he goes where he is needed, carting condoms, clean needles, a phone number to get a bed for the night, if night ever comes for the beam-soaked kids. I look out beyond the stream of bodies to the halo glow off the sea. It seems alive.

Yudi and I continue to watch together. I pretend it is my job, everything normal, though I wouldn't know the first thing to say to an Ortho kid, sidelocks framing his newly formed teenage jaw, high as the lights crawling up into the sky, asking for a condom. Others show up, the crowd tipping slightly older and seedier, less lit up by it all and more focused. Some are here to sell, Yudi explains. He sees the same faces. They trade in nascent sexuality and Orthos are the biggest prize. Yudi never interferes. Well, not until the boy.

The deejay spins more tribal with the passing hours. I can't even make out the English lyrics, but the beat is everything. Walking a few feet from the van, I move in closer to the wave of dancers. There are almost no bystanders. Everyone is caught up in it—and for a moment I give in to the leviathan. It's cliché, but my hips don't care. I roll slowly at first, then circle in time with my hands raised high above my head, pounding into the light. I could do this forever, the music showing no signs of retreat, until I grow conscious and come down hard.

I kick off my running shoes and socks and amble barefoot outside to a small cove just off the shore to sit for a few moments alone. I shut my eyes, clearing out the scene behind me, and open them into the black waves, trying to egg on a visit from my father, but here is the thing about hallucinations, if that's what it was: you cannot prompt them, they have their own agenda. I shut and open again. And again. By the third or fourth time I give up and stand, still looking into the sea, the music and kids thumping behind me.

I stand and walk a couple of steps out, cold granules of sand tickling between my toes. I have to pee.

Did I say that out loud?

There's a voice from behind. Directly in my ear. "Turn around."

It's female and not mine. The heart is its own humpback and tugs harder than a pole. I take a deep breath and turn.

It's Gila.

Or perhaps a figment, I'm not sure. She's wearing tinted glasses despite the late hour, and her hair is blue-black, no curls, the scent of shampoo, fresh, which gives me hope.

I say her name, reach my fingers out to graze her hair. She grabs my wrist. Tight.

"It's really you?"

"Of course," she says, still holding my arm. "Are you taking drugs?"

"No."

"You are just here for a party."

"I'm with my neighbor."

"I know who he is," she says.

"Does he work for you?"

"No."

"But the bartender does, right? The bartender works for you."

"Stop it!" She throws my hand down. Hard. Her cheeks tighten. "You just couldn't let this rest."

"Apparently neither could you."

"No. Do not try that with me. You are putting everyone in danger by being here."

"I've been trying to find you for months."

"You were not supposed to come back. After . . ."

"Is my father alive?"

"I said stop." She puts her hand up in front of me. "You have much to explain right now. I am taking you away."

"But Yudi . . ."

"I'll take care of him."

"Don't you dare hurt him!" My back constricts into a shell.

"Of course not. Go back to the van. I will walk several steps behind you. Go tell him you met a friend."

I smile. "Is that what you are?"

"You are very lucky it's me who found you."

"Am I supposed to thank you?"

"Just go."

I pick up my sneakers and walk barefoot back toward the van. There is Yudi in the shadow of the big lights arguing with someone, the boy maybe, but from the back he looks larger, broader, a baseball cap turned backward and a black sweatsuit with white stripes. He swings his arms wildly. I catch Yudi's eye and he freezes. Something tells me not to say anything now, that it's okay to slip away.

* * *

When I first met Gila last summer she picked me up at the Hilton and blindfolded me as we drove. I went willingly. She was so damn gorgeous and as strange as it sounds, it did not feel strange. My father had been missing just a few months, no reports of any deaths yet, and though the state of Israel had been his passion and recipient of his economic goodwill for decades, I didn't make the connection. I'd been invited to speak at a conference on international philanthropy. I did this often and was usually assigned an escort. Nothing seemed odd. Until we arrived at the resort nestled inside a giant rock along the coast, and there he was.

Whatever you want to call it, extradition? The law of return? The state of Israel protects its own, even its criminals.

Now, I half expect him to be on the other side of the door as Gila turns the key into what seems like an apartment in a tall, nondescript tower of glass and steel, far from the curvaceous white city the Germans built. We'd crossed a mess of cranes, orange tape, and pylons, all guiding us along a wooden platform scattered precariously above a trench of sand and stone, an aching moat. I am not blindfolded, obviously, though we have not spoken a word to each other since leaving the beach.

Once inside Gila removes her glasses and pushes buttons on two flashing panels; one lowers the single shade that had been raised, cutting off the glow from windows in nearby buildings. I feel like I've slipped from an urban parable into a spy movie, like the months since I'd seen her were make-believe, all leading to this flat with its shiny white walls and floor.

She pulls a bottle of wine out of her saddle bag, along with two plastic champagne glasses and an opener. She pushes everything toward me. I pull up the cork with a short pop and fill her glass. "I'll have water," I say.

"You don't trust me?"

"No."

"I can take the first sip."

"It's not the bottle."

"Then what?"

"You know I don't drink."

"This is not what I have heard."

"The bartender. I knew it."

"You don't know what you know."

"Don't tell me what I know or don't know."

A cold splash lands between my eyes, burning slightly, liquid running down my nose and cheeks.

"What the fuck!"

"You disobeyed me."

"I don't remember taking any vows to obey you." I wipe my sleeve across my face. "Do you have a towel or something?"

She walks behind the counter and grabs a roll of brown paper towels, tearing off a few sheets. She hands them to me. Our eyes cross. She sits down on a tall stool. I take the seat next to her, wipe my eyes with the rough paper. We sit next to each other, talking sideways.

"His people will find you," she says. "Or worse."

"Please don't threaten me."

"What are you doing here?"

"You lied to me."

"This isn't about you."

"He's alive."

"He is not."

"There was no one in that rabbi's grave, you have to know that."

"I don't know anything other than I watched him die. If someone has moved a body, that is another thing."

She stares down at the counter, like she's measuring

something behind those big green eyes. She pours a glass of wine for herself and sips. Takes a deep breath. "I don't know what is happening here."

I try and gauge what level she's at, the global where is my father, her dead lover? Or between us . . . And if it's not the latter, how shallow am I?

"What do you mean?" I goad.

"I don't know anything about the body."

"Why is he so mad at you?"

"How do you know he is mad?"

"I've seen him. He called you a cheater and a killer."

Her eyelids fall. Mechanically, like the controlled shade. In a split of time and space, even faster than the wine slapping my face, I know she is surprised. I don't think she's faking. I reach for the bottle of wine. In the rooms, one of the first things you learn is admitting you're powerless can be very powerful. It can also be an excuse. But somehow the knowledge comforts, it's always a choice. I fill my plastic glass and it glows purplish against the bright white counter. Then refill hers. We pivot toward each other and snap a quick plastic toast. I tell her what I saw on the beach.

"Someone is doing this to you," she says, regaining her footing. "Making you think this. We have to get you out of here."

"Who?"

"I am not certain. His people. The American government . . . they are not the brightest but they have Mossad to help. No matter. It is not safe for you here. I can get you on the airplane tomorrow."

"I won't go. There's unfinished business . . ." I say, emphasis on *business*, just as the ghost-man had said it a few days earlier. We glance tightly at each other and I know she's less sure than her words. "Look, Gila—"

"You must go!"

I jump from my stool, reach out, and grab her by the waist, feeling her spine tense up and release, like dancing on the beach. "Stop!" She pushes me away. "You have no idea what you are doing."

"Do you?"

"I will."

"But you don't yet, and you don't want me to go back to America." I stare deep into her under the cold white lights, waiting for something. A sound, a sigh, the wide eye of desire rendering everything else invisible. I try to speak, something inane, something inaudible, like, look, I don't know, you know . . .

"Stop," she says, lighter than on the beach, though there's a finality to it. I drop my shoulders, sigh. Back away from her chair, defeated. But she reaches out, grabbing the scruff underneath my knit hat and pulling me in.

What the—eyes saying this, I'm sure.

She kisses me. Long and desperate and deep. Like it's been ages or just ten minutes since the last time and everything between us slips down into the shimmering white tiles.

When we finally speak beyond love tones, Gila asks me a question: "How can you map a geography you've never known?" Poland is one of the few European countries I've never seen. But the imagery of grainy black-and-white streets, makeshift bombs, cold cellars, and striped pajamas looms through her incandescent accent—the way her eyes turn down as she speaks, somber, grave, the gloaming of Friday on the other side of the thick shades.

We are in the bedroom. In bed. Everything impossibly white.

It has been almost fourteen hours since we arrived. A risk, she tells me, that will have her dumping the flat once we leave. She didn't realize it would be so hard to let me go a second time. "Maybe if I tell you what you need, you can go home and shut your mouth," she says. "I am your escape hatch."

"What about you?"

"I am already gone."

Not your normal post-love lust, what's to make of it, and she's got a craving now to tell me things about my father.

"Even with Viagra he liked to watch," she says. "He set up scenarios for me to find my way through."

"And you?"

"I did what he asked. It is hard for you to understand, I know, but there was real caring between us. A sweetness."

"It is hard for me to imagine my father and *caring* in the same breath."

"I knew a different person."

"But why?" I'm after her, want to know what's her take in this, in me, him . . . so I push. I am an addict, after all, it's what we do.

"You must understand, we had known each other for some time, we worked side by side for half the decade. He trusted me."

"That's not what I'm asking . . . Why you?"

She shrugs. "Can anyone say why in these situations? Why are you here right now?"

"You know why."

I roll over on my side and lift myself out of bed, the first time in hours. Cool wind streams up from the air conditioner, centralized and running along the floor. Summer kisses long gone, we have become in this small eternity something different, something serious and vital. A protein.

She follows me up and catches my hips from behind, grabbing me around the stomach, sighing. "You've confused everything," she says, holding tighter. She smells sweet, sex releasing perfume from every part of her. It must have driven him nuts, watching the smell burn off. I would love to watch her too and I hate him for putting that into my head. He's so much a part of this it's freaky. Slowly she sets me free and picks up her cigarettes from the table, offering one. I decline.

"You're not an athlete anymore," she says.

"Why are you so mean?"

"You ask too many questions."

"I'm just getting started."

She flips a cigarette from the pack, lighting up and lingering over to the couch, then crossing her legs in front of her, an absurd gesture the more naked you are. Though she's stunning, I think back to her light-brown curls, the other hair a decoy. I am no longer objective.

"Okay, so, what can I tell you next?" she says.

"How do you know about Poland?"

"He told me," she says. "He liked to talk to me, he said he couldn't with most people. The truth is, he never stepped a foot in Russia. Your grandparents adopted him out of a Displaced Persons camp in Lebanon."

"Lebanon? Is he even Jewish?"

A shrug: "Maybe. We need to eat dinner." She puts out her cigarette, leaving a few stubborn embers burning orange into the blue-black ceramic tray. I hate the smell of dead cigarettes; they remind me of my mother, the morning after dinner parties, of growing up in the seventies with public service announcements everywhere, an assault of stringy gray lungs like a bombed-out village. But to focus on the ashtray is all I can do. I don't trust a word she's saying.

"Where do we get food around here?" I ask.

"We don't. But we start with the shower."

I hold my hand out to her. She takes it and I pull her so close into me it hurts.

She sighs, hot cigarette breath against my neck, the part of smoking l love. "God," she whispers, "I have never wanted to fuck so much."

"You mean get fucked."

"Yes."

"Did he—"

"Not now," she whispers, lightly kissing the back of my ear. I am going to die.

Pushing back slightly, I slide down in front of her, my lips at her stomach, kissing downward in quick bursts.

"You are passionate, for an American," she says.

I graze my teeth into her. She moans, squeezes my head with both hands, and slips down against the couch, keeping me with her, my tongue and lips closing in. She comes like that, like a general's daughter, like last summer, then begs, "More. Please . . ." and I get up inside her fast with just one finger, the way she shivers taking me down with her, and dinner as far off as Poland.

My father had big ideas, Gila tells me, even as a small boy. In the DP camps there were hippie Israelis, first-generation pre-statehood patriots, who sang sacrilegious songs and preached free love. "You have to understand, most of these little kids were from the ghettos, very religious," she says. "And here they are being seduced by jazz and the most preposterous jingles." She started talking the moment we were seated behind the bamboo screen. After the languorous cleansing, we'd gone into the night for sushi. Like lovers. The markers of an affair come in stages, when you get up and go out into the world together, that is progress. It's been so long since I've spent the day making love and then gone out for dinner. My goal: no sake, no beer, no whiskey.

I am comforted in thinking there's a way back to sobriety, back to the world where you are sober just because you say so.

"Why are you telling me all of this?" I ask. "Why now?"

"Because you asked and because you've dragged yourself deeper into his world. You should know what I know . . . just in case."

Did I mention that we are sitting on the floor in a private room? That her friend Talo is the sushi master? We have not ordered one thing and the colorful pieces simply come. Sake too, which I sip gingerly, immediately defying my own prohibition, thinking it's medicinal at this point, as I reach my bare foot against her inner thigh beneath the table. I cannot remember the last time I had a full meal.

"The camps had a geography of their own, but you see . . . Poland, Russia, it's sort of the same. Plus, he had ideas of getting much farther away. The way he tells it, he was keenly obsessed with America."

At seven or eight, it seems, nobody really knows how old he is, he knew Israel would never be home or could be his home away from home if he made it to America. The DPs huddled together in Lebanon, shipped from Poland, though Syria, Jordan. Nobody wanted them and this is sounding all too familiar already. When he heard a rich Russian couple was looking for one boy, the only catch was they were living in the States, he auditioned. She imagined it, reading between the lines. "He knocked out the competition," she says and we laugh, the first time in a while.

"Of course he did," I say. "I never knew much about his childhood. The Russians were kind of cold. Except when they drank."

"I am part Russian."

"And?"

Part of what is happening, this flirtation, is not knowing where the next minute will take us. I suppose that's the same for any lovers, but when do you get this? Someone who knows more about your history than you do? I am glad my father is not here, might never be here again, I want her for my own.

"Will you really move out?" I ask. We've been quiet for a few minutes, her hand on my foot. My foot in her lap, toes diddling, despite the knife in my lower back from sitting so long on the floor.

"It is no problem. The apartment is not mine."

"I'd like to see yours."

"You won't."

"Did he?"

Her silence answers. It cuts. Jealousy is a raging beast. My muscles shake inside out. I can barely feel my own skin.

"I'm sorry," she says, taking her hand off my foot and grabbing mine across the table. We are holding hands. "You cannot pretend I don't have a past."

"It's not the what, it's the who."

"I loved him."

"Loved?" I pull my hand and foot away from her. Draw down the shades. "Like past tense?"

"He is dead."

"What if he's not? Do you still love him then?"

"No."

"Why?"

"You push too hard."

"What happened with you two? You were working to-gether, you took me to him. Then a few days later he's dead . . . maybe, I mean, who knows? But something happened. What was it?"

"It is very simple," she says. "I told him you and I made love."

* * *

The next day I run fast along the beach like I shouldn't, charting my time with a plastic stopwatch and pushing, pulling to kill just one mile in seven minutes. Get back a small piece of who I was before. Gila dropped me back at my flat after dinner, saying keep my head down. From what she can tell, nobody outside of her camp knows I am here, and yes, she says, the bartender is hers.

With every pump of ankle, shin, thigh, every salty breath beneath the low gray sky, her voice infiltrates, knocking me off my game.

Don't forget he knows I'm here.

He is not real.

That's convenient for you.

Don't be angry at me.

You want him dead?

Don't you?

"No, I do not want my father to be dead." I say this out loud.

A knife pinch tears into the back of my calf, stopping me in my tracks. I scream. Take a deep breath and realize I am heaving. This is not the kind of injury that stops you, stops me. When did I become such a wuss? I take out Yudi's old iPod and flip on the Eurythmics. Put in the buds and leap back into the sand, as if the music were Percocet. Listening to someone else's songs can be intrusive, though I have this album at home, maybe even an old record. I held on to vinyl long after it was put under by plastic . . . and digital, don't get me started. I miss the scratches and skips, the foggy echo of those cassette tapes in training.

Tree had a huge boom box she brought to my apartment when we first met and carried with her everywhere, along with a briefcase stuffed with cassettes, titles scrawled on the spine in ballpoint pen, names that even then said classic rock, songs that capped sweet sixteen parties at Tavern on the Green and AM radio. I loathed this music and let my hatred swell into a desire greater than anything I could have envisioned before her, until I loved it too.

Then one day there was a new band she'd discovered, fronted by a woman with bright orange hair who dressed in suits and shouted, "*I want to dive into your ocean . . .*"

And dive I did. I do . . . *You can fucking do this!* I crank it for one last mile, sweat pouring out of every crevice, despite the cool wind drawing up from the sea, and a deep sense of regret for something I can't name. The finish line ahead, I see my father as a little boy, waving to my grandparents in their big Russian hats. But they pull away. They are not his real parents, those people have been slaughtered in the war and left him wandering the streets of a ravaged city.

The stopwatch passes seven and I run faster and faster toward my young father, until he disappears into the ocean too and I collapse along the shore.

I am in for a long soak. Amphibian. Barely born, I cannot feel my legs, my feet, the piece that might one day grow a tail. I squirt through the muddy outlet, lizard-like thoughts of redemption, smelling oil, the snap of Colombian gold seeds, Head and Shoulders shampoo. It is 1986 and I am deep into training for the Olympics.

When a bone snaps you can hear it shatter. Literally, it pops. Even if you don't seek assistance you just know. Which comforts me quietly, head buried below the bubbles like a slippery green frog, preferring water carousing through my ears to Mick Jagger and his greatest hits, wondering when she'll return. We are in season after all and have made the Nationals. All I need to do is ice the ankle for three hours while the hotel room fills with cinnamon sticks.

Tree had gone out to fill my 'scripts. Demerol mostly. Poppy fuel. I'd learned early on how to ice an ankle: ten minutes on, ten minutes off. Crush and snort the pills so they work faster. Someone fills the tub so the heat tingles deeply where it had just been cold. I am wearing underwear, a bra that slithers down the back. What sort of reptile wears a 34B? I ask someone to take it off and whoever complies. I usually wrap them down to skate faster, but sometimes at school too. I like the way it feels without them.

If the ankle'd snapped, there would be deeper pain, like ice cream hitting your teeth, only throughout your whole leg. A cold-cell shudder. All the pills in the world can't catch it and I would not be dreaming of a body without breasts, a pretty green tail guiding me through the muddy shallows. I slip my head under again and hold my breath until I'm sleepy.

A hand comes, this time with a glass of vodka. And I can smell it on her fingers, where she'd been dipping into the stash.

"Where's Tree?" I ask, unsure whom I'm addressing, though she looks like gold. Snap, crackle, pop fingers.

"I'm right here," she says. "Just returned with the goods to help you sleep and get up even stronger. Now how's that ankle?"

I sink beneath the surface again but the water's lost its charm, bubbles bursting faster, like stale gum. I feel her fist grab the back of my head, tip me forward.

"I brought you a salad," she says, her face right up against mine. "Something French-sounding."

"I'm not hungry."

"No?"

"No."

She smiles, lazy downturn of her lower lip. Most people's work in tandem, her upper and lower have different signals. It happens when she's snorting, not Demerol. Her own magic snake oil. Together we are reptiles, thousands of eggs left on soggy carpets in hotel rooms across the country.

She kisses me sloppily, wet, our mouths humid through the scrim of cool bathwater, the zipper of her leather jacket rubbing against my nipple, piercing it so tightly it warms my sore ankle better than a few lines of Demerol. It's all the same to me, in these amphibian years, where I somehow get over with no broken bones but shed a thousand skins.

"You don't want it enough."

I kiss her harder.

"Not that." She pulls me out of the tub, gently gripping under both arms to set me down on the toilet seat for drying. One fluffy towel slowly crawling up my thigh, followed by her tongue. I move her head closer. "I want it," I say. "So bad."

"Will it help you sleep?"

"Um-hmmmm . . ." I pull her by the hair, her breath in tiny heat waves against my inner thigh, just a shot away.

Gila shows up at my apartment the next morning carrying a cardboard box and two large paper cups. She is wearing big dark sunglasses and a straight blond wig, leather miniskirt, and platform boots, shimmering white. She looks like she's popped from the party scene in *La Dolce Vita*.

She sets the box down on the table outdoors and hands me one of the cups. "Cappuccino," she says. "I took a chance."

"Perfect."

"Now listen to me." She opens the box and removes a phone packed in industrial plastic. "You take this and open it."

I grab it from her but stay in place.

"Go on," she says. "Do it now. Then write down the number on a piece of paper and give it to me. Only I will have it. Do not under any circumstances give it to another person."

She says there are six more phones in the box. I should use one per week, then destroy it, even if there are still minutes. Once the package opens I write down the number once on a piece of paper and hand it to her in person only.

I lean in and grab her around the waist. "So you are my protector?"

"Not now," she says. "We have an appointment with my cousin."

"You're taking me to meet the family?"

"I am going to punch you in the face." She smiles. But stops me, reaching back into the box. "And you can wear this."

She holds out a thick straw Panama hat, gray with a black band, stylish. Not mine.

"It's cool, I have a hat."

"If anyone's spotted you, they say you are wearing that wool cap. Besides, it's for the cold. You look like a homeless person."

"I sort of am," I say, and back a few feet away to turn inside and cut the plastic on the phone, treading lightly on my right leg.

She jumps up in front of me. "*Rega, rega* . . . are you limping?"

"Old injury. Comes back when I run."

"Were you running from someone?"

"No. On the beach yesterday."

"Listen to me," she says. "Maybe you did something good in New York to keep them on hold, but if anyone finds you here, they will kill you. Or worse."

"You keep saying that . . . What do you mean worse?"

"If they think you have information they will hurt you and keep hurting you until you say things." I am finding this all hard to believe. My father was a thief, of course, but he kept his cuffs clean.

"I wouldn't know what to say."

"My darling," she says, softly again, "that is the exact point. You are in very messy shit here. I can help but you must stop being . . . what do you call it? A silly brat. You must pay attention and, most important, you must listen to me."

She seems steady but on a mission. It's a comfort to feel nestled into someone else's plan, the thought that someone's got ideas for you. It's what first drew me to Tree. Of all the coaches, she was the only one who started with Olympics. "If we look at '88 and map back . . ." she said to my father and me, sitting on the couch in our public den, where we'd been holding interviews, "what do we need to do? What's going to make her want this more than anything else in the world? 'Cause that's the only thing it comes down to. Desire." In that spit of a moment, an eye shift, a caveat, I knew she was going to be my coach.

I shift back toward Gila, not taking my eyes from her. Her lips soften into trust. Or close enough. She holds out the Panama again. I put my hand on it, lightly grazing her fingers as she lets go.

The snow sneaks up on us almost as soon as we leave the coast, a reminder that there is still a sliver of winter left for us. Within thirty miles of the city in every direction, save for the glorious sea, there are fields of tall grass, grains, rubber trees, Mediterranean pine. It's been raining again along the seashore, not uncommon for winter, but today there are giant flakes falling on the highway and apparently dusting the holy city. Not what you normally see on the nightly news in the Middle East.

Driving fast along the highway, Gila briefs me. We are traveling to meet a cousin of hers who makes rugs in East Jerusalem, the Arab part of town. The business is a front. Her cousin is an information broker. If I had seen my father in the flesh, he will appear elsewhere and her cousin will find him. She's doing this for me, she says, she still thinks it's futile, still believes to her core he's dead.

"I was there," she says. "He was in the hospital bed. And his heart stopped."

"Did you see his face?"

"Yes, of course I saw it."

"And you're sure he was dead?"

"Of course, yes. I'm telling you he was dead. Very dead."

"Because you killed him."

"It's not that simple."

"Why would you tell him that? You knew it would . . ." I trail off inside my own barren highway of a heart as the fields open up into greenish-yellow hills, lightly frosted. Rocky terrain like the moon on dry, crunchy moss. Still, it's a remarkable ascent into the bedrocked history of the Old City, capped by its golden dome. When Marc and I passed through here, a boy in one of the American tourist bars told us the dome would one day come popping off like a giant pimple and all of the Muslims would shoot out into space like thick white pus. He was a young Zionist with high hopes for the Jewish homeland and full of pimples himself. That was almost two decades ago and despite the endless conflicts and catastrophes, the dome shines like a beautifully wrapped truffle.

"I never wanted to hurt him, you must believe me," Gila says. "We did not lie to each other about lovers. Ever."

"He knew I'd fall for you. You are so my type."

She smiles, still looking forward. "I know."

We pull up into the slick, malled-out stone of modern Jerusalem and head east through the slush. There is a cement wall not far from here that is supposed to keep the Palestinians out. It cuts through major sections of town, destroying land held by families for generations. You can see the remains of the decimated olive groves, if you go in that direction. But I cannot bear to look destruction in the face yet, and we are speeding by too quick for eulogies. Gila is a typical Israeli driver, fast and focused, ready to swerve up onto the sidewalk at a moment's notice. Heavier flakes hit the windshield, barely wiped away by the dull rubber blades.

"I might want to see the wall later," I say.

"*Rega*, okay? We have business first."

"Gila?"

"I am saying this one last time: I did not kill him."

"No, it's not that . . ." I want to ask if that's why she's taken me on like a strung-out version of the war orphan he was, if it's about guilt, but I'm not sure I can handle the answer.

"What?" she says, impatient, dipping her right foot into the brake for a choppy turn.

"What's your cousin's name?"

"Teddy, I told you. Teddy."

In the time it takes to have this nonconversation, we pass from Jewish streets to Arab. There are people milling about, more open-air vendors, some using scrappy blue tarps to shield necklaces, plastic sandals, scarves, spices against the incongruous white flakes. This part of town still has a feeling long eclipsed everywhere else. I am overwhelmed with a sadness so big my eyes feel like they're blinking acid snow. I don't want to see Teddy today.

When someone goes missing, you put up a sign. Those of us in New York, when the towers fell, remember the faces on sheets of Xerox paper, men and women in the so-called prime of their lives, and then a sudden tragedy confines them to a flyer like a lost dog. We were all learning what life is like outside America, how to live at the behest of your enemies. Popping guns and army personnel commonplace. We could be so childish.

And in those weeks we were all on edge, not unlike what I feel at this moment sitting with Teddy.

Gila says he is one of five people in the country she trusts. That should say something about me, my father, that she's letting us in. Like Gila, Teddy is deceptive. He's casual, as is customary, but clearly well-heeled and well-fed. Expensive jewelry, jeans, shoes. Good haircut. He really does run a rug shop, where we sit on stout little stools drinking sugary tea, as if negotiations are about to begin, and they are, though I am a bit behind the language today. It's hard to pick up anything more than the obvious yes or no. Big mess. And their laughter moves me into twisted territory, wondering what she means by cousin. Whenever I'm fucking someone it's a given that everyone else in the world wants to fuck them too. Bloodlines notwithstanding. If I could freeze this scene I might understand how tortured my own thinking has become, but it's a visceral thing—remember, she was my father's lover first. Makes me wonder why we're even looking for him now that I've got her.

Teddy offers more tea, leans into me. "How do you know it was him, the other day?"

"I know it sounds crazy but he rose up out of the ocean wearing a cape."

"*Ma zeh?* Cape?"

"Like Superman. Only his was silver. Like a blanket you keep in the car for emergencies."

"This is serious, no?" He looks at Gila.

"If he is alive, it is very serious. If he's dead, a different kind."

Teddy turns back to me. "You are sure this is really happening?"

"I am."

"Here people see things sometimes. It's not odd."

"I smelled him."

"There is a type of sensation, the olfactory glands play tricks."

"*Shtok!*" Gila shouts. Literally, shut up, then something I don't catch, though it sounds protective. In that moment I am wholly and preposterously in love.

Teddy shakes his head. "I have people in Tel Aviv," he says. "I'll put them on it. Gila says you have money."

"That's right."

"You pay me in dollars."

"No problem."

"One question: what do you want me to do if I find him?"

I look at Gila but she's not giving up anything this time. "I don't know," I say.

"You think about it. Now, you want to buy a carpet."

I walk out with a knitted rug for my living area, which we throw into the back of Gila's jeep. The car is brand new. She says don't get too attached to it. Around us the sky bruises purple, still snowing but more lightly, like cotton mist. I catch a brief reflection in the wet glass and barely recognize myself. The hat is old-school gangster . . . but that's not the problem.

"I wish I had my other hat."

"You complain too much."

"It's cold."

Her upper lip curls slightly, confused, adorable in that white-blond hair, still herself but also someone new. Tiny incandescent crystals fall between us.

"Do you have any pictures from the army?" I ask.

"Why?"

"I wish I could have seen you then."

She looks, for a second, caught. Then soothing. "I will look."

"Thank you."

"You want to say hello to the wall."

I say yes but quickly realize she's misunderstood walls. It's too late. She's nudging me by the elbow across a busy street into what looks like the entryway of a nondescript stone castle, golden dome twinkling into evening, seemingly miles away, dim shadows alighting on the wet snow. Even drenched it does not fail. We walk down and under, onto the famous streets Jesus traversed, stopping short of the stations and instead wending the pathways of the Muslim quarter, stalls closing up early, if they'd opened at all. No one here does well with winter. We keep a quick pace and I struggle through, ignoring the pinch in my lower leg, telling myself it's nothing.

A few turns lit up by naked bulbs overhead, like the inside of a coal mine, we bypass several intrepid tourists in outdoor gear, their soggy maps unfurled. Then a final turn and there's a light at the end of the tunnel, nothing natural, it's well past sunset, more like floodlights teasing into the stoned-out remains of the second temple.

Sometimes I hear the sacred in pop music. And my taste is, I'm afraid, not much better than my first coach's, some might say even worse. As we cross seamlessly through the centuries my head rings in . . .

All in all it's just a—
Nutha brick in the wall

And here we are, Gila and me, standing in this ancient arena lit up like an Olympic rink, snowflakes dancing as we stare at the orange-brown bricks, charcoal bomb stains and bullet holes shimmering under the beams, tiny peaks like meringue piled up at the base. We tread lightly down through the square, emptier than ever. A man in black flicks a few flakes from the brim of his hat. Some carry umbrellas as they cocoon up against the wall. Boys in yarmulkes, giddy, pound one another with wet snowballs while their fathers pray.

We are on the men's side of the wall, but it doesn't matter. It's not often you see a tourist attraction without tourists. A holy site without sanctimony. I reach for Gila's hand and she grabs back, our fingers intertwined as we take it in together, holier than anything I can ever remember.

* * *

It is the first day of the third month and the city's got a spring in its step. Late-night beach parties pump their boom-boom, shake it, coming through slaughter, let's do it, baby, let's fall in love melodies. I am awake too early, in waiting, like lovers do, my window open to tempt the breeze . . . and fate. I have no phone number for Gila. No address. She calls daily to check in but there is no return number, caller *unknown*. She shows up in the evenings sometimes. My days are the same, though we are all in collective recovery, the conflict (as the war is referred to on the more well-heeled side of the border) has ended, despite the stray rockets escaping across the southern border, and whoops . . . another supply tunnel gone. The *Jerusalem Post* says more than 50,000 Gazans have been left homeless in the aftermath. This number astounds. What do you do with 50,000 displaced persons in an area the size of Philadelphia? A place where many had already been living in blown-out concrete buildings and canvas tents. What happens when there are no tunnels left? When there is truly no escape? I have been dreaming of boats and beaches, the insanity of escape. A world where *dignity* means something more than a ship and the walls stop throbbing and my lover comes to me in the middle of the night with fresh strawberries and stories of foreign homelands, not the ones I thought. If he's Polish, am I? Are we even Jewish?

A bottle of red wine stands next to my bed. Unopened. I'd set it aside for love games or emergencies. I reach my hand down to touch it, craving reassurance in the cool glass, the curve of its shoulder, how easily it grabs by the neck. Remember the wine scene in *Notorious*? Cary Grant sneaks into the cellar to look for clues and inadvertently knocks over a bottle. Out spills black sand. Then he kisses the hell out of Ingrid Bergman as a cover-up. I think the movie was about bombs and spies, the postwar Nazis, a dead father who was a war criminal, hot kisses that outwitted the three-second rule, and that's about everything I'm feeling, as the shadows lighten into a hazy trace of moonlight.

The next day, I walk along the beach with Yudi and the boy as the sun slowly pushes its nose above the waves. I do not have a favorite sunrise. Who does? They move through so quickly and then it's just the day. But for those few seconds, embraced by pinkyelloworange rays cascading above the water, I am decidedly alive. It's easy to see why the ancients thought the world was flat, how else could its borders contain so much liquid, so much eye-popping color . . . ?

I am with them. Gravity makes no sense to me.

The boy walks several steps ahead, an old metal detector attached to his elbow like an aerodynamic crutch, elephant-thick headphones clamped to his ears. Early morning is best, he says, especially Mondays. After the circuit parties you can catch stray earrings, necklaces, sometimes a money clip with a bonus jackpot. Unlike the time-sucked men half naked and gray who search for treasures, the boy is trailing what happened yesterday. Yudi says he is growing stronger and more independent. I do not speak the things I am concealing, the world where I buy small electronics and deposit them in key places on the terrace for the boy to steal and sell on the black market. I tell myself this is helping him stay off the streets. It would break Yudi's heart.

He and I are a few paces behind, silently trailing the boy through the glorious ache of dawn. I am barefoot. For the first time in days, I feel a slackening in my shoulders, though I am careful not to let it bring the U-Haul.

"I have been wondering . . ." Yudi breaks my spell. "What is New York like?"

"It's a city. A big one."

"Would I like it?"

"I thought you'd been."

"No. Boston. And all of those beaches in the north. Maine. Then New Mexico, the Grand Canyon. And California. Oh, and Toronto."

"That's Canada."

"Really?"

I smile and keep our pace behind the boy, eyes on his scraggly brown hair beneath the boomy headphones, his metallic arm cutting into the orange-creamsicle sky. He looks like manga, a cuddly cyborg hunting down his soul.

"No, I am seriously considering this," Yudi says. "I want to take him somewhere . . . somewhere safer. Do you think we could make a life there?"

"Listen," I say, "there are much easier cities."

"But for us. Who would have us? What could we do?"

"Let me think about it, okay?"

We continue walking in unison, walking like each step is about discovery over motion. I used to hate walking, wanted only to run, to move, to fly. When I had wings.

Not far ahead, the boy turns to us like he's seen a ghost, then drops to his knees. A throbbing kicks in—*He's been hurt! Someone got him!* We walk faster, almost hopping along the sand to reach him. He gestures up at us frantically, strands of hair dancing in the light as he pushes his hands into the sand, digging strenuously with his fingers. Next to him the metal detector flashes red. I kneel down to help, Yudi backs a few steps away toward the water.

The boy stops digging and looks straight at me, "It's *bah, bah, bah* . . . like never before."

"How far down does it go?"

The boy shakes his head, motions for me to *just dig* . . . He pulls himself up slightly, reaching into the side pocket of his parachute pants for a blue plastic shovel, a child's toy. He hands it to me. I point in front of me to make sure I've got the right place, but he is already back into it with his hands. I follow his movements and together we increase the depth and circumference of the hole, as the sand gets thicker, wetter, dark like clay. Yudi returns with a thin but substantial piece of driftwood and pushes it in deeper than we can get with fingers and plastic. The three of us keep digging until my shovel hits something so hard it bends. The three of us eye each other cautiously.

A treasure!

Yudi and the boy dig their hands around the impediment, isolating a smaller hole in the dark, wet sand. "Come to Papa!" Yudi screams, reaching farther down with the stick.

"Gaaaaaah!" the boy screams. His hands grip the top of something hard, shiny. Yudi continues to clear the circle. The boy pulls. My heart speeds forward though I've backed away.

One-two-three, Yudi measures and the boy follows. His right hand has literally disappeared into the sand. He heaves once more. Yudi sighs, falling backward. The boy yanks out what looks like an old chunk of metal, with grainy wood attached to the bottom. He brushes off the sand, though its shape has already become apparent and not surprising when you consider where we stand.

The boy gives the gun a quick look and slams it on the ground in disgust.

"Look!" Yudi picks it up and puts his free arm around the boy's shoulder. "This is good. This is from another time. This can help you."

Neh . . .

"You can almost see word *n-field . . . Enfield!*"

"Renfield?"

Yudi shushes me away.

The three of us stare at the piece, and I have to admit it's kind of lovely. In a land where soldiers carry semiautomatics into hair salons and people pine for security, guns forge the protective edge of a country on perpetual alert. But this one reads valor, a throwback to the heady days of Exodus, "good" terrorists, freedom.

"We will fix this up," Yudi says, leading the boy back toward the crowding boardwalk. I trail a few seconds behind, fiddling with the cell phone in my pocket, which I thought had been buzzing though I could have been confusing it with the persistent rumbling in my stomach. I fish it out to make sure, and slanting away from the sharp morning rays, I see a message: *Missed Call*. No return number. But I know who.

I trudge up to the guys, scurrying through the clap of joggers, dog walkers, bearded men pushing strollers. Just another day at the beach. We hit the lavender coffee truck for breakfast, then they return home. I sit down on a bench and hug the phone between my palms.

I have an irrational fear of old ladies in velour tracksuits. You know what I'm talking about. Caked and deep-dyed on top, some in shape, others shapely beneath their technicolor garments. They stalk the creaked-out boardwalks of every beach town in the universe, complementing my own lifelong habit of planting roots near the water.

My father and I share a passion for water, my brother never went in for it. He walked the beach with a catastrophic gaze, as if waiting for the wave that would carry him away. It's hard not to romanticize the dead, especially the young dead, the beautiful dead, the suicides. When we were kids we'd wander together before the day got too hot, chasing each other up and down the wooden planks, zigzagging between the velour ladies with a sense of purpose no one else could touch. "Watch it!" a lady would shriek, bringing us back to reality at hand. Another beach. Another spring vacation. A new girlfriend. My father's girls never wore velour— it was a pretend material, industrial sausage casing at war with their high-priced skin.

To be my father's girl you must above all revere the body. Your body. Ideal beachwear: a bikini, perhaps wrapped in a sparkling sarong, cotton or synthetic, but never give anything up too quickly. Even then my brother and I knew these ladies were velour sweat suits waiting to happen. And we treated them that way. I interrupt my own memory. I said *we*. But Marc only knew the first few and never gave them much of anything. He was tied to the original model, our mother who married a philosopher and moved away to a house by the river to paint every sunrise she could get her fingers into. She and her husband rehabbed horses, those marked by an extra toe, not enough muscle tone, respiratory problems, just shy of pedigree. She would never wear anything called a sweat suit.

She took us to the big boardwalk at Coney Island a few times, normally we were down the road in Brighton Beach, where the Russians lived, but they were his people. Sometimes she wanted us alone, with hot dogs and the Ferris wheel. We slammed each other with bumper cars even though we were officially too young for the ride. I remember being there a few weeks before she sat us down for the "I can't have an orgasm with your father, cringe when he touches me, he's a monster" talk. For years I thought that's why women left. Orgasms. I've been left for less and for a whole lot more, but that's not why I'm thinking of her, remembering the three of us on the beach that day, before Marc and I knew too much, when we still believed we were part of something bigger than our nights locked behind his bedroom door playing blackjack and sneaking cigarettes.

He started smoking at a crazy young age. He liked sucking and still wanted to be touched by her constantly. She was not touchable, though. Not in the sense of pull-me-to-your-chest comfort. No one in our family was. But he insisted, pushing up against her to take her hand, even as she carried her high-heeled sandals that sunk too deeply into the beach in one hand, a cigarette in the other.

He made her smile that day, just by taking her hand and leading her to the water. They stood up to their ankles in it, picking up rocks and lunging them into the ocean. Don't get too lulled into the pastoral, he was throwing them hard. I watched him bend effortlessly, his moves balletic. He picked up a stone and aimed it at a woman walking toward them. She was older, not wearing velour but something equally proletarian. I knew what he was doing before he picked up the rock, pulling back his arm and letting the stone fly into the air. It hit the woman in the forehead. She jumped, screaming from the pain, maybe, or the shock of it. "Marc!" my mother shouted, and ran to the woman.

He turned around to find me, predictably, and there I stood, a few feet back, hands tucked into my cutoffs, upper lip rolled up. I stuck my tongue out at him. He smiled slyly and made his way over. "I didn't like the looks of her," he said, and I gave it to him, a nod. The kid had balls.

We watched the lady squawk off in the other direction, my mother coming toward us. "It's okay," she said. "You barely hit her."

Marc smiled bigger this time, for one minute aligned with the crackling waves of the Atlantic. Before she left and his weeks of crying began. I tried to soothe him, I really did, spending time watching movies in the TV room or having contests on the roof to see what would fly or fall. I don't think we ever hit anyone there, we were too high up. But

I was training so hard, not really home even when I was, I didn't see any signs beyond a heartbroken kid, which happens with divorce . . . I was the lucky one, propelled by my deep hatred and getting faster every day.

I spend the entire day on the boardwalk looking out at the waves as the sun crawls across the sea. By the time it sinks, I am sitting at an outdoor café on the water, bundled up in nylon and wool, shivering from sunburned cheeks. I order too many glasses of wine as the air cools deeper, still winter. A waiter pulls a plastic cover over the outdoor seating area and turns on a space heater.

There are a few people left with me inside, looking out into the black of night, the sky loaded down with clouds, you can barely see the white tips of the waves and it's all fuzzy behind the plastic scrim. The same waiter sits in front of a tray of silverware, taking a fork/spoon/knife and wrapping the utensils in a white paper napkin so they are ready for tomorrow. Soon he will turn the chairs on top of the tables and mop the floor like every restaurant in the world. I flag him for a check.

Outside the wind is brutal, hundreds of tiny pinpricks at my cheeks. I walk through the dark tunnel under the boardwalk, where it's safe from the wind but stinks of urine and seaweed, and my heart jumps at the sound of my own footsteps. If I can just make it past the boulevard and onto my street—*ten*, exhale, *nine*, exhale . . . I move through quickly, toward the bar on the corner where a crowd gathers outside a purple velvet rope, despite the wind. It's gotten so trendy, all the collars turned up and women clamping their legs to keep skirts from rising. Head down, I pass the Movie Star and quickly cross the street into my courtyard, breathing heavily. The branches stir, something wrestling, nerves bleating, *eight*, exhale . . . moving faster through the bushes to the steps and a dead stop. The bartender is sitting at the bottom of the staircase.

He puts his forefinger to his lips, motions for me to come and sit down next to him in the dark. I do as I'm told. We sit silently, both looking forward into the black night, the freezing wind bouncing between us.

"I'm not going to hurt you," he tells me. "Nobody wants to hurt you. Which is why I have come. To tell you again, you really must go."

"Wait, aren't you with Gila?"

"You have seen her?"

I turn slightly, look at him. Something is off, though I can't remember if Gila had actually confirmed their connection or if she'd just let me think it.

"You are lying."

"Who are you?"

"When did you see her?"

"I haven't seen her. I swear." This new lie, I'm not even sure where it's coming from, but it feels alive, essential.

"I know you are here with a fake passport. You told me from the beginning you looked for her. Maybe you have seen her, maybe she is still only a projection of your own consciousness."

"A what?"

"Never mind. I will make this deal with you one time. You go home tomorrow. There will be a ticket waiting at the airport and you will clear security without a problem. After that it will be difficult."

"Oh shit. Are you the government?"

He stands, brushes off his trousers. I get up too. "Listen to me," he says, "I could not be more serious. People will cut off your throat!"

I laugh, sort of. Nerves, of course, but also because he sounds like The Foreigner in an American movie. He shakes his head, then turns and grabs my wrist tight. We are the same height, whites of our eyes catching each other through the dark, the wind. I try not to blink, to hold it.

"One time only, Jennifer," he says. "Then, as you say . . . all of the bets are off."

He lets go of my wrist and disappears into the blackness. I sit down on the steps again, trying to remember every word, every detail, as the wind slaps my face over and over and over again.

I am through with the beach, it's too fluffed up with risk and memory, and I have been leaving my house on brief outings only, covered in a blue fishing hat I found in a thrift store around the block and carrying a small umbrella, props. Gila had said earlier to change my hat every day, wear sunglasses. If she had her way I would not leave my flat until she figured out our next move.

She is restless since the bartender's visit. He does not work for her, she should have made that clear. Just stay put, she said. She will call again later. But here is what she does not know: I cannot stay in my apartment with the bottle. A glass of wine down already this morning, the rest will do me in. I need a meeting. *More than your life?* This is Gila in my head. Yes, I think so.

A few blocks from the house I check my phone again. Nothing from her. The metal burns in my clenched fist as I head toward the queer center but can't remember the exact street and am too scared to pop into a kiosk for a map, the idea of speaking Hebrew and blowing my cover paramount. Why is everything so fucking sinister? I decide to return home and start walking in the opposite direction. A twig snaps on the ground behind me and it feels close. My throat constricts. The footsteps get louder. I smell cologne or hair gel, the remnants of pipe tobacco. I hold my stance, keep the same pace, eyeing a truck parked a few feet ahead, half on the sidewalk. I can slip behind it, then run to the next corner, praying for topiary.

This is not the bartender. He does not follow; he appears.

When I'm alone his words feel even more ominous: *People will cut off your throat!*

A quick flash, wondering if that plane ticket is still at the airport, but he was clear: all bets off. I make it to the truck and duck down low, my heart speeding. Something says stay. I squeeze down under the bed and try to center myself, but all the yoga in the world can't get you out of shit like this. I breathe and count backward from fifty a whole lot of times, until I have the balls to check my phone and see it's been awhile, and it just feels okay, something you get used to, the senses and feelings. I slide out from under the truck and move into the crowd, crossing against the light, traversing several streets and boulevards, walking quickly on back streets to confuse anyone who might be following me, and somehow end up in the shopping district, people around me carrying big bags with designer names, beginning to buzz about lunch.

I stare into the window of a tawny clothing store. Silver mannequins draped in sparkling evening gowns hijack the window, bizarre *Star Trek* faces, bald and metallic with gigantic black lashes. My face floats between the bots, fishing hat and sunglasses, and I feel sorely underdressed for this morning, this life. I want to go home. I want to cry. I look awful, my skin so loose, nostrils drawn out, stubble on my cheek, prominent chin . . . I freak, I'm becoming him, even the smell. I turn abruptly and he's in my face.

I scream. He screams.

"Jesus, Jen, are you trying to give me another heart attack?"

My temples fire, my heart through my chest. He's wearing the same blue fishing hat as me.

"What the fuck?"

"It's a big day for us."

"I'm being followed, you can't do this."

"I've been trying to see you for days, but you've complicated things again. You and that mobster woman."

"You mean your girlfriend?"

"Oh, that is so last year. That little harlot betrayed me. So did you. Now everything's changed."

"That's right. I'm Polish now."

"Don't believe everything you hear."

"She thinks you're dead."

"Well, that's one thing she's got right."

"Oh, come on."

"Come, I'll show you."

"Fucking ghost of Christmas past."

"That's not the right movie. You're thinking of *It's a Wonderful Life*. I mean, yes, it's just as mercenary. The goddamn goyim!"

"Did you hear me? I'm being followed. I think it's the government."

"Forget about that. I've got you covered. Now, you with me or not?" He stares, like will I take the bait? I can't see what I have to lose. He nudges me toward a California-orange awning that creeps over yellow walls, white plastic chairs out front. Lettering in white says, *Juicy Restaurant*. Its trade is health food, whatever that umbrella takes under its spokes: juice, falafel, cucumber salad, wheatgrass, not unlike half the other restaurants along the boulevard. But somehow this one scored the word *Juicy*.

As we approach the restaurant, my father tells me he's become a vegetarian. Tragic for someone like him, but now he is happiest with a light stomach. We grab a sidewalk table and before sitting down he wipes the chair with a handkerchief to preserve the dignity of his bedouin pants—tie-dyed, with rolls of fabric gathered between the legs. I'd read a sect of bedouins believe the next messiah will be born through the anus of a man, landing in the dip of the pants; they're functional, but to imagine my father a bedouin was a gift I'd never allowed myself. He was always so tight-fitted, even as he started gaining weight in more recent years. In my fantasies he wore frayed jeans. But this, this is extraordinary and lifts my mood. He falls into his seat as if almost floating. "The benefits of weightlessness," he smiles.

"Whatever."

He stares up at me for a moment, through me really, the way cats can look at you so deeply and vacantly at once. Truly nobody seems to notice. Not the shaggy waiter. Not the elderly couple at the next table. Not anyone who's been passing by along the sidewalk.

"Jen," he says.

"Yes?"

"I'd like a shot of wheatgrass. Will you get it for me?"

I haven't seen him drink yet and feel excited for a clue. Do ghosts drink wheatgrass juice? I could tap the waiter on the shoulder and ask if he sees what I see, a paunchy gray man smiling from ear to ear at the thought of choking back a thimble of chopped-up grass the way he used to drink hundred-year-old Scotch.

I leave him on the sidewalk and walk the few steps inside, dandelion walls screaming at me. A commercial for a popular Israeli bank floats from speakers on the ceiling. I want to cover my ears, my eyes, slow down the pebbles rumbling inside my head. The woman behind the counter says something in Hebrew. She is stunning—long blond curls, dark eyes, tanned skin. How did she find her way here? I imagine she is Russian. Maybe she is a professor of earth science at home, here she pours wheatgrass juice. I want to make her my wife.

My father's a big guy, weightless or not. I'd always credited him for my height and heft. Which reminds me I am hungry. I add a plate of hummus to his double-shot of wheatgrass and count the paper signs with specials behind the counter until my tray comes. Balancing it to return outside, I see my father is not alone. He's got his hands wrapped tightly around the veiny crackled fingers of a woman, maybe in her eighties, certainly older than he is. Tan, weathered, not afraid to show a line in her peaceful mug—definitely against type.

I startle backward.

"This is Golda!" he beams. "We are in love."

I drop the plate of hummus to the floor.

"She was once president of this country, you know, and now—"

"Stop." Golda takes her hands from his and sits upright against her plastic chair. "You'll spoil me."

"Baby," he says, "we're long past that."

The rain comes out of nowhere. One minute there is sunshine on my shoulders, nudging me along the beach where Maccabee beers and Moroccan cigars are delivered under big white umbrellas. The next I am dodging raindrops like bullets, reminding me that government stalkers also like the beach. I do not have an umbrella so I run back as fast as I can, envisioning my flat with its displaced Japanese tub and terrace, the platform bed and concrete floors, Yudi, the boy, all of it ringing of hearth and . . . that word again, home.

Golda Meir was the third prime minister of this tortured land, the original iron lady, monstrous and crazy sexy with power. Coming up, she'd had affairs with all the best generals. She was a hero to this nation, an experiment in housing the homeless and landing the lost, no matter how heavy the bill for displacing others racked up. She died a long time ago, like decades . . . What is it she's been doing all these years that's brought her to my father? I continue to pound through the rain in the final stretches, remembering how she left me.

"Golda will walk you out," my father said, and she took me to the sidewalk, leading me a few feet to a street named after a baron and charting my path home. "There is a garden named after me," she says, "take a left there and keep walking. You will find what you are looking for very soon . . ." Then she pushed me, by the ass with both of her palms, into the traffic.

At home I shake out my sneakers and put them on the dry part of the terrace. Though I'm starving—I never ate my hummus, it stayed on the restaurant floor—I run the shower until it's steaming and step in, climbing out only after the skin on my fingertips crinkles. I cover my hot, pink limbs with sweatpants and a giant sweatshirt from the Hebrew University. Heavy raindrops bounce off the terrace. To stop rain, I once heard, walk three times around a ten-foot circle. Turn inward. Think of palm trees. I decide to try. The thing is, it has to be exactly ten feet, even a centimeter short and it's over. I can't figure out the distance and decide instead to wash the floor of my kitchenette and bathroom, because if I sit, I'll give in. I fill a pail with hot tap water, adding a quarter-cup of bleach and some dishwashing liquid. Nothing scientific. Bucket filled almost to the top, I seek out a tool. There are no mops in this country, not in the traditional sense. With a stone floor, it's better to attach a cloth to the bottom of a stick and pull. I dig the stick out of the closet it shares with a few sweaters, a skateboard, vacuum cleaner (good to know), all relics of past tenants. I have been here three months and have not thought of washing anything. This disturbs me, though only slightly.

Confession: I have never washed a floor. There was always someone else to do it for me and I liked it this way. Though it's left me entirely unprepared, standing before a pail of bubbly water not knowing if it's best to dip the mop or spill the liquid on the floor and glide. Don't go thinking I'm a rat's ass, I assure you I've swept a few times. Yudi keeps a broom on the porch. Actually, he is the person who told me about the walking in circles. It's a bedouin trick, I think, though he can tell me anything and I will believe him. I consider for a second crossing the wet path to his side and seeing if he has a real mop but fear the slickness of the porch, the sheets of water. Slanted rain terrifies me, makes me think of a meat slicer—I'm not normally scared off so easily. They don't have meat slicers here either, not the metallic contraptions that cut the paper-thin sheets of smoked turkey I like. You can roll them nicely around carrots. And I like to watch the sandwich boy on my corner deli push the hunk of meat back and forth. He smiles perversely with the motion. I imagine him fucking.

I imagine myself fucking instead of sitting before this ineffectual bucket. Maybe if I take a T-shirt and attach it to the stick, I won't need a mop after all . . .

Sofia, the Spanish au pair, used to wash our kitchen floor in a short dress. Week after week I watched the blue cotton roll up high on the back of her legs, thinking thoughts I can't remember, though they stirred up my insides. Then one day she turns around, catches me staring, and smiles. It's summer but gray outside. I am bored. Let's go to the roof, she says, and pulls me into the stairwell, not the elevator, never the elevator when you've got trouble in mind. She loves the *Sugar* sign across the river. The *S* burned out years ago and the idea of the rest, the *ugar*, makes her giggle. She's a teenager, I think, who can remember. I am big for my age and interested. I reach for her sleeveless shoulders and close my hands around the back of her cotton dress.

She kisses me lightly on the nose. Um . . . *ugar!* Then both cheeks. My lips. I reach my tongue out for her. She smiles, asks if I've done this before, and I lie. We kiss as the skies darken overhead. She's older but not like the friend of my mother's who touched me once when I was changing in Connecticut, I haven't thought about that in years. She said I was beautiful and just wanted to look. Sofia has class and loves to kiss, despite my fear that rain and New York City roofs don't mix. She says I need to watch more Fellini. She has an answer for everything.

Years later I will write her a letter. In rehab the second time, when I am ready to make amends and know more about her than I could have imagined then. I will tell her what she's left me with, the idea that kisses can bring on noises as deafening as thunder and disappear as fast. And the cold reality that you cannot own someone's kisses, that they can just as easily belong to your brother, for instance, who is newly dead when I write the letter, but he had confessed he slept with her too. Not as a child, but later, when I was in deep competition and she'd returned looking for work. They had a thing. Not love, he assured me. But I was still raving jealous.

When it rains, I still miss her terribly.

The floor can wait, I need a nap. The bottle next to my bed beckons with the third or fourth call to prayer, howling through the afternoon, you can hear traces of it here where I live. I pull off the cork I'd opened this morning and drink straight from the bottle. A sign, of course, but I just don't care.

The problem with rain, real rain, is that it makes you less perfect. But when it's over everything feels better.

I wake to winds snarling against the shutters, and the sky feels dark, maybe time for dinner, but no, it's still lightish out. I stand up and my head hurts a little, my throat clogged with rocks. The bottle next to my bed is more than half full. Not bad. I leave the bedroom, almost tripping over the pail of water in the center of the living area, too small to call an actual room. I must have located a T-shirt and dipped it in the water, as it's wrung out over the side of the bucket. I must have started cleaning, though the floor looks as filthy as ever, and it's not the booze that's playing with my memory, I barely drank anything. Sinking my hands into the bucket, it's cold, bleach stinging the open cuts in the corners of my fingernails from digging too deep in the sand the other day. Anything sliced into the skin will open more deeply under pressure. Healing is a complex process.

I take the T-shirt out of the pail and squeeze it tightly between my hands, then make circles on the concrete in front of me. When I lift, the underbelly is brown with everything I've dragged in these past few months. Wiping it away makes me sad.

She shows up just then. If I were writing it you would see how it just happens, shutters clanking more ominously until I realize there is someone knocking at my door. Out of nowhere. But does anything really happen out of nowhere? The new lover with a few stray hours. The law of averages says most American women have fewer than four lovers in their lifetime. I find this hard to believe. I clocked a higher number before I was sixteen, had tripled the returns by twenty. Is there a point where you use up your chances?

Though, here is number . . . forget it, I was never good at math. Or tracking personal history. She stands in front of me holding a small paper bag, her curls tight like bedsprings, maybe another wig, and I want to pull her into me so tight it hurts.

"You look terrible," she says, dropping the bag on the counter. She eyes the bucket in the middle of the floor, then comes closer. "What's happening?"

"I'm scared," I say, and can't believe I said it. It's not like me to put words to weakness. I do not fear anything. I am fearless.

"It's okay. We are leaving. As soon as night falls."

"Where?"

She puts a finger to my lips. "Shush. Don't worry now. There will be time for that. We will be together a while."

I part my lips slightly, lick the inside of her finger then draw it in with my tongue, sucking hard. "Mmmmm," she mumbles, inching her finger out and replacing it with her lips. I kiss her desperately, my arms locked around her back. If I could hold this moment, pause . . . She kisses back, like anger it's so ferocious. I break away and heave against her neck. "Make love to me," she says, and I am thrown by how perfectly each word tickles my eardrum, though embarrassed by the clarity. I hate sex sometimes, how it turns me hollow. All I see is beauty. Trite as it sounds, let me count the ways, as my hands pull at her trousers, pulling them back slowly, then in front with my chin, stopped temporarily by a harness, not what you're thinking, the baby Glock in the small of her back. She arches up, unhooking the leather strap in one swift move, and the whole apparatus falls to the floor. She grabs the back of my neck, I slip down in front of her, biting at her thong. I love wrapping my mouth in her, the clash of grit and spice, gobbling at her clit, while around us the wind continues to rant. She jumps into me, pushes my chin back, almost dislodging it from my face. I steady myself against her. She pushes harder against my jawbone, so hard I fall back against the bucket and the silty liquid spills across the floor. She presses down, and we roll together on the cold, wet floor. "Please," she says, and I flip us over, then pull her up with me and, standing, we kiss again.

"I missed you so much," I say, breaking off slightly.

"Show me," she says, her lips against my cheek.

"Why'd you wait so long?" I kiss her earlobe.

"Later." She backs up slightly, taking my hand and kissing it. "Just make love to me. There's not too much time."

I'm gone.

In my head I lift her over my shoulder and carry her into the bedroom, but even through the stupor, I fear my days of acrobatic foreplay have faded. Instead I let her lead me quietly inside and pull me down on the bed, kissing me deeply as I fumble at the buttons of her shirt, each a conundrum of dexterity over desire. Really, I should rip the thing off, but I don't, and with each button I kiss her skin, letting my teeth graze slightly, until the cotton falls away and there is only a delicate olive bra, dazzling against her light-brown skin, summer colors, and she smells like summer looming as I unhook the bra. She backs up slightly, a hand on mine from behind, and I am craven with anticipation, every time, it's this moment, the revelation that slays me, no matter how many lovers, nor how many years I've circled the planet, I want to quote Shakespeare upon gazing at breasts, uncovered and waiting, hers unremarkable in some ways, the continuation of skin, but the brown of her nipples, hard, bigger than I'd expected, she has small breasts, smaller than mine, and there I go comparing as I've done my entire life because she who has the strongest legs wins. But here it's a lowball down to her nipples and I suck gloriously, tweaking the other with my fingers, and she sighs, says something in Hebrew that sounds like suck, everything in Hebrew sounds like suck or fuck or uh-oh, and I love her voice, the language, I come up and look at her, really look, and the words slip from my lips, something in English that sounds like oh fuck, and she pulls my head down and I grab her hand and lay it between her legs, and she touches herself while I suck, nibbling ever so lightly, as her gasps beneath me turn to clipped words and waves and I stay with her like surfing, until she screams, jumping backward, and we're both heaving. She looks at me, smiling, and for a second, no two, I want to spend the rest of my life with her and it takes everything in me not to cry. That's ruined me so many times before, and this is different, and we both know it, so she takes my hand, pulls me back, kisses me, and we are at it again, nothing but possibility, though I am twitchy, desperate to get beyond kisses so sweet they'll bury me, I can't look at her, and instead turn her over, running my tongue down her back as she writhes, bending her legs up like a bird of paradise, and I spread them, licking down her thigh, spreading wider and, no joke, her asshole through the tiny buzzed hairs is like a bud opening up to my tongue, salty sweet earth and sea intensity.

This goes on for a bit, my taking her every way I can think of and rounding up her orgasms, only once coming, I defer with hands and tongue and tell her this is about her pleasure which brings me pleasure and that's the way I like it, not so much altruism but her coming makes me come so hard I can't see, like when I was in my twenties and could come just by thinking it. Seriously, I thought I was a mutant, but a string of lovers told me, no, this is a gift, this is something to cultivate, to embrace, to love. We fall back against very wet sheets, shutting our eyes together, and she's in my dreams, snippets like old filmstrips, though I catch myself before falling in, afraid she'll be gone when I wake. She sees me, smiles, takes my hands in between hers, and turns on her side so we're face to face. I kiss her nose, and she sighs.

"It's time," she whispers. "We must go quietly."

"Can you tell me where?"

"We are going up north for a few days and then you will not come back here for some time."

"I told you I'm not going home . . . I would have used that ticket."

"You misunderstand me. I am talking about this apartment. You will not be back here, but we will make them think you are still here. It will buy us time."

I stare at her, half in love with this idea of buying time. You can buy anything, really—my father has taught me that.

"Listen, before we go, I have to tell you something," I say, struck back by the enormity, the immediacy of what's happening. "I saw him again. It was even crazier."

"Not yet." She puts her finger over my lips and I want to swallow it whole this time. "We have a big drive. You can tell me everything."

We have arrived up north and we cannot sleep. Yet there is promise. The break of a cold, sunny morning . . . "Let's go for a drive," she says. "There is something wonderful to see."

She won't say what, and before long the two of us are careening in and out of the wakening hills in a brand-new black sports car that reads Grace Kelly, though the make is unfamiliar and we keep the top covered and it reminds me of my childhood, Marc, the line of cars in our garage in Connecticut, all the long, boring days together.

Gila drives with calm purpose. Eyes on the road, hands on the wheel. She doesn't talk much in the car, I'm learning, so I drift off, safe in her hands for the moment.

An afternoon long ago: the weather so stultifying even the beach made me gag, Marc and I spend hours in the air-conditioned garage. He had been watching roller derby at the rink where I skated in the winter and was obsessed with wheels. There was a girl he liked who liked an older guy who derbied so he followed her to the rink. This was an absurd town. Kids dressed in silver uniforms for the derby rink and rubbed vodka on their tongues through thick rollerball lip gloss containers. I hear derby is making a comeback or the media has discovered it once again, like they occasionally do with speed skating around the winter Olympics. He also played polo, the girl's guy, and Marc thought it was obscene, treating horses like a football helmet. He loved to ride and had been spending weeks at my mother's ranch in the mountains. He could jump horses and wanted to do the same on his skateboard. If only it had an engine.

As far back as I can remember Marc liked engines and machines. There were old golf carts in the garage. Fishing rods with an electric reel. Discarded pencil sharpeners, knife sharpeners, brand-new blenders and food processors, untouched because they were an offensive brand or played the wrong hand at a dinner party. So many motors to choose from, really, he just needed to find the right one and solder it to the bottom of his skateboard to engage the back wheels. They'll push the front along, he'd said.

We went off on tangents that summer, trying to build our way out of the heat. It was several years after my mother left, and my father had taken up with a singer. She did the Greenwich Village circuit and had nice round lips. In Connecticut she drove the '67 Midget, which was the smallest car I'd ever seen and cool green like sea glass. As long as she stayed the car was hers. Then it passed to the next one. My mother had picked out that car but left with nothing. Her plan had been to divest of all possessions, strip herself down like the north in March, and see what emerged. She had time to be herself without us, she said, which left Marc and me with her car, a cabaret singer, and a big problem: how to attack the hours on a summer day. It's true what they say about an idle mind, once you let go of the punitive aspects.

Gila tilts her eyes toward me from the steering wheel. "We are almost there," she says.

I catch her gaze.

"Are you okay?"

"I'm tired. My head hurts. But right now, in this car with you . . . everything is good."

That's a lie. She knows it too. She smiles, hands back on the wheel hard, eyes forward.

We are heading to a place she will soon reveal, a topography she holds in her heart, she'd said, and though a tad dramatic, my interest sparked because I still can't get a handle on her. Why are we here? I'd asked when we first arrived in the darkness and with a flashlight made our way up a dirt path through the brittle dew into what looked like a barracks. She said it was a depopulated kibbutz that had gone commercial, renting rooms to migrant workers and tourists. We have our own cottage in the woods where no one will bother us, she said, that's why. There are alarms on top of alarms, motion sensors, and accomplices. We are on the run.

Play music, she says. Like we are students on the way to the beach for spring break, and the song choice means everything. I reach for her iPod, which we've hooked into the speakers, and scroll through an abundance of British and American pop. Eighties and early nineties mostly. IPods distress me sometimes, they simply hold too much. I search by artist and find exactly what I'm looking for.

Gila's cheeks soften. "Perfect."

Annie Lennox sings post-Eurythmics, more mature, lovely, even sexier, sad sexy. What isn't when you're in the throes of it, but come on . . . *Catch me and let me dive under, for I want to swim in the pools of your eyes.*

"Oh, oh!" I say. "This is the adult version of diving into your ocean . . ."

"*Ma?*"

"The Eurythmics . . . remember? She was so hot."

"You are so hot," she says, and I feel it, the heat in my rib cage. "Can I ask you something?"

"Of course."

"About your accident. The big one."

"Oh, that. Why?"

"I was once in Freudian analysis, early in my twenties, just after coming out of the army with too much in my head. The idea is simple. You and the analyst become one. You bleed into each other, forget all the normal lines, only it's safe. Then you can revisit your past, but you get the better of it. Maybe you did this too."

"It's hard to know. There were so many shrinks."

"Tell me what happened."

"First: what were you and this analyst trying to get through together?"

"I had lost my will."

"What does that mean?"

"Not now, I told you I cannot think and drive. But I can listen. Tell me more."

The word *listen* plays aggressively against the softly rising hills, as we push up and down, moving forward. Is this what my father discovered that he'd never had? Why he could *talk to her*? I've got an itch to roll back.

"It's okay, if you don't want, we can be silent."

"I don't remember it. I was going so fast and I was ahead, even ahead of all my team. We'd been training wildly for the short races, and then something hit my foot—you know, I've been through the conspiracy theories, people hated me because I was young. They didn't think I was serious. Maybe I wasn't. But it was all me. I lost my focus, which is deadly when you're going that fast, and I tried to pull back like I'd done a million times, and the next thing I know I'm in a hospital room. I have no idea how I hit the wall."

"But have you tried to remember?"

"I watched it. Over and over. The biggest mistake of my

life on video loop . . . and thank fucking god there was no Internet."

"You think there is anyone who cares that much?"

I smile. "They showed it for weeks on the nightly roundup, those games were so fucking sad, people were falling all over the place, and the Russians won everything. But seriously, the agony of defeat? Do you even watch the Olympics?"

"No."

"Then why do you care?"

"I need to know how strong you are. Or if you are a coward."

"Fuck you."

"You are still hiding, I think. Still full of hate for the world."

Her words stop me, how she'd drawn me into revealing things I'm not sure I believe anymore. "You're trying to manipulate me, aren't you?"

She is silent.

"Right, right, you can't talk. Whatever . . ." I hear my tone change and realize I'm unnerved, need to tip the balance back, accuse. "Oh, come on, like you're so in love with the world, Gila. Maybe I gave up some notion of glory I wanted at fourteen, but what about you? You always dreamed of being a criminal?"

"I decided I would be the best at whatever I decided to be. And that has been largely the truth."

"Jesus Christ, you are so damn elliptical!"

She turns her head slightly . . . *Ma?*

"Like an ellipsis . . . the three dots. You're living in the spaces."

"I'm sorry. I don't understand."

"And where are we going? I feel like we're driving around in circles."

All red lips and sunglasses, she does not answer. Just pushes harder on the gas. There are no other cars on the road, maybe the occasional tractor, as she guns over a steep climb, the tiny pines growing heavier, more condensed, budding lightly at the tips, creeping up high into the white-capped hills. These are substantial bumps, bona fide mountains with ski lifts and hiking trails, though the highest peaks scream chicken from across a testy border. We reach the apex of our hill quickly and begin a descent into the pinkest valley I've ever seen, all sexual metaphors not withstanding, we enter the rosy sea faster than a speeding bullet, more powerful than a . . . Up close the flowers remind me of wild cherry blossoms in the Japanese hills. I've seen pictures in magazines, light and airy like cotton candy, but brighter. My breath catches, I am in love again. "Holy shit! What is this?"

"Almonds."

She slams the breaks and we pivot to the side of the road, kicking open our doors and running out. I follow her into the scent of honey dripping from the sky, a deep-throat buzz like thousands of electric razors, the hum of the planet this morning, frozen mountains dead smack in front of us, rising up behind the bushy pink forest. We can see our breath in the air. I want to lie down on the ground and writhe like a cat. Instead I wrap my arms around her waist from behind and we stand looking out, sucking in the air. She breaks away quickly. "Come," she says, and I love the way she says that word, echoed by Annie Lennox in the distance . . . *Come on now, come on now, come on now.* I'd put the song on repeat.

"The car is going."

"So." She takes my hand. "This is not what I want to show you."

We walk the few steps back to the car, stand next to it looking out and up.

"That's Mount Hermon up there?"

"Yes."

"I was here with my brother. A long time ago."

"After you'd fallen."

"Why are you pushing?"

"Because it's your secret."

"It's not a secret. Thousands of people saw it on television."

"This is what you hold? All the eyes on you?"

"Among other things."

"You misunderstand me, what I am trying to say is you are caught by the wrong hook."

"See! See! That's it."

"*Ma?* What?"

"Stop interrogating me. It's boring." I swing open the car door. Climb inside. Slam it.

She comes around her side, buckles up, and slaps off the radio. We sit silently for a few seconds that feel like minutes. I imagine myself flying in and out of the bulbous pink hills, entering and exiting, lips dripping with honey. "I'm sorry," she cuts in, eyes staring straight ahead, hands at two and ten on the steering wheel, though we are still in park. The engine rumbles lightly. "We must find a way to talk that's not explosive."

"Turn the car off."

She does, eyeing me suspiciously. I spin my cheek to the hills, so unabashed in their display that I blush. Gila reaches her hand over, squeezes my thigh. I stiffen.

"Is this why you're fucking me? So I'll give you information?"

"No," she says. "I promise. This was not planned. Except the first time last summer . . . that was him. This is me."

"Is he still alive?" I say, still looking out the window, away from her.

"I don't know."

I turn, skeptically.

"I told you, I have not seen him since his death."

"Who do you work for?"

"I am for myself."

"But before you were with him?"

"Yes."

"I want to know more."

"I told you much of this already."

"Tell me again."

Here is what she says.

They met several years ago. She was working for Mossad for a brief period after Technion, where she'd immersed herself in back-end technologies, systems to run systems. She specialized in surveillance, similar to what she'd done in the army intelligence unit. We tell stories differently each time, the details up and down like eye-popping hills, not what matters ultimately. Last summer she told me she'd been suffering from post-traumatic stress, something soldiers don't discuss though everyone sees a therapist. In the army she'd helped create systems that could detect a heartbeat ten feet outside of a tank, wireless carrots that when invited into the wrong hard drive disrupted missiles. And still they killed so many people, the wrong people.

This is how she lost her way, she says now, staring straight ahead, neck on high alert. It has everything to do with her own father. "He fought for a world that was better than anything we had ever known. He believed we could make the experiment work and be a model for the rest of the world. It is why he became a general. He had self-defense on his side. I had strength. And weapons . . . your country gave us to kick the hell out of Arabs." She leans back in the driver's seat, breathes deeply. "This is something to bear, the killing, especially when you are a woman. They are telling you, make this happen, be strong, we must continue to build, make hard choices, then get your legs up, and have babies so we can make a nation. We must grow our people. We must have our own people . . ."

She turns her chin toward the side window, unsteady. Outside of sex, I'd never seen her waver. I want to reach out but hear another voice saying be careful.

We look out at the hills in silence.

"This is how he walked in," she says quietly. "This father of yours, with his audacious mind, asking all the right questions, even the way he ordered meals was tactical. He made me feel smart and beautiful and useful."

"Useful?"

"I had lost all sense of purpose."

"So you two started stealing shit."

"You cannot possibly understand. You are soft like the country you come from."

"But he's not."

She shakes her head lightly, rubbing her fingers into fists between her thighs. A truck throttles past, shaking our little no-name car to its bones. It passes and I realize it's me who's trembling. I can't turn my head, can't look at her. She inches toward me, reaching over the stick shift, pulling my hands into hers. I give slightly, my heart barreling like a fast-moving truck.

"We can move past our fathers," she says.

"I don't understand you. You say you loved him."

"And now I love you."

I stare, are you fucking kidding me?

"It has always been," she says. "From the beginning."

"The beginning . . ."

"Yes."

I am not a believer, but this feels unlike anything I've ever experienced, the two of us lodged at the foothills of the highest point in this endlessly torn-up land. Her hands are warm, her eyes weighted with history, desire, almond blossoms in the morning light.

"From the first moment I saw you I knew something," she says. "I can't explain. There was him, of course. And it was my job to bring you to him, as you know. Make you want to help. He knew you'd respond . . . He does know some things about you, maybe. And this is why he is so angry."

"I don't want to talk about him right now."

"Then let's talk about us, there is power between us. I don't pretend to understand it, and mostly I understand everything, which is part of the difficulty here. This is why you should not have returned."

I slip my right hand out from our grasp, bringing my finger to her lips now. "Let's not talk about that either," I whisper, taking both of her cheeks between my palms, we kiss.

Lovers unleash lovers unleash love. Each carries a longing for the past, reentry, the colonization of another soul, came, saw, conquered, now I know you're mine.

Elbow propped on a pillow, I watch Gila's chest rise up and down, her limbs barely covered. She is deep in slumber, this daughter of a general who helped forge a people back when they were still pioneers, predatory baggage notwithstanding. The liberals were all terrorists back in the day, and what that does to your lineage, those born into the fire of this land, sabras, which despite the clichéd tough exterior of a cactus covering sweet Israeli juice, if the skin fits . . . Gila is taut right down to her toes, in perfect alignment but for a slight protrusion of the second digit and all the mythology that carries. A lover once told me the second toe was the key to a person's sensuality. If it's bigger than the first you're into something good. We were lying naked on her bed in the aftermath, talking about what we liked; I was barely twenty-five and talk still excited me. The thought that it might ramble into something purposeful, a new direction. I rolled over slightly and bent around her back, trying to get a look at how cocky she was. We'd met only a few hours earlier at an L7 concert down on the Bowery. She was up next to the stage, bleached-out dreads dripping down her back. Every so often she'd lean sideways into the people slamming rhythmically, just enough to dig an elbow into someone's side or jab her shoulder tightly against the human wall, teasing in and out of the springy heat.

I moved behind her.

She jumped up and down in place, music pounding like the inside of a car factory. L7 was legendary that year. One of the leads had pulled out a tampon onstage and thrown it at a stormy crowd—boys said it was gross. All the girls fell in love. The one in front of me was entranced, bouncing as if she had coils in her shoes. Then boom: she pushed too high, lost ground, and slammed down on my toes.

"Fuck!" I screamed over the music.

"Oh shit!" she said.

"Fuck you!"

"I'm so sorry."

I bit my lower lip, smiled. She put a hand on my shoulder and I kissed her.

This is a true story. As real as any of the moments I can no longer remember. What she said, what I said, then the two of us on her bed together a few hours later. I was reckless with girls after my accident, trying to glean some of the drive I'd left on the ice in Calgary. I never said much, I didn't have to. She said she knew everything from the size of my toe, the one she'd inspired back to life in a yellow taxi that smelled like stale cigarettes and pine cleaner, as we crossed the crumbling Williamsburg Bridge to a street

I'd never seen in a borough that had always confounded me. If there was any elegance to this sort of meeting, it crashed like electronic cymbals with her words. As if you could quantify sensuality. As if it had a purpose of its own. Looking back, I was naïve—who wasn't? But I would be lying if I said I hadn't checked the second toe of every lover since, lying too if I told you there was no difference between working a quick fiery fuck and making love to someone you are absolutely crazy about.

Gila is tight asleep. Despite the slight rise and fall of her chest, she is serene, and I want to sully it, waking her up to tell her about the L7 concert, tell her how many lovers I've had and why she's different. I want to hear more about my father too, and talk about sex and love like I'm twenty-five and it's all that matters. I reach my arm around her stomach and she pulls me in close, asks why I am not sleeping, and I tell her I can't, it's too much to close my eyes, I'm flooded with ghosts. She misinterprets and thinks I am talking about him, can we please just put him aside, okay?

I slip my right hand down and stroke her lightly. She moans and sinks deeper into me, tilting us together so I can get inside her with my middle finger. I fuck her gently, slowly circling her clit with the palm of my hand, almost on top of her. I dip my left hand down her lower back, sliding my fingers to the wiry entry point behind, all the while speaking it back to her, what she feels like, smells like, makes me want to do to her. She grabs my left hand hard, says un-uh, not now, and it's too much to negotiate at this hour. Instead I whisper in her ear, licking her lobe between words, telling her what I would do in both places at once. Makes her want to come, she says, but not yet, so I slow the rhythms beneath my palm and together we breathe and murmur the words *fuck* and *come* like a chant, it's so trite it takes everything in me not to ask did he get you like this?

Could he do this to you? But we are putting him aside . . . okay? *Okay?* I whisper and she whimpers back, yes, please. I add a second finger, my ring finger that's never worn a ring, fucking her faster, narrating it in her ear, those words I want to say forever, make her tell me she'll let me, anytime, anywhere, she's my colony now, and she says yes, anytime, yes, forever, yes, fuck me, yes, yes, yes . . .

I awake to silence, alone, the cotton comforter wrapped snug as a burial cloth around me. It is cold and damp, the windows covered with shutters from the outside, so I can't get a read on the time or place. I kick myself out of the blanket and put my feet on the cement floor. It's not as cold as I'd imagined, though once I stand the mountain chill brings goose bumps and shivers.

Gila is gone. The room is gray. I turn on the lamp next to the bed, behind my eyes a throbbing migraine or allergies. I am stiff all over, like I'd been running for days, particularly in my groin. Sex muscles. Makes me think of her, the way she says yes as everything seizes up inside, those three little words . . . *Did I go and spoil it all by saying something stupid . . . ?* I smell my fingers and she's there, touch myself and she's there, swallow the lump in my throat and it's her. Late into the night we rose together and drank shots of homemade arak at the little table in the main room. We kissed for a long time in the dark. Then drifted back to the bedroom and I shut my eyes, though it's normally hard to sleep with someone not yet familiar lying next to me.

I take a shower and stand for a moment in the heat before stepping out and wrapping my shriveled self into a big white towel. There is a fluffy robe, also painstakingly white, with Hebrew lettering I cannot read, though something says it's okay to wear, along with the terry slippers on a shelf next to the sink. There are multiple pairs, all the same size and covered in plastic. I feel like a patron at a high-priced bath, a rich bald dude from Russia or Poland, wherever I'm from.

My head rings, the throbbing abated slightly. But I need coffee. I walk out into the main room, thinking I'd seen a little kitchen, and find a mini fridge with a hot plate on top that looks menacing. No sink, everything pushed up against the wall, next to the table where we sat down together last night. I open the refrigerator and there's nothing inside. The levels of abandonment mount.

On the table is the bottle of arak, three-quarters full, my wallet next to it, a couple of stray pieces of paper peeking out like someone's been playing with it. All I carry is paper money, a fake license, and a few local business cards, having discarded everything else back in New York. The cards pop out, but I don't see the license. I turn out the wallet and shake it violently. The license is gone. An uncomfortable knot hits my chest, my ears ringing . . . *This is a test of the Emergency Broadcast System* . . . My passport (the fake one) lives in a secret lining inside my suitcase, along with codes for various account numbers, written on a piece of paper. You don't need a degree from Technion to break them.

I check my suitcase in the other room, everything's there.

But all hell's cracking, because this is the world we're living in, and I'm okay. I pace the few steps back and forth in the main room. This is all okay. Where does that word come from? It's ridiculous.

Gila took my license. She has a reason. Or she's a liar . . . There's no way I could sleep through her leaving. I pop open the bottle on the table, sniff the sour trace of licorice, nothing else obvious, and she drank it too. I am craving a nip of the pup, but resist. Think of those lists on the Internet. *Do you drink alone or hide your drinking? Is your drinking a ritual? Do you become irritable when your ritual is disturbed?* Fuck you! I open the bottle and take a long sip, its acidic madness scraping the back of my throat. I shake my head, an odd sensation without hair, and come back to my wallet splayed out on the table. A piece of old stationery sticks out of the side, Marc's initials on top with fancy serifs and curls, the black ink faded though still legible. I had completely forgotten it, stuffed deep into a fold within a fold inside the buttery leather, the note I've carried with me for more than a decade.

Two years after Marc slammed his car into a boulder, I discovered it, buried inside a box of trading cards—all pre-1987 Mets. They smothered a plastic bag of cocaine vials, a marble pipe, and a tiny spoon shaped like a serpent. The prize of a lifetime. He'd won it in an arm wrestling match with an ex-cop in Sydney. I wasn't there but he'd written to me about it, said he was sending me the box and I shouldn't open it, not for a long time. He had decided never to return, was renouncing our train wreck of a lineage and living off his wits. He was happy, he said. It made me mad all over again.

I take another sip of arak and it goes down easier, helping me place myself in time, when I'd first read the note and stuffed it inside my wallet. I never carried much, a credit card, a few bills, not even a license . . . I barely drove and shunned membership in anything, had no loyalty to stores or coffee shops, liked moving around. This was before I stopped drinking, one of the earlier times, but after I'd quit skating. There were girls and Frisbees and red-and-blue plaid suits. A shaved head like I've got now. The idea that I'd learn to make documentaries. I'd almost gone to him when he wrote from Australia, just as I'd flown to this stupid little country when he asked, giving up that final season in the rink, my comeback, to save him from the Israeli army. *If you leave me, we're through*, said the coach I adored, with the cocaine problem in check and imperialist notions about what it took to be a winner. Marc and I traversed this land together. Both tall, with long brown hair flopping against our shoulders. Big bones. Hard to tell who was older, which the favorite. People thought we were lovers.

He wanted me with him as he slipped farther across the universe. We could be good together, he wrote, do what families do for each other. There was enough money, time, some blown-out notion of youth. But our weeks together in the holy land filled the spaces between pen marks. There was no us after that. I never told anyone what we did, what I saw, and I destroyed so much of it. Only this note stalks the world with me, because it didn't arrive in a blue airmail envelope but rose from the ashes like an archeological relic.

If you're reading this it's all gone happily, he wrote, handwriting so neat it looked printed. *And don't start drawing narratives about how special I was, how misunderstood. I am not your poem. Or poet. I think poems are stupid mostly. But I like Bob Dylan.*

Remember this as you think of me somewhere far from your concrete shell, think of me laughing, probably at the wrong time, making someone want to rip out my eyeballs.

There's nothing I need anymore. You can have it all. My little world. My shitty little life. Just know that I once loved you. Know that I am free.

I am lying dead across the stoop outside when Gila pulls up. She's fast, almost jumping out of the car like on a cop show. "What happened?" she asks, a shadow towering over me.

Something about her seriousness renders me silly. Like if we're fucked, why not just give in? I can't help giggling.

She taps my shoulder, asks what's wrong, why am I outside, and I can only smile. I am locked out. I heard a noise and went to see. The door stuck behind me so I sat down on the chilly concrete in my bathrobe, then lay a bed among the few fallen pine needles. It's logical though I can't speak any of it, besieged by old lovers and shifting dynamics, how Gila's a kid really, younger than I am and acting all superior. I twist up my back and sit cross-legged, making a visor with my palm to block the sun. She asks if I'm drunk. Somber, disapproving, huge.

"You know I'm an addict," I say.

"Stop making excuses."

"You sound like him."

She steps around me and opens the door, says get up. Somehow I do, with a sharp understanding that this feeling of trouble, of being in trouble, is what I deserve.

Inside it's hot. The walls cave on me, boiling white slime running down the sides. I fall backward into the couch, dizzy. Gila hands me an icy bottle of water, which I hold against my forehead, and it burns. She says do not move, says drink the whole bottle of water, she will be back. She pulls the baby Glock from behind her back to her front pocket and, keeping her hand on it, walks out the front door. I sit in silence, trying to follow directions, but the water hurts going down. I shut my eyes.

The walls split into shadows. Black-and-white movie clip of horse and jockey, what you get in film school, projecting into the unfolding distance, white screens as far as the eye can see. The horse goes faster and faster, body on top bumping up and down.

There's a catch.

I'd know those legs anywhere, I say out loud as if whispering to the person sitting next to me in the theater. Watch how they spill over the sides of the dark-brown horse. Purebred. Both of them. She is tall for a jockey, like me, an amalgam of every pigheaded cliché about rich women gone under. I know her well. She lives with a philosopher who trades on his fame from a book about the old Greeks that has become a staple on the college circuit. He stands off to the side reciting a lecture on Plato's cave, an African American man from Montgomery who marched with

Dr. King but kept peeling back further for answers. He is so handsome. She loves him as much as she loves her horses. And splattering paint across large canvases. Once she'd had a different life. Adorned in Chanel frocks at twenty-two, ash-blond hair shimmering across her shoulders. In one picture she wears a garland of fresh daisies, everything supersaturated, solipsistic mystery bursting in Polaroid.

I try to catch the horse, pounding through metallic hallways, strobe lights blaring full circle around me, my stepfather channeling ancient thinkers in bass clef. Coming through the light, the set is green grass and soft rolling hills, fog lifting. I stand in her living room with the floor-to-ceiling view of the mountains. She comes down off her horse and squints at the window, surprised to see me. She ties the horse to a wooden pole, then quickly kisses his nose. Removing her helmet, she releases the shock of gray hair that still strolls gorgeously down her back.

You're here, she says, once inside, offering me a glass of iced tea, Diet Coke, orange juice. Asks if I'm staying the night.

I have to go, I say, realizing it's been years since we've seen each other, astonishing given the proximity. I never think just go, not in my daily life, not without a reason. She is light-years away from me. Always has been.

She hands me a glass of fresh-squeezed pink grapefruit juice. This is what you ordered, she says. Then: I'm so glad you made it. Your brother never did.

I wake with a start, my ears filled up in stereo, everything's bloated, and I smell coffee. Gila walks to the couch carrying a white mug. She's made Nescafé on the hot plate. It's terrible. But the caring excites me, this falling into us. She is soft now, maternal, and in her I see legacy, devotion. I want to be good to her.

The hot liquid clears my sinuses, swiping back and forth like windshield wipers behind my eyes until I am here with her—not the phantom goddess I've chased halfway around the world, but a woman with intentions, good. Though I remain skeptical as she talks, lightly, of nothing in particular. She tells me growing up her family had parrots. They took vacations to Latin America to look at colorful birds, after the big wars. She loved to travel. Her father owned a small airplane, how she learned to fly. There were brothers, older. She does not say more about them. I do not talk about mine either.

We are silent for some time, holding each other. Then she pushes back. Says we are leaving tomorrow, returning to Tel Aviv. It is too risky being here now, though she did not find anything outside and the people watching over us say we're clear. She believes I saw something, though, agrees people are following me and we must stay ahead of them. And this level of trust is what I need more than anything.

"What about my father?" I ask.

She shakes her head, looks at me again, those eyes saying yes, I want to believe this part too, but . . . I find myself wondering again about the connection between alcohol and hallucinations, in all the years I don't think I've read much about it. I like things to make sense.

Gila breathes deeply, eyes focusing in. She takes my hands in hers. "I saw him die," she says. "It was one of the worst things of my life. You must believe me."

She's agitated, something new, a tick beneath her lower left eye, a line of skin cracking just slightly next to her lips, shaking. If you didn't know her you might not get it. She removes her hands from mine, shuts her eyes.

"What is it?" I say.

She shakes her head.

"Tell me."

"You were right. It was my fault."

"I didn't mean what I said. I was frustrated with you."

"But it is the truth."

"Come on, he had a massive heart attack. More than one maybe."

"They said he was recovering. He was breathing in tubes the morning I went to him. He opened his eyes and asked where I had been and I could not lie. I told him with you."

She looks down. I prod.

"It was like you see on TV," she says. "His eyes rolled and his body shakes. Like an epileptic. Then all the men come running inside. *Get out! Get out!* All the nasty names, like I am a child. *Get the fuck out!*"

She is screaming. I settle her shoulder with one hand, lift her chin with the other, trying to think of the right words, but nothing comes, so I reach farther around her waist and pull her into me. There may be tears, but maybe not, I can't tell and it's really not my thing, comfort, so I don't look and hope they'll go away, holding on tight, and the harder I cling the more antsy I feel. Gila breathes into me, whispering, "I'm sorry, *motek*, I am so sorry." Repenting, I think, and is that what she's up to? *If I killed the father, maybe I can save the daughter.* I take it in . . . or try to. Though I'd be lying if I said I wasn't thinking of escape routes and what happens if I believe her. What that does to him.

After a while we break, her eyes shot up in red but dry, hair a mess. This is new. She smiles, sort of, says let's go for a drive, there is a nature preserve not far from here with a sports complex. It has an Olympic skating rink, what she's wanted to show me but seems weird given the circumstances.

"Is it safe?"

"We have cover and a different car."

"Okay, but there's one more thing," I say, then tell her what's been bothering me. About my license.

She seems genuinely alarmed. "You carry a license?"

"It's fake."

"You should have told me."

"I just realized it."

"But did you bring it here with you? Do you know?"

"I don't remember."

"You have to be more careful," she mumbles, then louder: "You have to pay attention. These are dangerous people we are dealing with. Mistakes can kill us."

Fingers on a light switch is all I see, how we go from the extremities of caring to condemnation in seconds. Is this love?

I will be better, I promise, and like every time I promised Tree I'll be better, I'll be a winner, a knife ticks at my heart. Gila says things too, a refrain of dos and don'ts, words evaporating as soon as they touch ground, a defense mechanism, I'm sure, but it's hard to stick with someone when they start telling you how things are supposed to be. Then she says something that brings me back, something so shocking the life bleeds out of me and I feel light-headed: "I wish you were not here."

I feel the walls dripping down and hot all over.

"No," she says, "I don't mean it like that. You are my destiny," she says, somehow making it not sound ridiculous. Not that she believes in mystical stars and forces, but ever since she picked me up at Ben Gurion last summer, old baseball hat (Yankees) turned backward on my head, upper lip slightly curved like his, the same broad shoulders but stronger, she knew I would be her undoing. Normally she is a realist but she could not stop thinking about me the months we were apart and knew we would come together again, despite her original warnings for me to stay far away. She chose this the moment she saw me, she says, and the three stupid words I'd been keeping for myself well up . . .

"I hate you," I tell her.

She touches my thigh. "I hate you too, love."

And we sit for a while in silence.

Before standing, Gila Zyskun does something surprising—she quotes Elie Wiesel: "*The opposite of love is not hate; it's indifference.*"

PART FOUR

LONG BEFORE THE WAR, THERE WAS LOVE

Tel Aviv, July 1989

We are together again. My brother and me, in the devil's backyard, just like when we were kids. Though this time he's summoned me from the tip of the coldest point in Argentina to the city of secret forts and beaches, where it's a hundred degrees and so humid I can't catch my breath. He's decided we should travel together. "I mean, we're here, right?" He smiles, like it's inevitable we've come to this point together.

We sit in an outdoor café near the airport sipping bowls of milky coffee. Around us courtly men with long gray-black beards suck *shisha* tobacco out of gurgling octopus pipes and read papers in Arabic. I have just stepped off the plane, twenty-two hours and two flights taking me from dead of winter to summertime blues, and then the insanity of security . . . *Do you have relatives in Israel? What were you doing at the edge of the earth? Why did you buy your ticket so late? Who paid for it?*

I want to crawl into a hole and not emerge for days. When can I sleep, I ask Marc, and he says this isn't about you, I am in trouble, remember, the guys in my unit might come after me, you don't just walk out of the Israeli army, and ditching a gun can get you jail time, did you bring cash?

He will not take the bus, he says. There is heightened fear since the crash last week. They're calling it a suicide attack, Marc explains snidely, even though the guy lived, poor fucker. About halfway from Tel Aviv to Jerusalem, he grabbed the wheel and steered a speeding bus into a ravine, and yes, he was Palestinian. From a refugee camp in Gaza. He killed a couple dozen people, including one American, maybe a Canadian too. And that is why it's a suicide machine, because the aim is to take out as many people as you can, then go down in a blaze of history. "But homeboy fucked that up," Marc says, "and now I'm afraid of the bus." All of this makes my four-a.m.-where-I'm-coming-from head throb.

Marc needs a haircut. Matted clumps jut out from his scalp, merging into sideburns, light porcupine quills on his chin. He looks like a cactus. Seven weeks earlier he'd been perfectly shorn and bedding down with his M16. Soldiers carry them everywhere, responsible for their presence at the most heinous of moments. Never be caught without your gun, he was told. Treat it like your mother, your lover, your pet rock. He couldn't relate to attachment. My mother, his, had betrayed him years ago. And while he'd been devastated when she'd left, I had not. I spent the first evening without her sharpening the blades on every pair of skates I owned, inexplicably happy. It wasn't even like we saw much of her when she lived there, but he was more delicate than I. The one they worried about.

Looking at him jitter on across the table, I want to return to Tree in Ushuaia. I miss the glaciers, sheets of ice that shine like skyscrapers at sunrise. I miss the way her hands move through the air as she beats me to the finish, even though she won't touch me anymore. Not the way I want.

She'd dropped me at the bus station and stood blowing steam between her hands in the still-dark morning. I wouldn't let her take me to the airport. It was too long a drive through curvy hills that turned her stomach. She stood blowing steam into her hands and said I wouldn't return. Your brother is a fox, she said.

Marc tells me I'll like the north. On a clear day you can see three countries. And from above, the land looks like a never-ending green camel. More docile than a fox, the camel, unless you needle it enough to spit in your face. There may even be some snow left over for me. "It will be rad," he says. "You'll see."

We catch a ride with a couple of middle-aged German Jews whose families had come in with the first wave of immigrants before the war. They were born on the same kibbutz and fell in love as teenagers. "But you're like brother and sister," Marc says.

"Not at all," says the woman. She's got blond helmet hair, big brown eyes. "We have more than one thousand people on our land now. And the children have gone all over. We even had one run away to join the circus."

She smiles at her husband.

"Okay, cousins."

We park at youth hostels, sometimes splitting into gendered rooms with bunk beds, other times co-ed, but never without other people. We cross two-lane highways in tiny cars owned by lawyers, computer programmers, or rented by couples on holiday.

Marc makes friends easily. He sells acid to American college kids and buys pitchers of beer for anyone who smiles, asks why we're here, how long we've been on the road. His story changes every time. We don't stay anywhere too long and make up funny names for ourselves. I run ten miles every morning as the sun comes up, tracking down places to lift weights whenever I can, determined not to let time slip through my fingers. I will return to Ushuaia in several days even stronger. I will not smoke hash before seven and will keep it light.

We play fight about inane things, like when we were kids, just to see who's got more interesting things to say. One night after a quick smoke we argue about the most amazing things we've seen.

"The inside of a whale's mouth," Marc says. We are eating dinner at an outdoor café in Haifa. Tomorrow we will make our way in and up toward the border. We are planning to hike Mount Hermon. It's not too high, Marc had said, when you think about mountains in the Americas, Europe. We can handle it no problem. But I'll miss my run. And I don't get it, I asked, isn't the army after you? How's there time for a hike? That's the whole point, he said, I think. I am too stoned. Fading sun cuddles between us, bright orange sky peeking behind the green-green trees. The north is so colorful, lush in a way you don't see in storybooks. I keep resisting the urge to drop my head on the table and sleep.

"Are you listening to me!" Marc says, his voice harsh, mechanical. Sometimes when you smoke everything outside your head echoes.

"Yes," I reply. "A whale, you said. Male or female?"

"I believe it was a girl. You don't remember any of this?"

"Sorry." I shake my head, dropping my chin between my fists and staring straight at him. This is the first night we're eating alone. We are both good at attracting people and they tend to glom. He's more gorgeous than ever. I say this too much, but I'm blindsided sometimes that someone like him gets to exist in the world, just walk around like it's no problem. Even with his porcupine cut, dirt smacked across his forehead, and the same faded black Clash T-shirt he's been wearing for two days—we're doing laundry back at the hostel since we're barely carrying anything—he nurses a halo, an aura that makes you want to be near him as much as you know somewhere in the back of your head you should keep track of your wallet and car keys.

"Those stories about whales," he says. "All of my life I was reading how big they are, how smart they are, how gentle really. And then you see one up close . . . I wanted to crawl inside and make it my home."

"That's the fucking Bible."

"No, seriously. I can't believe you don't remember. It was at Sea World."

"Sea World?"

"Man, where were you when we were kids?"

"I don't know. The rink."

"This was before. When we were really little."

"Yeah, I don't remember much of that."

"You're such a bitch." He smiles but there's an undercurrent. A spider with drab white specks like the letters on his T-shirt crawls up from the bottom of the table. It's missing a leg. We watch it drag its torso forward and then back down the other side of the table, the colors above us bursting red, gold, purple magic. Marc says he loves spiders. Says this spider without a leg might be three years old, they can survive unsurvivable conditions. "When we wipe ourselves off the planet, it will return to the spiders," he says.

"Spiders from Mars, yes!"

"Did I tell you how I ditched my gun?"

And though he's told me a few times already, I say I can't remember. He says he tossed it into a truck full of lemons, not a rivulet. Each time the story changes slightly. Stories always do. The important thing is they got their gun back.

The next morning we meet up at five a.m. by the reception area of the hostel. Why we're staying at hostels when we've got piles of cash and traveler's checks in large denominations makes no sense. But Marc says we need to walk among the people. Like Jesus.

He looks like a teenager plucked from a line about to head into the gym. Red athletic shorts with white trim along the side, tight white T-shirt, almost translucent, you can see his nipples. Timberlands with thick white socks. His green regulation army cap has a big white heart painted above the rim, giving him a Sgt. Pepper-make-love-not-war look. Most of the time people with long hair should not wear hats. But, of course, it works for him.

The man who runs the hostel is whispering loudly to us in Hebrew words I can't follow. I walk to the window, where it's all blue shadows outside. Summer dark. The convergence of moon and sun that lets you see the outline of car tops on the street, sunken doorways, even though we're packed back into an alley with no streetlights. I hear a few English words: if we'd started hiking now we could have been at the top for sunrise. We didn't think of that. Apparently there is a day hike up Mount Herman. We can be back here in Haifa later in the evening. This is what Marc is negotiating, how to get in if we return after they've locked the front door. I hear him jostling back and forth between broken Hebrew and English words . . . *Listen, I did not travel thousands of miles to ride a friggin' chairlift! Show me the trails, dude.*

He smiles at me, then turns back to the man whose face is soft, cheeks puffed like dough bubbles and sagging slightly. "Do you know who she is?" Marc says.

I sigh, roll my head back, thinking this is what it's like to be a prop, a curiosity. Though he's not supposed to leave tracks, he seems to be explaining the winter Olympics, way earlier than Calgary.

When we were kids, like Marc talked about last night, the thing that sticks most is Saturday afternoons watching *Wide World of Sports* in the den with its overstuffed couches, plush rugs, the uncracked art books surrounding a giant TV screen. A button on the wall set off an electronic hum that rolled thick shades down over the windows. When we screened movies, we could make it dark, like a theater. Sofia would pop popcorn in olive oil, dump it into the biggest bowl she could find, and sprinkle the top with oregano and Romano cheese. We devoured it as she lined up the remotes in size order to find the ones that tripped the TV and sound before it started: four thirty in the afternoon. Every Saturday. The clapping horns and cymbals, orchestral bravado. Marc and I throwing pieces of popcorn at each other, faking microphones, and reciting: "*The thrill of victory, the agony of defeat.*" I can't remember the next line, because that's where it stuck for us, every week wincing at the skier who goes tumbling off the ramp, skis above his head, flipping forward and around and somehow landing on his feet, so you know it's a minor-key tragedy—he doesn't die, or worse, end up paralyzed, but it hurts so fucking bad in so many ways. Every time, Marc and I turning to each other like, holy fucking shit!

He comes up next to me at the window, his check-your-pockets grin firing as he tells me the cab will be here in a few minutes to take us to the foot of Mount Hermon. They are leaving the side door open for us in case we're not back by ten. He hands me an empty nylon backpack that the owner gave him for me to carry.

"Oh, and turns out we don't have to pay," he says, slinging the regulation pack he also kept from the army over his shoulder. "He remembered your crash."

"After you reminded him."

Marc shrugs.

I want to kick him in the balls. Hard.

We set out with the sun low in the sky, walking through a vast open landscape of chalky mud, rocks, green bushes popping up like hives on yellowed skin, a large metallic building complex in the distance behind us. Army, Marc says. People shout from the chairlift above us in Hebrew. *You can't walk there! Watch out for the mines, stupid!* According to the map, Marc says, the trail breaks away from the lift in a few kilometers and takes us into the trees. I ask to see it and he objects. But I push. He hands it to me, sheepish as ever, it's not a tourist map but a hand-scratched view of the area and trailheads.

"Hey," I pull him back by the elbow, "are you fucking kidding me?"

"Trust me. I was down the road for training."

"Down the road?"

"It's okay, they don't come past the chairlift much. Nobody does. I'm telling you, that's why there are no maps, and when you get to the top you can see Lebanon and the most beautiful abandoned village in Syria. It's the perfect day for it. You'll see."

Mirrored sunglasses reflecting the orange rays in the distance, lips giving just slightly, he's too confident to question. And, really, what am I going to say? *No, let's turn around.* I fall in behind him, and true to the drawing, we come to a T etched into a tree that takes us up a craggy path, just barely cut for walking.

Marc maintains a strong pace in front of me, the sun every so often cracking branches against his shoulder blades, woodland shadows on his T-shirt. I follow the shapes as we climb along the rocks into heavier shrubs that look like floppy green missiles, the way pine trees grow up along the Mediterranean. I can tell how difficult the next few steps will be from his legs, how much like baseballs those muscles beneath the back of his knees become. I steel myself to keep up. I can climb a silly mountain in the middle of camel-land . . . *Do you know who I am?*

Strobe-y pink light between the trees, Marc a tall shadow. He steps up and grabs a giant rock with his right hand. "Stick with me," he says, tipping his head back slightly, then scrambling up. I follow, hurling myself toward the sun like a balloon cut from its string. A few steps and I'm higher, breath catching the back of my throat, as I increase the lift and pace . . . pull, step, breathe . . . pull, step, breathe . . . When we were kids, Marc once asked for a balloon sculptor to come to the house and make architectural structures. The balloonist had snug jeans like ballet tights and a mustache that curled. He said he was better at blowing animals. Marc sighed, "If you can't make a bridge, a building, and a hot dog stand, then you should just leave."

He would try, he said, and pulled a long red balloon from the bag, stretching it out in front of him, then filling it with enough air to curve slightly, repeating with a few more red ones till I saw what he was doing. Making posts. He rolled out a few longer blue balloons and filled them up, wrapping them in and out of the red posts. The water! He was making a bridge. A few more red balloons stretched across the top and it started looking like a giant tiara. He should have quit while he was ahead. Marc sneered at me. I stuck out my tongue.

"Go home," he said.

"But I can do a building. Let's try the building next."

"Out!"

The balloon maker dropped the bridge on the couch and backed his tight ass out of the room.

"You're such a jerk," I said.

"I hate balloons that look like that. I like helium. I like missiles. Where did he come from?"

"Daddy's office."

"He has to go back."

Now Marc's legs tense again, his ankle curving slightly

inward, as he hauls himself up a steep ledge, dust shaking off behind him. I watch a few pebbles roll down next to me, picking up speed so fast I realize we are high and unstable and likely not on a trail. Time seizes up. I hear the pounding inside my head, hot all over. My right foot slips slightly and I wish I had hiking boots. I'd been crabby about wearing my leather high-tops, not running shoes. *If they're good enough for Michael Jordan* . . . Maybe I can't do this. I cannot turn a balloon into a bridge. The agony of defeat hits in a split second and you never see it coming. I call out: "Marc! Stop!"

But he's completely over the ledge already, invisible. His fingers appear above my forehead. "Hold my hand," he says, "then lean back and walk. I've got you."

I do as he says, walking a couple of steps up. If he releases, I'm gone, and that's the worst part—dependence. I grab the tip of the ledge with my left hand, clinging to his with my right, and push while he pulls. In seconds I am over the ledge. I fall back on the ground and let out a huge sigh. Marc smiles. "We're almost there," he says. "You're doing okay."

Looking up I see the outlines of peaks through the trees. We have come to a slight clearing, more thick oak trees on the incline ahead, no sign of a path. I lift myself up and walk a few feet from the ledge. There's a slight dip down in the other direction, lines of messy barbed wire. A green sign with white lettering in three languages: *STOP! BORDER! DANGER OF DEATH!*

"Don't worry," Marc comes up behind me, "we're not going that way . . . unless you want to get even higher."

"This is good. Thanks."

"Where's your spirit of adventure? You used to be so brave. I was terrified of you."

"And now?"

"Wait . . . shssssh."

We both hear it: footsteps and faint voices rattling above us. Sounds are deceptive in the woods, it's impossible to judge proximity from volume. Marc puts a hand out in front of me, reaching into his pocket with the other for his knife, a wooden switchblade that flips open into something like a compact machete. "Get down," he whispers. I do as I'm told, crouching so I can't see over the edge, yet the barbed wire has burned its way into my soul. This is how Americans get kidnapped. I want to go home.

Voices growing louder, I steel into the balls of my feet, thinking I can make out a few words in Hebrew, which comforts me slightly, though that's probably racist, and Marc says the army can be ruthless with deserters. I'm aiding and abetting. My thighs tense up. The voices sound singsongy, flippant. Through the shifting rays, two figures appear, nebulous at first, then materializing into robots, their giant square shoulders approaching jauntily. Identical in height and build, the two guys have the same moppy brown hair, tan skin, high cheekbones, the look you see throughout this country. Classic Israeli. They wear leather hiking boots with bright red laces, backpacks framed like metal braces, holding them upright and dragging tents, foam pads, pots, and spoons. I don't understand hiking, how you can move with all that crap weighing you down? And for what? To sleep in the woods? The hikers eye us skeptically, saying a few words in Hebrew to Marc, who tells them we are Americans. On holiday.

Their faces brighten. "We love Americans!" one says, and I can see his eyes are deep green like the pines, skin flaking around the corners of his nose, as if he's been blowing too hard.

"Have you hiked the Appalachian Trail?" says the other, voice much deeper, gravelly like a weekend radio announcer.

Marc smiles. "She's the athlete."

"We're from New York City," I say. "We climb buildings."

"Oh," says the gravelly one. "We are looking for people to join us. To make the trail."

"Make it?" I say. "Like it doesn't exist?"

"Don't be ridiculous," says the nose blower. "You are standing on a trail, are you not?"

"We are markers," says the other. Up close I can see his skin is darker than the nose blower's, and he's cuter, deep brown eyes, nose chiseled perfectly beneath them. "I am Bibi. He's Didi. We are from the Society for the Protection of Nature."

"Is that government?" Marc asks, aggression rising, like he's weighing whether they're good guys or bad guys. The usual.

No, no, of course not, they assure us, they are a private society of people who love the woods. They are conducting a project to connect a series of trails from north to south, to carve out a national trail. They have been working for years, their goal for it to someday become one of great hikes of the world. They have never been to America, never hiked the Appalachian Trail, but the stories are legendary among the group.

"We are more like your West Coast trail. We will move from desert to high mountains. North to south. Cutting through this whole country," Bibi says.

"And the day will come when we are even higher," Didi adds.

"This is high enough," Bibi says. "How high do you need?"

"It is thousands of feet higher in America."

"Count your blessings, my friend. We are carving a trail through this land. We are creating a place. Making a new history for ourselves."

"If we could get over there, past the border, it could be the greatest trail in the world."

"You go walking through the mines and the Arabs. You will never make it one day, with your allergies, your special foods."

"To expand is not the worst thing. Ask the Americans. They know."

"We are not even connected here and you've already got your eyes over there."

"We must protect ourselves. For future generations. We need land and walking sticks and weapons."

"Hey, I've got an idea," Marc says, jumping up between them. "Why don't we have a picnic? We've got plenty of food, yes?" He turns to me. After the cab dropped us off, we'd filled my tiny nylon pack with a couple of hunks of hard goat cheese, crackers, nuts, dried apricots and peaches, olives, protein bars, some water. Plenty, I don't know, but Marc seems gung ho. Bibi and Didi agree this is fine idea. They say there is a waterfall close by, not the one the tourists find from the chairlift. Few outside of the Society know about it. We can be there in ten minutes.

Okay, we say. Let's go.

We follow Bibi and Didi through the leafy trees for what has to be more than ten minutes. It occurs to me that I am not wearing a watch and have no idea of the time other than it feels like somewhere between eleven and three. My mother never wears a watch and claims she can feel time down to the minute. We used to test her and she always got it right, give or take a few. My life has been scalded by stopwatches, broken down into fractions of seconds, and one one-hundredth matters when you're pushing off at the start and need to jump a lead, even in short track, though I hate it, I really do. Long track is pure strength. You can train for endurance; speed is a lark, it's mind games. But it's the future of the sport, Tree says, high on the chip she's shouldering since Calgary.

"Hurry up, Americans!" Didi calls back to us. He and Bibi are several yards away, bushwhacking into what feels like a clearing, though I can't find the sky. Marc and I walk close together, occasionally brushing shoulders. As we approach I hear a loud rumbling that feels urban, like the factories pumping out electricity along the East River. It is the purest noise I've heard in days. We emerge into wet, gray rocks, water crashing down in pools and bubbling up into steamy little rainbows.

"Fantastic!" Marc yells. He rips off his shirt and quickly unties his boots. I sit down on a rock behind him, watching him ease out of his shorts and underwear. His ass is slightly whiter than his back and thighs. I look down at the ground between my knees and listen to the world tremble.

Looking up, I see Bibi coming toward us, saying something I cannot hear over the crashing water. He shakes off his pack next to Marc and undresses. His legs and back are covered in neat black hairs like a knit wet suit, providing a shield against the world that Marc simply does not have. They dive in simultaneously and come up shouting, though I can't hear anything above the water. I could scream and scream and scream and nobody would come, like New York in the seventies.

Didi shuffles toward me and shouts. I still can't hear a word, but his mouth opens and shuts widely. He motions for me to get up and we walk a few steps back into an enclosure, two huge pieces of slate pitched like a tent, the refuse of old fires, kindle, thick logs half-buried in the dirt to make seats. We sit for a few seconds, enough time for my thoughts to return.

"That water is literally freezing," Didi says. "Below zero. They are going to be sorry."

"You never go in?"

"No. It gives me a headache. But feel free."

I smile. "Not my thing. Though I love the cold. I just like to wear pants."

"Do you dive?"

"No."

"You don't dive. You don't hike. What do you do?"

"Not much."

"Your boyfriend is in charge."

"He's my brother."

"Ah, that explains."

We both nod as if we've solved a mystery. He tells me he had a brother who died two years earlier. A rare form of stomach cancer that only hits young men in their twenties. I thought he was going to say the army. The war. We forget, Didi says, that most of the time we are all just trying to live our lives. This is why we hike: to get at the essence of what it means to be alive. Why are you here? he asks again, and I say it's similar.

"Ah," he says. "You must go far from who you are to know yourself."

"Something like that."

He smiles, again as if we're colluding on a secret project. "Listen, you must take this land seriously."

"What?"

"These hills. The country. Surely, it's not like what you hear on the TV, danger everywhere. People are people. But don't be stupid."

"What do you mean?" I am suddenly paranoid they *are* army, that they're after Marc.

But no, he's talking about mountains. He tells me he and Bibi have spent months traversing from north to south, south to north, following the seasons so it's never too hot. "We have met many people along these trails. People from other countries. Word has gotten out about what we are doing and they want to help. But they come with packs, tents, prepared to stay. I've never met anyone this far up for a day hike. This is why there is the chairlift."

"We don't do lifts in our family."

"I cannot tell if you are joking or simply very sad."

"What's the difference?"

"So you are Jewish."

I look up from where I've been carving circles in the dirt.

"Now I have the picture," he says. "But please listen . . ." He tells me we must break off big sticks to walk with. If the ground is covered with leaves, twigs, anything, always put the stick down first. There are mines on both sides of the border. The people on the chairlift were serious. Hikers have been badly wounded. The longer he speaks the greater my urge to tear off my clothes and jump into the water where Marc and Bibi are still diving in and out of freezing rainbows. But stay with this, I tell myself, it's important.

Didi says there are streams with fresh water so we'll be fine, just watch where it's coming from. If it runs from the right, think twice because it's from the other side and could be poisoned. But do keep the sun to your right. And if it gets too low, please park for the night, no matter where you are. This is no place to wander in the dark, he says, eyes like my father's when he's trying to emphasize just how fucked up every other person in the world is. "This is the most beautiful place on earth," he says, "but it can get ugly so very quickly."

We stare at each other again, then look away, the water proclaiming its astounding victory around us. I see white bubbles, the quick flash of human skin, then glide back to Didi's eyes. It's like we understand each other. And this is what I love most about travel: how someone you've just met can be your best friend, if only for a fraction of a second.

* * *

"Holy fucking mountaintop!" Marc shouts into a muted, sinking sun. Clouds hover around it, like they were borrowed from yesterday. We could be anywhere with that sky. But we are not.

We have made it to the top before dusk, sweaty, huffing, alive. Bibi and Didi hiked with us for a bit up the peak, Didi breaking off branches big enough to use as walking sticks and demonstrating how to test for mines. Marc was holding his tongue, I could tell, he hated being told how to do anything, and, you know, he'd just escaped singlehandedly from the most clever army in the world . . . but he was polite. The swim must have mellowed him. Bibi and Didi were heading in the other direction, to a kibbutz at the start of the trailhead where they would attend a Society meeting and spend the night. They invited us along, said we could get an earlier start tomorrow. "But we're here now," Marc said, and they shrugged. "Just move quickly," Bibi said. Didi nodded, then raised a finger in front of us. He reached into his bag and dug out two books of wooden matches, water purification pills, a fold-up emergency blanket, just in case. He handed everything to me, staring, like, *Remember what I said.* Only I'd already forgotten most of it.

It's as if there's no life at all before this moment, Marc and me standing next to each other, looking out across the endless peaks and clouds. We cannot see Syria. Or Lebanon. It's way too foggy, but every so often a haze of green bumps pokes through, fading white ski trails. Marc says be patient. We are here. The clouds will move.

"We don't have all day," I say.

"We have all the time in the world."

I look at him and it's as clear as the sky in front of us is not: we are not going back down tonight. "You stupid little shit! We don't have a tent. We don't even have sleeping bags . . ."

"It's okay. I'll make a fire."

"Great. We can sing camp songs."

"Why are you so mad? We're on a beautiful mountain-top. In summer. People would kill to be here."

"We're in a fucking security zone."

"Oh, that's what you're scared of."

"I am not scared."

"Nobody's ever been bombed on this mountain. It's totally safe."

"That's a lie. Didi said there are bombs all over."

"He's a fucking killjoy. Trust me, we are safer up here than in the city, it's crawling with soldiers down there."

I shake my head to tip the bullshit out of my ears. I want a bed, the thin foam mattress on my top bunk in Haifa, with seven other girls around me snoring like cats. Or better, my thick cotton sheets and bedsprings at the end of the world, Tree peeking her head inside to see if I'm sleeping, though not coming close like she used to. She's less fun without drugs. All business. We need to start winning, she says over and over like a benediction, not just second or third, but first, ahead of everyone else or what's the point? I need to want it more than anything.

And here's Marc staring at me like I'm the one who's out of my mind.

"Why am I even here?"

"I told you it's safe . . ."

"No. In this goddamn country."

"You had no choice, you owe me," Marc says, an edge to his voice like when we were kids and testing each other. "Just calm down, okay? This is so beautiful. We are going to have fun. Let me find some wood and then we can relax."

He stalks off, green pack attached tightly to his shoulders, practically bouncing off the balls of his feet as if he'd spring from the mountain with one false move. There will be netting to catch him down below, of course, like the end of a ski jump. It strikes me how serious he is about fun. Different from the trickery he pulls on most people we meet—to have fun, to relax, means getting so far out of what other people might call normal. Who keeps a hefty bag full of mushrooms in an apartment? Everyone knew, apparently. The students, the administration, the local drug dealers. Last winter a dealer followed him home and put a gun to his cheek. "You gotta stop selling," he said. "You're too cheap. You're bringing the market down."

Marc tried to bribe him, unsuccessfully, and so the dealers were watching him, like the army is now, I guess. Marc told me he stopped selling and created a barter system, collecting antique coins, mountain bikes, vintage baseball cards, bottles of French brandy, all of it left behind in a flurry of deals with law enforcement. My father could get anyone out of anything.

He returns, arms hugging thick branches, two large plastic bottles filled with water dangling from his pack. Behind him clouds melt purple. A raptor flies overhead, squawking loudly, and I feel the magnitude of this peak, the highest point in the land. I stand up and stretch my arms high above my head, catch the faint flickering of lights through dusk in a faraway village, maybe Lebanon. Marc leans thick branches up against one another and shoves a few twigs and pieces of notebook paper inside as kindling. He lights one match and papers ignite from the bottom up, slowly catching the twigs, then branches, the smell unmistakably smoky, like the base of every winter sports complex in the world. He's proud of using only one match.

"I've always wanted to be a Boy Scout, mostly so I could wear the yellow scarf," I say.

He smiles at me, brow half-cocked, his way of saying, *What you said is too dumb for me to address, really*, then concentrates on the fire. It's his solidity that gets me, his certainty that his way is the only way. I've been accused of that too, but I'm nothing next to him. He nurtures the branches as they turn to coals, making sure we've got enough wood to cover us through the night. I hold my knees together tightly so I can feel my body and whisper to myself . . . it's okay, I'm here, I don't need him, I don't need Tree, I don't need fans, I don't need anyone . . .

I stand and spread out the emergency blanket orange side up. Marc shuffles back from the fire and sits down in front of me. He dumps out the contents of his pack on the blanket, saying, "Show and tell." In front of us: two notebooks, one leather-bound, one spiral with a tattered blue cover, a small address book, his Keith Haring wallet, *Narcissus and Goldmund*, another pocket knife, a flare, some glowing greenish rope, a smooth wooden pipe with his initials etched into the side, extra screens, three packs of Israeli cigarettes called Time, hash wrapped in tinfoil, two amber pill vials, a sheet of acid with tiny images of Charlie Brown repeated like toy stamps, and a piece of silky white fabric with hints of familiar blue that rolls out into an Israeli flag, looking like it's seen better days. "I found it over the border, took it back," he says with a smile.

I spill out the remaining provisions from my pack. It's slim after our picnic, basically a couple of power bars and some dried fruit. We shuffle around the goods. Marc moves the drugs into one corner.

"I can't believe you brought all of that on a hike."

"What would you suggest? Leave it at the hostel? Besides, I like to have choices. Like now. What do you want more than anything?"

"A burger. A big fat one. Dripping pink inside."

He throws a power bar at me. "Make believe."

I open the package and take a bite. Nuts are so good

sometimes. In the open air particularly, way up high . . . this is proven food chemistry, why tomato juice tastes better on airplanes than in real life. If we were a different kind of people, Bibi-Didi kind of people, we'd have marshmallows to roast, graham crackers, and chocolate. We would have carried a fucking frying pan and caught a trout this afternoon.

Marc eats his power bar in three bites and takes a long sip of water. He sits down in front of me, crosses his legs, and revs up. "Let's do something together."

I watch him reach for a vial and crack the seal. He holds out a couple of white pills. Ecstasy, of course. I recoil, just slightly, but hesitation is never the loudest voice in the room. Marc sighs, fed up already, and in a few seconds I'm the balloonist with tight pants, doomed from the moment he enters the living room. "What's the problem now?"

"You are so fucking predictable."

"And you're so lame."

"Fuck you!"

"Oh, that hurts." He fake cowers.

"I'm in training, you asshole."

"So what?"

I turn my head slightly, take a deep smoky breath. "I promised Tree . . ."

"The cokehead."

"She's clean now."

"So you have to be Sandra Goldfarber."

"That's below the belt." Sandra's family had the house next to ours in Connecticut. She went to Exeter, then Harvard. Got A's. Had boyfriends with last names like Taft and Piedmont. Like us, they pretended they weren't Jews. But Sandra was a model upper-crust kid. She once told on me for smoking a joint before we took out our horses, and she always wore dresses. For as long as I can remember, she was thrown in our faces when adults talked about what we had the potential to be.

Marc smiles. "Okay, you're right. I'm sorry. And, actually, you'll love this. I know someone at Harvard who says he fucked her. Says she's missing a nipple."

"Are you serious?"

"Yes!"

"Why?"

"No idea. Just that one's not there. Like it's a plain old lump of skin."

We look at each other in the dim glow of the fire and laugh. So he pushes. Says he doesn't buy it about training, says what's the big deal? And I try to explain but the more I talk the more I know there's nothing I can say. As far back as I can remember, whenever he asks what's the big deal, he really means stop whining and do what I say. He gets this from my father, ours, but I would never say that out loud. Instead we retreat. He puts the pills back into the vial and shoves it into the waistband of his shorts, then stands and starts moving branches around in the fire, his cover. I stare at the popping orangeyellowred flames wondering what *is* the big deal. This time next week I will be back on protein shakes and lentils and spinach linguini, handfuls of vitamin B, everything lined up so I don't have to think about it. Nobody will ever know.

When he sits down again, I hold out my palm. He grins, victorious. Out comes the vial, the pill dropping like a diamond into my palm. He hands me a bottle of water and takes one for himself. "*L'chaim*," he says, and we swallow together, like praying. Then he nudges me up so he can pull the emergency blanket out from under us to make a lean-to. I can't believe he knows how to do this. He attaches one side of the tarp to a tree with the green rope, ties a knot which likely has a name, all knots do, and I'd know it if I were a Boy Scout, but if I were a Boy Scout I would not be messing with my serotonin this madly, among other things. An uneasiness creeps in. I feel it in my stomach. Whenever you take a drug, all the other times you took the same drug spill forward, what went right, what went wrong, how you swore you'd never do it again. It's like how travelers together can't help telling travel stories or why kissing someone new always brings you back to junior high school. Or maybe that's just me. And the fallout is a bitch. Last time my legs hurt so hard I couldn't walk for an entire morning and my head felt like it was being cauterized on a factory floor, bringing on a nausea so intense it makes me want to vomit right now, and if I can't run tomorrow I'm screwed . . . Maybe I should stick my finger down my throat. I take a long sip of water and breathe deeply through my nose. No big deal.

The air crawls through my ears, and I'm soothed by the quiet, nothing but the occasional cricket, birds settling into trees for the night, the click and burn of the flames. I am overwhelmed by the weight of it: *On the top of the world, looking down on creation* . . . literally, if you believe the Bible, anybody's version.

Marc gently stokes the fire, adding a couple of branches at a time from his big pile. We are quiet.

It's cozier than I imagined, the warm flames in front of us, the tarp recirculating hot air from behind. I am bottled up with love for the first person who thought of creating a lean-to and for the debased Boy Scout sitting next to me, his profile lit up in stereo like the cover of *Hot Rocks*. I want to hug him. I can almost feel him hugging me. We stay silent for a long time before he stirs, pushing his feet out in front of him and turning on his side so he's looking straight up at me.

"Truth or dare," he says.

"Truth."

"Who's the greatest love of your life?"

"That's a bad question."

"Why?"

"Because it's not specific enough. Do you mean love love? Animal love? Friend love? How much I love Madonna? Or sour cream?"

"Love love. The big one."

"Hasn't happened."

"Really? Not the coach?"

"I love her deeply, I really do. Sometimes I want to bury myself inside her and let her take care of me forever. But . . . I don't know. I'm scared of her too, like why does she need me so much?"

"Because you're her ticket to ride."

"I'm not talking like that. If I were her I wouldn't have come back. I mean I fucked up so badly, everything we wanted . . . I thought she hated me. But it's different now."

"You mean she's behaving herself?"

"No, not that. I haven't thought about this a lot, but she must really love me if she came back after I ruined everything. That's what love is, right? Being totally and completely there for someone. But it's confusing."

"This is the problem with romantic love. The idea that there is one person out there for you. I think you get maybe four or five people in your lifetime. Four or five of these real soul mates. And in all the bumping around we do, you're lucky if you even find one of them."

"That's sort of depressing," I say.

"It is what it is. And I don't buy it with you, you're on truth serum . . . Can we talk about Sofia?"

"You first."

"Are you daring me?" His cheeks tense up, a kick in his

eye like crackling-hot embers, something I don't want to mess with.

"Isn't that the game?"

"Nobody said dare." Still that freezing look like he could order the fire to roar up and eat me feet first if he desired . . . It's getting so warm the hair on my arms tingles.

"This is bordering on not fun," I say.

"Dares are only fun if you can humiliate someone. Are you trying to do that?"

"No. Are you?"

"No."

"You don't want to humiliate me? That is so sweet."

"I'm serious."

"What are we even talking about?"

"Love," he says, and the word pours over me.

"Did you love Sofia?"

He shakes his head. "I couldn't. She came back looking for you. I was just there when you weren't."

"I think maybe that's the way you tell it in your head."

He nods . . . maybe. I don't know what to say, am kind of through with words and starting to feel like I'm falling into a magic-fingers bed, peaking probably. I say the P word out loud and Marc says yes and we giggle like we've beaten back a decade, only we used to laugh snidely, with a corner on cruelty, and I can't believe we've never done this drug together before. I once read shrinks use it to open up couples who said they never knew they could feel so much, never knew they could love so much. As this comes to me thousands of feet above the sea, black clouds moving over my head, every so often revealing a slice of moon and a star or two, I think I must be psychic. I have always had premonitions. I felt my mother was going to leave months before she sat us down in the living room. I kept seeing her having breakfast on a wooden deck overlooking foggy green hills with a man who was not my father. Now this is her life.

I lift myself up and a chill crushes my arms. I am half out of the flames, my head above the tarp, still in a T-shirt and shorts, the bottom part of me so hot I'm afraid I'll combust, the top like I've been dipped in a watery ice bucket, each sensation so sharp I have an image of my body snapping apart at the waist. I take the flannel shirt that's been tied around my hips all day and stick my right arm through the sleeve. It's snug and soft and feels like those first seconds slipping my fingers into a vagina, the hot-cold tingling of deep kisses. Both arms through, I button up the cuffs and tightly grab my forearms, palms radiating through the cotton so strongly it's like my hands are giant matches. I sit down, hugging my flannel elbows, and fall back onto the ground between the fire and tarp. My body sinks into the earth for a very long time. Moss tickles the back of my thighs, balmy waves from the fire enveloping me, and all of that soft cotton, like the lips of a woman, not Tree, but someone else entirely, someone who doesn't exist yet, the love of my life, one of the four or five I'm allowed, and I've finally found her and she's beautiful, with big searching green eyes and a desire for a little too much of everything. I shut my eyes. When I open them there is a slinky quarter moon above me, so close I could grab it. I am unspeakably happy.

It takes some time before I realize I am not entirely alone. Marc slouches nearby, huddled against a thick tree trunk, smoking. I see the outline of his hair as he inhales and the embers go orange. I walk over to him, smile. He raises an eyebrow and without a word we return to the fire, first sitting upright, then spreading out next to the flames, diagonally away from each other, our heads almost touching. The flare in my veins settles into the sky, still flagrant with stars, though more like a canopy. He was right. Clouds move. If you wait long enough everything does.

At some point we start talking softly again. Marc tells me stories of the army, a girl he'd fallen for. She worked in the kitchen and snuck him extra tomatoes and cucumbers, cottage cheese with creamy, thick curds. They fucked when nobody was looking. She said she would marry him and move to New York. Give him children. Make his life. As he talks I'm wondering if that's why he fled, not the violence but the promises. I ask him and he chuckles.

"You know me fairly well."

"I do."

"I'm Dionysus. Have you read *Narcissus and Goldmund*?"

"Just *Siddhartha*."

"The famous one."

"I don't remember it. I was working with my tutor, remember? The guy with the bad skin and shiny yellow hair. He looked like a cracked leather car seat. But he was so smart. I loved him."

"Buddha's awakening is good, don't get me wrong. But Narcissus is more earthy. I love minor works by major writers. That's where their excesses go and the dualities. The mind and the heart. Art and reason. Male, female. Love, hate. The earthly mother versus mother earth."

"Wonder who wins that one . . ."

He laughs. "You're such an Apollo."

"Oh no, that is just not true. I'm all about the body."

"Only in the most weirdly regimented kind of way. An athlete? Where did you ever get that idea?"

I look up to the sky, now glittering like a phosphorescent beach, because there is an answer somewhere, not too far off.

The first time I put on a pair of skates was kid stuff. I was four years old and gripped my father's knee. He managed to stay upright, even as I banged my palms against his thigh. We were at Wollman Rink in Central Park, going round and round. It was cold. He picked me up over his head and I giggled. "You pee and you're dead," he said.

It made me want to.

He could skate with me on his shoulders. We did this often, until the guard politely said, *No go, sir. You can't carry her like that. Her feet must always touch the ground.* That seems funny now, but it's how I remember it.

A few years later I could sail above the cool surface. I was faster than him. The guard now watched out of the corner of his eye as my father whispered to a tall man who wore a blue tracksuit and down jacket, unzipped over it. When I stopped going around, the tracksuit talked to me about form. Soon Wollman Rink was too small.

"What's it she likes so much?" my father asked him one day. I'd stopped to tighten my laces and could hear them perfectly.

"She's really fast. It's like she wants to eat the air."

"But do you think she can do it? Be that good?"

"I think she can probably do anything."

That's how I remember it: *She can probably do anything.* And the look in my father's eyes, like he'd stumbled into a deal that was going to make him a fortune.

"I've got you a real coach," my father said a few months later, brick fireplace blazing in the windows overlooking the park. He was drinking brandy out of a thick handcrafted glass. It smelled like shadows. I sipped hot chocolate—the cup incidental. We clinked our glasses together and I was invincible.

It's colder now. Marc rubs his hands close to the fire. I curl up next to the flames, knees almost touching my chin to get small enough for the stitched-up Israeli flag to cover me.

He leans back and taps my thigh, says sit up.

I do, keeping the flag wrapped tightly around my arms.

He lights a cigarette puffed up with hash and hands it to me, says it'll help the transition, but I don't want to leave. Once I watched a little girl on the subway gripping the silver pole as she stood close to her mother, who also held a littler boy tightly against her waist. Tears streamed down the girl's face as she eyed her mother and the boy, connected at the hip and cooing at each other. The girl screamed, "I don't want to be big!"

I take the cigarette from Marc and pull, feeling my lungs expand into the sweetness. Marc puts his arm around my shoulder, lightly but enough to say it's okay, I've got you. He smells like ashes and his little-boy smell on steroids: onions and coffee grinds and vinegar before they go down the garbage disposal. It's comforting. I snake my right arm out of the flag and wrap it around his shoulder. Our arms touch as we silently pass the cigarette between us, the Star of David covering our backs.

I am so into the warmth. The closeness of him. Like our bodies are one.

"What's it like being you?" he says.

"Most of the time it's okay."

"Even with . . . you know."

I turn to him and our faces almost touch. "Are we playing truth or dare again?"

"You want to?"

"No."

"Me neither."

We stare at each other, so tight it makes my chest cave inward. Different as we are, we know how to come together. Growing up, we were allies long before either of us knew the word. Until I gave him up for the rink, for girls. I put the back of my palm against his cheek.

"I can't go back," he says, one teardrop rolling down each side of his face, wetting my fingers.

"It'll be okay," I promise, though I have no idea if that's true.

"I'm such a . . . shit! I'm . . ." He shakes silently.

"It's okay." I move my hand around the back of his head and hold him. His body convulses into sobs and he's screaming, some words, I think, I just can't put them together. I have never seen him cry, not even when he held his hand over the flame in the kitchen and Sofia had to call 911. This is way scarier.

I turn my head slightly, detach my cheek from his. Behind him, the sky turns purple-gray, with fewer stars. He grabs my shoulders so wildly it hurts, but I am beginning to understand. If he lets go he'll spiral out into nothingness. He tells me I'm all that's left and it suddenly makes sense. What I'm doing here.

Tree once drew a picture of my knee and it looked like an old man. Up close it was ghoulish, jagged nose with down-turned lines, charcoal eyes, their weight unmistakable. We need to guard this guy like Gorbachev, she'd said. I smiled, though the metaphor was off. Hers always were. But the message was clear: my body was a tanked-up machine built for the glory that had eluded us in the cold mess of Calgary.

Several weeks later I find myself walking along a semi-tropical coastline in the soft gray morning with her pulse inside me, slowing down from my run, feeling at home once again just to be near the waves, though farther south than I'd imagined. I promised Marc we'd steer clear of Tel Aviv. It was the only way he would come down from the mountain. The marquee cities were too risky, soldiers lurking at every corner ready to turn him in when they were done beating up Arabs. Americans were safe. At least for now. Unless you'd run away from the army, which was more like reform school for American Jews. Happens all the time, Marc says, transforming young potheads into well-bred killers. They return and vote Republican.

I have lost count of the days since Tree and I stood in the cold dark hours at the end of the earth and she said I would not return. I practice talking to her out loud as I walk past the telephone booth.

He still needs me, I tell her.

No he doesn't. He's just playing.

You don't understand.

I do.

No you don't.

All too well.

It's not what you think.

What I think is you've lost your appetite. I'm wasting my time.

I have not. Please.

I'm leaving, J.

Don't go. I love you.

I'm sorry.

I can't even fantasize a version where she says come to me now, catch the first plane out, I love you too! I'd caught her for one moment when Marc and I first got down here, I can't remember how many days ago, time is slipping, condensing. I told her just hold on, I'm coming. She said there was another American girl in Ushuaia who was younger and faster and hated her coach. I said please wait, just a little bit longer. She was silent. Before hanging up she said stop pretending this isn't your choice.

A glimmer of sun jabs between heavy gray clouds, rays like butterscotch light sabers, tangerine-lemon sky. Green-apple waves, so tart they make my back molars ache. Paradise is a fucking bore.

Back at the hostel I shower while Marc sleeps off the morning in his room with three other boys, all American, just past college and slippery. They are headed to the Sinai, then into Egypt to float down the Nile like Moses, see the Tropic of Cancer. We have been invited along. But we won't go.

Marc likes it here in this resort town. He stays out late playing poker with Greeks and Kiwis and flirting with girls. We meet up late in the afternoons for drinks that bleed into sunset, a communal dinner around plastic tables spiked with beach umbrellas.

I peek my head into his room and smell the sticky sleep of boys, young men really, except Marc who's not even twenty though he's always seemed older than his number. In sleep he's royal, something you'd see in a movie staged a couple of centuries earlier. When we were kids I once told him I would marry a count. We had just returned from France and I was obsessed with palaces. I had no idea what a count was, only that it sounded more sultry than king and involved a black cape. Marc smiled, you will never get married, you're too bossy. You want me all to yourself, I said. His eyebrows fell slightly, exaggerating to say sarcastic. He was only seven and had no idea about counts and kings. I was ten and knew everything about everything, knew that neither one of us would ever get married, we had too much stuck under our skin. And I could make him sulk like crazy. He was a sensitive kid with curdled lips. Soon it hit me that he'd make the perfect count, after I discovered you could become royal, you didn't have to be born into it.

I shut the door and return to my room. It's empty, last night's girls having vacated early. Girls tend to move faster, stay on schedule . . . *why then oh why can't I?* I dress quickly and head back to the beach, passing the public phone again as the record plays . . .

I'm moving on.
Please don't! I'll leave tomorrow. Once he wakes up.
There's no place for us here anymore, J.

* * *

By the time we arrived in Calgary I'd been training hard for six years and had snagged what now seem like a couple of fluky world championships. We were outliers at the sport, the Americans, but every so often someone emerged big time. Why not me? I had a swelled head, knew I was hated by a lot of the other skaters. Emboldened by their stares, the clips behind my back, I traded my results for glamour, the kind that comes from trashing hotel rooms, wearing mirrored sunglasses and fur vests from Russia, burning it all for love and pills. I probably should have joined a rock-and-roll band, not professional athletics. I was the youngest on the Olympic team that year and had scored a place by a hair, though I wouldn't give that to them, especially not to the ChapStick girl next door who the press was pumping up. I'd seen her at Sarajevo in '84 and knew all eyes drew her way. The rest of us were roadies. She did well but couldn't catch the Dutch sensation, and overall it was a mess for America. I remember the parties, the hash oil I smoked because it was easier on my lungs, so many faces sucked through the sludge of games after hours, wind slamming into the alleys as fast as we could skate, and being thankful that for the first time ever they'd moved the oval indoors, though it was ultimately my downfall. I smacked into a wall that wasn't supposed to be there.

I have a few pictures from that year, all before the Olympics, all with the same catch-me-if-you-fucking-can drift in my eyes. Then they just stop, as if we'd tossed the camera off the highest mountaintop in Canada. I really can't recall most of what comes after, and believe me I am trying. The first year of recovery all I wanted was to understand what happened in those few seconds that shot up my world. As soon as I could walk I started going to meetings and obsessing. My share was always the same. Someone said the need for clarity is the mark of a true addict, you can't let go, can't give over to the notion that there are forces you will never be able to control. So it's just there, playing faintly in the background on endless repeat like static across a transatlantic telephone line. And it's given me an edge.

Things like this happen: I'm traveling in Italy, part of the later stages of physical therapy, where you venture back into your life to remember who you are, were. I decide to visit an old friend from Jewish camp who's living with a family in Milan. They're sophisticated. All the college kids dress like it's a film set and everyone plays the guitar. They hold nightly sing-alongs in a place called The Dungeon. Faces lit by candlelight, wax pooling on wooden tables too small to fit your knees under. People get real close around tiny glasses of bloodred wine. I have always despised singing. I hate traveling in packs. And am trying to stay sober. But imagine it, a group of young Italians, Jews mostly, singing Woody Guthrie songs and strumming on their acoustic guitars. There's another woman not singing. She's got dark hair cropped against her cheeks, chic in an angular way that's become popular again. Black olive eyes, dark skin, what they call Sephardi. Once from a small southern village, she's here studying legal research. We stand in the back of the room together and strike up a conversation. Her English is good. She tells me she likes living in the north. "Sometimes, you see, there is so much fire inside of me, I need go out into the cold to put it out."

"Mmmm," I say. "I can think of other ways."

"I'm sorry?"

"To put it out."

She doesn't bite. I tell myself I am above it, what can this angle from a tiny Fellini town possibly know about the boundaries of hot and cold, how to dip her tongue into the armpit of someone like me? We kick it around a bit more.

Talk about who we are, she says she heard what happened to me in the Olympics, says it's too bad, maybe I'll do better next time.

"What's it like?" she asks.

"Losing?"

"No. Going so fast."

"It's like fucking," I say. "Like nonstop, manic, pain-seeking-pleasure, turn-your-head-around fucking. You understand?"

I think I'm being clever, having decided to dig in, see what she's made of, capture some of who I was before the fall. But she is as cold and remote as Calgary, demurely excusing herself to return to the group. The students are singing "Jamaica Farewell" with rolling r's . . . *I had to leeeeve a leeeetle girrrrrrl in Keeeengstontown.*

"I'm nothing without you," Marc says.

"You lied to me," I reply.

"It wasn't a total lie. Besides, that dude is crazy."

"I was strung up in a pulley for eight months. Do you know what that's like? Having your legs stretched like silly putty? All of these people tiptoeing around you, the endless chatter? It's like being dead, only you're not. Because you know what? That would have been better."

"Chill out," he says. We are sitting together on the beach. He'd snuck up on me and we'd gone for a swim in the heat of midday. Afterward we were drying off and a man in green army fatigues approached, saying you little cunt, you horse's buttocks, and other things too British to stick. He had an M16 slung over his shoulder, the same model from Marc's stories of escape. My brother was nervous, biting the inside of his cheek, saying something like part of leaving the army is not having to report in. He introduced me. Words continued only they didn't add up. According to this person, who seems credible, Marc did not run away from the army. He was kicked out for drugs.

"Why does it matter what actually happened? The point is I'm done. This country is shit. They're killing children up in Lebanon. Young girls!"

"Don't try and pretend you're a hero. You are so fucked up."

"Oh, you're one to talk."

"I should be training. I've got another chance."

"You got lucky once, it's not going to happen again and you know it. That's why you can't leave. You're terrified."

"See, you're doing it again."

"What?"

"You made me come."

"Nobody makes anyone do anything."

"Bullshit! You always do. I've got to get out of here."

"I can't do this without you," he says.

"Do what? What are you talking about?"

"Life." This time, a look in his eyes like waves, stomped-out sand castles. Behind him two teenage boys in Speedos hit a ball back and forth with wooden paddles. I want to grab one and smack it down hard on top of Marc's head, literally knocking some brains into him.

"This is not living," I say.

"What's that supposed to mean?"

"It means we can't keep running away."

"Stop being such a coward, J. We can change everything, don't you see? Have a totally different existence, say fuck you to everything we've come from, be here now, be here for a while, you and me . . ."

I stare beyond him again out to the boys whacking the ball back and forth, blue-green sea, a tanker in the distance. They will stay for hours, it's so much fun to smack a ball with a paddle, diving through the air with your arm outstretched for the shot, and even if you fall, it's just a beach. You might not call it a sport, but they are working up a sweat, and that is the best feeling I know, what brings me back to myself.

"I can't do it," I say, unsure whether I mean now or forever.

Turning his back slightly, he looks out at the water as the late-afternoon rays slouch against the shoreline, the rhythm of high-rolling waves in and out like earth clouds, faint smell of french fries and cigarettes, all my sand castles and counts shattered sideways.

"Oh, come on, just think about it," he says, gaze still floating across the sea, our upper arms almost touching. I drape my towel over my shoulders and walk off.

I am still here. If *here* is a place we recognize as a state of being, like *Be here now!* Not geography. I have given up the idea that this tourist town exists on a map, that anyone inside our crystal beach ball is real. Much is made in movies of desert hallucinations, the mirage, as if they're the same thing. But a mirage is naturally occurring and can be captured on film. Hallucinations grip their sacred talons between your ears. Like any thought, they twist and turn you upside down, and try rendering them concrete. It's hopeless.

What keeps me tethered is the water and Marc, one expands as the other shuts down and I'm never sure who's winning. I know only those words held out in front of me: *You got lucky once, it won't happen again.*

Each day I walk by the phone, Tree and the crystalline mountains of Argentina slip farther away, every time I think about packing my bags I know there is no place on earth for me but here. How easily the climate suits my failure. I may never skate again and who cares?

Marc and I are still parked at the hostel, still spending our evenings together, though we barely exchange words outside the company of others. One night we are sipping drinks the color of the sea under a striped beach umbrella with the American boys.

"We're leaving tomorrow," the big blond one says, smiling. For real this time, he promises. He was a Division 1 soccer star and can recite all the John Belushi skits that ever appeared on *Saturday Night Live*. "We'll spend a few days in the Sinai, then go south."

"You'll never get into Egypt," Marc says. "Not with an Israeli stamp on your passport."

"That's bullshit," says another boy, curly headed and dark, like he's Puerto Rican or mafia Jewish. "It's not Jordan or Syria. They're crying for American dollars."

"Come with us," the third says. He's the biggest pothead of the group, eyes perpetually bloodshot behind wet brown lashes, thin hair, skinny, freckles. I am not sure I know his real name. They call him Winter.

"You should go," I say to Marc.

"Oh, sure." His eyes are like bullets.

"Why not?"

"We're in this together, remember?"

We stare at each other until it's uncomfortable. The blond boy orders another pitcher of drinks, the Blue Elvis. You can get those Mediterranean hues mixing blue curaçao and melon liqueur with fruit juices. It is very popular here. And it knocks your socks off. Others join us and we expand the table once, twice, until we have colonized the bar with pink cheeks and accents. We order plates of hummus, roasted eggplant, shavings of chicken and lamb from the spit, diced tomatoes and cucumbers—the closest thing to salad they've got. We smoke thick cigarettes laced with hash. There are other drugs too. They have eagerly found their way to us. To Marc. But I'm staying clear, mostly, because tomorrow could be the day I pack it in and return to a life of competition. I have kept my body strong, running ten miles in the mornings and lifting weights at the gym filled with body-builders, and one other woman who claims to be a stunt double for a famous Korean actress. The other day I bought a pair of rollerblades and this morning streamed down the boardwalk at sunrise. They call it muscle memory: how it takes only seconds before I am faster than anything.

People continue to join us and I can't hold their words. They are steeped in transition, translation, everyone coming or going or they've dropped out entirely. One Australian girl got a job taking tickets at the movie theater. A cute Jewish boy from Mexico City is waiting tables at a four-star hotel where dignitaries stay. Everyone plays strip poker, which I've never been good at though I know the general rules, and that's how I find myself sitting under a beach umbrella by candlelight with the three Americans, the boy from Mexico City, and two quiet women I've never seen before, all of us in various states of covering. I am down to a sports bra and Calvin Klein underwear, black with a thick white band. Boy-friend style. I keep catching the Americans staring at my legs.

"It's so strange," Division 1 says, "sometimes you look like a guy and other times you're all curvy and shit."

"Keep it down," I tell him, "you're not getting anywhere near my Calvins."

"Come on, I'll show you mine if you show me yours."

"Nothing comes between me and my Calvins," says one of the quiet women, English heavily accented, German-y.

We can't figure out if she's being funny. Humor takes awhile to break through its mother tongue. Someone says let's play, goddamnit! Who's dealing?

We go in for another round. Order more pitchers of Blue Elvises, my throat lumping less from the achingly sweet shots than from the king, who's appeared in front of me shaking his torso in a brightly flowered bathing suit, hips on wind-up, a come-on. But his face is bloated. Strands of shiny black hair fringe his eyes, cheeks thin and white as a sheet of looseleaf paper, lips pale blue lines. The king is dead. Long live the king.

"One more round!" an American shouts, and I have no idea if he means drinks or cards. My underwear still covers me, though others are not so lucky. Division 1's penis is out, crawling from a nest of light-brown curls like a periscope. One of the women has lost her shirt. Her nipples are hard and sweet, like chocolate-covered raisins. I want to bite one. A waiter comes by and says really, they are closing, we must settle up.

"One more round!" says the mafia Jew, who's down to his white boxer shorts. They argue lightly. Few things are as humiliating as waiting tables in a tourist town. I slip off to find Marc. Someone had last seen him on the terrace.

It's a skinny staircase, concrete edges lost to rubble. One whole step is missing, likely from a bottle rocket, we're close to Egypt and a straight cross into the Gaza Strip, rumors of underground tunnels everywhere. It's heavily policed, why the guy from Marc's unit was down this way. I hitch up over the empty step, the air hot and humid, like walking through someone's mouth, and it's dark. The higher up and away, the louder the waves, and screaming cats. At the final step, I hear words, lightly first and then full throttle. "I said stop it!" she cries. I push myself up and am embraced by the starriest of nights above the black water. So vast I want to curl up into a hole.

In the corner of the roof-rubble not too far down, I see a fogged-up figure, cutoffs down to his ankles, white limbs exposed in the dark. "Shut the fuck up!" he says.

"Please . . . don't do this . . ."

I'm not sure it's him, it's dark. But then: "Chill the fuck out!"

"No. Please . . ."

He rolls back his arm and punches. I hear a snap. The girl screams. I can see her face now, but only an outline. She seems young. My throat clenches up.

"Shut up!" He clamps his hand over her face, and they fall harder against the wall together. It's low and feels orchestrated. Like they could tumble over into the night and bounce along the shore. Everything in me drains out.

"Okay?"

Her body sways beneath him.

"I swear I'll find you tonight wherever you're sleeping and beat the shit out of you. Answer me! Are you okay?"

A muffled yes.

"Okay, good. I'm going to take my hand away now and you're not going to scream, got it?"

He pulls her back into him, almost gently, her body crumpling forward on top of him, lifeless, a rag doll.

Once with Tree, just once, she had been drinking brandy and ran out of coke, and we were in Europe somewhere . . . Innsbruck, I think, or was it Buffalo? She fell asleep while I was going down on her, abruptly, like one second she's moaning low guttural, then her legs collapse into the bed and everything goes hard. She was tight asleep. Or maybe she'd taken something else and OD'd, I couldn't tell, and anyway I was stuck licking a fucking corpse. Which made me sick. I reached up and smacked her cheek so hard my fingers stung. She shuddered awake, then hit me back even harder.

I feel the sting in my cheek, trying to turn and walk back down the broken steps without making a sound. But I can't stop staring. He moves forward, faster into her, and I can see more of her face, eyes shut tight. When they open she's looking right at me. This is the moment I betray her.

My mouth is so dry I can't swallow. A flash of white

explodes, satellites maybe, or the stars coming down, and I want to dive off the roof. I hate this girl more than I've ever hated another living being. Except maybe him.

I touch my right foot down one step, then the left, carefully descending the staircase backward. The Americans are at the bottom waiting, fully clothed. We're going down the street, they say, you must come, but wait, you look like you've seen a ghost . . . Are you okay? Never mind, I tell them, solidifying the pact I made up on the roof. Just get me out of here.

"What do you mean she's not there?" On the other end of the phone from the bottom of the planet comes static. A different sort of accent.

"She say to tell you goodbye."

As much as I'd like to pretend I am stunned, I'm not. I had a dream the other night that Tree went off with the young skater. It was only a matter of time.

I look out into the softest Blue Elvis sea, light foamy waves. In my ear, the man still speaking, "Meeese . . . you are there?" Yes, I knew she would go, but somehow I'd imagined her in the hot tub surrounded by snow when they brought the phone to her. She would be mean but present.

You are ruining your life. Get back here!

I think of her in steamy hot water. From the beginning it was the best part of our language. My father had a hot tub installed on the roof of our Fifth Avenue apartment, looking down on the park. In the winter, glass walls rolled down for cover, panes that fogged like a sauna when you tossed water on the rocks. He'd seen something like it in the north of Japan. There was a vent and if you slid it open slightly it smelled like snow. You could see people scurrying in their overcoats below.

When Tree first came to talk about coaching me, what

she'd do for me that nobody else could do, we took a soak. It was late December, between the holidays, and freezing. We drew skating ovals in the steam on the windows. Added stick figures. Talked stats. Then out of the blue she got serious, reaching over and grabbing me by the thighs. "These legs have horsepower," she said. "More than you know what to do with. I can help. But you need to listen to everything I say. Do whatever I tell you to do."

I nodded, okay. I was barely sixteen, remember, my eye on the gold and girls and her upper arms like steel bridges. She moved in closer and kissed me through the fog, her fingers sliding up my thighs. "When I say everything," she said, scraping her thumbs against the inner lips of my vagina, "I mean absolutely everything. Or you might as well give up. Understand?"

"Yes."

She kissed me again and I disappeared into the steam.

"We have skates! *Su equipo!*" The man at the end of the earth calls me back to the phone, the beach. I want to scream and shout and stamp my feet on the sand. But there's no one left to listen. And life is like this sometimes: you realize you're utterly alone.

I drop the receiver and the voice fades behind me . . . "*Su equipo*, meeese!"

Later I find Marc at the beach, sitting alone on a big white towel stamped, *Property of Hotel, Do Not Remove*. He wears the same cutoffs, frayed and faded, like something out of another world, Jim Morrison's California. Mirrored sunglasses, which seems reckless.

My backpack weighs me down. You do not owe him one word, I tell myself. But he sees me and waves. Unable to swallow, I spit out a glob of green saliva.

I walk over to him and drop my pack. It lands with a

ringing thump. He spreads the towel out next to him on the
other side and motions for me to sit. I shake my head but
then give in. Like always. We sit silently looking out at the
waves and it feels like a foxhole. It's the middle of the day.
The American boys are gone and the air has holes.

"Where are you off to?" he asks finally.

"Home."

"Where's that at?"

"You know damn well."

"Don't be mean to me," he says. "I'm really sad."

"I don't care."

"I'm serious, J, don't hate me. I can't handle it."

I don't know if he knows I know. He showed up at the
bar down the street at sunrise, the girl pinned to his hip.
She held an ice pack against her cheek and splinted nose.
She told us she walked into a wall. He ordered her a vodka
on the rocks and took her hand in between the two of his,
smiling. Like Tree after she'd pushed too hard. I couldn't
look at them, I think I was jealous. The way he was looking
after her, as if that's what he'd wanted all along. The Americans mapped out their itinerary.

I returned to the hostel by myself and packed.

"I don't hate you," I say now, looking off into the sea.
The sun throws beams against the surface. In the middle
distance a cityscape in gray. Flatter than New York, it shim-
mers like heaven in the movies. "I just don't know what to
do, I can't save you from this . . ."

"What are you talking about?"

"Are you kidding?"

He shrugs, looking off at the fake city, lost horizon.
"Why are you leaving?"

What am I supposed to say . . . because you don't really want me here, Marc, you want some kind of witness?
Because all you care about is getting fucked up? Because I

watched you rape a girl, and I know that's what it was even as I sense I'm backing away from it? . . . *Stop pretending this isn't your choice*, Tree had said, before taking off with the younger skater, choosing hope over despair, and in some ways I'm doing the same, in others I am just a coward, I am always running. But I did not spend eight months in a hospital bed to let you drag me into your hell, little brother, I've got my own.

I do not say any of this.

"It's okay, you don't have to tell me." He nudges his shoulder against mine. "Just promise you won't abandon me like everyone else," he says, more statement than question but it begs.

"I won't. I just can't be with you right now."

He lets out a deep sigh.

The city in front of us sinks into the waves.

PART FIVE

DEEP DARK DOWN IN
THE CITY OF SHADOWS

Tel Aviv, Mid-March 2009

When I think of love I think of secrets. Moments lodged so deep in neuron and tissue only the graze of her lips can rouse them. I want to gouge the hushed muck of childhood and turn it into a lollipop, so she can suck it between her teeth. I want to tell her about my brother.

Yet we talk nonsense on my bed, crisp and new, in an understated apartment on the sixtieth floor. It's the highest I've ever resided and I realize I don't like heights. I avoid the smoky gray-pink windows, especially on sunny mornings, though the entire city catcalls to one side, the glowing Mediterranean purring softly on the other, all of it perpetually, preposterously rose-tinted, like living inside expensive sunglasses. I have a private entrance and bodyguards down in the street below. One is called Mule and he follows me when I leave the block, the other, Wolf, keeps watch here.

Gila's wearing an orange miniskirt, tight brown leather boots with a gold zipper up the side. I walk around the bed and kneel down beside her, legs opening slightly to reveal the secret du jour: she is not wearing underwear. I smile and with every beat of my heart let desire eclipse revelation. She breathes, *ahhhhh*.

It is my favorite sound in the world. Devoid of accent, just the back of her throat letting it all hang out.

I could come right here, right now. But I don't.

She wraps her leather calves around my ears, careful with the zippers. My head feels cool and silky and I think how long can we keep this up? I'm a wonderer by nature. Some call it anxiety. Even as I lap my tongue up the inside of her thigh, slipping my head beneath her skirt, I want to know what she's thinking, who am I in this equation? I can't turn off the questions. This is why I drink. She smells like violets mixed with a little yeast. You can eat violets, the flowers and the leaves, something else to tell her later. *If there's time . . .* Now I'm driving her a little crazy, moving my tongue slowly from thigh to thigh, breathing heavily against her violet patch like a flirty bee, but remaining aloof. I used to tease women for sport, my own, seeing how long I could last without making them come. The more they begged the greater my resolve. But here's the kicker with violets: they can be self-pollinating. Insect or not, they make shit happen. My tongue rises up to her lips and folds into her. Again she breathes, *ahhhhh.*

I increase in speed and orientation. The moment it gets like competition and there is only one way out, unless you fuck it up so badly you can't handle yourself.

She comes, screaming louder than loud. The walls are soundproof, among other things. She grabs my head hard and pulls me up against her. Little kisses tip my nose, my cheeks. "You are a ray of sunshine," she says. I smile, hold her like nothing's going to rip us apart, not my father, his people, Mossad, not even our secrets. But in seconds the scrim descends. Kisses can't keep in anything. She unbuttons my fly, sticks her fingers inside, and I'm thankful I wasn't as upstart-y about the underwear, though the fumbling brings much-needed pause. "I am going to have you now," she says, rolling me over and throwing her weight on top of her hand. It's like dry humping with a twist. I am twelve years old.

I squeeze her wrist hard. "I can't."

"Just relax," she whispers.

"But I don't—"

She presses her lips against mine, teasing my teeth with her tongue, as she twists her fingers inside me. Nothing feels like anything I know and maybe that's the cool jazz of love but I've never had it like this, that syndrome where you go gaga for your captor, I can't remember what it's called, something about the Nobel Prize, though this happened long before she trapped me, before the war.

I take a deep breath, unlocking my tongue. My lips float just beneath her ear. "Say you'll stay tonight."

Her chest rises on top of mine, laughter. She pulls back and inches her fingers in deep. I give up. I've got all I need right now and this feels so fucking good. I sink back farther into the bed and hear myself saying something I've never said at a moment like this, though it's the thing I want to believe in most.

"Touch yourself," she whispers. And I do, though it's the end of me.

Returning to earth, I ask the question: "How long can we do this?"

"As long as it takes."

"What?"

"To find him."

"You said he was dead. You said you believed it."

"But you don't."

"You mean that?"

"Oh, *motek* . . ." She puts a hand against my cheek. "Your father did some very bad things, some I helped, yes, and I am paying for that now. But you shouldn't. If I can keep you safe then it will be one of the best missions of my life."

"And if you can't . . ."

She sucks in her lips, shuts her eyes. I whisper it's okay, kiss each one of her eyelids. Hold her tight and see violets, a whole meadow of them, like the almond blossoms up north. I want to go back before speculation, craven in my belief there's a world where we meet differently, like books about time travel. Come to New York with me, I want to say, let's leave tonight. But she breaks away, says I'm afraid our time is up like a fucking shrink.

"Stay a bit longer," I say. "Please."

"I can't."

"Why?"

"Tonight is my high school reunion."

Two things I know about myself: I get bored easily and I do not like following rules. Both of these come from my father, who may or may not be floating through the streets sixty floors below, either a high-priced confidence man or the most evil criminal in Gotham, depending on whose story you believe. I have been told to sit tight until men in casual blazers figure it all out.

Before she left last night, Gila put three bottles of Gavi in the fridge. I said no, please don't do that. "They are special," she said, "for bargaining, not drinking. Pretend they are not there."

"That's not how it works."

"Of course it is. You, your mind, is stronger than any desire. Or it should be."

"Not for an addict."

"I don't believe in such things."

"Belief has nothing to do with it."

"But, sure, it has everything to do with it," she said.

There was a man in one of my early groups who repeated

a mantra to stay clean: *Mind over matter. If you don't mind, it really doesn't matter.*

Years later I learned they were song lyrics by a Canadian stadium band. Which ruined everything.

Here's another thing about me: I am a wallower, I . . . make excuses. As a kid I'd received regular tetanus shots, close as I was to metal blades and rusted workshops, but that doesn't help the fear of falling, of spiraling out so far I can never pull myself back in. It's like being out on a street in a foreign city alone at three a.m., or watching the metal gates come crashing down outside a restaurant when it's just me and a couple of pugnacious bankers left inside and all I can smell is ice, big buckets of Coca-Cola on the side of the rink, air so frosty it tastes metallic, and I lose my footing. I'm crashing into that wall all over again.

There is a bottle opener in a drawer next to the sink. I will have a glass of wine, just one. To take the edge off.

Late into the evening, Gila calls on my cell phone with its number attached to a card, scrambler embedded. I am with a group from high school, she says. They call her by her real name, which I still do not know. This is not important, she says, when I ask, come on, why do they get something I don't? And high school reunion? How old are you even? She laughs, says I am old enough.

"There it is," I say, "the ellipses . . . You never say anything real."

"I am trying to protect you."

"How does my knowing who you are matter?"

"This is exactly what I am saying, it does not matter in the details. But here is something that might be in the English papers too. We are from Ironi Aleph High School, twenty years out. I graduated early, I told you this, *motek*, I was a prodigy with numbers. I was just sixteen when I went into the army . . . I am young, yes, but I believe I am older than your father's first wife."

"But what's your naaaaaaaaame?" I am slurring. Keep it together, breathe.

"Do you want my story or do we say goodbye?"

"No, no, don't hang up."

"A girl we all knew had a stripper come and pretend it's her."

"You're making this up."

"No, it's real. She was a mouse when we all knew her, in the books. And she wanted to change but couldn't do it herself. Do you remember the song 'Addicted to Love'? There was some dance on a table like a video and the boy who'd been in love with her all through grade school said stop, you are an impostor. And then the whole thing unwhirled."

"Why are you telling me this?"

"Because we are sharing, no?"

"Was that you?"

"You do not listen!"

"I want to know about *you*. I don't care about this girl."

"Wolf says the light is on."

"Are you coming to me?"

"No. Go to bed."

This morning there are two bottles of Gavi left in the refrigerator and the inside of my head feels like a power drill. My throat is clogged, my soul beyond weak. I have no excuse.

I set out by myself to find a meeting, not sure whether this is breaking the covenant. To discover a meeting in one's own tongue is a stroke of luck, some might say, almost worth the cries to pitch a tent and live among the chosen. This room is packed, hard to find a seat, so I stand near the back, balancing from one foot to the other, falling into the haircuts, a sea of shoulder blades, barely making out the voices. People tend to murmur in and out of sobriety, everything's fragile. I slip further into myself in the company of others.

A woman from Los Angeles is talking about a breakup and I listen to the details, the divisions, the doubting herself, the fear there's nothing inside her without him, her great love. They had been together for two decades. In the end she pulled down her pants and shat on the carpet like a fucking baby. She's not embarrassed. She's not proud. It's just what she did. There is no respectable way of falling out of love, she says. I am with her.

What's really going on is I'm pissed Gila didn't invite me to her high school reunion.

Then another voice, the deep baritone, hits me like a bus, literally crashing into the room of whispered confessions. *Unwhirling,* as Gila would say. He is an ex-soldier who'd lived through Lebanon, the first Lebanon. Came over at eighteen to join the army just like Marc, only he'd set off on his own. Felt the Zionist bug since he was a child and had convinced his parents to come first for his Bar Mitzvah. I inch along the side of the room to see him more clearly. He's got a shock of gray-brown hair springing from the top of his head, a glacial nose. Grizzly sort of guy. He speaks of two decades spinning into unaddressed trauma. "You don't start out drinking a bottle of vodka a day," he says. "It's a slow creep, drink before dinner, tucking in the kids, out with your wife on a crystal clear night and you can't think of one thing to say. It wasn't the language thing, I could speak Hebrew fine—and her English was pristine. We just lost something somewhere and it was my fault. I couldn't say what was happening to me, couldn't tell anyone. Felt like the biggest wuss on the planet. We'd won in Lebanon, we did. But why did I feel so lost?"

The war in the north two years ago sent him back. He was binging again and hiding it from his wife who'd stayed despite everything. It's what she does, he says. Loyalty is her brand. And by the way he says it, I can tell it disgusts him. Sometimes you need to be pushed out, he says, shoved with a steel-toed boot into a blinking rainy night, left utterly bereft, but deep down at the core a strange sort of happiness bubbles up knowing there's nobody alive who can save you from yourself. That's freedom, he says, and though I'm not sure I agree, I do something surprising. I ask him to coffee.

We walk outside together into a purplish sky, the end of the rainy season ushering in the sweet smell of hyacinths. Around the new immigrant center, cafés with umbrellas and concrete tables whisper sweet nothings, but he knows where he's going. A quick glance over my shoulder, just to see if Mule's stuck. Bingo. He's more software geek than bodyguard, fashionable glasses and tight leather jacket faded just so, but don't let him fool you, Gila'd said, he is a trained killer. No doubt he'll report the coffee and the gray-brown man. In a few hours they will likely know more about him than I do, Gila will scold, but for now can I just pretend I'm drifting?

When we sit down, inside not out, he asks why I'm here.

"At the meeting?"

"This country."

Expats tend to get right to the source. I first came in the eighties, I tell him, during the first Intifada, with my brother, after he ran away from the army.

"He ran away?"

"It wasn't for him. He was too sensitive."

"I never would have said this then but I can see it. I mean, what were we fighting for? The idea of being more American than the Americans. They used to say that about German Jews . . . more German than the Germans. Horseshit. I'm from Shaker Heights. If I'd wanted to live in another fucking suburb I wouldn't have come to the desert."

But you get a wife, he says. You procreate. And then you don't know who you are anymore—amazing more people aren't trolling the rooms.

I let him talk more than I do. It's comfortable.

"Everyone just wants to be normal," says the gray-brown man, spitting that last word between his teeth. "It's the death knell of this country. Since I've been here there's been this constant striving to live like everyone else, to be like everywhere else. Pretend there's peace. *Normalize.* It's a term. Did you know that? Do you know how damaging that is? I am from Shaker Heights. I know how damaging that is. If you can't embrace the very thing that drives you, you are fucked."

He is angry, my friend. But so am I. I hadn't realized it until this very moment, how I've tamped down a whole seething world.

"Do you believe in ghosts?" I ask.

"Why?"

"Because I'm seeing them."

He orders another round of cappuccinos, says it's okay, there's time before he's got a few errands to run. Later he will meet his wife and their best-friend couple at the opera.

"People always think this when they first get here."

"You mean I'm *normal*?"

He smiles. "We're a lot alike, you and me. I see them too. All transplants do. Ghosts, prophets, anyone you've ever loved, lost, fucked over, it's the six million, plus five thousand years of history. You've got a lot to choose from."

"I had lunch with my dead father and Golda Meir a couple weeks ago."

He looks up, a spot of white foam caught in the grooves of his upper lip. "He Israeli?"

"My father? No. But there's a deep connection."

"Is he buried here?"

"He was . . . maybe."

He stops mid-swallow, looking appropriately confounded.

"It's complicated."

He finishes his cappuccino in one long sip, bringing the cup down dramatically on the table. "I've got to go, but this has been incredible. It's hard to find people to talk to. Do you know what I mean?"

I nod, feeling slightly bereft and this close to ordering a glass of wine the second he leaves. He puts an arm through his jean jacket. "Golda Meir, ay?"

"Uh-huh. They were in a café like this. Drinking wheatgrass."

"Of course they were." He reaches into his pocket. I don't get up but for the first time notice the big TV sets in every corner of the ceiling, all showing the same music video without sound, a blonde with a big dog, black latex, I can't remember who she is but I've seen her before, she's newly famous. "Here's my card," the gray-brown man says. "You can call me anytime, my wife understands. It's what's keeping me whole."

When someone, a stranger, tells you my wife understands, what are you supposed to make of it? My father said he was never unfaithful to any of his wives until recently. Now Suki leaves long phone messages at every number she knows. I no longer hear them, that's Melissa's job. Though the stepster's words crawl between my ears. *I know he's out there, I'll find him, the animal. He made me get my tubes tied. Did you know that? Ask him about that one . . .*

Gila's at the apartment when I return, wearing black and white–striped pants with flared cuffs. Obsessive to focus on the small stuff, but it's a new style that makes her look completely different, a bit like the singer I can't remember.

She smells like lavender shampoo and leather. Brow slightly crinkled, she stares at me, and I see Tree, who, let's face it, is some version of my mother . . . or him. My shoulder blades tighten.

"I am very disappointed," she says. Then she's quiet.

"I'm not supposed to go anywhere?"

She tilts her head down. Away.

"This is insane and you know it."

Her gaze returns. Just a little. Still no words.

"What's happening here?" I feel soft and wet all over. Might even be tears. Shit.

She walks a couple of steps toward me. "You are not who I thought you were."

"Are you kidding me?"

"You drank one whole bottle of wine."

"I told you . . ."

"It was for Teddy."

I bury my head in my hands, speaking to the floor. "That's what you're worried about? Like you can't get another one. And who's Teddy?" I lift my head, give the attitude right back at her.

"He is my cousin. Remember? He is working for you."

Somehow I am supposed to feel guilty about this, feel grateful about this. Was I drinking on purpose? Vengefully? I don't care, I want it better. NOW!!!! "Look, I'm sorry," I soften. "You should have told me."

"I hate apologies."

Now I am silent.

"Take responsibility for yourself. You flew across the ocean to come here for some reason. Now be here. Stop going off in your head."

"I don't understand. Can't we just get more wine?"

"It's impossible. They were special from Galilee. Biodynamic. From exactly two seasons ago. It is bad luck to bring two, not three. So we will cut it down to one and see how that goes."

"I have no idea what you're talking about."

"You promised you would listen. That's how you will stay alive."

"I am listening."

"I said don't drink them."

"But it felt like bait. Like they were there for me."

"When will you learn that nothing here is yours?" She turns and walks into the kitchen.

The worst pain I've ever experienced was not from the fall, where I blacked out almost immediately after slipping forward in slow motion, barely noting the wall in front of me as I tumbled through the quietest quiet, like they show it on TV, and I just kept spinning and twisting and then everything went black. No, the worst pain was self-inflicted. Speed skates are flat ground. You need a ninety-degree angle on each side of the blade, so sharp it'll shave the back of your fingernails. That's how you test them. But I was young and just learning. Even with the fingernail shavings in my lap, I didn't buy it. And I had something to prove, I was tougher than the rest, a wild card. I swiped my knuckles fast across the blade and it was unbearable, one thousand times worse than a paper cut. I screamed so loud everyone came running as the ice between my knees turned the most beautiful snow-cone pink.

When I'm nervous my fingers still throb.

Gila returns jangling a set of car keys. Says we're leaving. Says follow me. I hate her with all my heart, hate her because she's not mine and never will be, because my soul's a bubbling cauldron of soap-opera loathing, which we all know is love dressed up in stilettos and latex . . . Lady Gaga! That's who was in the video.

* * *

Two hours later we are drinking tea in Teddy's rug shop outside Damascus Gate. He says they have spotted my father. *They* are Teddy's people and they saw him outside the kibbutz near Herzliya where Orthodox men make hard goat cheese, the one my father's been funding for years. It seems obvious, so I push Teddy for more details. When exactly? And what was he doing? Or wearing?

The gray-brown man said ghosts walk among us. It's not weird. Sitting here with Teddy I think maybe he's not qualified; we need to call in the paranormals.

I sip my tea, watch Teddy and Gila speak in Hebrew. Laughing. I am in her hands, theirs, and I'd forgotten how conniving she could be. To get here we walked down thirty flights of stairs to the lower elevator bank, then left through the basement so Mule and Wolf couldn't track us. Pillows propped up against the bedroom window and the low light of an electric candle. Anyone would think we were making love. I wonder if we will ever make love again. We'd stepped into an old minivan waiting on a side street so her car remained in the parking lot. I asked why, I thought Mule and Wolf were working for us. "I can count with one hand who's working for us," she said.

Teddy is one of them. But he needs more money. He flashes his thick gold pinkie ring as he describes the hardships of locating someone who's outwitted both American and Israeli intelligence. "He is sublime," Teddy says, and I hear the worship building to a personal crescendo. This is what my father can do. I hand over twenty-five thousand American dollars. Several wires had come in from Paris over the past two days, each sent to a different name. I'd set Melissa up there for several weeks in my flat, still playing me. Gila collected the money with fake passports.

We stand and shake hands. Teddy smiles and points to a small wooden stool. "You picked a nice one," he says. "It's made from fallen pine trees, hand carved, nothing harmed in the process."

I grab the stool by a leg. It's light and has beautiful lines, less gaudy than American pine. I have the perfect place for it, under one of the tall windows that overlook the Hudson. I say this out loud. Teddy nods, and we've sealed our pact with a twenty-five-thousand-dollar piece of wood.

Outside it's chilly, winds rolling down from the hills though spring is, as they say, in the air. Boys in baggy shorts kick soccer balls down the street, a woman wrapped head to toe in black carries a big bouquet of yellow tulips. The sun carves shadows up against the gates of history. Gila and I walk into it, not saying a word. Last time we were here it was snowing.

I pull her by the elbow, stopping in front of a row of stalls covered in blue tarps, the sky fading into pastels. "Thank you," I say.

"For what?"

"I know you don't have to do what you're doing."

"I want to do this. For you. For . . ."

"Say it."

She turns away. I follow, aiming to prompt further, but out of the corner of my eye spot the figure of a woman at a fruit stall. She's got light-brown hair, curdled brow, and looks familiar, like an old-time Italian actress, but utterly Semetic. It hits me fast. "Oh my god, Gila!"

"Please, don't push."

"No, look, it's her! It's Golda Meir!" I point to the woman who's now scoping us in quick recognition that this may be the wrong place and time to have her hands buried in a bushel of pears. She scrambles backward and the basket turns, a sea of reddish-yellow orbs rolling in her wake. I drop the stool and run after her, behind me Gila's voice warning don't go! But it's too late. Within seconds I've left behind the blue tarps and entered the Old City, trailing Golda through the same winding streets of winter, now far more alive, the trill of knickknack salesmen, bells and beads, old women haggling over spices in plastic bags, the twisted stone beneath my feet. It's too crowded to run, though she's wending fast between the Christian and Arab quarters. I just need to stick with her, keep my eye on her drab brown sweater sinking into the swarm of backs and shoulders covered in gray, blue, dark green, brown, thousands of us pressed together on this tiny path. I make the mistake of looking up. The tin roof feels close enough to touch. We are being squeezed inside a sardine can. My breath comes faster and I am dizzy. I reach out to balance myself but there's nothing to hold onto.

I feel a hand on my shoulder and turn my head expecting Gila. It's a young man with long brown hair and a pot-brownie smile, like my brother. Ghosts. "Marc?" I say it low. He smiles. Am I dead too?

"*Lo siento. Por favor.*" He lifts me up and I feel the pressure of his hands on my shoulders.

"It's okay, I'm okay," I say. I am here, in the Old City, alive.

"Ah, English . . . I think I know what you're looking for."

He seems calm, as if he'd been expecting me. Beads of sweat crawl from my temples and I'm light-headed. I wonder if this is a trap. He holds his hand out to me, looking less like my brother and more like secret police. "Come, I can help you get your bearings. Take you where you need to go."

"Who are you?"

"Simply a person who wants to help." He points to a flashing Coke sign, takes my elbow. "It is a little café. No secret dungeon. I promise."

"Let go of her." It's Gila, her voice low and calm.

"Whoa, whoa . . . I did not do a thing! I swear!" he says. She's got the Glock out, low, pressed into his right hip.

"Where were you taking her?"

"Just for a Coke. To talk . . . I'm with the international Zionists! Take my card, you can see!" He throws his hands up in the air. Gila says something in Hebrew. He answers, reaching slowly into his back pocket, eyes full on her. He is sweating. Strange as it seems, I have the urge to fall asleep and crouch down lower, squatting like in yoga, Gila and this guy towering faces above me. After inspecting his cards and a few more words, she taps him lightly on the back. He disappears into the crowd. I look up, head still spinning. People stream the path in both directions and I can't catch my breath.

Gila reaches her hand down. I stare at it. There are moments traveling when you want to lie down in the middle of a crowded street and cry, you feel so far away from home. Soldiers in green fatigues pass furiously, the sun on its last leg, soccer boys giving way to young men wearing cologne like Teddy's, tourists with passports tucked down the front of their pants. "I am right here with you," Gila says. "Just take my hand."

I do and the pressure of my palm in hers lifts me up, guiding us through the busy crowds under the low metal roof into more spacious stone caverns, light filtering in crisscrossed poles, leading us through the exit at Jaffa Gate. Yellowish beams now turn the stones gold. Lights shut down behind the windows of fancy stores. I realize Gila is holding my wooden stool, and it slays me she's still here, picking up the pieces. I tell her I won't do anything like that again.

I made another promise. Late last night as we climbed up thirty flights, laughing about the poor Zionist kid and wondering whether that Golda was *the* Golda, I told her I would change. She carried a bottle of citrus cleanser she sprayed between floors. We whispered as she spritzed. She said she understood why I'd disappeared inside the city walls, why I need answers, because she'd forced herself into my head. It's an old agent's trick: you bury your own thoughts and let someone else's enter. She said she's come to understand my addiction this way.

"In less than an hour?" I huffed.

"That is all it takes. I am hypersensitive. I am always seeing things and making connections."

You can train your mind to do this, she said. But the seeds must be there.

"I think I'm like that too, maybe that's why we're so good together," I said, and she nodded, pushing me up ahead of her a couple of steps. Several flights later she said she would remove the remaining bottle of Gavi and help me find a way to the rooms. She had promised to look out for me and realized that must be part of it.

My side of the bargain: I would not pick up.

We locked pinkies on this, still climbing. I was grateful I'd been running on the machine in my own private gym. Lifting weights. If I remember correctly, thirty-six flights is a vertical mile, in steepness the equivalent of scaling a high peak. Gila and I dropped back and forth in tethered rhythm. I liked watching her from behind, following in her wake.

All love is dangerous.

Maybe that's why I am resistant to any real danger.

Upstairs we fell into the soft white sheets and held each other close, whispering thoughts of love. Then she left conspicuously through the front doors at sunrise.

Three days later I spot the gray-brown man pacing outside the new immigrant center. The meeting is canceled, he says. He is jittery, worried he might do something he shouldn't.

"Let's get coffee."

I am hesitant. Coffee happens *after*, once we've been *through* something. And there is Mule a few paces behind, no doubt waiting to see what happens next. Watching someone else's life is boring work most of the time.

We return to the same café. TV screens this time on a local news channel, silent, Hebrew subtitles. The gray-brown man looks at the screen, a politician speaking. "This fucker, the ex-president," the gray-brown man says, "apparently he raped some of the women who worked for him. People used to say this country would be normal the day we had our own stock exchange. When we cared as much about money as we do about security. But you want normal, look at men in power, it's the same everywhere. They're all rapists."

"You sound like my father."

"The ghost?"

"No, the real guy. He was in finance."

"So am I."

This is my lot, I suppose, or he's a plant. He asks me about Wall Street, a place he's never been but has mythologized for years. I tell him it doesn't exist, except in theory. "My wife thinks I should quit. She's Israeli. Did I tell you that already? Born here so she's headstrong. She teaches at the university, not the big international one, the community college. It's filled up with Israeli Arabs who wear big gold chains and write hip-hop lyrics. This is the new Jerusalem."

I like what this guy knows, and the way he brings everything back to himself comforts, no questions I can't answer today. Lulled by his voice, I look up at the television screen and there is smoke, a bomb perhaps, I can't read the Hebrew subtitles, but the time code flashing at the bottom of the screen shows it's live, happening now. It feels familiar somehow, like I've seen the clip before, a 9/11 memory, all the smoke, residual trauma. Behind the reporter there is a closer flash of boulevard, and I can see the Movie Star Café, the silhouette of Garland on the sign out front. I stop the gray-brown man in the middle of a soliloquy I wasn't following. "What's going on there? On the screen?"

He looks up, listens. "She's saying it's a bomb in a residential apartment. They've contained the damage but they're looking for information. It's a strange neighborhood to bomb, mixed and very left wing, maybe it's a drug thing, they don't know yet." No, it can't be . . . how could it be? But something in me shifts, air draining heavily, my lungs freezing cold. "There was one person inside, they're not releasing details yet . . . Oh, wait, she says they think he was Palestinian, undocumented, maybe a hustler."

"Did they say that? *Hustler?*"

"She didn't use that word, but . . ."

Nothing about this moment makes sense. I see myself, the gray-brown man, he's talking but I've lost his words to the drilling in my head. I stand up and run out of the café, vaguely hearing him call after me as I quicken the pace to Mule who'd been ducked behind a small white car. He tries to run, avoiding me, but I catch him and tackle him from behind. He shouts something in Hebrew, falling slightly forward then catching himself and bouncing up from the sidewalk. "Go away," he whispers harshly in English. "Fast. You cannot be seen with me. We will be blown." Then he screams. "*Ganav! Ganav!*"

"I need your car!" I say.

"I make them think you are a pickpocket. Run!"

"Please," I say, and try to explain.

"*Bat zona!* Crazy bitch!" He screams and pushes into me, sticking his car keys in the front pocket of my jeans, then runs off. I press the unlock button and the lights on the little white car flicker. Inside I turn the key fast, fumbling my way to Ha-Yarkon, the only way I know back to my old flat, and mercifully, given the hour, the traffic is light, though it congests the closer I get to the Movie Star, my old block. I pull to the side and walk the final few blocks, coming closer to the barricades. They won't let anyone too close to the building, but I can see up to my flat, or what was my flat, a blown-out black hole where the front door used to be. It stinks of tar and turpentine. I move a few steps closer to the barricade but a cop pushes me back off the curb. Flipping around, I see Yudi's van parked across the road, a few stores down from the Movie Star, and push through the street peepers to get a closer look. A curtain in the back window slides open, a set of eyes peeking out, deep dark brown and shot up with pain.

My phone buzzes and I reach into my pocket, Gila will have instructions. But the phone is smacked out of my hand. There's a body in front of me, not Mule but male, tall, I notice, then another shadowy figure. Rubbery fingers cover my mouth and eyes, the smell of lemon-scented Pledge, then a pinch at my right knee. My heartbeat echoes, the slow-mo tumble over and over again into a wall that is not supposed to be there, and I am fucked forever. Please just let me sleep.

I am dozing in the woods. No sleeping bag or towel. Just me and the dirt beneath my head.

In the distance there is a crash. A car piles into a jagged rock on the Taconic State Parkway. I open my eyes and see legs. Black shoes multiplying like fruit flies. Tomorrow there will be flowers strewn across the rocks where the car had been. Today I can't keep my eyes open.

What are you wearing to the funeral?

Over and over they ask.

As if it's the only thing that matters. Will I look like a boy or girl? Can't you dig up the gray suit with the skirt? You look like that singer from the Talking Heads.

My mother cries throughout the entire ceremony. I stare straight ahead in a time warp, wrapping my fingers around the tiny plastic bag of Oxycodone in my suit pocket. It's half empty. My whole body quietly throbs.

Gila comes home for dinner. We are living in the high-rise with beautiful night views. I hear her voice before spotting her with a pizza box that smells like truffles. She smiles, drops the box on the counter, and grabs me by the waist. I want to kiss you everywhere, she says. We make love on the kitchen floor and feed each other slices of cold pizza over votive candles. I ask her to marry me and she presses her forefinger against my lips. Please, stop trying so hard.

I duck back behind the leather couch, hiding from Marc. My parents talk loudly as they approach, about a dinner party the old bastard is staging for Marlon Brando. He'd heard Marlon Brando had become enamored with American Indians and rounded up everyone he knew at the Native American Community House in the Village to find a chief for Marlon Brando to speak with. And though she wants very much to meet him, Marlon, there is trouble. First she says she doesn't have the right stones to go with her blue dress. He says we'll buy new ones. Then the colorist had disturbed her hair by a shade. He says they can get it back, fly her to Los Angeles where her favorite guy now practices. Then it's the weather. She cannot meet Marlon Brando and the chief, who now lives in a trailer in Queens by the old World's Fair grounds, in this humidity.

She says remember that Neil Young song about Pocahontas? Of course he remembers. Of course he feels for Neil Young who just wants to make love to the chief's daughter, but then Marlon Brando appears by the fire and what can he do but sing? That's how I feel, she says. Like Marlon Brando is ruining things between us.

Katrina, you can't blame Brando.

Then it's your fault, she says.

The party's over, love.

I am telling Gila about my mother. How just before she left for good she told us she freezes every time he puts his hands on her, told us he likes to watch but can't make anything happen for her. I am twelve, Marc nine.

He succumbs to her confidences, setting off a deep Oedipal hatred of our father.

I shrug.

You've heard this story before?

My scars throb. The big one cutting down my lower back like a chrysalis. I used to think dragonflies would burst out of it. Then the smaller ones on my hand and over my left eye. Marc whacked me with a tree branch, I can't remember why. There was a little blood but I could barely feel it. We were alone so I didn't go to the hospital and a doughy piece of skin eventually smoothed it over. Years later a friend was tweezing my eyebrows on a lark. I never tweezed, wasn't part of my lexicon, until we decided to form a punk band. Though we played no instruments, it seemed the right idea for the time. My friend said the Ramones never knew how to play guitar and then one day they were a band because it wasn't about melody or proficiency. It was all fuck you and looking good in tight black jeans. The tweezing would help.

Then in the middle, she'd slipped her finger against my forehead and said, "It's hard."

"You can do it."

"No, your head. It's hard."

I feel hands on my head. Warm, fingertips like dumplings.

Nice and easy, Jennifer, a voice says. You're almost home.

My eyes adjust to the light, harsh and stagnant. Two faces hover over me, both male.

"Welcome back to the living," one says, American. His hands shroud my temples. Like a healer.

They are suits. This is real. Who dreams of suits?

I sit up slightly and realize my feet are strapped to the bed. "Sorry for the formality," says the other man hovering, cute, good hair, Israeli accent. *Him again?* Everything is sluggish: thought, speech, recognition. "I warned you," he says, and the cobwebs slowly break.

"Some bartender you are," I say, though I don't recognize my own voice. He's still looking at me, compassionately, I think. I lift my head and notice a third man over in the corner. He's turned sideways, squeezing a cigarette between his thumb and forefinger. Yearling. FBI.

"Am I back in the States?" I ask, and still sound funny, like my mother. The past, my dreams, clouding the present.

"We'll get to that," answers the American suit. He removes his hands from my head and turns to the bartender, says something in Hebrew that includes the word water. The bartender walks to the corner of the room where Yearling now stands, legs apart, hands on his hips. Pissed off about something.

"Jennifer, look at me," America again. "Apologies for the spy drama but if the shoe fits."

I stare him down straight. "How long have I been here?"

"You came back around Thanksgiving, right?"

"In this room?" Noting . . . still in Israel, as the fog continues to clear. I was on my way to the old flat . . . why?

"Oh . . . a couple of hours. Chloroform is amazing, isn't it? I sometimes put some on my handkerchief before bed, when I want to dream of electric sheep. I'll bet you had some good ones, you were trying to twirl at one point—"

"Fuck, you drugged me! Fuck!"

"You'll be fine. It's temporary."

"I'm trying to stay clean."

"Advice, little honey bear: maybe you should focus on staying alive."

Fair enough.

"Now sit up," says America, adjusting the pillows as the back of the bed slides up electronically behind me. I hate that sound more than anything in the world. The bartender joins us and hands me a glass of water. "Drink," he says.

"Are you kidding?"

America nods *I hear you.* "Izzy, give me the glass . . ." The bartender hands it to him and he takes a long sip. *Izzy?* "See, no poison."

I take the glass from him and realize how much I want it. The back of my throat is a desert. I lift the glass to my lips and let the water flow. I want to cry.

"Okay, let's get the facts out of the way," America says. Yearling moves closer behind him, the bartender on the other side now, and I am trying to place them together, why I'm here. "We know Papa Bear's alive. We know you've seen him. We have a suspicion you may even be hiding him."

I would spit out the water, but it's so good.

"No, Jennifer, we are not that stupid." He gives me a cockeyed look. "I know where you're living and who rented the place. I know who she is to you and to him. I know about her little mercenaries. We know what she and your father are up to . . ." He says things Yearling's said before only in more detail. I try to follow but am still so foggy, and the tactics are confusing, those paragraphs I usually skip over in the *Journal.* My father is a thief, sure, but listen to the suits. They say with Gila's help my father syphoned classified information from powerful companies, then used it to downgrade their assets and bet against them—he had that much money and clout, few people could have done this for as long as he did without notice. In some cases they busted entire economies in their wake, threw markets into a tailspin. If you made a top ten list of worst financial crimes of the decade, they say he'd be up there in the high ranks . . . maybe even number one, America tells me. He names names like WorldCom, Stanford, Enron, says maybe they were worse because they schemed off the backs of investors who lost millions. My father and Gila never got to that point, but they made billions off institutions, some of whom were made up of individual investors. Which is worse? They can't say. And much of the information is still in play out there. Gila knows where; though he was the visionary, she took on much of the execution. He'd dug her up on the Internet some years ago when he was looking for a clean way in. It was a match made in heaven. I must have googled her a million times last summer when I returned, trying to make sense of that week, and found nothing, even in Hebrew. They are lying. She can't be found, America says, unless you know where to look. He motions to the bartender, who brings over a black laptop and flips it open.

"You will now see what happens when the hero becomes her own shadow," the bartender says. "It is not often you find a case so powerful. You begin to wonder about brain chemistry, or an overdeveloped animus."

"Stop with that shit, you're driving me crazy," America says.

"You too are born of this, the self and the shadow. It's how you play happy cop, sad cop."

"Jesus fucking Christ, you people . . ."

"You are saying the Jews?"

America rolls his eyes. "Just show her."

The bartender tilts the screen toward my face, then pulls up a chair beside me, telling me to click around. The keys are in English. "This is the first level of betrayal. We trained her, first in our most special unit—I was there too, we were like brothers—then Technion . . . Anyone would sell their first child for this kind of knowledge. But look how she does . . . Go down, scroll more."

On screen there is some sort of advertisement for a company that excels at techno-corporate problem solving. They will cut through firewalls, crack company codes and passwords, send people inside, extract all the information you need. There is a promise of discretion, the latest technology, chips not yet registered with the government, the best consultants in the world: "*We are the only company of its kind. Beyond experimental. We blend the most innovative technologies with human ingenuity and the highest-ranking global intelligence.*"

"Your girlfriend's calling card," America says.

"This is the dark web?"

"Deep web. Yes."

"It is, in every definition, a shadow world," the bartender says.

I click into a directory, which looks like any other directory, a list with numbers next to it indicating how many posts the category holds. But scrolling through I feel sick . . . hit men, drugs, body parts, every kind of sex slave, child porn. America says don't click on anything else, even by accident. Just once will put a trace on your computer.

"You're saying this is Gila? Child porn?"

"That not so much," America says. "Click back to her page."

I do and it's all spying, information gathering. There is a company name and no picture. But something about the language . . . the blending human ingenuity with global intelligence, the only company of its kind, all sounds like her. America says she's something called a kite: hired to do the breaking and entering, and if caught the client can cut the string, no trace of involvement. "She's supposed to move on after delivery, but seems like that changed when she met Papa Bear."

"I know all of this already," I say. It's true in theory, if not practice.

"This is ridiculous, you're worse than she is," Yearling says, moving closer toward me on the bed.

"Was there even a bomb in Jerusalem?" I look directly at him. "Or were you just trying to get me back here?"

"Let's remember it was actually you who changed the plan, little honey bear, not our darling Jimbo, crafty bugger though he is, right?" says America.

"We knew you were lying all along," Yearling says. "We had no idea how far you'd take it. That's been fortuitous for us."

Yearling and America are together now, smiling, I think. I look down at my hands and see they are particularly veiny, like after a power lift. They are making fun of me.

Yearling chides: "Who are you with? Him or her? Who's pulling your strings?"

"Why don't you tell me? You seem to have it all figured out."

"Oh, she is feisty, you said she was, but . . ." America says, and they laugh like the men at the bottom of the world when I tried to carry a gold-plated switchblade out of Argentina. Always, small groups of men laughing. Right now, I'm for Gila, I don't care what she's done.

Yearling comes back to me. "You think that bomb was meant for the kid? Someone was trying to get *you*."

"Bomb?"

"In your old apartment."

"Oh my god, the boy!" The images come fast: the TV screen, Mule and the gray-brown man, a white car, Yudi's eyes . . . I choke it all down.

"Yeah, sad about that," America says.

"You killed him!" I want to rip his head off but am stuck.

"Oh dear, that wasn't us. We're the good guys."

"Liar! You're all fucking big fat liars!" I pound my fists into the mattress.

Yearling pushes slightly past America, grabs both of my arms with one hand, slamming the other over my mouth. His fingers dig into my jaw.

"*Tranquilo*, Jimmy." America puts a hand on Yearling's

back. "Let her go. She'll be a good girl. Right, Jennifer?"

"I gave you weeks!" Yearling says to America as I make a final attempt to free my legs from the straps, then give up. "You're trying to subvert me. This has nothing to do with Homeland."

"How do you know?" America counters, and Yearling's grip loosens. He drops my hands and releases my jaw. I taste blood inside my lip.

"I'm sorry," Yearling says to me.

"Clearly that bomb was meant for you," America says. I am sinking farther in the muck of it, the boy. It's my fuck-ing fault. "Maybe it was your father's people. Maybe Gila's. Maybe someone else. That's what we need to find out."

"Don't forget there is still big-time theft here," Yearling says. "And extortion. And laundering . . . More RICO bull-shit than you can name. I don't know why I agreed to this. I can arrest her right now."

"She doesn't know shit," America says. "And the bodies are adding up now . . . Dr. Freud here has more jurisdiction than us."

"I am a Jungian," the bartender says.

"Anyway," America turns to me, "lots of threads to pull. So many leading back to your girlfriend. And Papa Bear."

"If he's alive."

"You know he is. People've seen him near the kibbutz. Walking around in a friggin' toga."

I laugh out loud, nerves likely. But the thought of my father dodging all manner of international law dressed in a toga . . . well, it's something to grab onto. I cannot think about the boy, I will not think about the boy. I stare at my hands, focus. My father rose from the ocean in a metallic cape, then disappeared into thin air. We had lunch with Golda Meir, who appeared a few weeks later fondling pears outside the Old City.

"Gila swears she saw him die," I say.

"Wouldn't she?"

"She hasn't seen him since."

"She's playing you. Can't you see that? They both are. You weren't supposed to come back and now that you have, you're really dangerous for both of them. You have information."

"Are you kidding? Nobody's telling me anything."

"Yeah . . ." America pauses. "This is the tricky part. I believe you. I think even your friend Yearling here believes you, though you've been very bad for his career—Jimbo, don't say another fucking word. We've got something, Jennifer . . . something to show you."

He takes the laptop out of my hand and taps at the keys. He brings up a page with images of gold coins and instructions for purchasing and trading them. Yearling calls this Internet money. "It's small potatoes. You can't make any real money in it . . . it's all tech cowboys and black market bullshit. But your father's not a dumb guy, he's using it to cover bigger deals, all based on stolen information from you-know-who."

"She said she was out of it."

"Again," America says, "wouldn't she?"

"Enough!" Yearling stands up on a chair and raises his fists in the air. "I'm king of the world!" he screams. "Izzy, come and get me. I'm feeling it, all systems are go!"

"Cut the shit!! You fucking clowns!" America screams.

"I'm falling . . ." Yearling leans backward. So far he really is going to fall. My mind jumps to his head splattering on the concrete. "IZZZZZZZZZYYYYYYYYYYY!" he screams. The bartender dives forward at the last minute, sweeping him up just before his head hits the ground, and places him back on the chair.

Yearling sits back, crosses one thick leg over the other,

awkwardly. This is really weird. "You know what that was, Jennifer Baron? That was trust . . . and you know what the thing is about trust? If you put it in the wrong hands, you're screwed. What we're offering here is a little unscrewing."

"I don't understand."

"We need you to—forgive the pun—expose Gila Zyskun or whatever her name is. Maybe your father too."

"What makes you think I'll do that?"

"Because it's the right thing to do," America now, high horse.

I roll my eyes.

"Okay, how about for the kid? They killed that fucking Arab kid!"

"She will not be motivated by that," the bartender says. "She is too narcissistic and has a superiority complex. It is typical for the oldest child."

"How about prison?" Yearling says. "Jennifer, are you motivated by the idea of not going to prison?"

"Even I know you can't just do that. You need some kind of proof."

"Oh, that." Yearling takes out a picture that looks like an ultrasound. Only there is some sort of metallic strip in the center. "This is your uterus," he says, and the word sounds like a forgotten planet.

I run my tongue inside my cheek and still taste blood. It's the jump drive I'd wrapped in several layers of cotton and latex and stuck up inside, as instructed. Armond told me he'd burned the drive after downloading its contents to an untraceable laptop. I remember asking why and he said it was about the frozen assets. They had to move everything fast in case my father was found dead and the wills kicked in.

"You left on an Israeli passport," says the bartender. "Very smart. If you'd been in the foreign line, the files would have come to us sooner. Proactive measures. Our people, it's a bit more difficult. You cannot simply spy on your own people."

"So you see," the voice of America rolls over him, "if you'd just stayed home and baked cookies, we wouldn't have gone digging. But once we found you here, again, we started wondering why. That's never what you want, agents wondering why. Sounds like a country-and-western ballad, right?"

"Not really," I say.

America laughs. "Okay, listen, don't be fooled by my charming disposition. Just be smart here. We really do know everything."

"I have no idea what was on the drive."

"Tell it to the judge," Yearling responds. Did he really just say that?

"Thing is," America, pacing back and forth now, "it doesn't matter because we've got you leaving the country with that stick up your, uh, vagina. Then someone known only as Toko shows up down in this torrent of smut, trading information he shouldn't have and literally turning it into gold. The gold in the shadow, right, Dr. Jung?"

"This is not even close to the right metaphor," the bartender says. "You are a jackass."

America ignores him, comes back in my face. "You want to know something else? We don't really give a shit about your father, because even if he's alive, he's dead. He's running around the holy land in a fucking sheet! Think about it. What kind of life is that? But your girlfriend . . . that's another story. The level of thievery alone is astounding, and then you filter in the kid . . . maybe blowing up a rabbi . . ."

"She didn't do any of that!"

"Whatever you say, but surely you can see you're in a pickle here. What does that mean, in a pickle? Jews like pickles . . . wonder if that's got something to do with it."

"It is from Shakespeare," says the bartender.

"Shakespeare! I hate fucking Shakespeare!" America comes in closer to me. "The thing I'm trying to say here is you are damned if you do, damned if you don't. I don't envy you, little honey bear."

A bit later the bartender comes in alone with the computer tucked under his arm. I am still tied down to the bed though beginning to feel more like myself again. He opens the screen and sets it on my lap.

"So who are you? Mossad?"

"That's not important. Look at this."

I tilt the screen forward and see some kind of personality test. "It's Myers Briggs," he says, and I can't help laughing. A few years ago we had a group of behavioral consultants come into the foundation and they made us do this. We were supposed to use the findings to guide important conversations. I cannot remember what happened after they left, nor my results. I think my intentions had been good.

"The schematic is based on Jungian archetypes," says the bartender, "and it is the most clear assessment of how people will behave in the many situations of life."

"You're serious?"

"You will take this test many times until we are sure you are not lying."

"Who lies on Myers Briggs?"

"You would be surprised."

He leans over to make sure the test is ready to begin. I take it five times in a row without a break, answering the same questions again and again, stopping every time on the ones about order versus chaos . . . I crave order, routine, it's why meetings really work for me, once I lose my footing, it's a quick drop into the caldron . . . *double, double toil and trouble*. I kind of hate Shakespeare too, all the fancy screaming. I believe people need structure to keep them in line.

I am an ESTJ.

The bartender tells me I am The Overseer, the same type as George W. Bush and Condoleezza Rice. Martha Stewart. Also Saddam Hussein.

"When did Saddam take the Myers Briggs test?"

The bartender shrugs.

"Come on, this is sort of bullshit."

He stares at me, long. "You think you are not an ESTJ?"

"I think it's like astrology, you bring to it as much as you want."

He sits down on the side of the bed, brow crinkled, lips pursed, concentrating. "Remember the night at the bar? You said you were looking for hope, but hope cannot be something we seek or pursue. Hope comes from faith in something larger than ourselves and it is therefore a challenge when you do not believe in anything. Hope is the lie, you see what I mean? You are in Alcoholics Anonymous? How do you see the higher power if you do not believe?"

"I once went to a Bruce Springsteen concert at Madison Square Garden. Before he started he walked up to the mic and said, *Take what you need*. Then he played a fucking glorious show. I have no idea what anyone else took, but for me it was just music. Beautiful music."

"And the music comes from a place of magic."

"I think so."

"Hold that, okay? Use it. And remember you are The Overseer, you are pragmatic and strong-willed, a natural leader. Stop letting other people tell you what to do."

"But you're telling me what to do."

The door clicks open, letting out a mechanical screech. I look up and there's America, stark against the white walls, everything as clean and somber as a hospital, not just the bed. "Izzy, you done yet?" he asks.

"Is that really your name?" I ask.

"Izaak."

"All right, enough," America says. "I let you do your little talking cure, now we've got work to do before throwing her back to the wolves."

I cannot remember the last time I thought about work, even the idea of it. The government agents are giving me a job, and I like jobs because I am an ESTJ. I value tradition and stability and a world that makes sense. All of this feels right within the confines of this room, it's what awaits outside that scares the shit out of me.

I am led out of the shadows into the world of the living. America sits next to me in the back of an unmarked black van without windows. He'd covered my eyes until we got to the van so I would have no visual memory but for the white room. We stop blocks before my building and he tells me the exact streets to walk home, reminding me of their surveillance, they are with me always. Like the Almighty, I joke. He tells me I am not funny.

Upstairs it's dark. I turn on my phone as I've been instructed and find texts from Gila. I text back and she calls, where have you been?

"Two meetings, then the beach. I had my ringer off."

"Well stay put now. Something's wrong."

"What do you mean?"

"Mule isn't answering either. I thought you two were together and something happened. Don't scare me like that."

"Oh god, I'm sorry," I say, trying not to be too obvious or overly concerned about Mule.

"When was the last time you saw him?"

"I don't remember seeing him at all," I say.

Gila sighs. "Just stay put." Then, before she hangs up, says, "Maybe he just has his ringer off."

She shows up the next morning with the English papers. "The CIA is on a tear," she says. Rhymes with beer. Like the Hank Williams song: *There's a tear in my beer, 'cause I'm crying for you, dear* . . .

She has been reading agent blogs on the government's intranet, buried in the deep web. Hacked in, of course. Amazing what people will say when they think it's safe, she tells me.

"That's private," I goad. "Why wouldn't they feel safe?"

"You are tense this morning, my angel? Is something wrong?"

"I'm struggling."

"Do you need something from me?" She smiles sweetly and I want to faint, so she'll resuscitate me and take me away from this apartment, out of this flip-flopped world where I am now spying on her and I swear she's onto it.

She takes off her trench coat and is wearing a tight black dress that belts at the waist, short suit jacket, strappy heels. She looks great, of course, which makes this harder. I turn away from her and walk to the coffee machine, a fancy model that grinds the beans, perks, and steams milk one cup at a time. Groceries are delivered every couple of days by a third bodyguard called Fox, who looks like Mule, who Gila says is now officially missing. I brew two cups of cappuccino and bring them to the counter, where we sit down across from each other like normal.

"It's as if he just disappeared," she says.

"That's weird."

"It happens."

She stands abruptly, as if she's forgotten something, and walks into the bathroom. I sip my cappuccino, comforted by the familiarity, the dependable taste of coffee, and Gila coming to see me, bringing newspapers, just like home. Until I remember the chip in my flip phone that will record our conversations. I have been taught how to open the phone with a small screwdriver to remove and insert the bug when necessary. I get a new phone from Gila every few days loaded up with minutes, mostly to talk and text with her. It's also a tracking device. When the next one comes I will know exactly what to do. The phone now rests on the counter, though the bug won't work in the flat. The walls are thick with scramblers. I've been instructed to swindle her outside to talk, having studied a list of questions guaranteed to entrap, just pushing the right side of legal.

The toilet flushes and she steps out of the bathroom. She walks up to the counter and again asks, what do you need from me, *motek*? and I want to die. Or kill her first . . . I am not sure why I've come back here instead of insisting they send me home to the States, prison and all. If she killed the boy, I don't trust my own resources.

"I have to go to a meeting," I say.

"We can do that, but tell me, what does it mean, *on a tear*?"

"Not tear," I point to my eye. "Tear, like ripping a sheet a sheet of paper . . ." imitating the gesture.

"Tear. English can be very strange."

"It means they're on a roll. A surge, if you will."

"This is different how?"

"You tell me. You did the reading."

"Well, there is Afghanistan. They are not sure what they are doing there, this from the agents. But they are close to something. Then Iraq and Iran. The idea is a push strategy. These are sand queens in their Nike walking shoes."

"Sand queens?"

"They go into the tents in the desert. Drink tea. Make

deals. Giving away things maybe they shouldn't. Sometimes undercover. And every day they shake the drops of sand from their eyes."

"You mean tears?"

"No. Agents do not cry."

"Did you?"

She stares at me across the counter. Hard. And I'm sorry, but all I want to do is fuck her, fuck the anger out of myself for falling, because I am more pissed now than I was about a pesky high school reunion. I am under the spell of a killer.

"I never cried," she says, not taking her eyes from mine.

"Not even when you killed people?"

"What is in you now? Why so much violence? You are sure nothing happened yesterday?"

"Nothing happened," I say, thinking nothing except you betrayed me, Gila. Like last summer, when you convinced me to mule a jump drive out of this bloody mess of a country, ringing me in the middle of the night, let's meet at the lovely little restaurant on the water, please come now, dear.

"Oh, *motek*," she says, backing up her stool and climbing down. She walks around the counter, rolls her hands around my stomach from behind, feeling up and over, like she's trying to cover every inch of me, looking for the one thing she will not find. I am less stupid than I was one year ago, when she pulled me into the front seat of an old red Toyota truck and kissed me soft and wet and perfect, everything I'd been dreaming of for days. I fall in love too easily. Too fast. At heart I am a trusting person, this is common for ESTJs, I've been reading all morning on the old laptop she lent me, though it feels naïve considering where I come from, everything I'd worked double-time to blast out of my veins. I never suspected then that she, we, were part of a bigger plan, Gila driving lightning fast with one hand, the other scratching my inner thigh, as we veered off the highway onto subtle suburban roads and dark fields, industrial lots lit up like space saucers. She took me into an office trailer and we kissed. I ripped her shirt off and there was the baby Glock snapped between her breasts.

She turns me around, puts her palms against my cheeks, and brings my lips to hers. We kiss briefly. "Something is not right," she says, eyeing me like an agent. My temples heat up and I feel shaky.

"I need to get to a meeting."

"What time?" Still all eyes.

"I don't know. Later."

"Show me."

I stay silent, having given away too much already, why I could never be a real agent, because I cringe and squeal and stamp my feet. America warned me, said if you're in danger of talking, call. He gave me a private number. "And whatever you do, get out of that apartment and get her talking."

"Bring me the laptop," I say. Gila backs up and walks toward the front door, pulling her Mac, the private one, from a sharp leather bag. It's covered with a translucent red skin, the apple lit up like a back-alley logo. The keys are in Hebrew so I tell her what to search. And there is one, thankfully, at the queer center this time, a meeting in English at two o'clock.

"Okay," she says, "Wolf can take you."

"No, you do it." I stare at her.

"That's impossible."

"Why?"

"It's just not possible. It's too dangerous to be out together in daylight."

"Come on."

"We need to carve false paths."

"But—"

"Enough! I am calling Wolf."

* * *

The first thing that strikes me is how much I miss the gray-brown man. His ground is the new immigrant center, not with the queers. It's my first time in this new space, which is much bigger, the walls and floors spotless, and the chairs don't squeak every time you cross your legs one way or the other. The meetings skew young and hip, the English speakers more transient. The kids talk like kids. Big parties. Strategies for avoiding the joint someone passes you on the beach. How to be queer, a foreigner, and not drink when drinking feels so much better. I'd be a mess even without the sword of Homeland Security hanging over my head. Without the killer beast of a girlfriend I couldn't pry from our padded walls. I want to stand up among the kids and shout all Shakespearean, say I am the shittiest double agent. And I'm kicking myself for chasing her down to this blazing piece of earth. My breathing labors, just short of freakout. I'm craving a Xanax like mad but settle in, trying to concentrate on the tightly shorn dude with multiple eyebrow and lip piercings who says he's having a hard time in the rooms. Sometimes the worse people's stories are the more he wants to pick up. Recovery workers know this, he says. He used to be one himself. You want people to relate to others, to develop empathy, solidarity in sharing their truth, without remembering too much of what kept them in it for so long. It feels good, at least for a while.

Focus: another kid, a girl with half of her hair cut in an angle against her cheek and tinged pink, the other half shaved, says she was sent here at eighteen to live with cousins and finish school at the American university, do the army. All the foreign kids do the army, that's what the gray-brown man said, it helps to socialize them. If Marc hadn't been kicked out, maybe things would have been different.

The kid says her parents were Orthodox and lived in

New Jersey. Her father lost his job working in the timepiece industry and reverted to reading the Torah all day long, proclaiming himself some sort of penny arcade mystic. Her mother had gone to work cleaning houses and built up a small empire of immigrants. They moved on to office buildings. "Nobody had time for me," the girl says. "So I acted out. Smoking weed. A lot of weed. Some meth. I bought an electric guitar and hooked up with a couple of girls from the hood who also smoked a lot. We formed a girl band. The thing is, we actually could sing, but we wrote the worst songs."

Deep in reverie, memory, sweet nothings, and safe words, she fell in love with the drummer, and one night her mother, the force of the family, caught the drummer's head lodged between the girl's spread thighs as she called for the Heavenly Father. Next stop: Jerusalem.

"That's what they do," I blurt out, and the kids turn on me. Someone says, "What do you mean? Say more."

But I've broken protocol and want to shrink farther away. Too late. I look up at the girl but am swayed by the door behind her. There is a small, square glass window cut into the metal, crystal clear. Inside I see my father's head, hair hiked up in the middle like a samurai.

"It's okay," she says. "You don't have to speak."

"I . . ." cannot form words, my mouth's hanging open so damn wide.

My father tilts his chin up. *Let's go . . .*

"I get it," she says. "I totally get where you're coming from. But like how stupid can you be? You can't deal with your kid so you send her to the fucking Israeli army? Like maybe just talk to her, ask one question even . . ."

He motions again with his chin, as the girl continues. I bolt up from my chair and out of the room. There are a few people milling about, talking, flirting. Posters on the bulletin board flap in the wake of an air-conditioned stream. Everything smells like fresh paint. Looking around, he's nowhere. I lean back against the wall, breathe and blink tightly, thinking I'm crazy, seeing things, maybe Gila or one of her pack can get me a Xanax. Then I see him, in front of another door. This one has no window, only a thick silver bar across its middle and standard EXIT sign. He pushes it back with his elbow and mouths the word *up*.

I enter, walking up five flights to the very top and another door that says *NO REENTRY* in three languages. It takes some muscling to push through to the roof. The sun hits the top of my head, no wind for miles, spring heat wave on high, rays baking the sticky blacktop. Feels like walking on hot sand. I move a few feet away from the stairwell and there he is, sitting on a ledge in the toga that's driving everyone bananas, manic white hairs bunched on top of his head, face creased like a warrior. He waves me over and I come.

He's about to speak, but I shake my head roughly, put a finger against my lips. I reach into my pocket for the bugged phone.

"Oh, I get it," he says. "Not to worry. I'm wearing equipment of my own. Whose wire?"

"FBI, Mossad. Take your pick."

"Uh-huh. How are you, Jen?"

"Never been better."

"Sarcasm doesn't suit you."

"Then how about rage: Fuck you!"

"Better."

"You made me break the law."

"That was your choice. What did you think you were doing?"

"You said they were your accounts, everything legit."

"I never said the word *legit*. Never in my life."

"You and Gila. You knew she'd get me to do it."

"Oh, stop with the damsel-in-distress thing. I mean, sure, I knew you'd like her, but I had no idea it would go the other way. There was little inkling of lesbianic tendencies."

"You wouldn't know."

"Look, you messed with my plan, okay? You and the spy who loved me . . . first."

"I can't believe you're blaming me. You set me up, and I'm in big fucking trouble now. You want me to go to jail?"

"Don't kid yourself, Jen, if I were alive—"

"No. No. No! Stop it! You're standing here talking to me all real, okay, so you're wearing a sheet. Like ooooh, I'm from heaven. I only eat wheatgrass. What the fuck?"

"Hey, this is not a sheet. It's armament."

"You are too much."

"I have to protect myself. There's bulletproof lining under here, an ammo belt . . ."

"And if you're a ghost, why are you so afraid of bullets?"

"It's complicated. And hardly the point." He jumps down from the ledge with a muffled thud, sandals sinking into the roof. We are almost face to face, he's still got a few inches on me. A quick thought: I will never get to see him shrivel up and fade away. Which I am okay with . . . I think. Both of us are sweating at the brow. He takes a deep breath, smiles, leans his elbows back against the ledge he'd been sitting on. "Did I ever tell you about the night you were born?"

I am stunned.

"No, no. Trust me. This matters. It was early November. Pretty yellow leaves down all over. Your mother had a refrigerator installed next to the bed so she could keep yogurts in them. She ate yogurts all night long when she couldn't sleep."

"Yogurt?"

"I know, right? The symbolism! Anyway, one night, I

mean it must be like two in the morning, she nudges me, points to a wet spot on the bed, saying it's time. We took her in a cab to Doctor's Hospital—it doesn't exist anymore but in its day was the most elaborate in the city . . ." He hitches up his toga slightly and sits back on the ledge again. Be careful, I think, and am struck by the impulse. I do not want to care what happens to him.

"Can I just say how wonderful it is to be free of pants!"

"What a world."

He smiles. "You took eleven hours and forty-eight minutes to excavate yourself from your mother's chute. I couldn't watch. The enormity of it . . ."

"Maybe this is a little heavy on the details."

He raises his head and looks up into the clear blue sky. "Jen," he says, "I swear, I never wanted a kid."

"No offense, but that was kind of obvious."

"But then there you were. One minute you weren't, and then you were. The weight of you in my arms . . . it's enough to make you . . ." He's choked up. Legitimately, I think. "Look," composure regained, "I did what I could. Your mother had real problems. We had her on Lithium, for fucksake, and all the disco drugs."

"Are you kidding? Last I remember she wouldn't even take an aspirin. Are you really trying to blame her because you sucked as a parent?"

"What I'm saying is none of us are one thing or another. We contain multitudes. Whoa, I have no idea where that came from."

"Walt Whitman."

"New Yorker, right? Anyway, Jen, the point is, like it or not, I am your father. I seeded you. And now I must protect you. It's biblical."

"So it's an eye for an eye."

"Exactly!" He jumps down again, weirdly agile in that

toga, untainted by the heat this time. I am headache hot, sweat tears escaping from the back of my neck, my armpits, underneath my breasts, as he walks a few steps closer. I can smell him, not the cologne version but rougher, like when those pretty leaves start breaking down.

"I have a safe house," he says, "underneath your old apartment. The little faggot took me down there, that's where he's staying. Your entire floor was bombed out."

"How do you know that?"

"I went looking for you."

"You went looking for me? . . . Did you . . . I mean that bomb was meant for me, not the kid. Are you trying to kill me?" I stun myself with how calmly the words come, what a natural-born leader or super agent might do.

"Jennifer, I'm surprised. Do you think I'd kill my own blood? Flesh of my flesh? Light of my earth-born loins?"

"Nah, you'll just lead us to the gates of hell and let the villagers stone us to death."

"Somebody's been reading the Bible."

"Wikipedia, actually."

"You have it all wrong. I came afterward, to pick up the pieces, I see things that I could never see before . . . and this is what I'm saying about the night you were born, the weight of you is now fully inside me. It always has been. But I was blind to it. And now, I've been given this chance, granted this earthly form one more time. Only for you."

The human brain begins to form attachments before birth, attuned to signals transmitting down into the deep womb. Once released, you are already impossibly in love with your mother. From the beginning, mine was unrequited. But he was there, imprinting from the get-go, and no matter how bad things are, you don't want to believe you're an orphan, that it's just you against the big bad world. This is why we fall in love, though we are never more susceptible to suffering than under its spell, all defenses down. I think that's Freud or maybe the Jungian bartender talking through me now. I look into my father's eyes, soft and endless. Brown like stained hemlock or cherry. I have no idea what's lurking behind them and for one second think this is what other people get from me.

I take a deep breath. Nod, I understand.

"Good," he says. "Now listen up . . ." He starts in with details, speaking slowly so I can understand, but I can't help wandering, wondering if he's really some sort of ghost or holy spirit, an image of my shadow self. That the dead walk among us is not news. People often tell stories about being visited by their loved ones, especially in bereavement. The cranks call this after-death communication and it is strongest in dreams. This is how my brother's come to me throughout the years, sometimes with others, sometimes just the two of us, and I never know when or why. But I trust that he is trying to tell me something, maybe the thing left unsaid, just as I remain somewhat skeptical of our father, the notion that ghosts can appear to anyone in any form, to your lover or next-door neighbor, stretching the outskirts of credulity. It defies order! He is correct about one thing, though: the essential question of dead or alive is less important than the space we give it, and he has taken up residence.

Go back, he's saying, pretend I am waiting for Gila to plot our escape, pretend everything is the same. He will take care of the agents.

"Why can't you just turn her in? That's all they want."

"The Israelis, sure. Be more afraid of the Americans."

"I don't want to do this anymore!" My voice rises and I am literally kicking my heels into the spongy roof. "I can't do this!"

"Yes you can."

"No!

"Yes."

I think I am crying.

"Okay, okay, let's try something: raise your hand like this with me and shut your eyes." He lifts his left hand in the air. I do the same. He tells me to breathe, inhale deeply, then exhale just as long . . . This is something I know, comes easy, so I breathe out loud, longer each time, beginning to count down out of habit, and hear him with me in sync, breathing together as he says things like we are calm and we are strong and I can find this whenever I need it, just come back to my breath in the dark.

When I open my eyes he is still there, smiling.

"I will get you out of this," he says, and I nod, though I do not want the moment to end, him gone. "Oh, and Jen, never assume anyone is who they say they are."

"Except you."

"That's right."

"But you're not real."

"Stop chasing the details. Keep your own truth close. Now turn around and take the elevator back downstairs."

He will stay on the roof until I leave, he says. Then he'll fly off using the retractable wings on his toga. I look at him, still a bit of an unbeliever.

"What did I tell you?" he says. "Your own truth. Don't worry about mine. Now go."

I turn and walk out as he said, then stand on the street a few minutes waiting for him to fly away.

Gila said I could walk down to the beach after the meeting, which I do, the weather still showing far too much leg to return to my prison in the sky. Several paces behind me, Wolf is trying to blend in on the boardwalk, though he's wearing too much black for the climate. I made us wait outside the center for a short while, seeing if we could get a glimpse of ghost-Dad soaring from the roof, but spotted only a couple of seagulls and have to admit I wondered about shapeshifters and how, if graced with otherworldly powers, we'd all want to be birds at some point.

Now we've come to the queer beach in the middle of the strip, it's crowded for late afternoon, mostly men in various states of undress. I find an empty patch of sand and sit down. I do not have a blanket but kick off my sneakers and roll up the bottoms of my jeans. Feeling the sand between my toes causes the back of my neck to tingle, which makes no sense but it's glorious. The water is that perfect aqua blue-green I fell in love with years ago, the sky so deliciously clear I want to lick it. I lean back on my palms and stare out.

I can barely keep my eyes open and wish I had a towel, maybe Wolf has something in the car, better not ask, and I am sweating buckets. I take off my T-shirt and roll it up into a pillow, grateful for the gays, my people, and the fight for a little slice of beach where we can be naked if we want to. Nobody will mess with me, Wolf has that covered, you can see how rich people and celebrities get used to this, thinking it's okay to do anything because someone's got you covered . . . I don't remember this as kids, was an easier time, maybe . . .

I am walking with purpose. The sky is filled up with trees, all midsummer green and alive, and I am learning to ride at the country club in Connecticut. I am young, maybe six, seven, but today I assume a new form, adult, topless but in control. I am going to see Helga, a friend of my mother's who works sometimes in the money business with my father. She rides every morning and sometimes we sit in the stables and talk. She is tall, surly, and does not have a husband. She tells me not to get a husband, even the word is terrible, hus-BAND, you're banded for life. Not for her. I have not met Sofia yet but I sense it is not for me either.

Helga wears pencil-thin red skirts and purple lipstick. Her chest and arms are dotted with freckles, which makes her seem friendly. She likes me. Once time she asked me to take off my clothes so she could see what I was made of. She walked close to me, she was so tall, and touched me between my legs. This is power, she said, use it sparingly and use it wisely.

When I see her today, she is wearing her riding clothes. I am as tall as she is now. I pull her toward me and push her head down to my nipples. From down there she whispers that I am beautiful, that I am an old soul. There is a mad twitching between my legs, like when I hold my pee too long. I look up at the wooden slats, shifting farther above Helga, snaps of light break through, throwing thin streams against the dirt floor. A figure emerges through the rays in a silk robe, flowing curls loose around it. The figure takes one step in. Helga leans into me harder, sucking with purpose. I am happy, aroused. My eyes cross with the beautiful intruder and I want to die, then I want her to pull me away and strap me into a stroller even though I'm way too big. But she turns quietly and walks away.

I wake in horror, like in a thriller, you've seen it so many times, the heroine startling up, fear in her eyes, sweating, hair a Hollywood mess, though I have no hair, my whole head is a mess. I want her out, my mother, out of my fucking head. And how's that for irony: he's supposedly the ghost and she's the one who continues to haunt me. I reach into my front pocket for the phone I'm not supposed to use, but fuck it, let the feds bug her all they want. I press her digits, which for some reason I memorized before I left—Melissa said the less I had written down the better, and I left my BlackBerry back in New York. I knew I'd get her message, and her voice alone chills me deep. I tell her I need to talk, tell her to take down the number of this new phone and call me back, then quickly hang up. I am not sure what I want to say. The last time we spoke about anything real was after Marc's death. She turned to me and said, "If one of you was going to die young, I always thought it would be you."

"Really?" I said. "I knew it would be him. He was too broken for this world."

"Perhaps. Maybe I just wanted it to be you."

I'd learned to keep her at bay by then, had stopped giving value to the venom that slipped through her lips. Though I couldn't think of any reason to drop that pearl, except to be cruel. My face must have given away something, as she spoke again, unprompted. "Don't get me wrong, I'm not saying it should have been you. Only that there's got to be a reason. Maybe this is trying to show me how to do something different. I love you, Jen, I really do, but I don't think we've ever really liked each other."

That was probably the most truthful thing she's ever said. I used to think it was my fault, but it wasn't. She was not likable.

I feel a clamp at my throat and wish I could cry. In yoga sometimes we meditate. Take the thoughts and say, "Thinking!" then literally watch them float away. I speak out loud: "Thinking, bitch . . ." Doing this a few times, watching her drift across the deep blue sea, then I put my head down against my T-shirt again. I'm not sure how much time passes with my eyes shut before I hear the voice, familiar.

"Wake up! Wake up! I cannot believe you are here!" I open my eyes and focus on the figure towering above me.

"Yudi! Oh my god, I'm so sorry!"

"Thank you, my dear. It has been a horrible time." He bends down on one knee, smoothing out the chocolate-brown sarong covering his lower half. He's wearing a black cutoff T-shirt on top, his curls held back in a thick black headband, dark Jackie O sunglasses. "It's just terrible. I cannot stop crying."

I sit up slightly and touch his bent knee. "Watch what you say. I'm wired."

He pulls away, unsure of what I mean, maybe. I mouth the word *bugged*. Ah, he nods, and I am now suspicious. It's as if he knew I'd be here.

He leans down closer and pulls a tube of sunscreen out of a straw tote. "You are too white. You'll burn your nipples off. Let me show you my new tattoo." I pick up the sunscreen and twist off the cap. It smells like tea tree oil. I hate tea tree oil. I close it back up. He raises the inside of his arm to me, Arabic lettering inside his left bicep, the boy's name. "Adnan," he says, and his shoulders shake. I tell him it's lovely, putting a hand on his shoulder, as if that ever helps. He stands and reaches into his bag again, removing a sheet with bright orange and gold circles for us to sit on. I dig my T-shirt out of the sand and pull it over my head. It's from a recent Pretenders tour, just the right level of fade over Chrissy Hynde's guitar, though it occurs to me now that recent was over a decade ago. Her mommy album. I am queasy.

Yudi stares vacantly out into the waves.

"Come on," I say, "let's go for a walk." I drop the phone down on the sheet and pull him by the arm. Everything feels exaggerated. He takes a fanny pack out of his bag of things and clips it around his waist. It bounces above his sarong in the back. We walk silently down to the water's edge and set off farther south toward Jaffa. The warm waves slip between my toes.

Out of the phone's radius, I say it again, "I'm so sorry."

"I know, dear," he says. "But this was always the risk, his brothers are clinically crazy and violent. We knew they were looking for him. And now I have people looking for them."

"What . . . ?"

He stops our walking, looks at me, a bit perplexed, like should he say it or not?

"What? Tell me."

"I thought you sent him."

"My father?"

"He is a very good man. He wants to help."

I am here in this moment on the beach. My toes scraping into the sand and it feels cold. If I were dreaming I would not feel the cold, you do not feel temperature in dreams, or do you? I'll google it later. Keep feet moving, I tell myself, then push us forward. I am afraid to ask, to know any more.

"He promised he would find them."

"Who?"

"His brothers . . . the killers."

"Then what?" I can't stay quiet, it's too difficult.

"I told him they should not be killed but should be made to endure suffering. I want them to suffer horribly, I want them to think they will die but then not die, because their hell is here on earth. Is it bad? Am I a terrible person? They are more terrible . . . How could . . . He was just a boy . . ."

He is crying again, and it's me who's the terrible one, because I am jealous of his ability to be free with the tears, jealous of his grief. I am also angry that the bomb might not have been for me after all. Terrible.

I take Yudi's hand, tell him he is good, what he's feeling is right, I would feel the same, I tell him I want justice too. Though I know what he doesn't, we are on different planes, each in our own orbit. He cries for some time; I try to soothe, until silence blooms heavier than words. We keep the water to the right, wet sand between our toes, the setting sun alternately sweet and brutal against my face. There is a light wind and the temperature dips as we stroll, again, the hot-cold sensations assuring me that we are here, walking this earth through the dramatic shifts of April. We walk until we hit the beach by our flat and the sun melts low against the blue-black waves.

What is left to say about sunsets? Everything about sunsets has already been said. But it's a purple-orange Margaritaville kind of evening coming down. Makes me want to dive into the sea and not return, long as I end up someplace better, a place where I know how to cry and sadness can simply be what it is.

The sky tilts jaded blue as we return to the queer beach, foamier waves cuddling my ankles against the early-evening chill. Looking up from the water's edge, I see two silhouettes hovering by Yudi's blanket, a man and a woman. She's wearing white go-go boots. I tap Yudi's arm. "I know them. I'll handle it. Just don't mention my father."

"She is your woman?"

"What did he tell you?"

"That you have fallen in love with a very bad woman and we must save you."

"Whatever . . . Listen, I have to ask. Are you sure the bomb was for the boy? Adnan. I mean Adnan."

He is angry, insulted. "You think we are a country of terrorists? Just exploding random bombs everywhere? Blowing up anyone?"

"No, that's not it . . . it's just . . ." I turn and see Gila walking toward us.

"Ah, you think maybe she did it?"

I shake my head. "No."

"It was his brothers, I know it in my bones. Your father believes me. He knows this too."

Gila has made it down to the water. She stands in front of me, holding out my cell phone. My heart spills into the ocean, that damn phone . . .

She hands it to me. "Your mother called."

"What?"

"She says she will try again."

I introduce Yudi, remember my old neighbor? Gila says

hello. I see Wolf dipping back closer to the boardwalk as we return to the blanket. Yudi picks up his sheet and shakes out the sand, granules shimmering in slabs of white light coming from the boardwalk, all the lamps aglow. He stands and says he'll be leaving. Gila says something in Hebrew and he smiles. Sometimes I forget I am the visitor here, glazing over the fact that a culture, a people with their own tastes and thoughts and collective neuroses, existed before I arrived.

They talk a bit more, I think he's covering me now. "Maybe you two will come with me for a lemonade sometime," he says.

"That would be nice." I shrug and kiss his cheek. We say goodbye.

When he's a few steps away, Gila says, "Let's go, let's get out of here."

"No. I can't be in that apartment right now. Did you talk to her?"

"Who?"

"My mother."

"Yes," she drawls, and it's a whole goddamn world in that one word, so flagrantly sibilant it latches me back to the affirmative, so deep I want to hear it over and over again, preferably as I'm kissing the top of her neck, just beneath her right ear, which always niggles just so and makes me come down on the side of the boy being killed by his own flesh and blood, so it wasn't her, not something she would ever do, she's exonerated. Gila is not a killer. She's not into child porn or hit men or anything else in the deep dark down, she's just an old-fashioned thief in new clothes. And she is lovely. The earth vibrates, seriously, screw the implicit connotations and conventions, I am literally buzzing in love with her, in love with love, the two of us so fucked against the dusk-soaked firmament.

There is a drill under my feet, but really in my front

pocket. The phone. I take it out, no recognition of the number. "It's her," Gila says. "You can answer it."

I do. Then say hold on and press mute. "Is there anything I should know?" Gila shakes her head, just say what you have to say.

It is awkward at first. As usual. "I'm getting the garden in," my mother says.

"That's great."

"Douglas is on the road with his new book."

"Oh."

"We are happy," she says, scratching across the ocean for words. "So, what's all this about?"

"Nothing. I mean . . ." Stammering, I realize I have no idea what I want from her. She asks if I'm okay and I say yes. She asks who answered my phone and I stare at Gila. "She's a friend," I say. Gila's brow furrows.

"She sounds foreign."

"She's Israeli. I'm in Israel."

Gila comes a step closer in front of me, positioning herself so she can place her ear against the back of the phone. Lightly, slowly, her fingertips graze my forearm. My chest inflates.

"Are you still there? Jennifer?"

"Yes, yes. I'm here."

"This has to do with your father, doesn't it?"

"No. But listen, there's something I need to know. What was wrong when you left? I mean, with you."

"You're lying, you've seen him. He's told you things."

"No. That's not it." I pull back slightly to catch Gila in the eye, trying to convince her as much as my mother. There is no Daddy in this picture. "Everyone's still saying he's dead."

"Yeah, I'll believe that when they get him in the ground," my mother says.

"Please, just tell me, why did you leave?"

"You are hounding me from the other side of the world to ask about him. You're as obsessed as ever. It's not healthy. Douglas thinks you're not even gay, he's always thought so. You're just imitating him."

"That is the stupidest thing I've ever heard."

"Such florid language."

"What do you want me to say? You're right, I'm just trying to be my father . . ." And there is, of course, proof of her husband's hairbrained theory right up in my face. She touches the top of my head, brings her lips to mine, and kisses me softly. I move the phone away from my ear and lock into her. My mother's voice in my ear asking something, which I ignore. Because my phony gay lips, my tongue, are otherwise engaged.

"Are you there!?" she asks again, irritated. "Goddamnit, Jen!"

Not budging.

"I'm hanging up!"

I break the kiss and speak into the phone: "No, no, I'm here. Don't go!"

"Why are you calling me?"

"Because you owe me."

"What on earth do I owe you?"

"The truth."

"So high and mighty," she sighs. "Do you think you know why I left him?"

"You said he couldn't make you come and he was a peeper." Gila smiles, recognition maybe. I love making her smile, no matter how twisted the source.

"That is selective memory on your part."

"Well, what do you expect? I was twelve and hyper-aware of that kind of stuff. As. You. Know."

"What does that mean?"

"Don't you remember Helga?"

"Of course. She was very supportive of you, she said you had big ideas in your head."

"I'm talking about me. Helga and me."

"I don't know what you're saying."

"In the stables. You saw us."

"Saw you? What are you talking about, she took you riding, taught you how to get up on a horse."

"She touched me. Like really touched—"

"That's ridiculous."

"You saw it."

"You have a big imagination. Always did."

I am fuming. But what next? Sofia, how you let her seduce me, I think, that one's a bit more gray. Marc fell for her too, later, and in a deeper way than I could have imagined. But you let your husband send her away from us. Essentially you've bowed out of everything.

"Can you even name one of my coaches?"

"Oh no . . . Really? Are we really going to do this?"

"Yes. We are."

"He couldn't keep us honest, Jen. I felt like we were always in danger."

There are daggers and then there are daggers. Waves around us crash in discordant symphony. Hard to hear what she's saying . . . *Really?* "You felt endangered," I am screaming, "by him?"

"I did! He was not always involved with the best people. Not surprising for someone with so much money who came from the ghetto. The real ghetto, mind you. He fought like hell for his life, which is what I loved. But once he started to believe his own story, he started thinking he could buy anything, even our safety."

"Are you serious?" I look at Gila, who's no doubt been following every word. She grabs my free hand, hard. "You left for your own safety?"

"Yes."

"But you left your kids behind!"

"I needed to get as far away as possible. If I'd taken you, he would have been in my life forever. I was young. You act selfishly when you're young, but the truth is, I would probably do the same thing again . . ." Line breaking into static.

"You killed Marc! And practically destroyed me."

"That's a bit dramatic, don't you think? We do what we can."

"How can you live with yourself? You killed your own son."

"Are you kidding? I'm the one who tried to save him. But he was too sensitive, his soul too open to the world, the good parts and the bad. He couldn't live with himself. You had other choices. You could have been someone great, but you chose to be mediocre. It's got nothing to do with me."

"It has everything to do with you."

"I'm sorry you see it that way."

"She is talking nonsense now," Gila says. "Hang up."

I look at her, the contours of her face lit up like a black-and-white photo, the outline of her nose, bumped from the time she crashed a helicopter just short of Syria. She'd told me this up north, when she said she loved me and promised to be my shield and sometimes everything comes down to what you feel more in a given second, even if you know you might hate yourself in the morning.

I nod to Gila. "Okay."

"What?" says my mother.

"I'm done." I say this calmly, Gila presses her fingers into the back of my hand.

"Done?"

"Yup. It's over. I don't need this shit anymore and I don't need you. Goodbye."

I slam the phone shut. Gila rips it out of my hand and

hurls it up into the darkening sky toward the water. "What the fuck!" I shout. She doesn't answer. We watch silently as the phone arches into the black night, the waves a safe-harbor soundtrack, impossible to gauge where it lands. I exhale loudly. "That phone is wired."

She shakes her head. "Not anymore."

I stare at her, trying as much as I can to catch the full meaning. She steams back at me now, like I've crossed something. "How could you . . . ?" she says. "After everything, after us."

Her eyes condemn but not in a lurid way, unlike the iron lady we'd just tossed into the sea. I read concern, and a desire to make things better, change the whole trajectory, which brings thoughts of Tree after Calgary, when I begged her to return and then left her cold in the Antarctic for weeks. Unable to stick in my skin, I break away, walking closer to the water.

Chill out . . . Rak Regah! Thinking, bitch . . .

Let's take this back to zero. We are nothing but water . . . blood, sweat, tears, literally 97 percent water, more than in the average beer—I learned this in a documentary film—with millions, trillions, bazillions of blood cells constantly cycling beneath the skin. You don't think about them until something breaks down. Most days they are silent, just doing their job. Everyone knows blood speeds up breath, why athletes strive to maintain a steady heartbeat, even under pressure. I was young when I started playing with breath, pushing excessively when my blades hit the ice but keeping my lungs cool and dry. Some skaters study stance, form, psychological knockouts. I was all about speed. You do not need head games if you are simply faster than everyone else. I would keep moving, be faster than everyone else.

I can slow my own breath.

"Sit still," my mother used to say, long before she left

and she was just starting to set up easels around the living room, because it had the best afternoon light. Like a lot of painters she began with portraits. Realism. Hours, she posed me in front of the gilded molding, rays from the window piercing my eyeballs. "Don't blink," she'd say, and I would keep my eyes open until they felt like sandpaper. I could do this for a very long time. I once believed I could stop my heartbeat too.

By the time my mother left us for the philosopher you could barely make out any figures in her paintings. They were thin black lines and splashes of primary colors, like something I might have brought home from art class if I hadn't given up school for sports. I was mostly learning from tutors. I'd kissed Sofia up on the roof in the busted glow of the red *Sugar* sign and fell in love.

Only love can take your breath away.

Gila walks up behind me. I feel her body radiating through the wind. "You cannot play all sides," she says, slowly but loud enough to counter the waves. "And most of all you cannot play me."

A glint of moon pops in and out over the white waves. Like movies from early science lessons. The VCR had just become a phenomenon. My tutor played the sequence over and over so we could dissect its force.

"I told you about the army," she says, still behind me. "When I was there. How it became so violent. Not just on a mission but inside, especially if you are a woman. It was the thing we never spoke about. To be the darlings of the world there are always things you never speak of."

I turn around slightly. "Are you saying—"

"No!"

We sit down next to each other on the sand. She continues as if we never stopped, one ongoing conversation, love . . . "What I am saying is very simple. You need to decide whether you are in this with me or with the others."

"This is my father we're talking about."

"Yes, sure. But also the others."

The waves replay and replay like that VCR loop, the subtleties of liquid mass and motion still totally lost on me. I cannot speak beyond their black majesty. And what does it mean to survive? At five, six years old my father tricked a couple of Russians into snatching him out of a DP camp in Lebanon and carting him across the ocean to Brighton Beach. I was tied down for eight months with white coats pulling on my arms and legs. Now I can run, walk, pass go. I have never once considered driving a speeding car into a sheet of stone. I am, above all, not a terrible person. This, for some reason, seems most important.

I peer at Gila. "I've heard some very bad things about you."

"This is the same from the beginning. I told you who I am. Nothing has changed."

"You stole a shit ton of money."

"I told you already, I am not stealing money. I take information. Then feed it elsewhere. I am not responsible for what happens next, don't listen to anyone who says otherwise. And besides, I take from the very rich, weapons companies, oil, those with real blood on their hands."

"Robin Hood, right. I remember."

She smiles lightly. "You knew this, I told you everything. I am not the one keeping secrets." She touches my cheek.

"I'm scared," I say.

Her upper lip cracks, eyes softening. "I am also afraid, but I believe in our love. It is the only thing that matters to me now."

Words eclipsed, I nod, and it's an impossibly romantic moment, the two of us staring at each other in the moon-light, neon waves, stars dipping in and out of the gray-black clouds. Gila's face lit up. A single tear, maybe from the wind, escapes down the left side of her face. I wipe it away with my thumb.

"They do too cry," I whisper.

"*Ma zeh?*"

"Agents."

She shrugs. "Maybe."

PART SIX
BEYOND THE SEA

Somewhere in Tel Aviv, Sometime in Spring

My brother comes to me in the cold, after we'd both returned from the holy land and I could barely think of him without a rustle in my gut. He'd leased a walkup on Ludlow Street above a bar with pink flashing lights in the window, known for lightly toxic drinks and backroom antics. I'd been there once before with a girl with giant freckles who claimed she could stick her entire fist in her mouth and hum "The Star-Spangled Banner."

"Show me," I said. She smiled.

Later I fucked her under the alien green lights in the bathroom.

It's dusk when Marc comes down the stairs, a gleam in his eye to match the yellow-amber outside, subdued slightly by pink flashing neon. Like a train wreck or moonlit go-go dancer. Still so damn pretty. I'd had two bourbons and was just warming up.

He sits down next to me. Turns slightly and sighs.

We sit in silence staring at the bottles in front of us lined up like a row of gap-toothed soldiers, a mirror behind them. Our faces break the spaces between bottlenecks.

I order another bourbon, straight up, and one for him. He finishes his in two long gulps and asks the bartender for another.

The silence feels natural, notes to be gathered and sealed in a glass jar for the inevitable gray weather.

"I'm leaving," he says finally, slicing through it.

"Where to?"

"I don't know, Bali. Maybe Australia."

He could not get any further from this moment. Tipping the seasons upside down.

"Is that why you've summoned me?" It comes out so coarse it burns my throat, like I'd swallowed the row of pink electric lights. He exhales loudly. And there, in front of us, Ludlow Street in winter, the coming of evening. A girl I will meet in two hours and get so drunk she leaves her shoes in a cab heading uptown without her. I will carry her on my back to my apartment.

"I need something more," he says.

"More than what?"

"I don't know, this life. This city. The thought of running into people I know on the street gives me shingles."

"Are you kidding? This is New York."

"Not anymore."

There is bourbon, seemingly flowing from taps in the ceiling, amber waves of grain spontaneously made liquid. His long glazed-out stares, tight fist against the bar, professing the hope of something more. He says Israel depressed him. He'd never felt so far away from himself, because it was too much like home. We have angry little bursts every few minutes . . .

"It's all the same," he sings.

"I hear you."

"Don't say empty words."

"You started."

"Give me something real. I'm leaving."

"You first."

"You're still mad at me?"

"I wasn't until you walked into this bar."

"It was your choice to come. All I'm saying is don't do it again. Stop chasing me. Leave me the fuck alone!"

We turn closer into each other and laugh so hard I taste tears. On the TV screen down aways, a chart plots the recession, thin lines hiking up and down, peaks and valleys, and that's who we are, what we've been taught of life: avoid the flatline middle at all costs.

Heat moves into my temples. Warmth like fresh, fluffy donuts. Every country in the world thinks they invented the donut, but it was really us. Like most things.

I open my eyes and it's blurry, halos fluttering against the walls. "Oh man . . . not again."

"I'm afraid so, little honey bear." America removes his hands from my head. The chloroform fog comes stronger this time, the space behind my eyes throbbing wildly. Hallucination's a bitch. Like inhaling too much speed before laps around the rink, freezing-cold air throttling tortured synapses. But it makes you go so fast.

My arms and legs are all strapped to the bed this time. I look past America's shoulders for the others, but there is no one else today. Just America and me. Which makes me gasp.

"I'll get you some water," he says, and I know the drill. He returns and slides up the bed, releasing the straps around my right wrist so I can drink. Before handing me the glass he sips, and I have a profound sense of we've-all-been-here-before failure. But failing is big, never mediocre. You do not choose mediocrity, it chooses you, and everyone eventually. How did I get so depressing?

"Am I going to jail this time?" I ask, taking the glass from his hand, which seems shaky. Like he's got a hangover. I can see the holster strap underneath his blue blazer.

"Maybe," he says.

"I don't want to go to jail."

"Why not? What do you think it's like in there?"

"Cold. Concrete. Beastly."

"You forgot one thing. It's a mindfuck. Not a nice place. Even for a hotshot like you."

"Have you ever been in jail?"

"Of course."

"No, I mean not visiting. Locked up."

He looks down at me, oddly. Like it's the worst thing to ask an agent if he's done time. I feel my systems reconnecting, snapping back the edges of language, personality, the little things that make you you. I am an ESTJ. I am powerful.

"I'm not having this conversation," says America.

"What?"

"Look, this isn't working out between us. Gila Zyskun or whatever her name is, she's got her sexy little teeth into you and, let me tell you, you are going to be sorry."

"What makes you say that?"

"This isn't a joke, Jennifer. I'll put you on a fucking plane right now and you can deal with the Justice Department. Wait until you get into the rooms with the FBI. Want to see what a thug is? It's a hundred little Yearlings, all trying to be somebody. Trust me, there is nothing more sadistic than an overempowered bureaucrat." He backs up slightly, runs his fingers over the top of his head, grabbing his hair, which seems long for an agent, though sparse. You'd think you wouldn't want anything someone can fist. Makes me think of fucking, Gila's got hair too.

"You have nothing on me," I say, just as she'd prepared me. Three days and we were almost clear, living in a new apartment about forty-five minutes up the coast. Like suburban moms. Except we had no kids and fucked a lot. We were getting ready to leave, though I had no idea where to, better that way. She'd left me alone for just a few minutes.

Maybe these guys are not so dumb.

"Stop it, okay? Or I won't talk to you anymore. You're my prisoner, remember. Start acting like it."

"You sound a little pouty."

He flips his heels around and pulls his hand back. Smacks it across my cheek and my eyes shutter, everything tightening. She said this would happen the angrier I made them. If you're caught, make them think you're a loose cannon, she'd said. As if she knew I'd be caught . . .

Don't go there.

America is breathing heavily. He paces, stopping at the table where the pitcher of water rests. He fills another glass and drinks the whole thing down. "I'm sorry," he says, moving slowly toward me again.

I nod it's okay. But it isn't. Only one person has ever hit me. And only once, when my brother lay dying in a hospital bed.

"You don't have to cooperate," he says. "But you should know you're not getting out this time, not until I know exactly what you're up to."

"Can I ask . . . how did you find me?"

He cackles. "That's funny."

"But—"

He grabs my free hand so tight it could break, but only for a few seconds before strapping it back into place. I see the white handkerchief coming toward my face and flinch my head sideways. He pulls my chin back, covers my mouth. It smells like shampoo.

"Go back to sleep," America whispers. "We've got a bumpy fucking ride ahead."

He walks out the door. Computers beeping as my eyes shut down.

When I sleep I see the letter in my head, every word committed to memory—this one because it was so upbeat. He'd taken to F. Scott Fitzgerald–like salutations. Like this was our life from the beginning.

Dearest sibling, he reads, standing in front of me though all I can see is a giant head and arms, as if he's at a podium . . .

There are so many things to say, I don't know where to start. The big news perhaps: I am in love. We met at the racetrack. She's a painter. She rides a Honda motorcycle and tattoos for a living. Which leads to small news: my new tattoo. I know, I know, I always said I'd never. Always said it was so stupidly trendy. But everything changes when you feel something, right? When there's love. I can't believe I've never been in love before. It's amazing. The whole world looks beautiful. Even Sydney.

For days I wondered what to do, how to mark myself, and I kept thinking of you. If I were J, what would I put on my forearm? My thigh? Should the location define the image or vice versa?

And what do you think? No matter what part of your body I thought of, I came up with the same thing. You're guessing, right? It's okay but you'll be wrong. Not because you don't know but because you know me too well and you'd think Marc would never do that because it's so damn obvious. Love, right? And sometimes the obvious is all we really want. We're just too clever to admit it. Fuck, who am I?

She loved it though. She loves everything about me, even the hard parts.

I am now the proud owner of an anchor, with a thick chain curled around my right thigh. It's an antique anchor, like seriously. From the 1600s. We looked it up at the library and matched the exact design. You can even see the splinters in the wood, she's that good.

And she'll do anything for me. She says she wants to meet my people, and this might not surprise you, J, but I told her you were all dead. It's not bad to be an orphan living so far away, but then . . . you know this already. And it's, of course, why I'm writing, what I want from you. I need you to forget everything and I will do the same. Mind you, this is no apology, it's just the truth. I was never myself. And now I am myself. It's that simple. So just be happy for me and forget everything else, okay? And maybe you can start skating again. Give it another try. Or fall in love, that's what you need. It's what the world needs. Just try to forget me, okay?

Oh, fuck it. I was such a dick.

Know that everything's changed. I'm okay now.

There is no escape.

I am strapped to a hospital bed floating in a sea of beige walls, so familiar I want to vomit. My head feels like a shotgun shack. There is no clock, and I have been stripped of my

phone, any notion of hours, minutes rendered meaningless
. . . What is time anyway? Just sands in a plastic hourglass.
We made the whole thing up and we can call the whole
thing off. There is an old Yiddish joke about a rabbi wrestling with time. Like sitting on a burning stovetop, every
second an eternity, but drop a sexy woman in his lap, every hour's a blip. There is so much wrong with this joke I
must have invented it. What I wouldn't give for a window
to scrape night from day. This is how they drive you up the
wall, the silence far worse than solitude, every stray creak
amplified with promise.

America's come a few times. He covers my eyes to take me
to the toilet down the hall. Walking inside the bathroom with
me, he removes the horse blinders, lingering behind a bit too
long before saying knock when you're finished, which gives me
performance anxiety knowing he'll be back inside the room
to blindfold me again, roiling in the stench of everything me
and mine, and I won't give it away. Which is bizarre. I've
never had shy bowel, a trick on the skating circuit. Mostly
for the ballerina types. I couldn't care less who smelled my
shit, actually believed they all should, I was that arrogant.

But America . . . we are getting too cozy.

Back in the room he sits beside the bed and tells me
about his childhood. He grew up in Phoenix and had four
sisters, was a high school track star. We talk about running.
Athletics. We understand each other, he says. Sometimes I
think he's keeping me awake deliberately, preparing me for
the plane ride he keeps threatening, one flight to a roomful
of Yearlings and interrogation and I'll never be the same.
He says his first girlfriend was Jewish. She looked a bit like
Gila Zyskun and there is something in the way he says her
name that shakes my bones. I try and hold her steady, let
her occupy more space in my head.

Yesterday, whenever that was, or weeks ago, it's all yesterdays now, Gila and I are on a two-lane highway between Tel Aviv and Netanya, heading up the coast in a hearse. It's got the darkest windows, people are less likely to mess with you if you're driving a death motor, she said. The tires can kick it to 120 kilometers in less than ten seconds and it shoots bullets from the front bumper, like the Batmobile. We drive quickly against flashes of gnarled spiky pines, dusty brown dirt and stone, desert to the left, sultry Mediterranean to the right, sky cast in somber gray shadows. The highway insulates, brings it all home. You are one with the world yet left to your own devices. We are not supposed to be outside together but I'd insisted and it's perfect. Then there is a bump. And another. We roll into a choppy ravine off the side of the road. Gila frightens. She pulls back on the gear, carefully navigating to a halt, barely a shoulder to cry on.

"Fuck!" she shouts.

There is no word for fuck in Hebrew or Arabic. Not exactly. But people make up clever phrases like your mother wears devil horns and pack them into a word. Linguistic complexities masking the cold hard truth that nothing is as strong and beautiful as *fuck*.

I turn to her, stricken. We are sitting on the side of the road in a hearse with a flat tire, running from all manner of the dead and the living. I've never felt more like an open target and sense the beginnings of panic, where it just slightly tightens the throat. Gila shuts off the car, popping open her door. I follow and we walk around back together. She peels off her leather jacket and kicks the shit out of the big nuts with her white go-go boots, before attaching a jack to the back fender. I want to fuck her like it's fiction, or the set of a French film. Maybe it was a dream.

In a manner of minutes, she'd unhooked the spare and changed the tire, making everything right again.

I was never trained to fix things. Only to break them. Someone else always cleaned up, and if you're paying attention and you pay people to do things for you, normal stuff like changing tires or cleaning a toilet, there's always a hidden lever of shame, which I've found is best managed by shoving it underneath the carpet. Money cools your cheeks in a permanent way, but you can spend your days longing for an earthly utility, anything that connects you to how things work.

"Come on, come on, where are you?" the voice says, America. "You are not paying attention."

I am, I tell him. I swear. Then repeat it back he says, and I sigh.

"You are a bad girl," he says. "Now I'll have to tell you that whole thing again, back to when I was nine and had my first kiss. When I was playing games in closets with my older sister and her friends . . ."

I am walking down Atlantic Avenue in Brooklyn, heading to the train terminal after a night I barely remember. It's now all about the girl.

She was wearing red shorts and black Mary Janes with high platforms that matched her sparkling jet stream of hair. Think rock and roll in the early eighties, the Runaways because Joan Jett and the Blackhearts always felt redundant, though there's a Pantone color called Black Leather Jacket, which is more like deep green, and was eventually co-opted by Crayola into the more prosaic LEATHER.

I love the idea of six-year-olds saying please pass the leather.

The girl had four straps drilled into the ceiling above her bed. I'd never seen anything like it, her bed was a dungeon. Two of the straps had fur-lined cuffs attached to the bottom, badger or mink, endangered. I wrapped them around her wrists and tightened the Velcro grip. Next to the bed was a nightstand with three open shelves stocked with equipment. A paddle, butt plug, lots of lube, body paints. I inspected them slowly as she called out: Not that one! That's not what I want! I ignored her, a weapon in itself.

She was getting pissed off, called me weak. Inefficient. A pussy. I jumped on the bed in front of her and grabbed around her waist. Played with her nipple rings. Hard. I leaned back on my knees. She looked right through me and said hit my nose. I must have startled.

I'm serious, she said. Punch me in the face like your worst nightmare, like I stole your grandmother's wedding ring. Hit me like I fucked your first girlfriend.

I backed up slightly off the bed making a fist. She looked demonic. I told her to shut her eyes.

Not on your life, she said. Hit me, you fucking bitch!

I was paralyzed.

You fucking pussy!

I pulled my fist back, felt my shoulder lock in its socket. I'd hit punching bags in training for a while, when Tree became convinced my upper body was holding me back. The thing about hitting bags is it makes your knuckles bleed, why you wrap them down; I steeled myself for the pullback.

Fuck you, you fucking baby-ass shit-stained piece of nothing!

My knees glued to the mattress and for some reason I remembered being with my brother at the moonwalk at Rye Playland. We jumped so high we he hit the ceiling. I bounced up and down on my knees to give him an advantage.

Coward! You fucking coward!

Back with her, angrier now, and ugly. I wanted to hug her.

Who did this to you? I said.

She shouted this is why I fucking hate women!

I could not get off my knees but also knew I couldn't hit her. No matter what she called me.

You were supposed to be different! You're a fucking athlete, a superstar . . . Get the fuck out of here!

I leaned back and rolled out my feet. Reached up and unpeeled the Velcro. She fell to the bed, still screaming.

Walking out into the bruised dawn, I headed so fast to the train I didn't notice the wailing until the men dropped to their knees on the side-

walk in prayer. A line of them in front of me on a Brooklyn sidewalk at sunrise. Seemed you'd want more privacy, but the earth, even under concrete, gets you closer to holy.

I stretched around them as their cries filled up Atlantic Avenue, louder than the few cars waking into the day, like a great howling spirit or goat.

It felt like a cleansing: these men bowing down as I stepped into the subway station.

The same call wakes me now, stray crooning in the distance, five times a day, though I can't always hear it. Maybe it's in my head because there are no windows, no trace of outside. Where is it coming from, unless we are inside a mosque? I ask America, and he laughs, says I'll never know.

He's brought a Monopoly board into the room. Says let's play. Like we are sitting together on a rainy Saturday afternoon, just passing time.

I ask where are the others? He ignores me and opens the board between us at the foot of the bed, moves his chair closer. Says he'll unstrap my legs so I can sit up. One arm to play. But don't try anything. My knees buckle as I wiggle them out, every muscle achingly tight. The back of my shins feel raw.

"Come on, let's go, pick a piece," says America. He's antsy, hair greasier and rough stubble on his chin and cheeks. He chooses the race car, I take the horse, and we start to play. He is also the bank. I try to let him win because the sooner we get this over with, the sooner he leaves and I can go back to sleep, I am so tired today. But the luck of the dice is with me. I quickly buy up Boardwalk and Park Place, grab a string of railroads. The first card I pick is a free pass out of jail. America is not so lucky. He lands on my property twice and has to pay fees, then ends up in jail the old way, rolling doubles three times—Marc and I never played by this rule, but you could go to jail for getting up to pee. You show any kind of weakness, you pay. Thinking the dice must be with him, America attempts to roll his way out, the first time no go. He's disturbed, aggressively rubbing his chin. I buy another house for Park Place. He grumbles, won't roll the dice when his next turn comes.

"Come on," I say. "Are we playing or not?"

He is silent, staring.

"Are you mad I'm winning?"

"You are not winning. You are not! You do not win here!" He is shouting.

I try and ease back into my pillow but my legs won't move. As if they are still strapped down. America stares at me, eyes glazed and amorphous, somewhere else.

"You cheated!"

"Wait . . . what?" I say.

"You heard me, you're a fucking cheater!" he shouts. "You cheat and you lie."

"I did not cheat! I'm not the cheater, you fucking loser!" I throw the *Get Out of Jail Free* card at him.

"Fuck you!"

"No, fuck you!"

He smacks his hand across the board and the pieces go flying. I can feel the beat of my heart. He stands up and stares down at me like he wants to say something. He looks like Marc. Fiery and red, like something's tripped up and there's no return back to what we were. He turns and leaves the room. I know not to breathe until I hear the door beep. Once he's gone I try to wrangle my left hand out of the belt with my right, but there's some kind of lock. I'm eternally trapped but can kick my feet up slightly, bend my knees, small things but they feel big.

I went to Australia a few months after Marc's death. A private investigator my mother hired had turned up the name of his girlfriend in Sydney. They wanted to notify her that he was dead, tell her not to come looking for him, or whatever. I wanted to know who she was, what she did that made him want to drive his car into a boulder. I went by myself.

We met in a bar in Newtown, close to her tattoo studio. She was quiet at first though screaming in her appearance, bleached-out green hair, full sleeves of tattoos, so many you couldn't see where one ended and the next began, lots of colorful flowers, waves, and sea creatures. She had two small teardrops underneath her right eye, which somehow seemed the scariest, like she wanted to pass through life crying. I asked if they were recent and she sneered at me, of course not.

She did not ask about Marc's accident. She did not want to know any of the details, she'd been trying to forget him, so please tell my family to not contact her again, if we were even his family. He'd said he had none. And she'd told him to leave, insisted on it. She was trying to get her life back together. He was a sick fuck, she said.

"I'm sorry, what?" I turned toward her. Neither one of us had touched our drinks, I can't remember what I ordered but it was brown, with big ice cubes. I wanted to drink the whole thing fast and order another. She said he never talked much, could barely look her in the eye when he did. Then she said something that sounded so familiar I almost couldn't believe it, thought maybe he'd told her about what went down in that trippy tourist town, if I was even re-membering it correctly or just hearing it now for the first time. She said she walked in on him with another girl, a younger girl, someone they knew from around the clubs, and it wasn't so much that he was with someone else, they were open, had threesomes with other guys and girls, but this was different, she could tell from the second she saw him on top of her. He was hitting her across the cheek then in her stomach, while he was inside her. The girl was crying out for help, the girlfriend said, shaking as she recounted the story, real teardrops and mascara on both cheeks, so you couldn't see which was the tattoo, and in that moment I knew she was telling the truth and I knew I would choose not to believe her. She said she screamed his name, told him to stop, cursed him, and then, as she described it, the adrenaline kicked in and she ran to him and tore him off the girl. You can lift up a whole car on your own adrenaline, she said, but it surprised them both. He punched her and her nose cracked. She was bleeding. He dropped to his knees, sobbing and begging her to forgive him. The girl ran out of their flat. Don't touch me, the tattooed girlfriend said, don't ever touch me again, and like that it was over.

The girl never pressed charges, despite pleadings from the girlfriend to put the lousy fucker away. This was a crime, she said, and she wanted him to pay. But ultimately she settled for his leaving, the assurances that he would return to America and get help. That was when my mother sent him the plane ticket. If she'd known anything about Marc's circumstances she never let on.

As the girlfriend regained composure, wiping the mascara off her face with a towel the bartender had given her and breathing deeply, she said she was still angry but trying to be empathetic. It's hard to think badly of the dead, she said, and it was all he knew. I didn't ask what she meant by that.

A little later America returns and reties my free hand and feet. He does not talk as he does this, seems far off, and is wearing what looks like a skirt and knee socks. I can see the brown hairs on his legs. At the door he turns and asks if I like his outfit. I blink tightly, trying to see if I'm dreaming. "This was the closest I could get to the Catholic school uniform, remember?" he says. "The ones I was telling you about, that my sisters wore and I always wanted because I'm like you. I'm half man, half woman. What do you think?"

I stare at him, not sure what to say.

"Do you think I'm pretty?"

"Can you just send me to jail already?" I reply.

"I asked you a question," he says.

"Come on."

"Am I pretty?"

"Yes. Sure."

"I don't feel like you're present, Jennifer."

"What do you want from me? I've told you everything a thousand times." This may or may not be true, I can't remember if we've talked about my father. Did I tell him that story about my brother and the girlfriend with the tattoos? Why is he wearing a skirt?

"I guess I'll just have to ask your girlfriend."

I raise my neck slightly, questioning.

"Yup, we've got her now too," he says, and I stop to calculate veracity, the equation of truth over lie, probability. You cannot simply believe everything you hear, sometimes you will not even believe your own eyes.

"Is she here? Can I see her?"

"Oh, come on now. The point is you'll never see her again. That is her wish as well."

America is a liar.

"You don't believe me?" he says, pulling a syringe out of his pocket. "That's a big mistake, little honey bear. After all we've been through . . ."

I squeeze my lips together between my teeth.

"Let me tell you something," he says as he locates a vein in my thigh that has not been used. I feel the pinch of the needle, liquid in. "You will have no confirmation whether

I'm telling the truth, none whatsoever . . . not now, not ever. And believe me, this pains me as much as it pains you because in our heart of hearts we believe the same thing, you and me, we want truth but we know we'll never get it from anyone . . . What we also know is everyone's out for themselves, right? And everyone lies . . . you, me, everyone . . ."

There is a blue airmail envelope with Marc's handwriting and a nondescript stamp waiting in my mailbox. I grab it and press the button for the elevator, passing a neighbor on his way out who asks if I am okay, voice rattling as if on speakerphone. I have been out all night and in the metallic doors of the elevator see that my cheeks are cosmo-flushed. Fine, I say, though it's not clear my words register. He walks out the front door into the screaming morning. I want an egg sandwich like a curse.

The elevator doors shut behind me and I press three, my floor. But it does not move. I press again, thinking maybe it wasn't hard enough, but nothing. Then once more, again and again, manically like Morse code or there's someone after me like in the movies, and it still won't budge. I press Door Open and nothing. I am alone in an elevator that won't open or move with an airmail envelope burning through my fingers.

The heat comes next, like someone took a Bic to the edge of the envelope. I smell smoke. Tiny flames crawl across the powder-blue paper, working their waves into my palm, until my hand bursts into fire. I scream but what is the point? I am trapped in an elevator.

I try blowing out the flames but cannot breathe. Looking up at the brushed-metallic ceiling I see my brother's face, smiling. A spark shoots up through my feet and the elevator rumbles. One stop and there is a stewardess in a hot-pink uniform, a John Waters stewardess. "Sir, please put your seat back up!" she says to me, as the elevator shoots through the top of the building like a hot air balloon.

Five times a day I wake with the wailers. We seek commonality, ascendance. We believe in hope, which means there's a god, whatever shape or form. I like believing in something.

The cries envelop me, this time louder than usual, a chink in the chainsaw, someone at the door. I hate when America disrupts my prayers.

He's hovering today so I ask what's up, squinting hard.

But it's not him.

Finally, someone's come to fly me home across the ocean or throw me in prison, which has to be less exhausting than all of the talk, the costumes, the endless games of Monopoly, which always end abruptly, end in my being ridiculed.

The man cuts through the straps with something that looks like a giant pair of scissors. He frees my legs, then my arms, and I see his fingernails are manicured, feminine hands. He smells like olive oil and garlic.

"We are leaving now," he says, and the voice is familiar.

"Izzy," I say, and the bartender smiles warmly.

He says put your arms around me and I do, literally collapsing into his chest. I realize I am crying. He grabs me tight around the waist and carries me straight out of the room.

In a country of goats and prayer there is always something stewing. A perpetual sense of mistrust. I am being deprogrammed as if dismissed from a cult and weaned from daily doses of barbiturates and ketamine.

Special K? What the fuck?

America is a very bad man, Gila says.

I tell her funny, he says the same about you.

Then I fall back asleep.

Hours pass, days maybe. Gila brings me tea and crackers. She insists I drink lots of water. I have chills, night sweats, can't keep down too much food or remember my dreams. The pillows are cozy and smell like bleach. Then one day the plates shift, and I feel my legs again. I can hold a thought for more than a few seconds and smell food without gagging. I eat oatmeal, chicken soup, hummus and toasted pita, the best tomato I have ever tasted in my life. The bartender comes to see me and I ask what's going on?

He is still with Mossad, he says. They have broken up their team, since America went rogue and they called him home. He has disturbed the bartender's research, they had tried to create the perfect team based on personality types, imagine how that could transform the way agents operate across cultures. But America had strayed from the group. He is plagued by his past, the bartender says, has too much blood on his hands. They all thought he'd turned.

The bartender has a new team and they will work to free me. He'll send me home once they get Gila, and he will arrest her when the time is right. I am not sure what I'm hearing, he and Gila had seemed cozy earlier.

What if I tell her this? I ask him.

She knows, he says.

When I ask Gila about this she smiles. He's with us, he's just saying the opposite. It is what he must do.

My head cannot contain opposing ideas, a sign of a feeble mind, I've heard. Gila promises we are repairing my focus as we work on fixing my body. She walks me back and forth along the garden path, saying I must do this for longer increments every day despite the pain. My spine feels like tiny people with Led Zeppelin in their ears are jamming ice picks between each vertebra. I beg to return to bed and she says no, the bed is for sleep and sex and nothing else.

We do not make love. We do not hold hands or exchange furtive kisses. We keep our noses north as we walk in silence.

The beach is private, a section up the coast fenced off with barbed wire on the outskirts, our villa built into a seaside cliff. It costs millions and can be rented with American dollars only. We never see the wire, everything's just far enough out, and I'm glad because it feels like a historical mindfuck.

We eat meals on the stone terrace, watching the clouds spread above us to reveal shades of heavenly blue. The rains have ended. Pink flowers drip along the white concrete walls, set against classic aquamarine waves. Spring is in full force and we will be leaving soon.

Gila works on a laptop and does not let me near it. Earlier I asked if I could check my e-mail and she said no.

"You don't trust me?"

"Not you, *motek*, but all of the others."

"Like who?"

"The Americans. Izzy's people. You know what we're up against."

She is working behind the scenes, she says, figuring out a plan. Every morning she brings me the English papers, sometimes with whole articles removed. I ask why and she says for my own good. Seems reasonable. We play old country music on her iPod. I am becoming a better listener, getting wind of what's next. We will travel out of this land together, to someplace far away, where nobody will look for us. Linda Ronstadt helps me sleep better than drugs. I am starting to dream again.

One day, I can't say which, I wake up and we fight about peanut butter. I told her I like smooth and she brings chunky. She tells me I am selfish. Do I see everything she is doing to make sure we are safe and free? All I do is complain.

I am dumbfounded. She'd said she was happy taking care of me. Said it was her mission.

"I cannot do absolutely everything!" she yells.

I nod okay, say I want to help. "Just tell me what to do."

She steps to the edge of the terrace, leaving me staring at her back against the turquoise waves. A chill spirals up both of my arms. I am not sure what to say. I know only that I have been transported from one cell to another. Then I hate myself for thinking that.

She faces me again, brushing her hair back. "There is so much here that is stressful for me. If one little thing is wrong, one detail, we will be killed or taken away."

"I understand. I really do."

"I need to know you are with me."

"Totally. I am. And I have an idea, don't get mad though . . ."

She shakes her head, go on.

"Maybe my father can help."

"Your father is dead."

"No, he isn't."

"Just because some people in the kibbutz say he walks around in a sheet doesn't mean anything. They are very interested in his being alive and able to—"

"I saw him again."

She eyes me coldly. "When?"

"Just before America got me, at the AA meeting."

"Why didn't you tell me? All these days . . . you see everything I'm doing. And you hold this back! What a *balagan!* A betrayal!"

"I'm sorry." She's right. I had been holding onto the notion that my father was somewhere nearby, watching us, ready to spring me from the compound at a moment's notice, but only if I asked for it.

"*Yalla!* Get out!" she screams.

"Come on, Gila."

"I cannot look at you now!"

I walk inside toward the bedroom we share, though Gila is not really sleeping; all night she keeps her head stuffed inside the computer. My legs feel shaky. I sit down on the bed and wonder if the jump from the terrace would kill me or simply break both legs. I'd likely land on the beach but could just as easily slam back into the cliffs. It is right now my only hope of escape, you need a code to exit through the front door, and, really, I have no idea whether my father will be there or not, he's on his own timetable.

The walls and ceiling look whiter than before, not a crack in the paint, so different from the rough stone in the living room. I stare up at the clean ceiling for some time, wondering if it's drywall, the stone underneath plastered over. Why would anyone do that? I was once at a vineyard in Italy that had similar stone in every room. It was like living in a castle.

The first time I got drunk I was in Europe. I was a child. We were vacationing in Switzerland so I could skate with a former champion in Zurich. It is the only time I remember my family, the four of us, together in the mountains. Marc and I shared a cramped room in a tiny hotel. Anything we ordered from room service came through a dumbwaiter between our single beds. The first night we ordered wine and a bottle appeared. The second night we ordered two, saving the extra underneath my bed. The third night Marc said enough. He didn't like the way his tongue felt. He was seven years old. I drank three bottles by myself or maybe one was water, I have no recollection beyond staring down into the snowy streets below, making wishes. We were staying in a gingerbread village. At some point I fell asleep in my clothes.

In the morning Marc was already gone. I scrambled out of bed to meet my father in the lobby. He would take me to the former champion at the Olympic oval. She spoke little English, and I had the worst headache. But something happened. Instead of feeling bad, I was inspired by the secret in my bones, as sultry underneath my skin as I was freezing above it. That made me go even faster.

The former champion was impressed. She said get low.

And lower and lower. She pushed my head down hard. The deeper you bend your knees, the faster you will go, she said. Your knees are your life. I kneeled down lower than I thought possible, pushed farther ahead, all the while thinking, I've got a secret.

Everything good has an underside, its shadow, the thing left unsaid that can do you in or give you great power. When I think of love, I think of secrets. I can't help it. This is what my brother's left me with.

I open my eyes into darkness. Gila comes in and turns on the light. She sits down on the bed in front of me. I want to ask her for a shot of bourbon. But don't.

"Sit up," she says.

I do.

"There is too much to lose," she says. "I need to know you are not keeping things for yourself. I need to know everything."

I hold down the frog in my throat. She asks for details of my father's plan and I tell her what I can recall, how he'd promised to smuggle me out of the country, reroute and re-wire all incriminating accounts, assured me that the ultra-sounds America and the bartender showed me were fake, and even if they weren't, they would never hold as evidence. You really think they can get an ultrasound? At an airport? he'd said. I've got a bridge I'd like to sell you . . . The point is, I can go back to New York and live my life.

She nods and I can tell she's hesitant to go further. "And me?"

"You?"

"What does this plan do to me?"

"He didn't say anything about you." This is a lie, I can't help it. Why tell her he said she could burn at the gates of hell for all he cared?

"Do you want to go home?"

I stare at her long, silent, digging into what I know right now in this moment in a borrowed villa that feels so much like everything that's come before it. I do not own anything. We cannot own anything. Or anyone. This has nothing to do with love.

"I know I don't want to go to jail," I say. "And I don't want you to go to jail."

"We will not go to jail," she says, and reaches for my hand, squeezing tight. "I am asking a different question. An important question. Do you want to go back to your old life? From what you say, you were not very happy."

"I'm not sure I can do it. You'll have to forgive me, I'm an athlete, okay? Not a criminal. I don't have a map for this."

"But sure, yes, you do."

"You're saying it's genetic."

"I am saying this life is not as far off as you think. You were one time training to be the best in the world, but to be number one, you must separate yourself out from the pack, from all of the others. This is why you never feel like it's home. Why you drink alcohol. And have random sex."

I smile. "You are not random."

"Yes. In some ways I believe you've called me to you and I have done the same, because we have both separated our-selves out, for different reasons. Maybe now we can build something new together, something we don't even yet un-derstand, but we have to change who you are and who I am right now in this world." She releases my hand, looks down and away from me.

I lift her chin, bringing her back, determined not to leave this to guesswork. "What exactly do you mean?"

A deep breath and I sense we are skirting the extremi-ties, the enormity of what remains.

"We can become different people," she says. "We will

need to change what we look like, not just superficial like the hair, but this is not hard. And there is money. A lot of money."

My skepticism is up.

"I told you I am a very good thief. And like I said too, every single person or people I stole from did more terrible things than you can even think of."

There is a logic that comes from an ethical barometer of your own making, which does not feel entirely ethical, no matter how familiar it is to me. It's everything I grew up with and she knows it. She was my father's lover first.

She says she understands if this is too much. She will not blame me if I want to leave, but she will never be happy. And neither will I.

Our faces are close, thighs touching. I sometimes can't look at her, she's so beautiful, but how to trust it? When she's gone I can barely remember her forehead, whether her eyes are green or brown or somewhere in between, the small scar on her nose. Still, how deep can the layers of destroy and develop go before someone catches up with us, or more terrifying, if she's no longer her and I am no longer me, how do we know we'll still be in love?

We sit in silence a little longer, looking but not touching, and I am positive she is doing the same, mirroring, memorizing, because this moment now, on a bed in a borrowed villa, is as close to honest as we've ever been.

Later that night we make love. Slowly, with purpose and softer than usual. I let her go down on me, more for her than me, though we don't say this out loud. She wants to feel powerful, lost in the sweet folds of twist and shout with only her tongue against my clit. I don't scream for her to fuck me, it's not my style, though I want her to, which is not something I usually go in for, and I've relinquished the shame that keeps me locked inside myself, why I don't normally let anyone do this, the sensation too much to bear without giving up something, in this case the thing I've had on her, being the one who makes her come over and over, like nobody's business. We are tempting fate, perhaps, in this reversal of fortune, or she's auditioning—*see, this can be a lifetime*, even if our faces change and we're on the run . . . Where have you always wanted to go? she asks, moving her tongue away, a nibble at my thigh, and I whisper no, please, not now . . . Where, Buenos Aires? Rome? The shores of Tripoli? No, I want to say, this is about forgetting, and grab her head on both sides, tugging at her hair, where goddamnit! she screams, on the verge of tantrum, tantra . . . the two conflated in the libertine hour, an aching need to leave all conscious thought behind, where I started, so it's easier to give her a few words, someone else's words, Marc's . . . Bali, I whisper, maybe Australia, just make me come, she giggles and I immediately regret my words, pull her harder by the hair, reach for her hand and push it against me. She puts a finger in, looking up slightly and whispering those other words, as if it's all we need, just the two of us up against it, in a more serious way than any song ever sung blue. I push her head back down and feel the magnetic lock of her tongue, let myself fall deeper, dropping so low to the bottom of the sea there's jellyfish and squid and seaweed slapping up against my face. It's a soft swim, a floating inward, slipping between deep caverns of yes, this is it, this is everything, make me feel this way forever, though the water's getting rougher, my breathing shorter and more labored, I realize someone's clipped my snorkel and I push up, so fast my arms break, the pain excruciatingly complex, I scream so loud but can't hear myself and know I'm coming to the surface, heaving for air and . . . *crying?* Gila pulls her head back and sees me. I cover my eyes with my elbow. She dives up and holds me hard into the night.

* * *

The plan is a simple one: We leave by boat to Cyprus where Gila has medical people who will take care of the surgeries, small ones, she promises, and give us space for recovery. We will bring two of her men with us to keep watch, new ones, since Wolf and Fox are now exposed. We can figure out where to relocate as we recuperate. This will take a lot of money, Gila says. Only the really rich and really poor can disappear.

A doctor comes to the house and says I am well enough to travel long distances, followed by a pop-in from the bartender. We sit out on the terrace drinking tea. It's a gray afternoon but he wears dark glasses and a black cowboy hat to look like a tourist. When I ask if he's here to arrest Gila, he looks at me like I'm crazy. "I am with the two of you," he says. "We are one team."

"You said you would arrest her."

"I think maybe you were still in your dreams."

"Is she paying you off?"

"It is not like that. I am in deep cover. There are bigger fish to cook in this pond."

"Who is bigger than me?" It's Gila, walking outside. She's wearing a tan jumpsuit that cuts off in a rectangle above her breasts and a wig with darker curls.

The bartender smiles at her, then comes back to me. "This is very typical. The extreme confidence. Can you guess her letters?"

"I have no idea," I say.

"She is INTJ, The Mastermind."

Gila rolls her eyes behind his back. "Are you here with something?"

"I have word from the captain. About the boat. You leave at midnight tonight."

"What?" I look up. "It's too soon!"

"Darling, there is no choice. We are not going to the

Bahamas for spring break. This is your life we are talking about."

"My life?"

"I am saving you. That is the plan."

"See," the bartender turns to me, "The Mastermind does not care what others think. Luckily you will have time to have these things out together."

"Shut your lips, Izzy!" Gila snaps, and they begin to argue in Hebrew.

"You're saving yourself!" I say. "This isn't about me."

I storm out and back into my room, slamming the door behind me and flopping down on the giant bed like a friggin' teenager. The ceiling closes in on me in its extreme white and I'm burning up. I am not leaving, they can't make me. Why is she The Mastermind and me The Overseer? And is anyone ever the minion or the flunky . . . or how about the heretic? I do not believe in systems and gargoyles and how to succeed in business without really trying. Flight is my way, but I've left too many ghosts behind. I need my own plan and set about thinking, though that rarely comes on command. The best ideas usually surface in liminal territory, when you're not in one world or another, transitional times like running on the beach or, for some reason, the shower, where the whole world congeals into a steamy womb. My back too raw to run, I decide a walk might be liminal enough and get up to put on my sneakers. I lift one and a giant bug squirms out, big and brown, with a thick shell and flying-saucer eyes, far too many limbs swaying in warning or surrender. I shudder, slam the sneaker down on top of it, again and again, it's not easy to kill with a rubber sole. My back tingles from the exertion. I lean back and see the thing splattered into the concrete floor, a pool of fluorescent green slime circling it.

I am overwhelmed, again on the cusp of tears. I am not

normally a crier. I slam down emotions until they're invisible. Nor am I a killer of bugs; in my apartment I've trapped roaches underneath a glass and let them out the front door. Roaches! I sit down on the concrete floor with my legs spread and feel a deep swelling in my chest. Then big sobs like hiccups come.

In the heaving a feeling emerges, a flash so simple it defies all planning. I cannot leave anything loose this time. Nothing unsaid.

I gather myself together and walk out of the bedroom. Gila and the bartender are still huddled on the terrace, height of afternoon blues and yellows on display. "I need to see my father," I tell them.

"You don't trust me," Gila says.

"It's too dangerous," the bartender says.

"I don't care. It's what I need."

"You are being selfish," Gila says.

"You could go to jail," the bartender says.

"So could both of you. And you know what? I don't give a shit. I'm tired of this kidnapping business. You want me, Gila, I need to go on my own. I need a say. And I need to see him."

Gila and the bartender look at each other, silent for a few seconds.

"Okay," she says.

We drive down the coast, just after sunset, the gloaming such a vibrant orangeredpurplehaze I can't look without seeing millions of tiny black dots. Even with sunglasses. Gila is talking about what we must do to make this work, assuming we don't go down before midnight. This is very risky, she said before we left. We don't even know if he's there. If he's still with us he'll be there, I assured her.

"What happens if we do find him?" Gila asks now. "You haven't mentioned."

"Then I'll be free, I think."

"You think?"

"I don't know . . . I like my face the way it is."

"This is an opportunity, *motek*. Isn't there always something you wanted to change?" Her foot pushes harder on the gas of the crusty, nondescript Honda sedan. I love the way she drives the car like a sex toy. Radiant pink flowers climb the low-lying hills. I take off my sunglasses. Darker roses, not quite red, beginning to roam. A rose is a rose is a rose, sure. In any name, any language, like love. But appearance matters, is more troubling than we like to think. You do not bring a new lover tulips.

She asks again. Isn't there something that's always bothered me? Not just the face. We can do other things too. "Wings? Can you make me wings like a hawk?"

"I am being serious."

I think for a few seconds, staring off into the pink-soaked sea. I am not a Hollywood starlet scaling the mountains of youth. I am not a power broker tipping the nodes of dollars and discipline, I'll leave that one to my father, whatever world he now inhabits. The bartender says he's an ENTP, The Inventor.

I am not a celebrity though I was once on the cover of *Time* magazine. In a year heady with promise. People I'd never met put numbers on me in casinos in the middle of the desert. Those who bet against me won big.

I am not living in an unexamined shell, have never wanted to be another gender, as much as I've dabbled in the rush of shifting roles and testosterone. I am a creature of the margins.

I like being tall.

No, I tell her. There is nothing I want to change.

She takes her right hand from the wheel, pushes her sunglasses down on her nose, giving me the top of her eyes . . . deep emerald green? Which could be lenses, I seem to remember her taking them out one time, seem to remember a darker brown, why I can't get a handle on this appearance thing? She turns back to the road, going very fast along the curves. It's too late for dark sunglasses.

"Give me your glasses," I say, and she hands them over. "Here's the thing, okay . . . I once spent almost a year in a hospital bed trying to get back everything I'd lost in less than a second. I'm full of bolts and stitches that cry like hell in the rain. I hate recovery, I'm terrible at it, but it's all I do."

"You do not need to recover now. You can be just you and you can choose what you want. A blank slate. This is exciting, no?"

She slides off the highway onto a lit-up service road, coming toward flathead buildings and warehouses, the back roads down to the beach through Jaffa.

"Can I be The Mastermind?"

She pulls the car into a run-down lot, full of blown-out concrete levels that must have held hundreds of cars in their day. Headlights reveal broken pieces of stone and wires on the ground, the faded stencil of a dove poking out of the rubble. Gila sees it too. "Some things are too fundamental," she says.

"Everything changes. Look around you."

"Yes, but underneath, what endures is truth. When we blow ourselves up off of this land one day, which we will do, I cannot doubt, we will be stripped back down to what is essential. And it is now like this for us: we can go back to the beginning, to the garden of love."

I take a deep breath. "You and me? Together?"

"In this way we can rewrite the world, my love," she says, and turns off the car. Everything goes dark. "*Yalla.* Let's go."

We walk under cover of a majestic dusk in black leggings and windbreakers. Dark sneakers to absorb sound. Hats made of the lightest possible wool. My head itches, I need another buzz, but put that away for now, concentrate. Creatures of the night, we traverse the streets and alleyways, down a stone staircase left over from the old beach town this city once was. Gila knows exactly where we are going, has plotted and replotted the coordinates of my old flat, looked at skeletons of the building on the Internet, can tell how deep into the ground it goes. If there really is a bunker, she knows how to get in.

People are watching us, she said earlier. They will not let bad things happen. Gila knows this in the way one with resources knows. *Only the very rich and the very poor can disappear.*

My father has been gone more than twelve months.

We come to the edges of my old block, then the building with its dingy stucco walls, the cracks catching bits of streetlight, courtyard out front redolent of spring perfumes. Across the street the Movie Star serves fresh vegetables and wine from France. I want nothing more than a seat by the window with a carafe of pink-orange wine and pack of Gauloises, to stare out into the dusky world. I will want this every day for the rest of my life.

Gila nudges me down low through the courtyard, but instead of taking the stairs up, we walk around back to a concrete staircase attached to the building. It goes down into the earth, ending at a metal door. She removes an electronic device that looks like a radio and destabilizes the alarm, then cuts a hole around the knob with a small blowtorch. Within seconds we are inside the tiny room. There's a desk and bed, everything some motif of black and chrome. Concrete floor. Gray walls. Two laptops on the desk, one dark, a Bart Simpson screen saver on the other, tiny lights flashing from a router in the corner. The bed is unmade, as if someone had gotten up and not looked back. There is a note taped to the Bart Simpson screen that says, *Gone Fishing*.

"They're at the beach," I say, and before Gila can warn me off, I tell her I am going to find them.

"I know."

There is a path Yudi and I walked not long after we met, just underneath the boardwalk, so it's safe from the midafternoon cancer rays, something I never used to think about, but this will to live long and prosper, to be healthy at all cost, is oppressive. I was a sanctimonious shit when I first got sober.

Gila and I walk silently in the direction of Jaffa, sticking close to the overhang so we're not too visible. It is dark, clouds covering a quarter moon at best, air heavy and damp. The sea looks almost black, accented with crashing white waves, nothing too alarming. Farther down it mirrors the windows of the big hotels, as if the guests had fled their bunkers before shutting off the lights. We have all been here before, walking on a beach with a lover, perhaps in this exact spot, only now I can't think of a word to say. I bump up against her, our arms flutter. Still nothing, each waiting for the other to emerge.

Everything in me says move into it, resurrect yourself, what you'd leave behind is already gone. But there's a tug in my soul I can't explain.

"Gila," I say, "I'm still not sure."

"It is very simple."

"But what happens if we're wrong? If everything falls apart?"

She turns to me, scraping her fingernails against my cheek. This woman can impersonate, cheat, steal, even kill, but she won't tweak the truth just a little to say the one thing I need to hear. Honesty laid bare can be gorgeously brutal.

"This is the biggest risk of all," she says. "Isn't it always?"

"Yes, but, to give up my identity?"

"All lovers do."

"I don't think that's true."

"How should you know?"

"That's not fair . . . I am . . . I mean . . ." I stammer, struggling to speak clarity to my confusion, and it goes something like this: I am not a risk-taker by nature, true, and relationships, sure, yes, they've eluded me. I lead with the head, not the heart, typical for my letters, but that doesn't mean I don't know anything about life, people . . . She stops me, eyes shooting out wide. I hear it too. Off in the distance, an engine, the horn of a yelping fire truck, maybe, it's difficult to discern over the waves, though I swear it's on the beach and coming toward us. She grabs my hand and rushes us the other way, back toward the concrete stairs. As the sirens ring closer I am overrun with an enormous sense of relief. Let's get caught, let our souls be heaved apart by the moment and spit out into the night, each of us alone.

She pushes me beneath the boardwalk, shading us under a concrete embankment where hot dog stands rest in the somber hours. A black cat sighs under a half-open umbrella. It smells like a litter box. My heart beats wildly, a howling racing in. Gila's face up next to mine, she shuts her eyes as if in prayer. "You know the plan," she opens her eyes, "but if we lose each other, do whatever you must."

I say okay, then beg, please don't leave me, and I am surprised by the force of my words, the thought of losing her deeper than any risk lurking underneath, and I am for a few seconds present, diving into her eyes, what remains even as the colors shift, it's fundamental. Around us a screeching fills the sky, thunderous wheels spinning in the sand . . . then comes a harshness above the wailing, a whispery, mechanical tone, familiar cadences, *"Come out come out wherever you are . . ."*

Gila tries to hold me back. It's okay, I tell her, and step out of the embankment as the image congeals, a white VW van up against the black backdrop, headlights off but I can tell it's Yudi's. An old man hangs out the window of the passenger side singing rhymes into a megaphone. The vehicle stops abruptly, skidding along the lower part of the beach, where the sand packs tight and dangerously saturated. My father jerks forward in the front window; looking windblown, he spits out the words, *"Olly olly oxen free."* Despite Gila's protests I walk down toward them. He pops open the door.

"Jen! I thought I'd lost you for good!" he says without the megaphone, holding open his arms. He's toga'd up, samurai hair, thick gray stubble around his chin and cheeks. "You have no idea what I've been through."

"Hi, Dad."

"What, no hug for your father? I gave you life, remember, without me you'd still be a few measly grains of stardust."

"Not now, okay? We don't have time. I'm leaving tonight."

"Wait. We had an agreement. You and me."

"That's why I came."

I turn away slightly and see Yudi hopping out of the van.

"You would not believe . . . *eizeh seret!* We narrowly escaped the police today," Yudi says as he approaches us. He seems harried, but not afraid. And he's dressed oddly like my father, only his sheet is more diaphanous and he's got his curls pulled back in a gold headband. "They stopped him by the water and were asking about the sheet, saying he had Jerusalem syndrome . . . *So you think you're Moses?*"

"And I said to them, if I were to choose, do you think I'd pick Moses? Moses was a gregarious little fuck, sure, but all the questions, the indecision, the whining . . . are these the right laws? What happens if people don't like these laws? If nobody believes my laws? And what now, they're partying, I'm going to go sulk forty more years . . . Fuck you, Moses . . ."

"Are you serious? The police?" I ask Yudi. He nods.

They quickly tell me the rest of the story, how the Orthodox men from the kibbutz showed up and lifted him away in a prayer circle, admonishing the police for stopping the famous rabbi and his wife (the Golda impersonator), who'd traveled overseas despite her tremendous fear of airplanes. Yudi says it was like a carnival with the Orthodox men praying and ultimately leaving the police confounded. Somehow they let him go.

Now there are three Orthodox men in the back of the van, another three behind them on the boardwalk. All armed and, of course, none truly religious.

"Jesus Christ," I say.

"Exactly!" says my father. "That's who I'd be! You get me, Jen. You really get me."

"I need your help," I say to him.

"You know that's the only reason I've come back to this shithole. You're the one thing standing between me and eternal grace."

"Well, is this embarrassing," comes a voice that feels too close.

"Hello, sweetheart," my father smiles. Whole governments after us, secret police, bad guys, and it's the way he says *sweetheart* that makes me want to vomit.

"You are alive," she says tentatively.

He shrugs.

"You fooled me! You tricked me into thinking you died . . . or I never would have . . ."

"Never would have *what*?" I say.

"It wasn't a lie."

"I saw your heart shake! Your eyes roll away!"

"All true."

"Never would have done what, Gila? What?!" I am shouting.

"They said you were dead . . . *kus emmak!*" Gila in his face.

"And they were right. I was dead."

"I see you! You stink! And all along I am telling her she is crazy," Gila's eyes lit like giant moons, she's fuming. The beach has cleared out slightly around us, fewer stragglers, the waves slightly more rumble-y white than before.

"Oh, come on, you're smarter than that," says my father. "This belief that one is either dead or alive is so parochial, there's a whole scale in between. Ask the little faggot here . . . he knows about scales."

"Stop calling him a faggot!" I say.

"It's fine," Yudi says, barely above a whisper. "We have an understanding."

"Shut up!" Gila shouts.

"You shut up," my father counters. "You blew this thing to pieces. The two of you little lovebirds. I'm on borrowed time here and everyone knows it. But you . . . Jen, you were not supposed to come back, whatever possessed you? Though I appreciate the sheer industriousness of it, I didn't know you had it in you . . . And you," he points at Gila, more stern than I've ever seen him, "what the fuck did you think would happen? You went after her. We said lay low . . ."

"I thought you were dead! I saw you die! They all said to me that I . . . There was a funeral!"

"For the rabbi."

"Who was you."

"For a time."

"So you are alive?"

"Maybe. Maybe not. That's not for any of us to decide and it is not the fucking point right now!"

"*Ach*, I despise you!" Gila yells, clenching both fists in front of his face. He raises his left arm up to the shifting black clouds, as if he's expecting something, someone, to airlift him back to the heavens. The right arm follows and he is more biblical by the second. But he stays grounded, coming back to Gila. They stare at each other, between them a venomous coil you can almost see.

"Lay low does not mean lie down with my daughter," he says calmly. "There are all kinds of rules against this. You should know better than anyone."

"So you are now the rule follower?"

"You know what I mean, we set this up together. We had an understanding, a marriage of sorts, and you've broken your vows. That's cheating."

"You are the biggest cheater of all."

"You just don't like losing. And how could you bring her so deep into this? That wasn't fair, Gila. Even for you."

Gila looks down, away from him, and away from me. She's giving up, I think, and what I see is my brother, how he'd cower before this man, father of fathers, soul of my soul. Marc used to regroup on his own and get even sneakier.

"Admit it," he taunts, "you owe us both an apology."

"I owe you nothing," Gila says, lifting her head slightly. "I loved her."

"*Loved?*" I hear my pitch shoot up.

"I wanted to protect her."

"Fat load of good you've done there, my dear."

"Hold on, what do mean, *loved?*" I turn to Gila.

She stares at me, silent, a black shadow cast over half her face. Like a birthmark. Behind us the elegant crashing, crushing soundtrack. I almost can't hear her. "What you said earlier . . ." she says.

"Yes?"

"I cannot assume the risk for both of us. It's too much."

I feel my throat closing in. Want to swallow but it's too dry. "That's not what I said. I meant the opposite, I'm ready."

"That is not what I heard."

"Look! Over the clouds!" Yudi shouts, pointing to what appears to be a helicopter coming in above the sea. My father glances at his watch, as if expecting someone, then taps Yudi on the shoulder. Yudi scrambles toward the van.

"You are ambivalent," Gila says to me.

"Yes, but—"

"Look at me, both of you." My father is now close up, almost between us. We look. "Go with him to the van."

"I will not," Gila says.

"Don't be stupid. You're the one they're after. But I'm pretty sure I can get you out of this mess you've created."

"I should trust you?" She turns to me. "Go."

I try to speak but she covers my mouth. "Leave us for a minute," she says to my father, and he nods, just one minute, walking a few steps back toward the van. The helicopter crawls lower, though not making a move to land, and it won't. Gila'd said this last night, I recall. She anticipated someone would find us and try to scare us into surrendering. It could be anyone, she said, even someone you love.

"I am right this minute changing the plan, so you listen to me. I want you to go with them, let them take you out of here," she says, her hand still gripping my face. I wince, forcing open my jaw and biting down on her thumb. "Ow!" she screams.

"I'm meeting you at the boat," I say. I have a picture of it and a number for its spot in the port. Whatever happens, we had agreed to meet there before midnight when we were set to sail.

"No you're not. This is what I am saying. Listen to me!"

"What? Why!!!"

"I can't take this on. I will never forgive myself if something goes wrong . . ."

"This is my choice."

"And you will never forgive me if it's not what you think, because things are never what you think . . ."

"But I want to! I've decided!"

"I'm sorry, it is just hard to believe what you say." She is shaking. Looking right at me. I stare back through the dark, a softening like warm waves between us. Last night she said she loved me in a different way than she'd ever loved my father. Each person has her own way, her own songs and styles, she'd said. Each of us is a country unto ourselves.

"You said you loved me."

"I did. And I do. Never forget that."

I look up at the helicopter and see my father walking back toward us. "This is it," he says. "You come with me now or you're going up in that plane with the agents and it is not going to be pretty."

"I'm leaving," Gila says. "Please don't follow me."

"I'm going with you," I say.

"No you are not."

"I want to be with you!"

"It is not possible." She turns her back against me and begins to snake toward the concrete wall under the boardwalk. I break from my father and start to follow her footsteps. "Gila, wait . . ."

She doesn't turn around.

"Goddamnit! Please! Let me come with you!" I shout, and continue in her wake. She's walking fast toward the pinhole exit in the concrete, the one we'd descended earlier. I am gaining on her, step by step, watching her sleek black shadow, shoulders wrapped in nylon, yoga pants. I know every ounce of what's beneath, every curve and dent in her flesh, but that means nothing. I call her name a few more times but she just continues along beneath the dark overhang, signaling at me to turn back, and I keep stomping along the sand, shouting her name into the crashing waves.

She is under the boardwalk, almost at the pinhole, where she'll climb up and disappear forever. I call her name once more with all my lungs and she turns abruptly, pulls down the zipper at her neck, and peels the baby Glock from her breasts.

There's a loud click, like a car door slammed shut, then a burning rubber smell, and my thigh throbs. A teardrop rolls out of the corner of her eye and she's breathless. My leg feels like crying.

"I'm so sorry," she says, tears falling.

"You shot me."

"I love you so much, I do . . ."

"You fucking shot me!"

"But I cannot do this for us both."

"I don't want to go back, I can't . . ."

"Yes you can, Jen," says a voice behind me. I will not turn around, can't look away from her. She cracks the gun once more and buries it back in the holster, the same one I'd peeled from her skin almost a year ago, the first night we made love in an empty trailer and it felt like everything I'd been missing for years.

Now, the two of us frozen on the beach, pitted against the in-and-out of a deep black tide, eternity.

"Gila, go!" says my father. "Get the fuck out of here before I challenge you to a duel."

I turn and see he's got a gun of his own, an antique, the one the boy dug out of the sand a lifetime ago. My lungs collapse inward, a throbbing behind my eyes. The boy is dead. How senseless it all is.

Gila nods to him, an understanding, perhaps. His face softens.

"Goodbye, *motek*," she says, then turns and stalks off, picking up speed as her figure grows smaller and smaller and sinks into the concrete. I bite my lip to keep from bawling. My father puts his arm around me, though I don't feel it, I can no longer feel anything.

A man in black sits in the driver's seat, another one next to him looking into a handheld computer. A third helps Yudi pull me into the back where there is a piece of thick foam on the floor. They place me down lightly and I lie back, my head against Yudi's shin. The orthoman sits down next to me. He hands me a pill and a plastic bottle of water. "Don't worry, I am a professional," he says.

"Professional what?" I say, and Yudi smiles. I turn to him. "Will you come with me?"

"To New York?"

"Or Paris. We can be roommates again."

He says maybe. When he is done mourning. The window for loved ones goes on for a long time and he is still so very sad. I tell him I am too.

The professional whatever says it's time, he must remove the bullet from my thigh as we drive. Better for me to be asleep. I will be fine, he says. After I eat the pill I will feel a slight pinch, and then very soon I will be on my way home.

"That's what I'm afraid of."

Yudi strokes my head. I hoist myself up against his leg and look out the back window. I see my father holding out his arms to the helicopter, shouting something we can't hear. Yudi sees him too.

I take the pill from the doctor and swallow.

"He will walk into the water and pretend to offer himself to the agents," Yudi says.

"That's when we catch him with the net," says the professional.

I feel the van's wheels move beneath me as I close my eyes.

The bay windows in our living room look out over Fifth Avenue. We do not have a water view but if you climb to the roof you can see the East River and on a clear day all the way into the streets of Astoria. Marc says he likes the water, says he's always wanted to live down underneath the river, like the Beatles song, next door to the Octopus's Garden. So he could borrow handcuffs.

We sit together on the couch waiting for Sofia to turn on the television, like she always did when we were kids. But we are all grown up now. I have gray hairs along my temples and even a few colonizing places I'd rather not visit, harrowing proof of the long road to oblivion. If you're lucky, my father would say.

Marc is as old as I remember him, the way the dead age for us in temperament only. You are immortal in memory and photographs. Everything else moves forward.

He lifts a cocktail glass with shiny green liquid on the bottom, a layer of foam on top. He calls this Beyond the Sea. Says cheers and takes a long sip that gives him a foam mustache. Another sip and I can trace the liquid flowing down his Adam's apple. He puts down the glass and holds a hand out to me. Let's run, he says. And I say okay. We stand at one end of the long hallway, each crouched down with our left leg bent back, right leg forward, and fingers of the left hand scraping the ground in position, the same way it goes on the ice, but my brother and I did this first, up and down the hallway that takes up an entire city block.

We are big now, can barely fit next to each other in the hallway like we did years ago. But size doesn't matter.

"On your mark," he says.

"Get set."

"Go!"

We push off and sprint side by side until I can overpower him, I am taller than he is well into our teens and stronger in every way. Our fa-

ther can reduce him to tears in a few words. He looks to our mother for comfort and she holds him close to her breasts. When she's gone he never learns how to soothe himself.

Sometimes I let him win. Everyone needs to win sometimes. But it taints your view of what's fair.

Even if it's just a hallway. Even if we sprint up and down for hours as our legs turn to Jello-O and we collapse on top of each other laughing and know there is nobody who can take this away from us. Except one of us.

Then a break in the laughter, we stare at each other, long. I have questions, the ones I could never summon. Why, Marc? Who did this to you? But I am afraid I've known the answers all along, I've just kept running from them.

"Again!" Marc says. "Let's go!"

"I'm tired."

He nudges me with his ankle. "Chicken!"

I spring up and lock into position. "On your mark . . ."

We run and run and run, not stopping until the sun has lingered off down Fifth Avenue and the octopus has locked her doors for the evening. And this feeling, this running up and down a long hallway, rolling in and out like the sea, not covering much distance but moving faster and faster with him, is all I need.

EPILOGUE
RIDE A PAINTED PONY

Zurich Airport, November 2012

J ust after the onslaught of a fiery dawn, the line at international security is short, though I am ushered to the front by a man wearing a Swiss Air uniform. He is in charge of bereavement. They no longer discount fares but have assigned people to help expedite boarding and will give me triple miles for the flight. We cleared customs and immigration in less than two minutes, then walked down the long corridor, rays shafting up against the windows on both sides, everything inside sparkling clean, anonymous. Perfect for a country committed to secrecy. Or maybe that's just in spy movies. We arrive at the stainless-steel tables that lead to the scanning machines, like in every industrialized nation in the world, except here they're research-lab clean, and it's freezing. The man in charge of bereavement says he'll meet me on the other side, despite my protests. I am fine, slightly in a daze at how quickly everything's moved, but really okay. I kick off my shoes and remove my belt, hat, leather jacket, laptop comes out of my shoulder bag, pockets emptied, everything else has already been checked. A deep chill creeps up the back of my neck, happens every time I get close to the scanners, knowing how far up inside they can see. I hold my breath walking through, but I have nothing to hide. I am traveling on my own passport and student visa, deep in training to become a shrink. A Jungian.

When we arrive at the gate I see my name flash on the

upgrade screen and approach the two attendants at the desk. They are both wearing scarves tied at the neck, with fashionable haircuts, pretty. The flight is near empty, says the brunette, I can ride first class instead of business. We are scheduled to depart on time. They will take care of me. As I turn away she says, "I'm sorry for your loss." The words catch me, so strange in the metallic hum of an airport, like they'd misplaced my luggage.

"Thank you," I reply, and quickly walk off to find a seat close to the ticket counter where I can plug in my laptop and phone. I'd packed in a whirl of e-mails and logistics and had forgotten to charge, though they must have chargers in first class, I can't remember, and the forgetting is small comfort, proof of how far I've shuffled things in just a few years. In that time the global economy has collapsed and slightly re-bounded. Half the foundations in New York were dissolved in the wake of a giant Ponzi scheme, and while we had no dealings with its architect, it gave me an out. I collapsed the family foundation and sold every building in my name to big-time developers. All of my father's visible assets are still frozen pending his arrest and return someday.

Every so often the attendant looks over, her eyes leaden, and I can't hold her gaze. I'm afraid I'm not mourning hard enough.

My mother's death was fast and furious. She had been out riding and suffered a stroke. Her horse returned to the house agitated and alone. Douglas located her as fast as he could but it was too late. Her brain had exploded. He called to tell me what happened, taking awhile to get the words out. She was his whole life, he said.

I felt hollow, focused on finding a pen to write down the few details he had about the funeral. Before hanging up he said she never stopped talking about you, Jen.

I have chosen to believe him, though I have not said

much about her outside of therapy and my meticulous study of dreams and relational dynamics. I am learning how to maximize the ghosts. I've been attempting to call my father back to me in dreams, actively waking myself up in the wee hours so I can return to sleep and dream more heavily, keeping a notebook by my bed like the master himself. But what comes forth is too fuzzy to consider—you cannot dream on command. I have no concrete idea of my father's physical or metaphysical state, nor does the rest of the world. Every so often I get an impersonal report from someone at the FBI saying there is a new team working on the case, a detail has emerged, a sighting somewhere off the Mediterranean. A sleazebag producer is making a movie about his life for Netflix, though I refuse to speak with him.

The irony of my father possibly still roaming these shores as my mother is socked into the earth is something. She will be buried next to Marc in the big cemetery not far from the strip malls. I will visit with him tomorrow too.

I look up from my laptop and gauge a shift in energy, a few people starting to board, one in a wheelchair accompanied by the flight attendant with sad eyes. They see everything, should probably have degrees in social work. I stand and another one comes to meet me. She walks me down the gangway, says if I need anything I should let them know immediately. My seat is on the aisle in the third row of the plane. It reclines all the way back and there are pillows and blankets and Bose headphones. The attendant asks if I'd like a drink and I ask for tomato juice.

"Good choice," says the woman at the window who is drinking a glass of champagne, the New York Times spread out on the tray-top table in front of her. I smile, settle in. "I'm Alice," she says.

"I know." She is very famous. A pioneer of the feminist movement.

"Do I know you?"

"I have one of those faces."

She pauses. "They said your mother died."

"Yes."

"I'm sorry. That's always complicated."

"Death?"

"Mothers."

I nod, settling into my seat as people begin to file in. The attendant brings my tomato juice, whole can with an iced glass. I stare at the faces for a bit, then pick up my copy of the paper. On the front page there is news of Gaza, another war, this one called Operation Pillar of Cloud, a biblical reference to how the heavens shielded the Israelites as they made their way through the desert during the great migration. Exodus. My strongest reference is still the movie with Paul Newman.

But you cannot fool everyone with the defensive stance, the Israelis are pummeling the streets of Gaza again, and while some of this is surely provoked, you wonder what happened to turning the other cheek, recognizing the collective psychosis behind bullying, or is it only an eye for eye that ever feels like justice?

I miss Gila like crazy when I read this shit.

Alice lifts her copy of the paper and scrawls a note on a legal pad. She is writing a speech she will give later this evening, she explains. About oppression. She has been working with international agencies committed to saving girls from the atrocities of the world. On a good day, I am just trying to keep my head out of the clouds.

The pilot clears us for takeoff and I peer over Alice's shoulder toward the tarmac. It is now a bright morning here in Zurich. Airplanes are coming and going, doing their daily business, carrying people up, up, and away. Airports can be the loneliest places in the world. They can also be the most beautiful.

When we hit cruising altitude I ask Alice for a few pieces of paper and a pen. I should write a speech too, for my mother's funeral. Or something more grounded than a dream journal, words leaden with the weight of the world. At the top of the page a sentence comes, *Fury is an airport in summer* . . . I do not fully understand its meaning, but it sends a chill up the back of my neck. I put down the pen, angling my seat back as far as it goes, and blink my eyes shut.

THE END

ACKNOWLEDGMENTS

This book began as a short story for Akashic's *Wall Street Noir* collection. I can't remember all of the parameters, but the story was supposed to be set in an "emerging market," and, of course, have a crime-y element. Such strictures can allow for great creativity, and when I turned in the piece the characters would not stop talking to me. A decade later the story settled into the book you now hold in your hands. So many wonderful souls helped get me to this point, and I am grateful to everyone who read pieces of the book, talked me through technical questions or some facet of the creative process (writing is hard!), or simply let me natter on over a glass of wine. You are all beautiful and you've all helped me understand what it means to be part of a community.

That said, I want to express my sincere gratitude to several people who were instrumental to my writing and, finally, completing this book. To Aaron Zimmerman and all of the brilliant folks who dipped in and out of the Tuesday-night writing workshops at NY Writers Coalition—so much of what's here began in thirty-minute writing sprints and the conversations they generated. To 100 Monkeys, who took me in when I was wandering through this world without a writing group: Michael Buenting, Judy Chicorel, Deborah Clearman, Rita Hickey, Laura Kruus Reismann, Susan Miller, Nancy Weber, Iromie Weeramantry, and especially my comrade Mary McGrail. To Elena Georgiou, Angela Himsel, Melanie Hoffert, J.T. Rogers, and Virginia Vitzthum, for being such astute readers as the book was making its way out of the womb. And for sustenance of some sort over the long haul, thank you to Kim Bernstein, Meg Griffiths, Sarah Hill, Gerry Gomez Pearlberg, and Susan and Fred Sanders. So many of you are also treasured friends and I feel beyond fortunate to have you in my life.

Thanks also to Johnny Temple and Johanna Ingalls and everyone at Akashic Books, for providing the best home I could imagine for this and my two previous novels.

And to Susan Ryan, thank you for showing up at exactly the right time.

Claire Holt

Lauren Sanders is the author of two novels—
Kamikaze Lust, which won a Lambda Literary
Award, and *With or Without You*. Her writing
has appeared in various publications and journals including *Bookforum*, the *American Book
Review*, and *Time Out New York*. She is a resi-
dent of the great nation of Brooklyn.